D0406887

THE GUNS ABOVE

Robyn Bennis

TOR

A TOM DOHERTY ASSOCIATES BOOK

NEW YORK

THE GUNS ABOVE

Copyright © 2017 by Robyn Bennis

A Tor Book
Published by Tom Doherty Associates
175 Fifth Avenue
New York, NY 10010

www.tor-forge.com

Tor® is a registered trademark of Macmillan Publishing Group, LLC.

The Library of Congress Cataloging-in-Publication Data is available upon request.

ISBN 978-0-7653-8876-6 (hardcover)
ISBN 978-0-7653-8877-3 (e-book)

Our books may be purchased in bulk for promotional, educational, or business use. Please contact your local bookseller or the Macmillan Corporate and Premium Sales Department at 1-800-221-7945, extension 5442, or by e-mail at MacmillanSpecialMarkets@macmillan.com.

First Edition: May 2017

Printed in the United States of America

0 9 8 7 6 5 4 3 2 1

Dedicated to
PHILIP BENNIS,
Master Sergeant, USAF

Acknowledgments

I would like to thank my editor, Diana M. Pho, without whose suggestions this book would be much less interesting. Thanks are also due to my agent, Paul Lucas at Janklow & Nesbit Associates, who is an absolute rockstar.

Thank you to my incredibly helpful beta readers: Sheila Haab, Jill Bailin, Richard Bruce, and Becky Chambers. Around the time she was helping me out, Becky made her own debut with *The Long Way to a Small, Angry Planet* and has since followed it up with *A Closed and Common Orbit*. They're both great reads, so make sure to pick them up when you're heading to the bookstore to buy a second copy of this book.

Above all others, I must give credit to the people most responsible for making me who I am today: the baristas at Clocktower Coffee. Thank you. In the story of my life, you're the real heroes.

Now, if I went on acknowledging everyone who made this book possible, it would seem that I only did a tiny fraction of the total work. This hews a little too close to the truth for my comfort, so I'm going to cut these acknowledgments short. But if you don't see your name here, I'd like to thank you twice: once for your contribution, and again for your anonymity, through which you preserve the illusion that novel writing is a solitary affair.

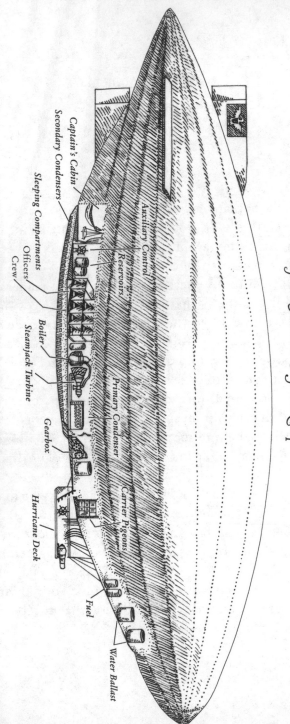

THE MISTRAL
of the Aerial Signal Corps

Captain's Cabin
Secondary Condensers
Sleeping Compartments
Officers
Crew
Boiler
Steamjack Turbine
Gearbox
Hurricane Deck
Auxiliary Control
Reservoirs
Primary Condenser
Carrier Pigeons
Fuel
Water Ballast

The Hurricane Deck of
THE MISTRAL

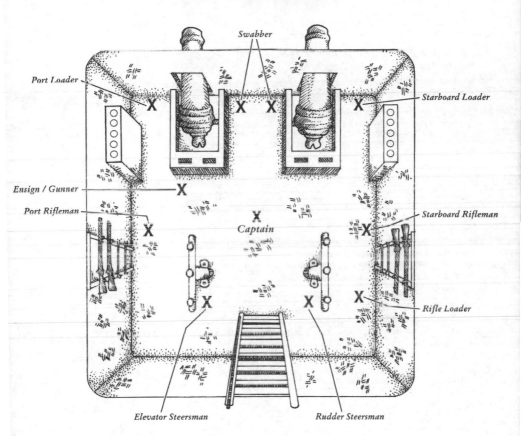

Swabber

Port Loader

Starboard Loader

Ensign / Gunner

Port Rifleman

Starboard Rifleman

Captain

Rifle Loader

Elevator Steersman

Rudder Steersman

THE GUNS ABOVE

1

JOSETTE DUPRE WOKE atop a bleak and stony hill, her head throbbing, her uniform soaked in blood, and the thunder of the cannons still echoing in her ears. Incandescent embers danced above her, swarming past her body and disappearing into the oily smoke all around.

Her only living companion was a carrion crow that stood atop her boot. She tried to kick it off, but lacked the strength for even that trifling movement. The crow held firm, staring back at her with little black eyes that reflected the flaming wreck of the airship *Osprey*. She had no memory of her escape from the stricken ship, but she must have gotten out somehow. If she were still inside, she would be on fire, and she was reasonably convinced that this was not the case.

From somewhere down the hill came the sounds of hoofbeats and musketry. The musket fire was sparse—not the crisp, hearty bang of a fusillade, or even the rolling crackle of skirmishers. Rather, these were the sounds of a rout; of an army not merely defeated but shattered, its remnants a panicked mob fleeing from pursuing horsemen. But which army had been routed? Hers or the enemy's?

At that moment, she couldn't recall who was winning when *Osprey* went down. She remembered the crash, and the hostile soldiers who swarmed over *Osprey*'s railing. She remembered commanding the crew to burn the ship. But after that, there was a most curious gap in her memory, beginning from the moment a skirmisher cracked the butt of his rifle into her skull.

Now that she thought of it, she couldn't even recall what enemy they were fighting. Was it Brandheim or Vinzhalia? But this couldn't be Brandheim—it wasn't cold enough. Yes, yes. Brandheim was last year's war. This year's was Vinzhalia, which meant the battle had been against the Vins.

But who the hell had won the damn thing?

She had to work it out quickly. Scavengers from the victorious army were already approaching. She couldn't see them through the smoke, but she could hear their boots clomping on the rocky earth, their bayonets slicing open pockets and packs, and the gurgling cries of wounded men who were too addled or stupid to play dead.

They chatted while looting, but Josette couldn't discern their language. By the sound of it, this regiment had been drawn from some border county and spoke a dialect neither quite Garnian nor Vinzhalian. She did her best to place it, but she had no ear for that sort of thing.

They came so close that she could see their silhouettes, like shades lurking in the gloom. She closed her eyes, for she couldn't hold them open in this stinging smoke, but now she couldn't see their uniforms. Moreover, she was only delaying the inevitable, consigning herself by inaction to a lingering death on this miserable hill.

Footsteps approached and the crow took flight. Above her, a young man spoke. She could barely make out his mutt dialect, but he seemed to be lamenting the waste of a woman killed in battle. This sentimentality did not stop him from kneeling down and rifling through Josette's pockets. Finding nothing of value, he drew a knife, cut away her flight harness, and sliced open all the hems and folds in her uniform where a soldier's wealth might be hidden.

She stayed limp through it all, even when an exploratory hand groped under her waistcoat and lingered there far longer than was required to check for coins. Her resolve wavered only when she heard the pliers click together. She'd heard that a good set of teeth could fetch as much as five liras, and now lamented the lack of decay in hers. Could she stay still, stay quiet, while her teeth were being yanked out one by one? How many would he take? How long would she have to endure it? Perhaps it was better to cry out now and risk the bayonet.

And then she heard the airship above. By its sound, she judged it a light semi-rigid with six airscrews, a Deacon steam-jack engine, and Merle reduction gearing. That made it an N3-class scout—probably Captain Ravi Salicar's ship, the *Sparrowhawk*. And since the fusiliers weren't alarmed by its presence above them, they were surely Garnian as well.

Her eyes shot open and she called out, "Stop!"

The Garnian fusilier froze with his pliers an inch from her mouth. Another man came to help, and together they pulled Josette to her feet. As she rose, the throbbing in her head turned into a sucking, hollow feeling. Her vision filled with stars, and the world went black.

2

When Josette next woke, the air was filled with the mingled odors of blood, putrescence, and the unnerving sweetness of gangrene. She opened her eyes and flinched at the intensity of the morning sun shining through a dirty window.

Her hand rose to shield her eyes, brushing the bandages over her forehead. Pressing on them, she could feel a dull ache just above the hairline on the left side. The area was numb in the middle, and she worried that she'd been trepanned.

She was nearly certain she hadn't, but it probably didn't matter in any case. No officer, to Josette's knowledge, had ever been dismissed from the army for having brain damage. Indeed, she knew several gentlemen for whom it seemed to be an advantage.

She sat up and looked around the room, idly picking flecks of blood from her matted brown hair. It was a narrow room, large enough for only two cots. In the other cot lay a patient wrapped head to foot in bandages. Burned, no doubt. Josette knew that it must be a woman, but only because the army wouldn't put her in a room with a man—even a dying one. They might cheerfully send men and women alike into the jaws of death, to be shot, bayoneted, and torn to pieces by cannonballs, but they would never violate propriety.

A stone bottle sat on the table next to the burned woman's cot. It tempted Josette, for there was no water by her cot, and she'd had nothing to drink since before the battle. And after all, the woman wouldn't be wanting it. She would soon want nothing at all, judging by her thin and ever-shortening breaths.

Josette decided, in the end, that she would not steal water from the dying woman. If nothing else, it would be a hard thing to explain to the orderlies.

She stepped out of the room and into the dim hospital corridor, where the smell of decay was even more oppressive. Across the hall, a door opened into a ward crammed with wounded men. The corridor was almost as crowded, with cots lining both walls. But there were more men than cots—so many that men were stretched out on the floor or propped against the wall as their wounds dictated.

She recognized one of them. He was a wiry, graying, weather-beaten man of about fifty, sleeping with his chin against his chest outside her door. It was Sergeant Jutes, chief of the *Osprey*. His legs were splayed, with the left one bandaged and resting under a cot, where it was less apt to be stepped on. He looked pale—paler than usual, even—and she had to watch for the rise and fall of his chest to be sure he was only sleeping.

"Sergeant," she said, the words rising as a croak from her parched throat.

Jutes's head whipped up and his eyes shot open. "Sir," he said, crisp and clear. He was halfway into a salute when he froze, his light gray eyes going wide at the sight of Josette.

Oh no. Had she walked into the corridor half-naked, in one of those flimsy hospital gowns? She looked down and was relieved to find herself still in uniform, save that her bloodstained pea jacket was missing both rows of brass buttons, in addition to the other damage inflicted upon it by her rescuers. Perhaps it was only the copious amount of dried blood, then, which alarmed Sergeant Jutes.

"Not to fear," she said. "Only a small portion is mine.

I wish I could remember who the rest belongs to, but I don't imagine they're in a position to ask for it back."

Jutes was pulling himself to his feet in such a hurry that he nearly overturned the nearest cot.

"For God's sake, man. You don't have to get up." But it was too late for that. Josette knelt down and helped him the rest of the way.

Standing upright, Jutes completed his salute, touching knuckle to forelock in the older fashion. Sergeant Jutes wasn't tall, but he stood a full head taller than the diminutive Josette. "Wasn't sure you'd make it, sir," he said. His eyes flitted to Josette's forehead.

"I've had worse," she said, feeling the wound. "I'm doing a hell of a lot better than my roommate."

"That's Auxiliary Ensign Naylor, sir."

"From the *Mallard*?" Josette looked back into the room, aghast. "Good God. And I was about to steal her water." She turned back to him. "How's your leg?"

"Hain't turned putrid yet," Jutes said, in a tone that mingled gratitude and hope.

"Hurt it in the crash?"

Jutes looked at her in surprise. "Sir?" he asked.

"Did you gash your leg when we went down?"

"No, sir," he said, and was silent for a moment. "I caught a bayonet pulling you out of the wreckage. Sorry I couldn't stay with you after that, sir."

She'd never been any good at thanking people, especially those subordinate to her, and this was the first time anyone had saved her life. Overwhelmed, she could only pat him on the shoulder and say, "Well, it's damn bad luck about the leg. Where's Captain Tobel?"

Jutes hesitated. "Sir?" he asked.

"Captain Tobel. I thought I recalled that he was wounded."

Jutes stammered out, "No, sir. I mean . . . he's dead, sir."

Her gasp turned half the heads in the corridor. She simply couldn't imagine a world in which Captain Tobel was one of the bodies rotting on that hill. "Good God, is anyone but us alive?"

"Sadiq and Ancel were killed by skirmisher fire, along with the cap'n, before we landed. Borden lost both legs in the crash and may live yet, and Rouget caught a bullet in the chest going over the rail. Talbot, Ferat, and Jobert died in the melee on the hill, and the Guilbert brothers lost an arm, an ear, and a dozen teeth between them."

That was half the crew—half the men she'd worked with every day for the past two years. She caught herself wondering how Captain Tobel had allowed such a massacre to happen, before she remembered that he had been the first to go. When he fell, she had taken command. She wasn't supposed to take command. Auxiliary lieutenants such as Josette were not permitted to take command of an airship. Indeed, the auxiliary officer ranks had been created to accommodate the peculiarity of female air officers, who had to be protected from the burden of command—particularly in battle, when a single moment of womanly hysteria might result in disaster.

Or so they'd explained to Josette, back when they made her an auxiliary ensign. Now she was an auxiliary lieutenant, a rank which permitted her to be the second-in-command of any airship bearing a crew of up to thirty souls, and even to stand night and morning watches if the weather was especially mild. But it did not entitle her to take command of a ship in battle, no matter the circumstances.

But she'd taken command anyway. She'd taken command, and half the crew had lain dead or mangled within a quarter of an hour.

"And Ensign Sandali stayed aboard to fire the ship," Jutes said. "It went alight something beautiful, but the poor lad never came out. Everyone else is alive and well. That's thanks to you, sir, and I'd venture somewhere north of two thousand fusiliers owe you their lives, too."

Jutes's last comment hardly had room to register inside her mind. It took everything she had to keep from weeping in front of her sergeant—or rather, the man who had been her sergeant until she crashed her airship.

"You all right, sir? It was a high butcher's bill, to be sure, but it needed doing. There ain't many who could have pulled it off as well."

Through the mental fog, she noticed that the squawking chatter of the packed corridor had abated, to be replaced by infectious whispering. Somewhere on the edge of earshot, she heard someone say, "That's her."

"Nah it ain't," another voice replied. "She's taller. Over six feet, I heard."

She looked at Sergeant Jutes. "Perhaps we should continue this conversation elsewhere."

Jutes said, "I ain't allowed in the officers' rooms, sir."

Josette found that she could not endure the stares of the men in the hall, nor the thought of returning to her room alone to count the seconds between Ensign Naylor's labored breaths. "Then what do you say to getting the hell out of this hospital?" she asked.

Jutes looked relieved. "Been tryin' to since they sewed me up, sir, but I can't outrun the damn nurses on this leg."

She nodded. "Good. Any other surviving Ospreys in here?" By which she meant other crew members from the late airship.

"No, sir. Apart from us and Private Borden, they've all been given to other ships."

"Then we'll just have to do it ourselves." She supported him with one of her arms under his. "Put your hand on my shoulder there, and I'll help you walk."

Jutes looked like he might jump out of his skin from the sheer impropriety of it. "Begging your pardon, sir, but I ain't sure it's proper for an officer to be holding up a sergeant like this."

Josette began to move, forcing him to walk along with her or else be pushed over. "Don't be an ass, Jutes."

"Yes, sir," he said, and hobbled down the corridor at her side.

The soldiers in the corridor parted at their approach, stepping or crawling out of the way to leave a space so wide that Josette and Jutes had a foot of clearance on either side. The whole spectacle made her cringe.

A pair of nurses came down the corridor, obviously aiming to intercept the escapees, but when they saw Josette, they moved aside so quickly that one of them stepped on a man's hand in her haste to get out of the way.

The fleeing patients passed another ward, where the casualties were worse than those in the hall. Some of the men there were already dead and had been so for hours, left to stiffen in their dying contortions by a hospital staff too busy to remove them.

Josette saw the entryway ahead. The front door opened and a corporal pushed his way inside. He shouted down the hall, "Another trainload of wounded is coming in."

A wrinkled nurse stuck her head out of the nearest ward and shouted back, "No more room! Put them in the street!"

Josette whispered, "We did *win* the battle, didn't we, Jutes?"

"Yes, sir," he said firmly. "It was a stunning victory."

Josette ran her eyes over the dead and wounded, packed shoulder to shoulder in the wards. "God help the enemy," she said.

Lord Bernat Manatio Jebrit Aoue Hinkal, son of His Lord the Marquis of Copia Lugon, woke shortly before noon. This was rather earlier than was his fashion, but the snoring of his bedmate made it impossible to sleep any later. The bed-mate was a matronly woman of at least fifty, which made her twice his age, but this thought caused him no shame, for he valued maturity in his lovers.

Bernat rose to stand, tall, thin, and quite naked in what little sunlight made it through his hotel room's soot-encrusted windows. He stepped to the washbasin, scraped away the night's growth of whiskers, and brushed his short, midnight-black hair. He donned the accouterments of nobility, putting on silk stockings, a fine pair of breeches, a ruffle-sleeved shirt, and a rose-colored sherwani. He applied a layer of powder to his cheeks and a dab of lightener under his brown eyes. He contemplated his wig for a moment, but decided against it. The damn thing was itchy, and he wasn't planning on visiting any-one important.

On his way out, he kissed the woman who lay snoring in his bed, and left his last gold lira on the pillow next to her. Out-side, the smoke was oppressive. It drifted in from the manufac-tories east of Arle and shrouded the entire city in gloom. Even worse, it clung to everything, covering the inn's expensive mahogany siding with a layer of soot.

The noonday street was clogged with carriages and carts, all going in the same direction. Bernat looked for the nicest covered carriage and hailed it.

"Sorry, my lord!" the coachman called back. "I'm hired."

Only then did Bernat notice the men lying in and atop the carriage. Indeed, there were men in all the carriages. There were even men in the carts. "What's going on?" he asked.

"Casualties from the battle," the coachman said. "They're comin' in by the trainload. Ain't a coach to be had, I'm afraid. Army's hired 'em all."

"Then how am I supposed to get to the semaphore office?"

The slow progress of traffic was taking the coachman out

of earshot. He raised his voice and said, "It's only a few blocks that way, my lord. You might resort to walkin'."

Bernat set off in the indicated direction, but not before giving an indignant snort. Three blocks later, his shoes covered in mud, he arrived at the semaphore station. It was quite a large office, and bustling with clerks. The one nearest the door stood hunched over his desk, scribbling on a slip of paper. Without looking up, he said, "Be with you in just a moment, my lord. The battle's got us a bit busy handling dispatches for the army."

Bernat sighed. "Why even *have* battles when they're such a vile inconvenience to everyone?"

"Words of wisdom, my lord, words of wisdom."

"I mean, don't get me wrong," he said, though the clerk gave only a cursory impression of listening. "I'm not one of those silly pacifists who seem to be popping up everywhere. I only mean that if we're fighting a war over Quah, they ought to hold the battles there, oughtn't they? It's only fair. It wouldn't even be such a terrible burden for Quahnics, for they must certainly be used to this sort of thing by now."

"Only fair, my lord." The clerk finished writing and looked up at Bernat. "And what can I do for you?"

He was sure now that the man hadn't been paying attention, but it didn't matter. It wasn't so important that the common people listened—only that they agreed. "I must send a message to Lady Hinkal, staying in the palace at Kuchin. It's very important."

The clerk licked his finger and pulled a fresh slip from his drawer. "Arle to Kuchin costs twelve dinars per letter," he said.

"That much?"

"Sorry for that, sir, but it is one of our busiest lines, and the cost of materials for semaphore towers being what they are these days . . . and, by God, if you saw the wages the signal operators are demanding, citing the current labor shortage, as if that excuses . . ." The man seemed suddenly to remember himself. "Sorry, my lord. What would you like the message to say?"

Bernat looked into his purse and gave it a shake. A few small coins jangled against each other. "Better keep it short," he said. "Just make the message, 'Mother, send money.'"

The clerk jotted it down and counted the letters. "That's nine silver rials so far," he said. "And how would you like to sign the message, my lord?"

Bernat looked into his purse again and frowned. "Just leave it unsigned," he said. "She'll know who it's from."

Once Bernat had handed over most of the money in his purse, the clerk stamped the slip PAID and said, "It'll probably be afternoon before it's sent, and tomorrow at the earliest before you can get a reply. There's a huge backlog, and the horse couriers are having a hard time getting through the streets."

Bernat pointed at the ceiling. "Horse couriers? But there's a semaphore tower on top of this building. It can't be only for show. I saw it signaling yesterday."

"Yes, my lord, but the smoke's too thick today to get a message through, so we have to send a rider to the tower outside town."

Bernat sighed and said, "This is the most horrid day ever."

"WHAT DO YOU mean, no billets are available?"

The quartermaster looked at Josette and Jutes as if they were stupid. She was a stocky auxiliary lieutenant, sitting behind a desk piled high with ledger books and stacks of paper.

"I mean," said the quartermaster, "that I cannot provide you with billets, because there are none available."

Josette had once expected fellow auxiliary officers to treat her better than her male comrades, but experience had long since taught her differently. "Lieutenant Bowden," she said, for this was not her first battle with the Royal Aerial Signal Corps's quartermaster's office, and she knew most of her enemies by name. "We passed empty barracks on our way in."

"Which are reserved for all the convalescents we're expecting. You may not have noticed, but there's been a battle."

Josette pointed to Jutes, who was propped up in the doorway. "You may not have noticed, but we were in the middle of the damn thing. Granted, we only played a small part, being bayoneted and bludgeoned on the front lines, while you were back here, fighting with a ferocious quill for God, Garnia, and bureaucracy."

The quartermaster looked up at Josette's bloody uniform, then back down at her paperwork. After sorting a few pages into their proper piles, she said, "If we provided quarters for every bugger who escaped from the hospital, we'd have none left."

Josette leaned over the desk. "Indeed, because they'd be filled with airmen. One might even argue that this is the sole function of airmen's quarters: to be filled with airmen, however much that state of affairs may inconvenience you. As we are airmen, and as we are convalescents, we require quarters."

This time, the quartermaster didn't even look up from her work. She only thumped a ledger and said, "That ain't what it says here."

Josette stood where she was for several seconds, trying to formulate a plan of attack. None occurred to her, so she turned and walked out of the quartermaster's office, defeated again. Outside, she stopped to plan her next move. As she pondered, she heard the whine of an airship's steamjack out on the airfield. She could barely see the ship's silhouette through the smoke blowing in from the city, but it sounded like Captain Emery's chasseur, the *Ibis.*

Jutes cleared his throat, interrupting her train of thought.

"Sir," he said, "if I may have your leave, I'll be heading back to the barracks now."

She arched an eyebrow. "I thought I was the one with the head wound," she said. "There aren't any quarters for us."

"No, sir," he said. "But I'll be bedding down anyway. If anyone comes along, saying they've been assigned to my bunk, I'll tell 'em there's some mistake and send 'em to the next one. Ain't exactly my place to say, sir, but if I was you, I'd do the same thing."

"And what happens when there are no spots left, and they figure out what you've done?"

Jutes shrugged. "Begging your pardon, sir, but in this army it'll take weeks for them to figure that out, and by then we'll probably be assigned to another ship anyway."

He saluted and turned toward the barracks. The officers' quarters were in the same direction, so she helped him along. On their way, they saw the *Ibis*'s enormous, cigar-shaped envelope loom out of the smoke overhead, on its way west. *Ibis* was low enough that Josette could hear the bustle of half a dozen crewmen running about on her crowded hurricane deck, which was the wide wicker gondola hanging under the ship, a third of the way back from the nose.

Josette cupped her hands around her mouth and, at a surprising volume for her small frame, shouted out, "*Ibis*! Fair winds!"

Captain Emery's head appeared over the railing. He shouted back, "Dupre! Congratulations on your victory!" *Ibis* was already passing out of earshot. Emery waved and then returned to his station.

Josette frowned. "Was he mocking me?"

Jutes looked surprised. "Sure he wasn't, sir."

Josette mulled it over for a few paces. She'd served with Emery several times. They'd even graduated in the same class at the Royal Aeronautical Academy, back when women had to pass themselves off as men to get in. He had never said a word to give her away, though he could have done, nor had she ever known him to resort to mockery. "But he wished me congratulations on my victory. Congratulations for what?"

"The word around the army, sir—which I will surely back up, seeing as how I was there—is, it was your doing that turned the battle," Jutes said. "General Lord Fieren was shy to attack the Vins, what with them holding that rocky hill. Overlooked the path of our advance, see, and it would've been hell on the ranks, with all that rifle fire coming down from it. I been in the infantry, sir, and I can tell you he was right about that, at least. Anyway, he tried scraping those Vin skirmishers off with artillery, and by sending our own skirmishers up the slope, but the damn Vins had nice cover up there and wouldn't budge, so he resorted to sending *Osprey* in to clear them out."

Josette sighed. "But we didn't clear them out, Jutes. I crashed the damn ship."

"Not crashed, sir. A hard landing, to be sure, but not a crash. Or, if it were a crash, you crashed her prettier than I ever seen. Brought her down like a barrel o' bloody bricks, right on the heads of them Vin skirmishers. Bloody Vins didn't know what bloody hit 'em. All they knowed is all of a sudden they was underneath half an acre of canvas."

It had been a damn fine piece of work, now that she thought of it. A crashed airship, unless all its bags of buoyant luftgas were completely obliterated, didn't want to come down in one place. It wanted to be blown by the wind, bobbing along the ground at unpredictable intervals. But she'd wedged *Osprey*'s tail into the rocks, so that it had pivoted down to land atop the skirmishers. To them, it must have looked like the sky was falling.

"And it stirred those skirmishers up real nice," Jutes said, grinning wide. "And we made a damn fine account of ourselves, if I may say so, sir, being less than twenty airmen against a hundred hard soldiers. Don't know how long we could have kept it up—prob'ly not long—but we kept 'em busy long enough for our men to get up the hill in force."

She scratched around the edge of her bandages. "And so what if that's true? I wasn't even awake for most of it."

Jutes shrugged. "Not for the last part, sir. But you was still the cap'n, even then. I hear the newspapers are all calling it 'Dupre's miracle.' Saw one paper saying—now how was it they put it?—'Auxiliary Lieutenant Dupre accomplished, by pluck and daring, what all General Lord Fieren's fancy stratagems and tactics could not.'"

She didn't like the sound of that. Not at all. It meant trouble. "And they're saying all this because I crashed my ship and set fire to it?"

Jutes nodded eagerly.

And now she finally understood what was going on, and that things were even worse than she'd thought, for she'd been sold out by the goddamn newspapers. Some of the news sheets were pro-government, while others were more critical, but every last one of them loathed General Lord Fieren, the architect of the army's campaign in Quah. Or rather, the architect of the army's dismal fighting retreat across Quah, a territory which had been taken from the Vins at the cost of so much Garnian blood only a decade earlier. Since then, Garnia had defended it against multiple attempts to retake it by the Vins, against opportunistic attacks from Brandheim, and even against Quahnic revolt, and Garnia had won every time.

But even in victory the army was beginning to wear thin, and this war wasn't going quite as well as the ones before. Shortages of equipment, experienced officers, and men fit to hold a musket had all conspired to make it much less fun to read about in the newspapers—or so she'd gathered.

In fact, the battle that brought Fieren south to Arle had

been his first outright victory against the Vins since the latest war began, and would surely prove a great morale boost for the army and the country at large. Faced with such a victory, it should have been impossible for the papers to condemn Fieren, but they'd managed to do it by giving Josette all the credit. All of which meant that her career would be quietly demolished if the public ever lost interest in her.

Judging by their past infatuations with war heroes, she'd be lucky if she had a week.

3

As the first light of dawn crept over the windowsill of his hotel room, Bernat lay in an empty bed, somewhere between sleep and alertness, waiting and hoping for a knock on his door that would bring the semaphore reply from his mother. As dawn grew brighter and anxiety slowly won out over slumber, he finally opened his eyes and stared at the plaster ceiling. At length, the bell towers chimed out the hour.

Ten o'clock. Dreadfully early. Surely no one with any sense would be found out of bed at this hour. But he couldn't sleep for worrying, so he rose, dressed, and went downstairs. After breakfast, with too little money for real entertainment, he passed the time by reading the morning paper in the hotel's stylish parlor. Whenever the front doors opened, he looked up to see if it was a semaphore messenger with his money, and each time he lost his place and couldn't remember a thing about the story he was reading.

"You know, that same newspaper had an article the other day. They said women ought not to be allowed in the air corps at all."

If not for the thick Sotrian accent, Bernat might have taken the gentleman sitting across from him for an inhabitant of Arle. He wore the white robe and tight embroidered cap popular among tradesmen and other petite burghers in this city—popular here because they were popular in the neighboring land of Sotra, and the locals still thought themselves half-

Sotrian, though it had been centuries since Arle sat inside those borders.

"I beg your pardon?" Bernat asked.

"That woman all the papers are talking about," the Sotrian said. "They didn't even want her in an airship before. You Garnians are so damn fickle. I think if I ask any person on the street out there, they can't even tell me why you're fighting Vinzhalia in the first place."

Bernat had never been burdened with excessive patriotism. National pride was a habit better suited to the commoners, and simply wasn't proper among the ruling class. But propriety was one thing, and this jackass giving insult to his country was another. He put his paper down and said, "We're fighting them, sir, because they are a bunch of godless royalists who scheme to take our lands, rape our women, and destroy our very way of life."

The Sotrian frowned. "Putting aside the question—purely incidental, I'm sure—of how the disputed territory of Quah fits into this analysis, are Garnians not royalists as well?"

Bernat turned his nose up and sniffed with infinite indignation. "We are monarchists."

"What's the difference?"

Bernat had no idea, but he made an educated guess based on what little he did know. "A monarchist governs for the benefit of the commoners, selflessly blessing them with the superior wisdom found in those of noble birth. A royalist, on the other hand, is a godless usurper who schemes against the peasantry, taking their land, raping their women, and destroying their very way of life."

"I see," said the Sotrian. He stroked his small beard. "I must, of course, bow to your superior wisdom on this subject, except for one small matter. I assure you, the Vinzhalians have a god."

"Well of course they have *a* god, but they don't have *the* God. Their god is one of those wretched pagan affairs, with goat horns and three eyes." Bernat waved a hand at his forehead in vague illustration. "You call that a god? Of course not. If you came across it in the countryside, you'd end its life out of pity. You'd have to be a true fool to kneel down and worship it."

"Honestly, sir, in the course of my life I have become half-convinced that one god is as good as another."

Bernat sighed at the man's stupidity. "One god as good as another? Would you say the same about . . ." He searched for an analogy, and found one when he glanced at his feet. "Would you say that one pair of shoes is as good as any other? Of course not."

The Sotrian nodded, apparently nearing enlightenment. "So . . . your God is like a superior pair of shoes, and their God is an inferior pair?"

"Exactly!" Bernat said.

"And this is why you must kill them? Over their poor taste in footwear?"

"Yes!" Bernat said, and then, "No. Not just because of that. It's . . . it's complicated."

"I'm beginning to appreciate the complexity, sir. I feel quite a fool now, for naively assuming the whole affair was over Quah's considerable mineral wealth."

Bernat racked his mind, trying to come up with a way to explain it that was simple enough for this man to understand. "Let's say you come across a man in the street, wearing a rotten old pair of shoes."

"Shoes with goat horns and three eyes?"

"Precisely. And you happen to have an extra pair of much better shoes."

"Which, if I remember my Garnian theology," the Sotrian said, "would be the personification of the sun, birthed from the mouth of the world, and advised by a pantheon of deified saints?"

"Indeed. Very nice footwear, you see?"

"That is surely beyond question, sir."

"Well?" Bernat asked.

"Well what, sir?"

"Wouldn't you give your extra shoes to the man whose own shoes were dilapidated and festering with eyeballs?"

"I might," the Sotrian said. "But what if he didn't want to take them? Should I force the matter, even to the point of killing him?"

"Well it's hardly our fault, if that's what it takes to put the man in a decent pair of shoes!" Bernat said, raising his voice, though he didn't mean to. "Now, if you'll excuse me, sir, I believe that semaphore is for me." He rose, bowed to the Sotrian, and went to the front desk, where a boy had just delivered a folded semaphore slip.

The man behind the desk handed the slip over, saying, "For you, Lord Hinkal."

Bernat noticed that no money came with it. Perhaps he had to pick it up at the semaphore office, which would be a dreadful inconvenience. He unfolded the message, which read:

My Dearest Bernie,

Visit your uncle Fieren in Arle and he will help you out. I'll send him a message, telling him to anticipate you at the museum. Hope you are well.

All my love,
Mother

"What a horrid day," he said. But at least, at the end of it, he'd have money enough for wine and the card tables.

Outside, he hailed a coach. It cost him most of his remaining money, but he felt it an acceptable outlay now that he had

more on the way. After a short ride, he arrived and found that
the Arle Museum of Art and Antiquities was free to enter, but
only on three days per week. This was not one of them.

By the time Bernat paid for his admission, his remaining
wealth added up to little more than a rial. It would barely buy
lunch at Oceane's, let alone pay his bill at the hotel. These
thoughts gained particular salience when he stepped into the
museum's grand hall and didn't see his uncle anywhere.

In desperation, he searched the galleries, and finally found
a man in uniform. The uniformed man was sitting on a bench
with his back to Bernat, but it was quite a fancy uniform, and
the man was being attended by an aide-de-camp. Bernat approached from behind and asked, "Uncle Fieren, is that you?"

Fieren did not turn. He sat, sipping a cup of tea and staring
at a painting. "Bernie," he said. "Come. Sit."

"I was worried when I didn't see you in the hall."

"I prefer to take meetings in front of appropriately themed
paintings," Lord Fieren said, taking a sip of tea. "It's a common habit among powerful men."

Bernat's nose wrinkled as he examined the painting, which
depicted a pack of hounds chasing after a fox. "But why this
one?" he asked.

Fieren's mustache twitched. "Because I couldn't find a
painting of a wolf eating a clown," he said.

There followed an uncomfortable silence—uncomfortable
for Bernat, at any rate—during which neither of them said a
word. Bernat finally broke it with, "Are you allowed to have
tea in here?"

Lord Fieren took his eyes off the painting and stared hard
at Bernat. "And who the hell would stop me?" He took another sip—a curiously dainty sip that kept his handlebar mustache clear of the liquid. That mustache was his Uncle Fieren's
pride and joy. For as long as Bernat could remember, his uncle
had tended it like a gardener pruning a topiary.

Bernat looked away, focusing on the painting as if he were admiring it.

"You know why we're fighting this war, Bernie?" Fieren asked.

Rarely had Bernat been so primed to dazzle someone with a detailed answer to an unexpected question, but his uncle barreled onward before he could speak.

"We're fighting because Quah-Halach was part of the Tellurian Empire, and that makes it rightfully ours, as the inheritors of that empire. Vinzhalia is fighting to 'take back' what was never hers in the first place. They don't pay any heed to proper claims and natural rights, so why should we treat them any differently?"

"Indeed," Bernat cut in. "It is not unlike meeting a man on the street with inferior—"

But his uncle wasn't listening. "In the last war with Vinzhalia," he said, "we could have finished them once and for all. Did you know that?"

"I did not," Bernat said. "Though I might almost compare the situation to—"

"We should have done it, too," Fieren continued, heedless. "Burned the whole damn country to the ground, if that's what it took. If they'd listened to me back then, we wouldn't be in this mess now—a mess the papers are blaming me for. Can you imagine it, Bernie? Blaming me? The one man who saw what had to be done, and the one man no one listened to."

"It's a travesty, Uncle," Bernat said, not entirely sure whether he was referring to the war, or to the missed opportunity to impress his uncle with his ingenious footwear analogy. "But take heart. Things will turn around. We haven't lost a war in three generations."

His uncle deigned to smile at him. "Good lad," he said. "That's the spirit. I wish the Crown had your attitude."

There followed another long silence, and he considered

whether he might find some excuse to go into his shoe metaphor. In the end, however, he decided it was better to get to the point. "Mother sent me a semaphore saying you have money for me."

Lord Fieren began to laugh, and laughed so hard that he had to hand his tea over to the aide-de-camp to keep from spilling it. "Is that so?" he asked.

Bernat began to sweat. "Yes," he said. "What's so funny?"

Uncle Fieren grinned. "She sent me a semaphore asking if I would commission you into the army."

Bernat's sweat turned icy. "I don't find that at all funny," he said, his voice quavering.

"Well, I do," the general said, wheezing in delight. "Thank you, Bernie, you've brightened a truly rotten day."

Bernat stared in horror, slowly realizing that his uncle was perfectly serious.

"Don't be so glum, Bernie. The army's the perfect place for a second son. You have no idea what joy I take in lording my position over your father, the marquis. Gaston here will draw up the paperwork, and you'll be commissioned an ensign by suppertime. It'll all have to be confirmed by the Ministry of the Army, of course, but that's just a formality."

Bernat stalled for time. "Pray tell, Uncle, what is an ensign's job?"

"Oh, it's, uh . . ." The general was at a loss, and had to look to his aide.

"It is the most junior rank of commissioned officer, sir."

"Well, I know that, Gaston!" the general harrumphed. "But how would you describe what an ensign does?"

Gaston considered it, then said, "When I was an ensign, sir, they said my job was to sit around being useless while I learned the trade from my superiors."

The general nodded. "Well, there you have it, Bernie. I

expect you'll have no trouble with the first bit, and the second will come in time."

Bernat's lower lip quivered. "And the pay?"

"I'd say about half a lira a week, wouldn't you, Gaston? But think of it this way, Bernie. Once you've paid your weekly mess bill, and once you've paid off the cost of your uniform, your buttons, your sword, and your horse, well . . . the rest is pure profit, isn't it?"

Bernat tried not to cry. "And how long will it take to pay those off?"

"Oh, well, let's see. An average horse costs me about two hundred and fifty liras. So that would take, what?" He descended into thought.

"About ten years at an ensign's pay, sir," Gaston said.

Bernat slumped, hopeless. "Ten years? Do horses even live that long?"

"Gaston," the general said, "how long does a horse live?"

"On a battlefield, sir? I'd say about fifteen minutes."

"Ha-ha!" The general reached up and punched his aide hard on the shoulder. "What a droll fellow!"

Gaston stood there, holding the general's tea and being punched in the arm, his composure infinite. He rocked back and forth with the punch, tea sloshing in the cup, but not a drop was spilled.

The general turned back to Bernat. "Perhaps it's best to forgo a horse, at least at first."

Bernat suddenly remembered something. "And how much does a colonel of militia make?"

The question shocked even the placid Gaston. The general twisted his face and said, "A what?"

"If I can raise a regiment of militia, the army will make me the colonel of it. Is that not correct? I only ask because it sounds a lot more fun, being a colonel."

"How in damnation do you even know about that?" the general asked. "We're keeping the policy secret until we can work out a way to announce it that doesn't smell of desperation."

"Well, it's gotten out somehow," Bernat said. "People are talking about it. I listen, you know." Actually, now that he thought of it, he was reasonably sure that he'd learned of this secret policy by reading about it in the morning paper.

Lord Fieren harrumphed. "In any event, a fresh regiment is at least a thousand men, Bernie. Where the devil are you going to find a thousand men?"

"Ah," said Bernat. He pondered, then looked up. "Perhaps you could lend them to me? Just until I find my own, of course."

Fieren eyed him. "I tell you what. Because you're family, you can bring me nine hundred, and I'll make up the rest."

Bernat did his best to look appreciative, but he was at a loss. He didn't even know where spare militiamen were kept. "That's very generous, Uncle, but I don't think I can manage it."

"Then we'd better sign you up as an ensign, eh? Oh, don't be such a child. If you like, I'll put you on my staff, so you don't have to deal with the rabble in the ranks. Come now, it's a far sight better than starving in the streets."

Bernat wasn't so sure of that. He'd passed plenty of people who were starving in the streets on his way to the museum, and, while he didn't precisely envy them their circumstance, at least they weren't reeling about with a bullet in their guts. "Are, uh, ensigns shot at very often?" he asked.

"Oh rarely, Bernie. Rarely. Wouldn't you say, Gaston?"

"I was just about to, sir. Lieutenants, on the other hand . . ."

Fieren gave Bernat an appraising look. "Well, yes, but I don't think Bernie here will have to worry much about promotion."

Bernat was still not convinced, but he supposed he could try being an ensign for a while and, if it didn't work out, he could always change his mind and starve in the streets later on. He gave a feeble nod and said, "Very well, Uncle."

"Good boy. Now, I have a few other matters to take care of. Why don't you hang about and look at the paintings until we're ready to deal with you. Gaston? Will you see about freshening my tea?"

JOSETTE DIDN'T KNOW why she'd been summoned to a museum, of all places. She just hoped General Lord Fieren wasn't one of those inscrutable men who held meetings in front of thematically appropriate paintings.

She made her way into the appointed gallery, where Lord Fieren and his infamous mustache were sitting together and enjoying a cup of tea. Captain Gaston Katsura, the general's aide-de-camp, stood stiff and tall at his side, and some aristocratic fop leaned against the wall nearby, dabbing his eyes with a handkerchief.

Mere minutes from now, she might be assigned to some backwater signal base on a lonely stretch of the border, sent to a distant outpost in the Utarman fever swamps, or even kicked out of the service entirely, left to live on a manufactory woman's stipend in Arle, or as the wife of some idiot yokel back home in Durum.

She took a deep breath, walked to the edge of General Fieren's sight, and saluted.

The general returned an approximation of a salute, waving his palm vaguely in the direction of his eyebrow. "Lieutenant Dupre," he said, without looking at her.

"Sir."

He finally deigned to look her way, then furrowed his brow. "I heard you were taller."

Josette was surprised. "We, uh, have met before, sir."

"Have we?" He took another sip of his tea, careful not to wet his mustache. "I don't recall it."

"The Halachia campaign in '22, sir." She stared straight ahead, never meeting his hard gaze. He made no sign of recognizing her, much to her amazement. Little more than a decade earlier, she'd stood anxiously before him in the amnesty court set up after the women's auxiliary was established. Only a few dozen women had turned themselves in, trading in their men's uniforms for the ridiculous, impractical skirts that the air auxiliaries had been expected to wear back then. Josette was the only officer among them, though a mere ensign, and had thought herself memorable.

"I was second officer aboard the *Whimbrel*."

"And . . ." He paused. "That was one of my airships?"

"High altitude scout, sir."

"Aha," he said. "I still don't remember you."

Josette didn't know how to answer that, and by the time she did think of something, awkward seconds had passed, and it no longer seemed appropriate.

Apart from the occasional footsteps of another visitor to the gallery, and the intermittent mewling sounds bubbling out of the young fop, the only noise was the general sipping his tea. Was it her imagination, or was the sound of it growing louder with each sip?

"I expected you'd still be in the field, sir," she said, merely to create some idle conversation.

"Not that I have to explain myself to you," he answered sharply, "but I'm here ahead of the army, preparing to go north and return to Quah."

At first, she thought she'd heard him wrong. "But the second front of the war—"

He cut her off. "Has been invented by poltroon journalists to sell newspapers." His mustache twitched back and forth. "I assure you, Lieutenant, the remnants of the Vinzhalian expedition we defeated are rushing north as we speak, cursing themselves for siphoning vital troops from the Quahnic campaign. This recent action was nothing but a . . ." He waved his hand vaguely. "An exploratory stab. They know we're wearing them down. They know we're on the brink of turning the tables, and in desperation they tossed the dice with this attack. Now that it's been repulsed, they'll be back to the real business of this war. Ah, but if we're quick, if we can move our expeditionary force north faster than the Vins can?" He flashed a wicked smile. "Then we'll have them!"

"Yes, sir," she said. According to a certain set, Garnia was perpetually wearing the Vins down, on the brink of turning the tables, and had been since the war began. Never mind that men were being sent to the front half-trained. Never mind that women were being shoveled into the manufactories, into the signal corps, into the logistics corps, in a desperate attempt to free up fighting men—so that *they* could be sent to the front half-trained. Never mind all that, and didn't you know, we haven't lost a war in three generations?

She looked from him to the painting. "Lovely painting," she said, desperate to change the subject before she accidentally spoke her mind.

The general ran his eyes over it and smiled. "It is. And appropriate to our business today."

Oh hell, she thought.

"Do you hunt, Dupre?"

"Yes, sir. Or rather, I did years ago, back in Durum. Only for food, though. And not with dogs, of course." She laughed, hoping her nervousness wasn't showing. "If we'd had that many dogs, well, we wouldn't have had to hunt, would we?"

The general peered at her for several seconds and said, "What a delightful story." He looked at Captain Katsura. "Gaston, wasn't that a delightful story?"

Katsura seemed to consider the question, frowned, and said, "I didn't care for the dog-eating part."

"Well, I thought it was a delightful little story." Fieren beamed such a smile that it made his mustache bend in the middle. "I've heard a lot of delightful little stories about Lieutenant Dupre over the past couple days."

"Sir, I'm not . . ." Josette stammered. "I mean, I didn't . . ."

"Of course not." Lord Fieren's smile grew wider. "An officer in the King's Army, even a mere auxiliary officer, wouldn't go around spreading fanciful tales that denigrate and undermine her superior officer. What do they call that sort of thing, Gaston?"

"Treason, sir."

The general looked at him, then back at Josette. "I believe the word I wanted was 'slander,' but either will do in a pinch."

The prospect of a quiet life as a yokel's wife suddenly seemed more appealing. Josette swallowed, but it didn't relieve the sudden constriction in her throat. She could already feel the hangman's noose tightening around it.

The general reached into his coat and came out with a folded piece of paper. A lawsuit? A discharge? A death warrant? He rose and handed his tea to Captain Katsura.

Josette stiffened and stared straight ahead.

The general stood before her. "Congratulations, Lieutenant."

Her eyes whipped up to his. "Sir?"

He thrust the paper at her. She unfolded it with shaking hands and read. In her addled state, she missed half the words, but there was one sentence that her eyes ran over again and again. It read, *We, reposing especial Trust and Confidence in your Loyalty, Courage, and Good Conduct, do by these Presents Promote you to the Rank of Senior Lieutenant in His Royal Majesty's Aerial Signal Corps.*

Her eyes scanned down the paper. It was signed not by a promotions board, nor by Lord Fieren Hinkal, nor even by an officer of the Ministry of the Army. Rather, it was the flowing, artful signature of Leon the 18th, King of Garnia.

Well, of course it was. A moment's reflection would have told her that, for only the Crown would dare set such a precedent—a precedent that might well pave the way for a fully integrated army. No doubt some confidant close to the king, an avid reader of the broadsheets and a realist who appreciated the army's manpower shortage, had whispered the idea in his ear.

"Don't get any ideas," the general said, with sharp emphasis on every word. "I expect you to use discretion when commanding junior lieutenants."

Oh, of course. They couldn't have her ordering male lieutenants around on the flimsy pretext that she outranked them.

"And I suppose you'll be wondering about a command," the general added.

Actually, it hadn't even occurred to her that they'd give her a ship. Putting a woman in command of an airship was as unprecedented as . . . well, as unprecedented as promoting one to senior lieutenant, now that she thought about it. But wouldn't it make a hell of a pitch, if and when the recruiters went looking for women to join the army?

"The ship we're giving you is one of those . . . what do they call them, Gaston?"

"Chasseurs, sir."

"It's a chasseur," the general said. "Do you know anything about flying chasseurs, Dupre?"

"*Osprey* was a chasseur, sir." The nearest thing to a warship in the air, a chasseur stood alone among airships, for only chasseurs were built to withstand the furious recoil of a cannon—albeit a specially designed, lightweight cannon known as a "bref gun."

"Well, I expect you'll manage," the general said. "The ship's *Mistral*. It's a new design."

Josette's enthusiasm was momentarily checked, for the general had said the two words every airman dreaded: "new design." Army flight engineers were forever searching for new and more efficient ways to get airmen killed. When they'd collected enough of them, they put them together in a devious package called a "new design." But she took heart. At least he hadn't said "revolutionary new design."

After a sip of tea, the general went on. "My advisors tell me that it's quite revolutionary."

Her heart sank. Like most revolutions, the aerial sort left a lot of dead bodies in its wake, and the survivors no better off than before. She wondered if the general knew what he was doing. Was he trying to get rid of her, the woman the broadsheets had credited with his victory, by her fiery death if necessary? Or did he see her merely as the Crown's latest pawn, to be obliterated if convenient, neutralized if necessary, or ignored if neither?

"Do make sure you acquire the proper insignia," the general said, casting a glance at her collar badge, which bore an image of crossed cannons and a single wing. She would have expected the army to provide her—at a public ceremony, no less—the double-winged collar badge appropriate to her new rank, along with epaulettes and sleeve badges for her dress uniform. It appeared that General Fieren, however, was of a mind that she ought to purchase or borrow them herself.

"Well, I'm sure you have preparations to make," the general said. "Don't let me keep you any longer."

Josette saluted, and the general returned the salute with a lackadaisical motion. She left the museum in a daze, bumping into several exhibits and nearly knocking a bust off its column.

Outside, she found Jutes resting against a parked cart. He looked up as she emerged.

"You haven't been waiting here, have you?" she asked.

Jutes straightened up and made an innocent face. "Just out for a walk, sir. Happened by. How did it go?"

"I have a ship," she said, hardly believing it herself. "It's going to be dangerous, though."

"Not a revolutionary new design, I hope."

"Actually, it is."

He grinned. "Then you'd best pick a sharp sergeant, sir, hadn't you?"

INSIDE THE MUSEUM, the general looked perturbed. "She didn't ask about a public promotion ceremony," he said. "I was hoping she would."

Gaston cocked his head. "Were you planning to have a ceremony, sir?"

"Of course I wasn't, but I wanted to see her face when I refused it. Well, Bernie, are you ready?"

Bernat was still staring off into the gallery in the direction Dupre had gone. "That woman is terrified," he said.

Fieran guffawed at the comment, and even the stolid Gaston twittered. "She's what?" his uncle asked.

"Terrified," Bernat said, looking at them. "When you gave her a ship, she turned absolutely pallid. Couldn't you see it?"

Gaston twittered again, but the general was suddenly thoughtful. "That woman's expression didn't change once, the entire time she was here. What do you think, Gaston?"

"If this had been a gallery of statues, sir, I think the museum staff would have dusted her by mistake."

Bernat shook his head. "You only have to . . ." He tried to think of how to explain it. "It was the way she stood, the way her eyes moved searchingly about the gallery, the way the corners of her lips twitched, the slight pauses where there shouldn't have been any. It all points to one thing: the prospect of commanding this ship positively unnerves her. No doubt because she knows her competence is lacking. You really didn't see it?"

The general handed his cold tea to Gaston and harrumphed.

"I hope you don't play cards, Uncle. Any decent card player should be able to see that she's bluffing."

"Perhaps you're right." The general pulled thoughtfully at his mustache. "I don't know if you're aware of this, Bernie, but that woman has been going around and selling her story to all the broadsheets, taking credit for my victory."

"I've seen the stories," Bernat said, "though until now, I didn't appreciate the implications."

"And now the Crown is rewarding her. Can you believe that?"

"Truly, Uncle, it stretches belief."

"It all stems from this nonsense about a manpower shortage," Fieren said. "We've suffered losses, certainly. You can't fight a war without casualties, you know. But the army's never been stronger. Morale's never been higher!" His voice had slowly been increasing in volume, until by now it was echoing through the galleries. "But there are those, Bernie, in the palace and in the newspapers, who would see the army suffer under these fanciful experiments. They would see it turned into a prancing bunch of women, instead of the masculine army that God intended. They would do it merely to slake their hatred and jealousy of me. Of my success! Of my achievements!"

And here Bernat saw his chance at deliverance. "But what can be done about it?" he asked calmly.

"Nothing needs be done," his uncle said, simmering and waving his hand. "She doesn't suspect it, obviously, but she's only a pawn in the Crown's little game of pushing an integrated army. And you know what happens to pawns, don't you, Bernie?"

Bernat grinned back. "They march across the board and get promoted, if you don't do anything to stop them. Shame there's nothing to be done about this one. The broadsheets have their lies, and what can anyone say against the broadsheets, when they speak with one voice? You'd need someone on the inside to get the truth out."

"Then I have just the man," Fieren said, as if he were about to drop something out of the clear blue sky. "I'm putting you on her new ship, and I want you to keep an eye on her."

"Me, Uncle?" Bernat asked, feigning surprise, but taking care not to overdo it lest he give away the game. "I'm not sure an ensign, useless as they are, is up to the task."

"Think on it, Bernie. If you can document evidence of her incompetence—something they can put in the papers, something that will end this foolishness—it will go very well for you."

Bernat looked up from thoughtful reflection, and a grin grew slowly on his face. "Very well," he said. "But I'll go as I am, not as an ensign. And I want ten liras' salary per week, paid in advance starting today, and another two hundred and fifty when I've gotten rid of her for you."

The general could not have been more stunned if a tiger had leapt from the next room and swallowed Bernat whole. The teacup slipped from Gaston's hand and smashed against the floor with a tinkling crash that echoed through the gallery.

Bernat smiled. "It's only the cost of a horse, Uncle."

4

"THAT OUR SHIP?" Jutes asked. "She looks like a bloody sardine."

Josette tilted her head. *Mistral* did look like a sardine, her envelope bulbous in the middle, with a sleek tapered silhouette that curved smoothly into a sharp tail behind and a convex nose in front. The envelope of a typical chasseur looked more like a cigar.

"The shape's supposed to give her better gas capacity and improve her turning performance," Josette said.

"Got my doubts about that, sir," Jutes said. "An' I don't see how they can make a curved girder as strong as a straight one. Don't matter if she turns fast, if her tail snaps off doing it."

Josette couldn't deny it, but in that moment, as she walked underneath her ship, she didn't care. Above her, the white cloth envelope had already been stretched over the superstructure's plywood frame. Along the ship's belly, though, the canvas hung open and the keel was exposed, awaiting installation of the engine. Above the keel, great luftgas bags nestled inside a rib cage of hoop girders.

Mistral might indeed be a sardine, but it was her sardine, goddamn it.

She leapt up and grabbed a longitudinal girder, by which she pulled herself up into the exposed keel. From there, she walked forward and climbed through sixty vertical feet of hoop girders to reach the rope ladder that led to the forward crow's nest.

She negotiated the ladder with ease and was soon in the crow's nest, looking down at the envelope from above. The crow's nest on *Mistral* was nothing so grand as its naval equivalent. It was really only a porthole cut in the top of the ship, a flap of fabric that could be peeled back and looked out of.

From it, Josette could see *Mistral*'s top side, the ship's fabric skin a dazzling white except where the Garnian eagle was painted on the tailfins. Josette lingered there, admiring the ship, until she saw the steamjack and boiler coming into the shed on a flatbed rail car. She descended the entire height of the ship so quickly that an observer might have been forgiven for worrying she'd fallen through it.

As her feet came down on the shed floor, a faraway voice called out, "Ah, there you are!" She turned to see a young aristocrat walking toward her. He walked for some time, and was out of breath by the time he reached them. "Good God," he said. "This place is bigger than it looks."

Such a large indoor space had a tendency to trick the eye, especially when two of the four airship berths were empty, and only the relatively slender *Lapwing* sat across from *Mistral* on the far side of the shed.

"You're Dupre," the aristocrat said, when he finally caught his breath.

She eyeballed him. "Surely. And you are?"

He stood up straight, in a poor imitation of military attention. After giving one of the clumsiest salutes Josette had ever seen, he offered his hand and said, "Lord Bernat Manatio Jebrit Aoue Hinkal, son of His Lord the Marquis of Copia Lugon."

She realized that this was the fop she'd seen with Fieren yesterday. "So you're General Lord Fieren's . . . what?"

"NEPHEW," BERNAT SAID, giving another salute to put her at ease. He'd been practicing all the way there.

Dupre seemed ready to ask another question when, without warning, she pointed at one of the yardsmen working on the airship and bellowed, "You there! That strut is not your fucking footstool!" The words echoed through the cavernous space inside the shed.

Bernat jumped back, thinking for a moment that she was yelling at him.

The man Dupre was pointing at was easily three times her size. His foot hung poised and quivering above a thin plank running between two thicker boards. "Sorry, Cap'n," he said.

Josette glanced at Bernat. "Sorry, I didn't mean to scare you. They like to stand on the struts. They're more delicate than they look."

Bernat swallowed. "The men?"

"The struts," Josette said. "The struts run between the corner boards of the box girders, like rungs on a ladder. The more ignorant yardsmen—the ones who exaggerated their skills so they could get a signal base job and dodge the conscription gangs, no doubt—have a terrible habit of trying to climb on them."

"But proper airmen are too smart for that?"

"I don't know about that, but I've never met an airman who made the mistake twice."

Bernat laughed nervously. "Quick learners."

She spared him a glance. "Yeah. I imagine you learn a lot on the way down. Things like, 'The ground sure comes up fast' and 'I should have stayed a farmer.' By the way, what the hell are you doing here?" After a few moments, she added a grudging, "My lord."

"I'm here as an observer," Bernat said. He began to look through the pockets of his jacket. "I have the paper here somewhere."

"Don't trouble yourself for papers, my lord. Your word's good with us. Just try to stay out of the way of moving ob-

jects, and if you have any questions, ask me or Sergeant Jutes."
She indicated the Brandheimian-looking fellow who was over-
seeing the installation of some mechanism into the ship's belly.

Well, that was easy. Bernat had expected some resistance,
had foolishly worried that she might suspect his true mission,
but the dumb bitch suspected nothing.

She was mouthy, though, and he liked that. If only she were
twenty years older, he might even consider taking her into his
bed. As it stood, however, he would just have to ruin her as
quickly and conveniently as he could, collect his money, and
return to more important pursuits.

JOSETTE LEANED INTO the open boiler, her hips resting on
the lip of the inspection hatch and her legs sticking out for balance. She ran her hand across the smooth surface inside the
steam drum, checking for defects. When satisfied, she swung
back and dropped to the ground next to Jutes.

He only said, "Damn small boiler for a chasseur this size."

"They had to make up the weight," Josette said. "*Mistral*
was slated to get a boilerless engine. Some kind of new gas-
combustion piston. Lightweight. No open flame. No ballast
lost to steam."

Jutes gave a skeptical snort.

"They never got it working, but by then she was half-built
and they had to make do." She watched as the yardsmen bolted
the boiler back together, keeping an eye on them to make sure
they tightened everything properly. It would be a pain in the
ass to fix any shoddy work once the boiler was mounted in
the keel, and quite deadly to take off without fixing it. "It's a
high-pressure design, though. The engineers say that it should
provide the same power as a larger boiler."

Jutes snorted with even more derision. "If that's true, sir,
then how come they don't just make 'em all like that?"

"That's the first question I asked the engineer liaison, and he told me . . ." The yardsmen had finished closing the steam drum and were hopping down from its railcar. Josette took a wrench from one of the yardsmen as they passed and hopped up to check the tightness of the nuts herself. "He told me," she said, reaching into the guts of the boiler and working her way around the drum, checking each nut in turn, "that a standard steamjack isn't built to handle the pressure this boiler can provide. Our steamjack is."

Jutes did not look satisfied. "So why ain't they building all the steamjacks like this one, too?"

"That was my next question," she said. She found a nut that didn't pass muster and, after shooting a poisonous look at the yardsman who'd tightened it, put her foot against the outer surface of the boiler and heaved on the wrench. It took the strength of both arms and a leg, but she managed finally to tighten it to her satisfaction. "The answer is that our steamjack is *also* a revolutionary new design."

"Bugger me," Jutes muttered. "So the entire damn engine, saving the water and the airscrews, is made of parts that no one's ever flown with before?"

"Actually," Josette said, "the airscrews are also a new design. You'll see when they install them. They only have two blades, like a scout's airscrews."

Jutes looked at her like she was making a bad joke.

"But," she said, "they're longer, with a more severe camber, which is meant to make up the difference. They look very stylish."

"Aye," Jutes said. "They'll sure look stylish, snapping off and tearing through the envelope. I'll have to have a letter ready, saying how stylish that looks, so all I need to do on the way down is sign it."

"And it's interesting that you mention the water, because—"

"Ahem, excuse me?" Bernat waved his hand daintily. It

seemed that he'd been trying to get their attention for some time before they noticed him. "It's getting rather near lunchtime. Would either of you like something from Oceane's? My treat. I just need one of your men to go fetch it."

Josette arched an eyebrow. "The army will provide you with lunch," she said. "We can't spare anyone right now."

"Begging your pardon, sir," Jutes said, his lips smacking together. "But the crew prospects should be gathering outside. Could send one of them."

Damn. She'd forgotten about the crew. "All right," she said. "Jutes, why don't you get to work picking out a crew, and you can send one of the prospects for your lunches." She leaned close and lowered her voice. "Don't let them see the ship, or you'll scare half of them away—and the smarter half at that. Might be best not to mention who's commanding her, either, if you can avoid it."

Jutes furrowed his brow.

"Not all of them were in the infantry," she said. "They may not look so kindly on *Osprey*'s casualty list."

He nodded. "Yes, sir."

Bernat butted in, still smiling like an idiot. "Any particular dish you'd prefer?"

She looked at him. "Nothing for me, thank you."

"You don't know what you're missing," Bernat said. "They make the most wonderful beef kofta, with fresh garlic and ginger. You'll never taste better."

"Another time," Josette said. "But why don't you accompany Sergeant Jutes and observe the crew selection? It's a truly fascinating affair." And it would pawn the fop off on someone else.

"So, how's life in the army treating you, Sergeant Jutes?" Bernat asked on their way across the airfield.

Jutes didn't look at him as he limped along. "Apart from a punctured leg, bad food when there's even food to be had, and—like as not—a fiery death aboard an untested airship, I can't complain, my lord."

Bernat turned pale. "Not aboard that airship, surely?"

"What airship did you think I was referring to, my lord?"

Bernat looked over his shoulder, back at the shed. "Surely you jest. A fiery death? I was under the impression that luftgas was not flammable. I've been assured of that, by several of my most intellectually snobby acquaintances."

"They ain't wrong, my lord. Luftgas ain't flammable, which sets it apart from every other damn thing aboard an airship. Envelope, bags, gondolas, girders, rope, fuel, and, of course, gunpowder for the muskets and cannons. All it takes is a few embers blown from the boiler fire, or some fool forgetting to wet the martingales afore firing the cannon, and you're looking at a long, hot plunge."

Bernat wanted to throw up. "And what of enemy action?"

"Yes, my lord, every once in a while the enemy manages to sink an airship. Mostly we take care of that for 'em, though. More convenient all around."

Bernat stared at Jutes, looking for signs that the old airman was teasing him. He found none, and they continued for a while in silence. Halfway across the compact earth and yellow grass of the airfield, Bernat worked up his nerve again and asked, "Your family hails from Brandheim, yes? When did they come south?" A little idle chitchat might build a rapport.

"Generations ago," he said. "My—now, which was he?—my great-great-grandfather lived in southern Brandheim when it was taken by the Vins. He fled to Quah-Halach, which belonged to Brandheim at the time. When Quah-Halach rebelled, his son, my great-grandfather, sided with Brandheim, and when the rebellion looked like it was going to succeed, he couldn't get back to Brandheim on account of there was

Vin-occupied territory in the way, so he had to flee south, into Garnia."

Bernat was about to go into his own family's long history, when he realized that Jutes wasn't finished.

"But my grandfather, a young buck at the time, didn't like it in Garnia, so he ran back to Quah to join the rebels. They'd already won by the time he got there, though. So when Brandheim invaded independent Quah-Halach, aiming to take it back, he fought against Brandheim. But of course, Brandheim won that one, and didn't take too kindly to Brandheimians fighting alongside the rebels. When they executed him, Grandma took the family back into Garnia, my father among them. He always said he wanted to run off and fight like Grandfather did, but when the Vins took Quah from Brandheim, he was too young; when Garnia took Halach from Brandheim, he was just married; and when Garnia took Quah from the Vins . . . well, by then he was too bloody confused about which side was which."

Bernat knew all the history from university lectures, but hearing the various wars and rebellions rattled off end to end made him wonder how there were any Quahnics or Halachians left alive. "And what did your father think of you joining the Garnian army?" he asked.

"Well, he wasn't happy," Jutes said, "especially when I fought in the Halachia campaign. Though maybe he was a little consoled that a Jutes was finally fighting on the winning side of something. Though this war might put the lie to that."

"Surely not," Bernat said. "Garnia hasn't lost a war in three generations."

Jutes didn't look convinced, but then, of course a Brandheimian would lack faith in Garnia, even though he was technically a native citizen. It was only natural—all the more natural, as the most recent war with Brandheim had only been last year.

As they approached the squat medical building, Bernat saw the crew prospects teeming at the door. "If this business is so dangerous," he asked Jutes, "why are there so many volunteers?"

"You have to die of something, don't you? And if it's gonna be in the army, might as well be the Aerial Signal Corps, where the pay's high and the girls in town hang on every word of your war stories." He grinned. "Besides which, promotion here is faster than anywhere else in the service, on account of positions opening up so often."

"I see." He turned his attention to the prospects. There were nearly a hundred of them gathered in front of the medical building, most wearing the sharp blue-and-brown uniforms of the Garnian army. A few already wore the coarse, more relaxed garb of airmen.

Jutes stopped in front of the group and shouted, "All right, you lot, assemble!" Every man and woman among them turned toward him and scrambled into four ranks, standing ramrod straight. Jutes went on, "This here is strictly volunteer work. If some officer sent you here as punishment, or to get rid of you, you just march your ass right back and tell that bastard the air corps ain't his personal flogging post."

After brief hesitation, six of the prospects stepped back from the ranks and slunk away. Jutes limped past the remainder, while Bernat kept what he hoped would prove to be a safe distance.

As he walked, Jutes said, "Here are the rules. No one may serve on an airship 'less you make out a will first, and you may not serve if you're married. If you get married after signing up, you will be kicked out of the air corps, and I will have to find a replacement for you. This will cause my cheerful disposition to sour, and I will discharge you from your service at a very great height, with the dearest hope that you land upon your new bride or groom."

He made it to the end of the ranks, where most of the female candidates had clustered, and turned toward them. "Women are permitted in this service as auxiliaries, and on rare occasions, they even end up being less trouble than they're worth. Surely someone has already told you that women auxiliaries are not permitted to fire a musket or service a cannon, and that is a fact. Someone has also told you that, whenever practical, women auxiliaries are put off the ship before going into battle to ensure their safety, and that is a bloody lie. It has never been and shall never be practical to set anyone on the ground before a fight, and whoever came up with that daft regulation is carrying around cowpats where his bloody brains ought to be. If any of you women are selected, you will go into battle with the rest of us, and you will be shot at with rockets, and you will be shot at with cannons, and you will be shot at with muskets, and I ain't met a bullet yet that's shy of tits."

Jutes stopped, took a step back, and eyed each of the women in turn.

"If any of that don't sound like it appeals to you, then I suggest you go find a job in a brothel, where you can better serve the needs of the army."

All the women stood their ground, though several looked significantly grumpier than before. Even Bernat was feeling uncomfortable. It took a conscious effort not to squirm.

"Still not moving, eh?" asked Jutes. "Well, feel free to sneak off when my back is turned. For any what stays and is picked, man or woman, you will receive a bonus of five rials, but almost all of that will go to the cost of your harness, helmet, goggles, and serge jacket. The weekly pay's double what you get in the regular army, and any crewman under one hundred ninety pounds—and that's including your baggage, ladies—is paid a weekly bonus for the difference, at two dinars per pound."

One of the bigger men shouted, "What if we're over one hundred ninety pounds on account of muscle, Sarge?"

Jutes shot him a look. "In your case, Luc Lupien, I'll cut bits off you until you're under."

This produced some chuckling in the ranks, which Jutes silenced with a glare.

"Mechanics first. Go through this door and see the sawbones. If he likes the look of you, he'll send you on to me. The rest of you wait here and think real hard about whether this is the right bloody place for you." Jutes whistled at the big man who'd interrupted him. "Except for you, Corporal Lupien, 'cause you just volunteered to fetch my lunch. Talk to Lord Hinkal here." He indicated Bernat with his thumb, then went inside.

Bernat, flush with the ten liras he'd earned in advance of his first week of espionage, gave Lupien enough money for three meals and told the corporal to take one for himself, then ventured into the medical building. He found an examination room behind the first door and a small, sparse office behind the second, where Jutes was sitting at a desk.

"Thought you'd be easier on the women," Bernat said, "seeing how respectful you are toward Captain Dupre."

"It's a hard service," Jutes said. "Wouldn't be doing 'em any favors by going easy on 'em. If it was up to me, I don't think I'd let women in at all."

In this, Bernat saw an opening. He was just about to inquire further when Jutes banged on the wall, in an apparent signal to the medical officer in the next room.

"How long will the exam take?" Bernat asked, setting his other inquiries aside for the moment.

"Not long, depending on the prospect," Jutes said, as a paunchy, gray-whiskered man came through the door. Jutes rose to shake his hand. "Good to see you, Vincent."

"And you, Abdiel. You're looking good."

"And you're looking . . ." Jutes grinned. "Well taken care of."

Vincent laughed and smacked his belly. Instead of the jiggle that Bernat was expecting, the slap made a thump and the firm belly hardly moved.

"Gears is yours if you want it," Jutes said. He sat down and turned his paper around, offering a pen. "*Mistral*'s a revolutionary new design, though. I'll understand if you refuse."

"To hell with it," Vincent said, signing his name. "I've gone down three times already. A fourth doesn't scare me."

That was too much for Bernat. "I don't mean to interrupt," he said, "but do you mean that you've been in three airship crashes and survived?"

"No, my lord, I died on every occasion," Vincent said. "By the third time, I'd become so inert, they had no choice but to make me an officer."

"Warrant officer," Jutes said, looking at Bernat. "Vincent here is always putting on airs. And the thing he ain't telling you is, he was probably the cause of all them crashes."

This earned a laugh from Vincent.

"What do you think of the other prospects?" Jutes asked.

"Paul Rosen will do for Chips," Vincent said. He looked to Bernat. " 'Chips' being the ship's carpenter, my lord, just as 'Gears' is the chief mechanic."

Jutes made a note on his paper. "And what about mechanic's mate?"

"Thin fare, I'm afraid. Only one of them fools has experience on air-cooled condensers."

"Which one?"

"You're not going to like it, Abdiel."

"Which one, Vincent?"

Vincent curled his lips into a smile that was somehow reminiscent of a wolf. "The tall brunette with the ass to die for."

"Bugger me." Jutes sighed. "The pretty ones can't handle the strain. Everyone knows that."

Vincent shrugged.

"And she'll cause all kinds of fights and strife among the men."

"She might, at that."

"And we'll want a woman for monkey rigger. That'll make two women on the crew, and the cap'n, and I hear they're sending us a girl ensign, too. That's four. Four bloody women on one boat."

"That seems to be the math, Abdiel."

"Bugger me." Jutes lowered his head and thought. "Well, send her in."

Vincent left and Private Grey entered. She looked at Bernat with some confusion, then saluted Sergeant Jutes.

Jutes made a show of studying his single sheet of paper. "You're a woman," he said, and only then deigned to look at her.

"Auxiliary Private Miriam Grey, Sergeant."

"I didn't ask your name, Private."

She swallowed. "Er, uh, yes, Sergeant. I am a woman, or so they tell me."

Jutes leapt to his feet and shouted, his voice so loud it rattled the window. "Was that a joke, Private Grey?"

Bernat was surprised to hear her say, as loud as Jutes but in a ringing soprano, "Yes, Sergeant, it was."

Jutes was around the desk as quickly as his wounded leg allowed, staring at her with his face half an inch from hers. "Did you just raise your voice to me, Grey?"

"I believe I did, Sergeant!"

Bernat put his hands over his ears as Jutes shouted even louder. "Are you trying to get your fucking teeth knocked in, Private? This is the Royal fucking Aerial Signal Corps. I've shot women prettier than you, Private Grey. You think I won't hit one?"

"No, Sergeant." Her voice broke as she tried to match his volume. "I think you're trying to get me to lose my nerve, so you'll have an excuse to reject me, even though I'm the best damn man for the job by a long shot."

Jutes's face was even closer to Grey's now. His voice was suddenly quiet, but there was a growl in it that was somehow more terrifying than the screaming. "And what makes you think that, Private?"

Grey was shaking all over, but she managed to speak in an even voice, with only a small tremor. "I heard you talking through the wall, Sergeant. From the exam room."

There followed a long silence, broken only by a hoarse cough in the next room. Bernat studied the wall, which did look rather thin.

Jutes shoved a pen into Grey's hand and said, "Sign the bloody paper and send Rosen in on your way out."

Private Grey's voice was instantly giddy. "Yes, Sergeant! Thank you, Sergeant!"

Bernat caught Jutes studying Private Grey's backside on her way out, though he obviously wasn't as impressed as Gears had been. When he was sure she was out of earshot, Bernat asked, "Have you really shot women?"

Jutes just shrugged. "Probably not. Shot *at* women, though. The Vins have 'em in their air corps, same as us, and I once saw a woman in amongst their skirmishers. No women in the Brandheim army, at least not officially. Mayhap I have relatives up there who say otherwise."

None of which helped Bernat in the slightest, but at least the rest of the interviews went more smoothly. Rosen was confirmed as carpenter. Corporal Lupien, when he returned with lunch, signed on as rudderman. Then came the selection of an elevatorman, two relief steersmen, two musketmen, and nine other airmen to rig the ship and service the cannons.

By the time they were finished, it was near dinner, and Bernat happily offered to treat Jutes to another meal. When it was delivered, they sat down to eat in the cramped little office.

"So," Bernat said around his first bite of lamb kebab, "tell me all about the women of the air corps."

JOSETTE STOOD UNDER the bow and looked back along the length of *Mistral*. The yardsmen had just finished attaching the hurricane deck to the underside of the ship at frame seven. Suspended by thick hemp cables, the hurricane deck was open to the air, providing maximum visibility below. It was also the widest open space aboard the ship, but it would soon become cozier when the yardsmen installed steering equipment, ballast and vent pull ropes, flight instruments, and two bref guns.

She wasn't sure what to think of those two cannons. Two-gun chasseurs were becoming more common, but there were advantages to single-gun ships. Foremost among them was the savings in weight—not just in the gun, but in needing to carry three fewer crewmen as cannoneers. Less weight meant less luftgas, which meant a smaller envelope, which meant a nimbler ship.

She still hadn't made up her mind when Jutes hobbled up and saluted.

"You haven't seen my goddamn officers anywhere, have you, Jutes? They were supposed to be on the afternoon train, but they haven't shown up."

"Haven't seen them, sir."

"Ah, well. Have you finished with the crew?"

"Yes, sir. And ordered them to get some rest, sir."

"Good. We'll be lucky to take off at dawn, at the rate the final assembly is going."

"Dawn?" asked Bernat, as he came up from behind Jutes. "Should we have breakfast beforehand, or will it be served aboard?"

They both turned to stare.

Bernat looked back at them sheepishly. "Or perhaps the army prefers to brunch?"

"My lord," Josette said, her tone approximating the deference to which the fop was technically entitled, "I'm afraid we won't be able to invite you aboard this flight. Perhaps when we've returned from our aerial trials, a week or so from now, we can have you along for an afternoon cruise."

Bernat smiled like a fool. "There must be some misunderstanding. I'm already invited aboard." He searched through his pockets and pulled out a folded letter. "By General Lord Fieren."

"Bugger me," Jutes muttered, then added a hasty, "my lord."

Josette took the letter and read it twice, hoping to find a way out. But it wasn't a letter of permission, as she had first thought, but orders addressed directly to her, instructing her to take the fop aboard. The orders mentioned no time frame, so she was stuck with him indefinitely.

"There's been some mistake," she said. "We can't spare the weight. I'll talk to the general and have this cleared up."

Bernat chuckled. "My uncle isn't in Arle. He went north ahead of the army, this morning." He looked around. "I thought everyone knew that."

She read the orders a third time, hoping to find some caveat or loophole, but they were rock solid. "It says you're an observer," she said. "What, exactly, are you meant to observe?"

"Airship operations," the fop said.

She looked him up and down. "The general sent *you* to observe the operation of an airship?"

He only smiled back. "I'm a quick learner."

So he was a spy. He had to be a spy. Did the general think a woman couldn't handle an airship, or did he merely doubt her loyalty? No, it wasn't that. In all likelihood, he didn't give a damn if his airship officers were loyal or competent—they were only airship officers, after all, and not even worth re-membering. She was merely a pawn in his feud with the news-papers and the Crown, and he'd sent another pawn after her.

Which meant she had a choice. She could make a futile, frustrating attempt to keep the spy off her ship, or . . .

"Welcome to the crew," she said. "Sergeant Jutes, at your convenience, please enter Lord Hinkal in the ship's books as a supernumerary observer, and see to his baggage."

"Shall I disappoint one of the crewmen, sir? There are one or two we might get by without, if weight's a problem."

Josette shook her head. "No, we'll find the weight some-where else."

"Yes, sir," Jutes said. He turned to Bernat. "If you'll step this way, my lord."

Bernat gave her a shallow bow and a warm smile before fol-lowing after Jutes. She returned the bow but not the smile.

When they returned to the shed a quarter of an hour later, Jutes and Bernat had two officers in tow. As they approached, Josette recognized the scrawny, tall one as Junior Lieutenant Nicolas Martel, her new first officer. She asked as he ap-proached, "What've you been up to, Nic?"

Martel grinned. "Counting days until I have the time in rank for a promotion to senior lieutenant, so I can get my own damn ship."

"I wonder what that must be like," Josette said. She'd spent nearly ten years as an auxiliary junior lieutenant, so long that she could have earned her senior lieutenant's wings five times over if she'd been born with different anatomy. "Where the hell have you been? You were supposed to be here hours ago."

"Our damn train was stuck on a side track while the regular army used both the main ones to send regiments north. Oh, and this is Ensign Kember." Martel stepped aside and indicated the raven-haired girl of about fifteen who lingered behind him.

Kember straightened up and saluted so awkwardly that she

poked herself in the eye. As the eye reddened and watered, she tried to hold it open, but she couldn't stop blinking.

"Ensign," Josette said, taking special care to not notice the girl's ocular flailing. "Please supervise things here. Nic, let's visit the warehouse and get our ship outfitted."

Martel looked through the shed door, at the darkness outside. "Will the quartermaster be in at this hour?"

"No, she won't," Josette said, "and that's the point."

He grinned and said, "Very good, sir."

At that time of the evening, the quartermaster's office was staffed by a single clerk, who slid the book he'd been reading under a stack of papers when Josette and Martel entered.

Josette walked up to the desk and casually brushed the papers aside. *"Memoirs of a Woman of Ill-Repute,"* she said. "That's a damn fine book."

The cover was blank, giving no indication of the book's title or pornographic content. The clerk looked at her with wondering eyes.

"I recognize the scuff marks," Josette said. "That book's been passed around more than the titular character. What are you up to, chapter seven? That's my favorite one."

Behind her, Martel chimed in, "Chapter eight is my favorite. Those twenty-seven pages have gotten me through many a long flight."

The clerk quietly slid the paperwork back over the book and asked, "So, umm, what may I do for you, sirs?"

"We're outfitting *Mistral*," Josette said.

"Oh." The clerk fidgeted awkwardly. "Sorry, sir, but I can't let you into the warehouse, or issue you ordnance and supplies, until the quartermaster returns in the morning. She left very specific instructions."

Josette narrowed her eyes. "These instructions specified me by name, I imagine?"

The clerk cleared his throat and looked away. "Not entirely

by name, sir. Not unless you have an unusually long and profane first name."

She leaned over the desk and said, "It's Private Corne, right?" The clerk nodded. "Private Corne, perhaps if you forget those instructions, we'll forget what we saw you reading while on duty."

The clerk thought for only a moment. "Sorry, sir, I can't help you."

She should have known threats wouldn't work. The quartermaster might yell at Corne for the book, but she'd skin him alive if he opened the warehouse.

But what the hell else could she do? If she somehow managed to drag the quartermaster out here, and somehow convinced her to open her stores, the spiteful bitch would see to it that *Mistral* got the worst of everything. She'd end up with rotten cordage, caked gunpowder, and spoiled rations. As Josette was weighing the question, Martel walked up and sat on the edge of the desk. He looked at the slender clerk, smiled, and said, "What are you doing in the quartermaster's office, anyway? A man like you ought to be in the air."

Something in the clerk's demeanor shifted. Josette couldn't put her finger on precisely what it was, but it reminded her of a dog scenting food. "I volunteered for *Mistral* today," Corne said. "I volunteer for every new crew, but I haven't been picked yet, sir."

As he scooted further onto the desk, Martel said, "I think that's an unfortunate oversight. Don't you think so, Captain?"

"Oh, indeed," she said. "Not ten minutes ago, Sergeant Jutes was indicating his regret at not picking a certain man, and I do believe you match his description. If you could see your way to letting us into the warehouse, Private, we could clear up that mistake."

"But the quartermaster . . ."

Martel flashed him a smile and said, "Will be a thousand feet below your heels, come morning."

Corne fished in a desk drawer, then slapped a key into Martel's waiting hand. "I'll hitch a cart for the supplies," he said.

Josette watched the clerk run from the room, then looked back to Martel, who was beaming at her. "Well done," she said.

"My pleasure," Martel said, trotting ahead and unlocking the door to the warehouse. "I only hope the extra weight won't be a problem."

As they stepped inside the sprawling but neatly ordered warehouse, Josette said, "I'll have Jutes dismiss someone to make it up. Now, look for good powder, shot, flints, and rations. Don't take anything we aren't entitled to, but take the best of it. I'll look for good cordage, cannons, and muskets."

She found the muskets first, and was just hefting a crate when she noticed, in a separate stack a few feet away, twenty crates with BREWER RIFLE written on their sides. She could hardly believe it, until she opened a crate and checked for herself. She reverently lifted one of the rifles, pulled the hammer back to full cock, and sighted down the three-foot barrel.

"I want to take this gun to bed and make a baby with it," she said.

"Sir?" Martel asked.

She quickly set the rifle back into its slot inside the crate and said, "Nothing."

Martel wandered over anyway. "Are these meant to replace our muskets?" he asked, as he looked the rifles over.

"I don't know," Josette said. "I've been requesting rifles for air crews for years now. But every time I put in a request, I get a letter back informing me that rifles take too long to load, and politely suggesting that I stop asking for them. But perhaps they've finally come around." She closed the crate and lifted it. "All I know is that I took a crate of them, thinking they were the muskets to which we were entitled. By the time I opened it and noticed they were rifles, we were already in the air and it was too late to return them." She took a crate of ten rifles and headed for the outer doors, where Private Corne was busy hitching a cart.

As she walked, she heard the stack of crates rattle behind her, and looked back to see Martel lifting a second crate. He grinned and said, "All I know is, I had no idea my captain already took possession of the ship's small arms. By the time I discovered the error, we were already in the air, and it was too late to return the excess."

"An unconscionable mistake," Josette said. "When you do finally discover it, please consider yourself reprimanded."

Martel grinned again. "Yes, sir."

"How much longer will this take?" Bernat asked Sergeant Jutes. "The ship looked perfectly ready to go when I arrived."

Jutes eyeballed him. "It didn't have an engine in it, my lord."

"Well, of course not, but it has an engine now, I think. So how much longer will it take?"

Before Jutes could answer, Ensign Kember approached, and the sergeant snapped instantly to attention. Bernat was about to wave his hand in front of the man's eyes when the ensign spoke for him. "It'll be at least four in the morning before all the rigging is done, but we'll most likely put the launch off until dawn."

"Dawn?" Bernat asked.

"Best time to launch an airship, my lord. Light winds, and the envelope warms up faster than the outside air, which gives us a bit of extra lift."

Bernat made a sour face. "What's the point of human flight, if it's so dreadfully inconvenient? I think I'll retire for the night and come back at dawn."

The little ensign nodded. "If you're sleepy, Sergeant Jutes will see you home, my lord."

Bernat had never said he was sleepy. "Oh, that isn't necessary."

"It's no trouble at all," Kember said.

It seemed to Bernat that the ensign could not possibly know how much or how little trouble it would be to Sergeant Jutes, but Jutes dutifully accompanied Bernat without complaint or apparent displeasure. When they were out of the hanger, Bernat said to him, "She's awfully bossy toward you for a little girl, isn't she?"

Jutes showed no sign of agreement. "She's a commissioned officer and I ain't," he said. "If she ain't being bossy, she's doing it wrong."

"It seems odd though, doesn't it, that she's ordering you around, when you've been in the army longer than she's been alive?"

"That's the way of the world, my lord."

Bernat smiled inwardly. He had Jutes escort him to his hotel, and as soon as the sergeant was out of sight, he proceeded from there to the nearest card hall. He purchased an ivory pocket notebook from a man desperate to cobble together money for his stake, and between hands he began composing the missive that would end Dupre:

The common airman, and he must certainly be considered the preeminent authority on the subject, does not look favorably upon his female shipmates. Indeed, those with the most experience are inclined to forbid women from the service altogether. The female officers, including Lieutenant Dupre, see this and fear that their shrewlike behavior may not be tolerated for much longer. They therefore treat these experienced men with the most egregious, spirit-breaking disrespect, as if they were

*commanding the meanest hired servants rather than
proud fighting men with decades of meritorious service.*

DAWN WAS ONLY a pale promise in the eastern sky when the
crew arrived for weigh-in. Many of them blanched when they
saw the shape of their new ship, and more still when they saw
the shape of her captain. Josette kept one eye on the ship and
one on the crew as they assembled in single file, baggage slung
over their shoulders. Jutes stood nearby with chalk and slate
in hand.

"Nothing goes on the ship if you don't take it on the scale
with you," he said. "And you don't get on the scale unless you
got your jacket, harness, cap, and goggles where I can see
them. Private Corne, you're first."

Corne stopped fumbling with his safety harness and took
a spritely step onto the big scale. Jutes slid the counterweights
back and forth until they balanced out at two hundred pounds.
And then, without word or warning, he snatched Corne's bag
from his shoulder, shoved his hand deep within, and pulled
out a bottle of cheap wine.

Corne babbled a barely coherent string of apologies and de-
nials, but Jutes wasn't even listening. He upended the bag and
spilled its contents on the shed floor. They included two more
wine bottles, half a dozen woolen socks, underclothes, a quarter wedge of cheese, and two shaving kits. After prodding the
shaving kits with his boot and making a show of counting
them on his fingers, Jutes leaned over and rifled through the
woolens.

He came up shouting. "Luc Lupien! Will you kindly explain why this man is carrying socks with your bloody initials sewn into them?"

Corporal Lupien stepped forward and stood at attention,
his bag hanging limp and half-full on his shoulder. He cleared

his throat and said, "Those are common initials, Sarge. Maybe they're the initials of the lady who sewed the socks? You know, kind of signing her work."

"Did you hear that, Private?" Jutes asked Corne. "Corporal Lupien has generously volunteered to carry all of your baggage along with his. Lupien, repack all this or you'll miss your turn." As Lupien bent to retrieve a wine bottle, Jutes roared, "Leave the spirits unless you want to be one!"

Satisfied that the situation was well under control, Josette left things to Jutes and went to finish some last minute paperwork. By the time she returned, the crew had been weighed in and loaded aboard, and the fop still hadn't made an appearance. With any luck, he would miss the boat.

She took one final walk around the ship, gathered her things, and ascended the ladder. "Coming aboard," she said at the top, and vaulted over the rail to the hurricane deck, which was crowded with newly installed instruments of flight and war. The bref guns had been emplaced with their muzzles run out through ports in the front railing. A pair of wooden steering wheels had been installed ahead and to either side of the companionway ladder, but aligned to face outward—unlike those of a naval vessel, which faced forward. Safety lines, called "jack lines" after the fashion of the navy, were suspended overhead, under a wicker catwalk that ran through the keel above. Between the jack lines there was an array of colored pull-cords, which ran into and along the keel, then turned up or down to attach to valves which could vent luftgas to make the ship heavier or release water ballast to lighten it. A cluttered bank of gauges and indicators filled what little space was left overhead, displaying the time, temperature, pressure, airspeed, inclination, heading, and altitude.

And then there was a spot, just forward of the wheels in the middle of the deck, in view of the instruments and in easy reach of every pull-cord. It was not marked or designated in any way. It looked exactly like every other patch of the wicker deck.

But the crew gave it deference. As they bustled about, making their last-minute preparations, they stepped lightly around it, as if around a basket of eggs. Josette stepped to the edge of the invisible barrier surrounding that sacred spot on the deck. She looked down at it and took a breath.

She stepped into it, faced forward, and at that moment ceased to be Senior Lieutenant Dupre and became Captain Dupre of *Mistral*. The change was purely ceremonial, an empty title borrowed from the traditions of the navy, and yet she felt suddenly heavier.

In the hush that came over the deck, she said, "Weigh off and rig for the mast."

The crew set to work. Once moored to the mobile mast, *Mistral* would be ferried out to the airfield. What's more, they would be "flying the mast"—off the ground, albeit only by a couple of yards—meaning that Josette would no longer be obliged to bring the fop aboard.

She almost made it, too. They were nearly secured when she heard an annoying voice shout from the shed floor, "Ahoy up there! The airship, ahoy! Permission to come aboard!"

Jutes went to the rail and looked down. "We ain't in the navy, Yer Excellency. You don't need to ask permission. Just make sure you announce yourself when you step on, so we can adjust the ballast."

Bernat stuck his head over the rail and asked, "If permission isn't required, how do you keep interlopers off the ship?"

"By virtue of it being an airship, Yer Excellency," Jutes said. "A thing which no sane or rational soul would ever wish to sneak onto."

At length, Bernat came over the rail with two heavy bags. He had his harness on upside down, with the leg loops secured around his shoulders and the shoulder straps hugging his crotch. Josette chose not to point out the error.

"We are weighed off, sir," Kember said, once sandbags had been dropped to account for Bernat and his baggage.

"Take us out," Josette said.

Two dozen yardsmen pushed the mobile mast forward, and *Mistral* lurched forward along with it, out of the shed and into the dim purple light outside. Other yardsmen walked alongside, holding lines attached to *Mistral's* keel, which they could heave on to correct for any crosswinds as she left the hangar. Yet more yardsmen walked beside the hurricane deck, holding handles on its underside, in case their weight was needed to bring *Mistral* down from an errant gust.

The eastern sky was rosy when they arrived at their launch circle, with streaks of orange slicing up through scattered clouds on the horizon. At the order, "Bring her into the wind," the ground crew tugged the ship around until she faced the light morning breeze bow-on, and then the bustle of activity abated.

Bernat, who had been loitering about the starboard side of the hurricane deck, seemed confused by the repose. "What now?"

"We watch the sunrise, of course."

She expected some further inquiry about this, but the fop only frowned and seemed to make a mental note of it. They watched the sunrise and, more pertinently, let the luftgas soak up heat that would grant them additional buoyancy in the still-cool morning air. This in turn would allow *Mistral* to carry more ballast in the form of sandbags handed aboard by yardsmen, the additional weight of which might forestall the need to vent luftgas later on.

When Josette judged that they were at their peak of buoyancy, she turned and looked up the companionway, where

Jutes had his station inside the keel. "Spin up the steamjack," she said.

Jutes relayed the order, and Josette could hear the mechanics making a flurry of adjustments that brought on an angry hiss of steam from the boiler. The hiss was eclipsed by the sound of the steamjack, which slowly rose in volume and pitch until it became a shrieking whine.

"Is this normal?" Bernat asked, raising his voice to be heard. He looked rather perturbed.

Josette shrugged her shoulders and said, "I've never heard this exact sound before, except once from the *Fulmar*, just before it exploded."

He stared at her for a while, eyes wide and mouth open, until he seemed to notice that the crew was unalarmed. "Very droll," he said, with resentment in his eyes.

"Cast off mast," Josette said, in lieu of a reply.

Above her head, the wicker catwalk bulged down as the monkey rigger ran forward along the keel. Plywood creaked forward as the rigger scrambled through the ever-narrowing keel toward the bow. Seconds later, Josette heard the rigger call, "Mast cast off."

Jutes repeated it at a bellow. "Mast is cast off!"

"Cast off all lines."

Kember went to the rail and shouted the order to the ground crew, then reported, "We are free forward, sir."

"We are free aft, sir," Jutes called down the companionway.

Now the only thing holding *Mistral* to the earth was the weight of the ground crew. Josette paused for a moment—not for any technical reason, but merely to savor the moment. Then she took a deep breath and shouted, "Up ship!"

Ensign Kember and Sergeant Jutes repeated the order at once, she over the starboard side and he along the keel. The ensign ran to the port side and shouted it again. The remaining ground crew heaved the ship upward before letting go.

"Set gears to reverse."

Jutes shouted, "Reverse gears." There was a clank as the gears engaged, connecting the spinning steam turbine to six booms, three on either side of the ship, each of which turned a two-bladed airscrew. The ship slid gracefully back from the mast, rising as it went.

At the rail, Bernat's short hair blew in the wash of the reversed airscrews, his lace flapping against the fringes of his coat. Josette donned her leather cap and goggles, as did the rest of the deck crew, but Bernat did not appear to have any. As he tried to hold his hair in place against the blast of wind, he shouted, "I was wondering, why do they call this the hurricane deck?"

"Nobody knows," Josette answered.

As the ship ascended and backed away from the stubby mooring mast, the ground crew came into view ahead of them, growing smaller and smaller. At two hundred feet altitude, Josette ordered, "Set gears to forward. Steamjack to one-quarter power."

The hurricane deck became a less turbulent place as *Mistral*'s backward movement slowed. The ship came to a halt, and for a single moment the air was completely still.

And then *Mistral* drove forward.

5

BERNAT WATCHED ARLE go past below. With the wind coming from the east, it would be another smoky day, but at this time of morning the manufactories had only just begun to belch soot, so the view was still clear. They passed over Arle's semaphore tower, so close that Bernat thought he could reach down and touch one of the articulated signal arms, and so close over the top floor of the Pagoda of the Pallid Jird that he could have tossed down an almond cake, or whatever it was monks ate.

He looked to Dupre, but her attention was fixed on the instruments mounted above her station. Bernat had no idea what the various needles and floats meant, but whatever it was, it inspired something vaguely like a smile in Dupre. Which is not to say that her mouth smiled, but her lips did tighten at the corners, and her habitual scowl diminished incrementally.

Bernat found it unsettling.

Dupre went to the rail and looked back along the length of the airship. When Bernat followed her example, she pushed him back. "If you're going to do that," she said, "put your harness on right side up and clip on to one of the jack lines. Then you won't fall out."

"But you're not clipped on."

"I'm not going to fall out." She leaned over the rail, so far that her feet left the deck and she pivoted on the rail like a seesaw. She hung there in that precarious stance, from which any stray gust or eddy of wind might have sent her plummeting.

Bernat wanted to grab her feet to keep her from going over-board, if only because he didn't think he'd get his money if she accidentally killed herself.

Martel came down the companionway, a logbook open in one hand. "First aerial test," he said to Dupre's boots, "is rate of climb at one degree up elevator, while weighed off."

Dupre tilted back onto the deck, looked at him, and said, "Later. I want to do the speed trial."

Martel grinned and said, "Yes, sir. I was hoping you'd say that."

"Pass the word to the mechanics: increase steamjack power to one-half. Let's see what her cruising speed is."

The steamjack's whine grew louder and higher. The corners of Dupre's mouth tightened further as she watched what Bernat now took to be the kinemeter, which measured air-speed. Its needle climbed steadily until it reached twenty-five knots, then settled to a stop.

"Pass the word: increase steamjack to three-quarters power."

Bernat watched Dupre's face to see what she looked like when her scowl went away entirely, despite a nagging worry that the sight could turn him to stone. But as the steamjack and airscrews grew louder, the tightening at the corners of Dupre's lips relaxed, and they drooped downward into their habitual orientation. Bernat looked up to see that the needle of the kinemeter indicator had hardly budged, rising only one knot, to twenty-six.

"Increase to full power."

Again, the needle twitched upward only a little. Now Dupre looked more unhappy than usual, something that Bernat had heretofore believed humanly impossible.

"Increase to emergency power," she said.

The whole ship vibrated as the steamjack's whine became a screaming wail, but the airspeed needle didn't rise by even a full knot. It seemed to be stuck halfway between twenty-seven and twenty-eight. Dupre pulled herself up by an overhead girder and tapped the dial. The indicator needle shivered, but didn't rise.

"Reduce power to full," she said, dropping back to the deck. She crossed her arms over her chest.

"She's not slow, sir," Martel said, as he recorded the data in the logbook.

"Well, she's not fast." Dupre took the logbook from Martel, double-checked the figures, and put her initials in the margin.

Bernat, meanwhile, was working on his letter to Uncle Fieren. He couldn't very well pull out his notebook, but he already had the latest section composed in his head:

Lieutenant Dupre has so little command of the flying characteristics of airships that, in the midst of performing her air trials (out of the order so carefully prescribed by army engineers), she was caught entirely unawares by the ship's top speed. She went on to whine petulantly that the army had not supplied her with a faster ship, as if the entire Garnian army existed only to serve her whims.

Or maybe, "as if the ship were her plaything" would be better. As he was contemplating it, Dupre looked over, as if noticing him for the first time. "Why don't we get you situated, my lord. Lieutenant Martel, you have the deck."

Dupre took one of Bernat's bags, testing its weight. "What do you have in here?" she asked.

"Just the essentials," he said, smiling and picking up the second bag. They went up the companionway together. Inside the keel, the air was relatively still, though Bernat's hair continued to blow in a light breeze.

He was surprised at how much of the giant ship's insides he could see, standing at the top of the companionway ladder. There were no internal cabins or bulkheads, as he'd imagined. Rather, the interior reminded him of the great whale skeleton on display in the Kuchin Museum of Natural Science. If one turned the skeleton on its back and multiplied its size several times, the creature's ribs might be comparable to *Mistral*'s transverse frames, as he believed they were called. The only difference was that a whale's ribs didn't meet at the ends, whereas the frames made a complete circle around the ship at regular intervals along its length.

And if the frames were the whale's ribs, then the keel was obviously its spine. Though, contrary to his expectations, he was not standing atop the keel, but within it. Five long lines of girders, running from bow to tail and twice as thick as any of the other girders, surrounded him and seemed to give the keel most of its strength. Two ran overhead, one ran at waist level on either side, and one ran directly underneath the wicker catwalk. The fact that he could see it through the spaces in the wicker did nothing to help his faith in the ship's sturdiness.

At each frame, the spinelike keel girders were joined at right angles to the riblike transverse girders. Short, narrow girders linked the keel girders to each other, also at right angles, so that the narrow girders traced the outline of a pentagon around the outside of the keel. Another pair of narrow girders connected the two overhead keel girders to the one under the catwalk, making an inverted triangle inside the pentagon outlined at each frame, with the perilously narrow catwalk running down the middle. With something like ten frames, this made for quite a lot of keel girders, but they were spread so far across the length of the ship that the entire affair still appeared skeletal.

There was no ceiling above the keel. He could see straight up into the giant luftgas bags that filled the superstructure— something like the whale's lungs and other organs. Only over the engine area, farther aft, did a fabric barrier separate the bags from the keel.

Forward of the companionway ladder, halfway to the bow, there were cages full of pigeons attended by an airman, though he seemed to be agitating them more than caring for them. Bernat also noticed a board, apparently serving as a desk, which had some writing materials on it. Good. At the rate he was going, he would soon run out of space for Dupre's faults in his notebook. Beyond the pigeons, the keel corridor narrowed, the five lines of keel girders squeezing in close to each other as they curved upward toward the nose-cone.

Aft, the keel catwalk narrowed as it ran between a pair of cylinders, and beyond that it split in two, bisecting around a tangle of tubes and gears in the middle of the airship. He couldn't see it with those tubes in the way, but he knew the steamjack turbine and boiler lay farther aft.

"Hold the jack line," Dupre said, indicating the single line running above their heads.

"Even inside?"

"You're in more danger of falling here than on the hurricane deck," she said. She pointed to the canvas walls covering the bottom two sides of the keel's pentagon, which were apparently the only barrier between the keel and the outside air. "You could punch through these walls quite easily, my lord."

Bernat cocked his fist.

"Although I'd appreciate it if you didn't."

He lowered it and shrugged.

She looked past him and asked, "Private Corne, what the hell are you doing?"

Corne looked up from the pigeons, but continued to rattle their cages with both hands. "Er, Corporal Lupien told me I had to keep the pigeons flying, so we'd be light enough to stay in the air, sir. He said we'll crash if more than half of them land at once."

Despite the noise of the engine and the airscrews, Bernat could hear snickering coming from the hurricane deck.

"And you believed him?" Dupre asked.

Corne swallowed. "Er—no, sir."

She put her hand on her hip and took a deep breath. "Then why are you harassing those birds, man?"

"Well, you see, sir, he is my superior, sir. That and, well, better safe than sorry?"

Dupre seemed to consider this. "Very well, Private. Carry on." She walked aft along the catwalk.

Bernat followed. "You're just going to let him keep at it?"

"Well, I don't want the ship to crash," she said, turning sideways to pass between the cylinders that constricted the catwalk.

Bernat squeezed between them, and was surprised to find them cold and leathery. A poke confirmed that they were massive water skins. "Good to know there's plenty of water to draw a bath with," he said.

She looked back. "Wouldn't take a bath in that water, my lord," Dupre said. "It's ballast water mixed with kerosene to keep it from freezing. The drinking water's back in frame three."

"Frame three?" he asked.

"The third transverse frame, counting from the tail forward." She pointed up, to the nearest of the whale's ribs, just aft of the water skins. "This is frame six." She pointed forward, to the frame closer to the pigeons. "That is frame seven." She pointed up at the enormous luftgas bag directly above. "And that is bag six."

Continuing aft, he paused near the pentagon of girders at frame six and looked up. He could see straight to the top of the ship, in between bag six and what must have been bag five. The space in the middle of the circle formed by the transverse frame was filled with rigging lines that crisscrossed the encircling girders. The bags were connected at intervals to those criss-crossing lines, and to great nets, which in turn connected directly to the keel.

He did not envy the riggers, who might have to climb up there and splice severed lines back together in battle. Just working out which went where must be a nightmare. A rope ladder threaded through the lines in that narrow space between bags, starting at the very top of the ship and ending within arm's reach of the keel, but the mere thought of ascending it made him dizzy. Thus it was with astonishment that he realized the tiny shape at the distant top of the ladder was a crewman, performing some adjustment to the rigging.

Past the water skins and partially eclipsed by them was a small compartment on the port side, set off with heavy leather curtains. Bernat peeked inside to see a caisson, like the ones he'd seen towed behind cannons in parades, and a few rockets.

"For pity's sake," Dupre said, "please stay out of there while you're dressed like that. You'll set off all the powder in the magazine with the static of your various garments rubbing together. And don't get any of your frippery caught in the gears."

Bernat quickly set the curtain back in place and followed her past the gearbox. He lifted his bag high over his head and took care to keep his lace out of the gears as he pushed past them.

Farther aft, the air became humid and sweltering, despite a breeze coming in through the air scoops on either side of the catwalk. Here, cutting through the middle of the corridor, what appeared to be a single, six-inch-wide copper tube looped back on itself dozens of times. Its aft end connected to the engine, while the forward end split into two and led, he thought, to tubes he'd seen running along the outer skin of the keel.

"It's terribly humid here," he said, tapping her on the shoulder.

It was very loud, too. Dupre turned and held her hand to her ear.

Bernat shouted. "I said, it's terribly humid in here."

She nodded and shouted back, "It's from the condenser. It's hell on the wood. Soaks up the moisture, no matter how much we varnish. The girders in this frame will only be good for eight months—a year at most—before we have to replace them."

They continued aft to the steamjack turbine, which looked to Bernat like nothing so much as a fifteen-foot-long iron trumpet, perhaps because he'd run out of whale comparisions. The narrow front end of the trumpet hardly intruded into either branch of the catwalk, but farther aft it expanded to take up nearly the entire keel. It was this mechanical monstrosity that was producing the dreadful whine that so grated on Bernat's ears. He plugged them up as he ducked under the aft end.

Behind the steamjack was the boiler, and then two more giant water skins, and then a smaller pair of brass fuel tanks. Beyond that, the catwalk ran between twin rows of curtained sleeping bays, most with two cloth bunks each, but some with only one.

Several crewmen were milling about and settling in. They stood at attention when Dupre approached, but she gave them a nod and they went on with their business.

She led Bernat to the last bay on the right. Blessedly, it was a single bunk, so he could retain some tiny vestige of privacy on this ship. It wasn't much privacy, of course, for only canvas separated the adjacent bunks, and the "ceiling" was only a net hanging between the overhead keel girders. She helped him stow his bags, one atop his bunk, the other underneath. The bay was so small that his bottom bag stuck out into the corridor, and the top one intruded into the bunk, which was just cloth stretched over a rectangular wooden frame and attached to the waist-level keel girder by hinges. The bunk bulged above his baggage, tilting to make an acute angle with the ship's outer skin. "If I roll over in the night," he said, "I'll go right through the wall."

Dupre shrugged. "Then don't roll over. Seems to work for everyone else."

Just past his sleeping bay were four more water skins, two on each side, each tucked into individual curtained alcoves. They were at least two hundred gallons each, but squatter than the skins forward and capped with hinged wooden lids.

"Reservoirs," Dupre said. "You drink from the front ones. You shit in the back ones. Please try not to mix them up. It would be a great inconvenience for everyone."

Curiosity compelled Bernat to lift the lid of the reservoir on the portside, aft. The scent of kerosene wafted out, but dissipated quickly when he closed the lid. He noticed an open port behind the skin, which sucked air out into the slipstream.

"One of the advantages of airship service," Dupre said, closing the curtains. "Fresh air. If this were an army bivouac, it would already be filled with that musty, farty smell that follows the army around wherever it goes, like some olfactory badge of shame."

"You missed your calling as a poet," Bernat said, rubbing his fingers together where they'd touched the lid.

"Many have said so."

He looked farther aft and saw a pair of steering wheels, just like the ones on the hurricane deck. "Can the ship be maneuvered from here?"

"In an emergency," she said. She walked back and he followed. As he reached out to touch a wheel, she stopped him. "They're connected to the control fins. Best not touch them, unless you'd like to kill us all."

"Ah," he said, pulling his hand away. "Perhaps there ought to be a sign."

Dupre snorted. "If you put a sign on everything that could

kill you aboard this ship, we'd never get airborne for the weight of them all."

Bernat looked farther aft, where the keel curved up like it did at the bow. Halfway up the slope, a pair of curtains, thicker than those on the sleeping bays, cut across the walkway.

"Captain's quarters," Dupre said. "And if I find you snooping around in there, you'll get a clear but receding view of the underside of the ship. Now, if you'll excuse me, I have duties to see to."

When she was gone, Bernat sat on his bunk with his feet on the catwalk. He closed the bay's curtain across his lap as far as it would go, though that still left a fair inch of space through which passing crewmen could peer in at him. In the moments when no one was watching, he wrote in his notebook:

> *She seems to relish her dubious right to give orders to men. The airmen, loyal and dutiful all, must surely suffer under this blatant abuse of power. It pains me, truly pains me, to see valiant fighting men in their prime withering under the tyranny of this brutish woman.*

That might not play well with the newspapers, but it would please his uncle, who was, after all, his most important audience. But Uncle Fieren would not be truly pleased unless this woman was gone, so Bernat settled in to contemplate how best to hang her in a noose of ink and paper.

SHE LEFT THE fop to worry about his death trap of a sleeping bay. All he had to do was sling his bags in the netting above the bunk, but with any luck it would take him the entire morning to figure that out.

In frame five, amidships, she found Gears, Lieutenant

Martel, and the mechanic's mate gathered around the steamjack. The carpenter wasn't far away, looking over their shoulders. "So what's wrong with her?" Josette asked.

"Can't find anything wrong, Cap'n," Gears said. He glanced at Martel, as if for assistance.

"She's not a slow ship, sir," Lieutenant Martel said. "She'll outrun any scout or bomber at full power, and I've never heard of a chasseur with such a fast cruise."

"Her cruising speed only tells me she has more in her, Nic. Something's holding her back at full power."

"I think I might get some extra power with adjustments to the condenser," the mechanic's mate said. "Might be good for another knot." Her expression was conciliatory, as if she were trying to meet an unreasonable person halfway.

"That'd only be pushing on a wet noodle. The steamjack's giving us excellent rotation already, so the problem lies further along the power train. Find out where the problem is and fix it." Josette noted their skeptical expressions. "I want fewer blank stares and more goddamn answers on this ship, starting now."

"Yes, sir," Gears said, though his face told her that she was on a wild goose chase.

An hour in the air and they all think I'm hysterical, she thought as she walked forward. Past the companionway, where Jutes stood watch, Corne was still practicing his avian agitation skills. "Stop bothering those damn birds, man," she said, "and go fetch the reduction schematics from my cabin. You know what those are?"

Private Corne nodded and hopped to it.

"And try not to drag that damn fop behind you when you come back!" she shouted after him.

"She really isn't a slow ship, sir," Jutes said from his post at the head of the companionway.

She shot him a scowl that shut him up.

When Corne brought the schematics, she sat in the slope of the bow and worked out the gearbox reduction factor, gear by gear, with pencil and paper. When she finished, she thought she'd made a mistake, but a second and third set of calculations confirmed her original conclusion: the reduction factor was far too high, leaving the airscrews with excess torque and a sluggish rotation speed. That's where the wet noodle was.

She called Martel over to check her math. He stooped carefully into the narrowing keel at the bow—in a naval vessel, failure to mind one's head might result in a painful lump, but in the air corps it could crack a girder strut, causing minor damage to the ship but rather more to the offending party's reputation. He sat for a while and worked through the calculations. Sure enough, he arrived at the same conclusion. After he checked over his numbers again, he frowned and said, "But those engineers must know what they're doing, right?"

She snorted. "I take it you've never met one."

He still looked skeptical. "These new airscrews are longer. Maybe we really need this much torque to turn them."

"One way to find out," Josette said. She called Gears over, and the three of them worked out a new reduction scheme using the gears they had on hand.

"Sure you want to do this, Cap'n?" Gears asked, when she got him to agree to the narrow premise that the plan was technically feasible. "It'll take hours."

"That's what aerial trials are for, Mr. Sourdeval." She turned to Martel. "Rig the ship as a free balloon and take charge of reballasting."

As Gears and Martel went aft to see to their duties, Josette was suddenly struck by the strangest feeling of doubt. Those airscrews, after all, were a revolutionary new design. Could Martel be right? Could the flight engineers have really intended them to turn this slowly? Such a thing seemed idiotic, even by their standards, but they did have a funny habit of trying to cheat nature with their half-baked notions.

While the mechanics dug into the gearbox, Josette made a few calculations, thinking that perhaps Martel's intuition about torque was correct. It took her only a few minutes to prove, with mathematical certainty, that he was wrong. The reduction scheme they'd planned would provide higher speed and more than enough torque. In the privacy of the forward section, she permitted herself a moment of smug reflection. Martel was not only wrong, but fantastically wrong. In fact, under the new reduction scheme, the airscrews would be spinning so fast that their tips would be moving at . . .

Her smug expression suddenly sank, and she felt a chill of sweat. "Oh hell," she said, realizing that her new reduction scheme was nothing but a very creative way to commit suicide. At emergency power, the tips of the airscrew blades would be moving at something approaching the muzzle velocity of a cannonball.

At that speed, the airscrews would disintegrate, exploding into a shower of deadly mahogany splinters. She looked aft, where the mechanics already had the gearbox in pieces. Taking it apart was easy, of course, but it would take them an hour or longer just to put it back in its original configuration. So she'd already wasted that much of the crew's time, on top of nearly getting them killed. And she'd been captain of an airship for less than four hours.

She wondered if she did have brain damage, after all.

"Shifting ballast!" Martel shouted along the keel. With the engine off, the steersman could not control the trim of the ship, so sandbag ballast had to be moved to compensate for any movement between frames.

"Ah, there you are!" Bernat said, squeezing between ballast bags. "Lieutenant Martel is not referring to me when he says ballast, is he?"

"Of course not, my lord," Josette said. "Mr. Martel is referring to something useful."

Bernat smiled, seeming to miss the insult. "I did notice we've stopped."

"You have a keen eye for detail," Josette said. She tried to ignore him as she looked over the schematics, searching for a way out. There was, she realized, one way to keep the blade tips from moving so quickly, but she'd look an even greater fool if she tried it and it didn't work.

Yet she couldn't stand the thought of going to her own crew, hat in hand, and telling them she'd wasted their time with her foolishness. She'd be admitting that she didn't know what the hell she was doing. So, to hell with it. "Jutes, pass the word for Chips."

When he arrived, the older man saluted first her and then Bernat by touching his knuckle to his forehead, the way Jutes did it.

"While we're stopped," Josette said, "I'd like you to shave eleven inches off the end of the airscrew blades."

Chips leaned back, as if physically bowled over by that order. "Yes, sir," he said, in a subdued voice. It was just about the reaction she'd expected. "I'd like a few men to help."

She nodded. "Take anyone you need, but leave me the musketmen. I want to train them on the new rifles."

"Ah yes, I'd forgotten that you shoot," Bernat said. "Not many women poachers out there."

Chips, Josette, and even Jutes, who was standing at his post at the companionway, all whipped their eyes around to stare at Bernat.

The fop chuckled softly. "You mentioned that you hunted in Durum. But, of course, anyone who's ever studied a map knows that the forests near Durum are King's Woods, which makes you . . ."

"That was a long time ago," she said.

"Oh, I'm not making an accusation, my dear captain. I'm only asking if you'd like to have a match."

She snorted. "You? Use a rifle? Do you know which end to hold?"

He smiled back, cool as ice. "I always figure it out by the second shot."

"Fine," she said. "Once the airscrews are unshipped, we'll do best of twenty."

"Unshipped?"

"Taken off the booms and brought aboard. I don't want shooting during the operation. If someone is distracted and drops an airscrew over the side, it'll be right turns all the way home."

Once the airscrews were aboard, Josette had the rifles unpacked and brought to the hurricane deck, where they were set on an upright rack secured to the rail. Ballast was shifted so that the crewmen could crowd onto the companionway, while the mechanics and crew working amidships found excuses to open ports in the keel and look forward to the hurricane deck. Wagers ran the length of the ship.

Mistral was drifting parallel to an arterial road that ran northeast from Arle, cutting though orchards and farmland. The musketmen were busy with the laborious process of loading rifles, which was a much slower business than loading the muskets they were used to.

Josette tucked her goggles into a pocket, took a loaded rifle, stepped to the rail, and pointed to a stone mile marker on the road below. The marker was no larger than a man and was at least two hundred yards away on the diagonal, a nearly impossible shot for a musket.

She adjusted the notched backsight to account for the distance, tucked the wooden stock against her cheek, and sighted along the barrel. She aimed nearer to the upper-left corner of the stone, to account for the influence of wind. She let half the air out of her lungs in a slow sigh and squeezed the trigger.

The hammer came down, sparking against the frizzen and igniting the powder in the pan. She shut her eyes against the hot flash as smoke and fire poured from the muzzle and the rifle slammed back against her shoulder. The heat on her face was already gone, but when she opened her eyes, she couldn't see her target through the obscuring smoke.

"Hit!" Martel shouted, lowering his telescope.

In the still air, the rifle smoke hung in an expanding, churning cloud under the airship's envelope. She stepped aside to get a clear view, and saw through her own telescope that the mile marker had gained a new pockmark a foot from the top, at about neck level.

Josette set the rifle back in its cradle. "Your shot, my lord."

Bernat took the next rifle off the rack and aimed at the same marker. A few snickers sounded from the gathered crew as he raised the gun to his shoulder. He squeezed the trigger and nothing happened, except that the hammer clicked down into the pan. There wasn't even a spark.

"Oh dear, a misfire. What rotten luck." Bernat kept the rifle tight against his shoulder and aimed safely over the side, much to Josette's disappointment. She'd bet Martel a whole lira that the fop would look down the barrel to see what was wrong.

"My lord," Josette said, "I believe you'll find this rifle is missing a flint. A small oversight by the loaders, I'm sure." She took a spare flint from the box, made sure it was sharp, and handed it to him.

Bernat, unsurprisingly, required help getting it into the doghead. He offered an abashed smile to the musketman who helped him, saying, "In Kuchin, we have a fellow who handles these sorts of details."

By the time Bernat was ready to fire, they'd drifted twenty yards closer to the target, but the advantage did not leave Josette particularly concerned. He aimed and fired, and the bullet kicked up a clod of turf as far from the marker as the marker was tall.

"I dare say that's a miss," Martel said. The crew guffawed and slapped their knees. One man leaning out of the keel nearly toppled over in his merriment.

The fop, meanwhile, was inspecting the rifle, as if he imagined some fault with it—some tampering that went beyond the missing flint.

"I zeroed the sights on these rifles myself," Martel said. "I can assure you, my lord, that this one is as perfectly sound as the others."

"It certainly bears no flaw that would make it shoot sideways," Josette added. "Apart from the man holding it."

Bernat made an indignant sniff and handed the rifle to the nearest crewman, Corporal Lupien. Lupien shrugged and set it back on the rack, which was nearer Bernat than he was.

She pointed past the mile marker. "For the next target, how about that fence post on the other side of the road?" It was ten yards farther and a fraction of the width of the mile marker, but the fop hardly took notice. He was busy wafting his hand in front of his face and wrinkling his brow in thought, as if he were trying to blame the air itself for his poor aim.

She aimed and fired.

And missed.

Well, it hardly mattered. It wasn't as if the fop would make such a difficult shot.

Bernat selected a rifle—one with a flint this time. He fired. Through her glass, Josette could see a splash of turf behind the post as the bullet plowed into earth. It was a miss, but a near miss. A bit nearer than her shot had come, in fact, which was surely a matter of luck.

Josette called the next target: one of the squat snow markers along the road. It was only two feet high and about as far away as the mile marker had been. She fired, and missed by a hair. It was not shaping up to be a good day, but she could console herself in having such an incompetent opponent.

Bernat took his time, seeming to contemplate everything from the rustling of the trees in the distance to the tip of his own nose. "Perhaps he's hoping the contest will be canceled if he can delay until the end of the world," Josette remarked. At that, a strange smugness came over the fop's face, and without looking at her he lifted his rifle, sighted, and fired.

Josette was shocked to see a puff of dust on the face of the marker, at its exact center. A second later, Martel said, "Hit," without enthusiasm.

Bernat smiled at Josette. "A balloon is such a lovely, stable platform to shoot from, once one learns to account for the peculiarity of movement. I'll have to recommend that the palace acquire one."

"This is an airship, my lord," Josette said in an even tone, as she took the next loaded rifle from the rack.

Over the course of the next seven targets, Bernat hit six to Josette's four. At this point, they took a break from the game so the rifles could be cleaned and reloaded, the powder scorches washed from the contestants' faces, and ballast dropped to keep the ship from drifting too near the ground. When these matters were seen to, they returned to the rail. This time, the crew who gathered to watch were subdued, and no wagers passed between them.

By previous agreement, Bernat called the shots for the second set. "The next mile marker," he said. With the ship's drift, the next mile marker was scarcely farther away than the first had been at the beginning of the contest. Both of their shots hit it dead center. It seemed to Josette that the fop was trying to hold his lead by calling easy shots, but he surprised her with his next call. He pointed to the next snow marker, perhaps two hundred and fifty yards away on the diagonal.

Again, they both hit.

"The stone after that," he said.

This one was almost three hundred yards, but again they both hit.

"And the one after that," he said, to whispers of surprise. Now this was a shot. A stone about twice the size of a man's head, at over three hundred and fifty yards' distance.

They both missed, but neither by much.

He grinned at her, and she knew what was coming. "The one after that." It was about four hundred yards away, its gray shape hardly visible against the gravel of the road.

Bernat hit. Josette missed.

He took the next rifle and sighted along it without saying a word. The bastard was drawing out the suspense, but she knew what he was going to do. Sure enough, he finally grinned and said, "And the one after that," just before squeezing the trigger. And he hit the damn thing.

She selected a rifle and sighted carefully, first aligning the weapon so that the front sight post was visible in the notch at the top of the backsight, then pointing both at the target. It was so far away that the front sight nearly covered it. Worse, the backsight was only adjustable out to three hundred yards, which meant she had to aim high to account for the effect of gravity, holding the target's location in her mind and aiming into the formless turf beyond it. At this range, the mere beating of her heart moved the barrel enough to make the difference between a hit or a miss. All she could do was remain as calm as possible and wait for the moment when the minute, capricious shifts in her acuity of sight, concentration, and muscular precision all aligned to minimize the wobble in her aim. When that moment came, she eased steadily back on the trigger until the rifle fired.

"Hit!" Martel said, excited. "And blasted to bits!"

The crew gave a cheer that went on and on, until Bernat finally quieted them with, "And the next marker."

Josette peered at him. "You can't be serious."

He smiled. "I don't have much choice. You've just blasted the nearer one to bits." He fired and missed.

She also missed, hardly making an effort on such a ridiculous long shot.

"Perhaps we'll try the same one again," Bernat said.

Josette glanced at Martel's slate, which recorded the scores. With three shots remaining, Josette would have to make all her shots just to tie, and could only do so if Bernat missed all his. She watched through the telescope as he fired. A moment after the rifle's bang, the stone jumped, though she couldn't see the point of impact.

"I think it bounced off the side," Martel said, "but it might be a ricochet off the ground."

Bernat put the rifle back and gave a shallow bow. "I defer to your judgment." That judgment would determine the outcome of the match, but the fop showed no sign of impatience or even concern over it.

"I suppose it's a hit," Martel said. This inspired disapproving murmurs from every crewman who could do math above ten.

Josette held her hand out to Bernat, saying, "Congratulations, my lord."

"Did I win, then?" he asked, though he didn't look surprised. "I had rather lost track of the score. But you must have done quite well, to stretch it out this long."

"My lord is too kind."

Jutes cut through the uncomfortable silence that followed, shouting, "Okay, you lazy bastards, back to work. I want these rifles cleaned and stowed!"

The work on the airscrews and gearbox, which had come nearly to a halt during the contest of arms, now resumed, albeit with little enthusiasm. As she was going up the companion-way to sketch out better airscrew configurations for Mistral's first refit, Josette overheard one of the riggers expressing his hope that the captain was better at gear ratios than she was at pointing a rifle.

For Josette's part, she hoped that the crewman was better at shaving airscrews than he was at keeping his voice down.

Josette sketched out a few potential airscrew configurations, worked out the theoretical stresses on the booms, and called Martel forward to get his opinion. He shuffled through her sketches, stopping at one that removed the outboard airscrews entirely and replaced the remaining four with standard four-blade chasseur airscrews.

It was the design she liked the most, so naturally she expected disagreement, but Martel nodded and said, "I think this one's a worth a shot. Gears was saying something about a more streamlined power train. I believe his exact words were, 'She has all the power she needs, and not a clue how to use it.' "

Josette snorted. "He *was* referring to the ship, wasn't he?"

Martel went pale. "Yes, sir," he said. "To the ship, sir. I'm certain he didn't mean to imply, sir . . ."

"Calm down, Nic. It was just a joke."

She only wished she believed it herself.

IT WAS FINALLY lunchtime, thank heavens. Bernat tried to grease the wheels of rumor-mongering by offering to share a jar of lampreys in white wine sauce with the enlisted men, but he was coldly refused by all but the mechanic's mate, Private Grey. For her, Bernat doled out a portion on bread and presented it as, "the best luncheon for the prettiest aboard." It just about made the poor woman go weak in the knees, but that was only to be expected when receiving such a compliment

from a man as handsome and charming as himself. The rest
of the savages were happy to eat the most disagreeable pickled beef Bernat had ever seen, so he took his luncheon alone
on the hurricane deck, sitting atop one of the snub-nosed cannons and watching the scenery drift past below.

Even with the engine off, the crew contrived to make a disagreeable amount of noise. They were up in the keel, having
their luncheon conversations, each small group speaking loud
to be heard over the noise of the rest. The intervening girders
and fabric did little to dampen the volume. It was a perfect
shame, for the slow drift over the countryside would have
otherwise been so peaceful.

And so he employed the time by working on his letter,
writing:

> *This morning, she tore the very airscrews off her ship in
> a fit of pique. What the yardsmen had worked so hard to
> install, she ripped out in barely half an hour. She then, be-
> ing spiteful of the airscrews' length for reasons of female
> impulse, had a full foot cut off the ends of them, at once
> undoing the mathematically precise work of the army en-
> gineers and laying bare her own latent paranoia regard-
> ing the male organ.*

Now there was something that would play in the newspapers. He wished he could let this thread of inspiration roam
further, but he had to cut his lunch and his letter short when
the ship drifted beyond the farmland and over foul-smelling
fens farther north. He wasn't sure what its proper name was,
but the crew referred to it as "Magdalene's Twat."

Shortly after aborting his meal, he was relegated to the aft
end of the hurricane deck so the cannon crews could prepare
their guns. Apparently, the captain thought Magdalene's Twat
was a wonderful thing to fire cannonballs into. Bernat was on

the cusp of a brilliant and raunchy observation on this state of affairs when the first gun went off and he nearly shit himself.

It wasn't just the deafening sound of the cannonade. He'd heard cannons before—cannons twice as large as these. It was the effect it had on the ship. The entire hurricane deck lurched backward, and the envelope above was pushed inward by the blast, sending a rippling wave through the canvas. Soot coated the underside of the envelope ahead of the cannons, and several embers were burning near the guns. The gun crews wet the ends of their swabs and put the embers out, in no particular rush.

"Good God," he said.

"Don't worry," Ensign Kember said, coming to stand next to him. "The envelope is soaked in borate, and it's triple-thick nearest the guns."

"And that prevents it from igniting?"

"Most of the time," she said with a smile.

"Oh good. It's reassuring to know that I won't be on fire, most of the time."

The second gun was fired with similar effect, after which Dupre and Martel minutely examined the fabric, the guns, and the cables. Then Dupre planted her hand on the rail and jumped over the side.

Bernat blinked twice. No one else seemed alarmed. "I didn't realize things were going quite that badly for her."

"She's clipped on," Kember said. "She's examining the underside of the deck for signs of stress."

"Someone needs to examine me for signs of stress." Bernat couldn't believe his uncle was afraid of a woman who took such casual risks. If he wanted to be rid of her, it seemed he merely had to wait a few days and she'd arrange the matter herself.

Dupre climbed back over the rail, nodding her approval.

"Reload starboard!" Jutes called as he came forward.

The starboard gun crew, consisting of Private Corne and two other men, ran the bref gun in and locked it into its slide. Corne wet a swab and rammed it down the bore.

Jutes, moving with a speed that didn't seem possible on his injured leg, ran forward and grabbed Corne by the wrist just as he was pulling the swab free. "Have you decided to blow your bloody hands off?"

Corne stared up at him, terror in his eyes.

"I figure you must have decided to blow your bloody hands off," Jutes screamed, red-faced, "because that is the only reason a dumb bastard such as yourself would do such a bloody poor job of swabbing out a goddamn cannon! I could do a better job if I shoved my dick in there and pissed down the barrel. I'd demonstrate, but it's too big to fit."

"Is it not odd," Bernat asked Kember at a whisper, "to task such an inexperienced man with loading something as dangerous as a cannon?"

"Oh, that's the least dangerous job for him," she said. "A lot less dangerous than rigging or mechanical work. It's the same reason the captain put me in charge of shooting them."

Bernat studied the girl. She did not appear to be joking, though he thought he remembered Sergeant Jutes saying something about women not being allowed to man—so to speak—a gun.

The powder monkey ran up the companionway and came back with a flannel-wrapped gunpowder charge. He handed it off to the cannoneer on the left, who shoved the charge into the muzzle, then stood aside. Corne, waiting with a rammer on the right side of the gun, pushed the charge home. The left-side cannoneer hefted a cannonball from the ready rack along the forward rail.

"If you drop that goddamn shot through the deck," Jutes screamed, "you'd best jump after it." This did not seem to help the man's attentiveness, but he eventually got the ball fitted into the muzzle. Corne rammed it down the barrel, and both of them hauled on ropes to pull the gun forward on its slide.

"Oh, here's my part," Kember said, giddy. She went to stand behind the gun, holding its lanyard in one hand.

Dupre looked out over the featureless carpet of peat and mud below. "Target that tree ahead."

Bernat leaned over the side to see past the guns and their crews. The tree wasn't much of a target, but in these fens, it was about the only thing standing.

Kember sighted down the length of the cannon. She turned the screw at the back three times to elevate the barrel, then back half a turn. She sighted again, stepped out of the way of the recoil, and pulled the lanyard. Though Bernat covered his ears, they still rang as the cannon flew back on its slide. He thought he saw the shot, a blurry streak in the air, and then a divot of peat was torn from the fen, ten feet in front of the tree.

Martel whistled when he saw it. "Damn fine shot," he said. "Your first time firing a bref gun?"

Kember beamed. "First time in the air, sir. Thank you, sir." She had puffed herself up so much that Bernat worried she might pop a button on her coat.

"Well, what are you laggards waiting for?" Jutes yelled. "Reload!"

They reloaded and fired one gun after the other, again and again and again, until the booming discharges became more annoying than startling. He went up the companionway and, after ballast was shifted to accommodate him, back to his sleeping bay, where he resumed his running letter with,

She has violated that most sacred regulation of the air service, which forbids females from drawing blood, by placing her ensign—a mere girl—in charge of firing the ship's cannons. It is one thing to employ women in this service as a matter of necessity, if indeed it is even a

necessity, but Captain Dupre clearly has greater plans: to sap the very femininity from woman. Lacking any of her own and secretly envying this most noble and delicate trait in other members of her sex, she seeks to root it out wherever it is found. For the sake of man and woman alike, may she never succeed.

CHASSEUR CREWS ALWAYS enjoyed live fire practice, but this one was beginning to wear on them. *Mistral* drifted with the winds, so no cooling breeze blew across the deck. The gunpowder smoke lingered, and the air above the bref guns' brass barrels rippled with heat. The cannoneers were stripped to the waist, glistening with sweat, and panting from exhaustion.

"Reload!" Josette said.

She would pay for this, not just with the further resentment of the crew, but in lost ballast. Every shot reduced the ship's weight by twelve pounds of iron and one of powder. Under power, the engine could compensate for the imbalance, but even that could only do so much. Beyond a certain point, buoyancy won out, and they'd have to vent luftgas just to descend, dumping hundreds of liras' worth of that precious gas and earning a letter of reprimand from the Army Supply Board. But she had to find out, sooner or later, whether this revolutionary new design could stand the recoil of both its guns firing continuously.

The gun crews finished reloading and waited, expectant. "Secure bref guns," she said.

She made another inspection, finding damage to the transverse supports under the hurricane deck, but this was not unusual. It was expecting too much to think you could fire cannonballs from an airship without breaking something. Chips could repair the damage, but the ventral envelope was now irrevocably streaked with soot. That couldn't be helped.

Nor could the fop be bottled up for long, once the guns stopped. No sooner had she completed her inspection than Bernat came down the companionway, saying, "That's a good deal quieter. My, we're a long way up."

They were just climbing through three thousand feet, in fact. As the smoke slowly dissipated, all of Lake Magdalene became visible ahead of them. As far away as it was, Arle would have been visible aft, if it weren't hidden by its own smoke.

"The ship's light," she said. "If you'll excuse me, I have to see to some things." She went up the companionway, announcing her movement so that sandbags could be shifted to keep the ship in trim. The fop began to follow her, but she put her hand out and said, "Sorry, my lord, but if you could remain here. It's a ballast issue."

In frame five, the new gearing was finally installed. Martel and the mechanics were crammed into the space around the gearbox, counting rotations to confirm the reduction factor. She left them to it and inspected the airscrews. Finding the varnish dry, she gave the order to have them remounted.

With the gun exercise finished, Jutes had taken station farther aft, and was now supervising the shifting of ballast. "Damn shame about that contest, sir," he said.

She spoke in a low voice. "I can't believe I lost to that foppish twit. I suppose the crew are snickering about it behind my back, eh?"

Jutes didn't deny it, which was as good as confirming it.

Josette sighed. "Once word of this gets out, and he'll make certain it does, I'll be lucky if they make me a goddamn quartermaster."

Jutes clucked his tongue. "I'm sure it won't be that bad, sir. They'll probably just give you a blimp, or send you to the fever swamps."

She snorted. "You're a true optimist, Sergeant Jutes."

"Runs in my family, sir. You know about my father?"

She shook her head.

"He was eaten by wolves, sir, right outside our cottage window. But after every bite they took of him, we heard him say, in the most hopeful manner, 'Mayhap the brutes are full now.'"

"Thanks, Jutes. That's very uplifting."

He stood tall. "Anytime you need cheering up, sir."

When she returned to frame five, the mechanics were carefully passing an airscrew through an open port to a rigger dangling from the boom outside. The chief mechanic saluted and said, "We're having to hurry, Cap'n, on account of our rate of climb." That was a more tactful way of saying that some dumb bitch had decided to drop five hundred pounds of ballast by practicing the guns, and now they all had to scramble to get the ship under power before she went above her pressure height and forced them to vent luftgas to keep the bags from bursting.

"Don't rush, Gears," she said. "If we have to vent, let it be on my head." To hell with it. They could only make her a quartermaster once.

But the remounting went smoothly, and the airscrews were ready before the ship passed four thousand feet. The steamjack was spinning up as Josette took her place on the hurricane deck. She closed her eyes and listened for the thrum of the airscrews. At full power, let alone emergency power, the tips of the shortened blades would still be moving faster than the designers had imagined, and that was before considering any weakness caused by shaving them. The laminated mahogany might fray when spun up, sending foot-long splinters into the envelope, the engine, and the crew.

She could hear them spinning up now, a low-pitched growl under the high whine of the steamjack. This was the critical time, as the airscrews approached their full speed. At any moment, she might hear the keening wail of a splitting blade, the gunshot crack of its disintegration, and then the tearing, the shattering, the screams.

"We're at full power!" Gears called from amidships. Jutes repeated the report. She wished they would shut up. She could hear that they were at full power before Gears said it, and the update only distracted her from the sound of the airscrews.

The healthy, satisfying, droning sound of the airscrews. They were well-seated and perfectly balanced. She opened her eyes and said, "Sergeant Jutes, please pass my regards to the mechanics and the carpenter. Elevators down ten. Bring her to one thousand feet and keep her there."

Even after reaching their target altitude, the keel was on a slight incline, as the steersman on the elevators had to point the bow down a few degrees to counteract the lightness of the ship. The sun-speckled surface of Lake Magdalene, now directly below them, offered no landmark with which to judge their speed, but the wind was whipping faster over the deck, and the kinemeter's needle slowly turned across the face of its dial.

It settled, twitching, at the tick mark for twenty-eight knots. Disappointed whispers rippled across the deck and up into the keel, and would no doubt spread aft even faster. The ship had gained speed from its modifications, but the gain was pitiful.

Lieutenant Martel came down the companionway, looking first at the kinemeter, and then at Josette. "We are very light, sir. When we're weighed off, we'll gain half a knot, at least."

Which would still be unimpressive for a chasseur at full power. "She isn't slow," Josette said, words that were quickly becoming the ship's mantra. She knew *Mistral* had more potential, but the bitch was miserly about giving it up. "Perhaps if we smoothed out the camber of the airscrews, they'd do better at high speed," she said, more to herself than anyone else.

A respectful but anxious look from Martel said that she'd be wise not to push her luck.

"Well, let's see how the rest of the trials go," she said.

6

THE TRIALS WENT well enough. Apart from her sluggish top speed, *Mistral* wasn't a bad ship. For three busy days, she worked her way north against headwinds, showing acceptable albeit unremarkable performance in her flight tests. Page by page, Martel's logbook filled with figures quantifying every aspect of the ship's performance.

By morning on the fourth day, there were only three pages left unfilled, representing a dozen minor tests and two very significant ones. These were the high-speed rudder and elevator trials, which together constituted the real moment of truth for any new airship design. Nothing put more strain on a ship's tail, save a blast of enemy canister shot or a thunderstorm. Indeed, structural failure of the tail due to high-speed maneuvers was one of the most popular causes of death in the Aerial Signal Corps, though flight engineers were forever claiming their new tail designs could survive three or even four times the maximum possible strain, and they always had the math to prove it.

Most captains—among those who were still alive, at any rate—had the habit of bracing a ship's tail with extra girders, planks, and line, no matter what the math said. But that option was not yet open to Josette. She was conducting aerial trials on a new tail design, and it must be that design which she tested.

Her first order when she came on deck in the morning was

to steer a course for the nearest semaphore tower. There, she could report on the progress of *Mistral*'s trials to date, and there would be a record of their last-known position, in case anything predictable happened.

The tower was in sight by the time Bernat woke and came on deck, a little before noon. Josette ordered Ensign Kember to break out the quicklime signal lamp and then asked Bernat, "Slept well, I trust?"

"Very poorly at first," he said, stretching his arms high enough to touch the keel girder overhead. "But once the sun came up, I managed to slip away." He waited for Kember to go up the companionway ladder, then leaned in to speak to Josette in a whisper. "That girl has the bunk in front of mine, and she breaks wind continuously from the moment she falls asleep. Makes it dreadfully hard to nod off." He kept looking at Josette, as if expecting her to present a solution.

Josette shot him a sideways glance. "What do you want me to do, have a word with her?"

"Couldn't you?"

She was about to offer a very curt answer, when Kember came back down the companionway, trailing a length of hose behind her and carrying a signal lamp. As Kember prepared the lamp, Josette said, "Just be happy you're not in the navy, where there's no fresh air."

"And while we're on the subject," Bernat said, "it's terribly noisy aboard this ship." He paused, as if waiting for commiseration, or perhaps admiration for making such a cogent observation. "I wonder if you might consider having the engine shut down while people are trying to sleep?"

The entire deck crew paused in their duties so they could turn and stare at Bernat.

"Or perhaps only reduced to an idle?"

"I've often proposed as much," Josette said. "Along with

having a nursemaid aboard every airship to tuck us in and read a story at night. Sadly, the army has been perfectly intransigent on the subject. Something about there being a war on."

That shut the fop up. He slunk over to his now-habitual spot at the starboard rail and started writing in his little notebook, holding it over the side where no one could see. He looked up from time to time and cast sly looks at her.

When the signal lamp was ready, Kember flashed a message to the semaphore station, summarizing the progress of *Mistral*'s air trials.

Josette, telescope trained on the station, read the acknowledging triple flash from their signal lamp. While the semaphore arms spelled out some routine message bound for the next station, the lamp flashed weather updates, along with a sketchy report of a Vinzhalian airship snooping around Durum, up to the north.

Josette didn't mention the report of the Vin airship to the crew, but Kember must have read the flashing message with her naked eye and whispered it to someone, because there was a palpable sense of resentment when Josette ordered the ship westward, to avoid the possibility of enemy contact during their trials.

After several hours, they were cruising over scattered farms and woodland, well away from the putative enemy ship. Josette called up the companionway to Sergeant Jutes, "Inform Chips that I want a repair party standing ready, and let the crew know we're performing high-speed maneuvering trials."

"Yes, sir," Jutes said, his voice more subdued than usual. Perhaps, with life hanging in the balance, he was feeling sentimental. He relayed the order and the information.

Josette steeled herself. "Steamjack to emergency power. Corporal Lupien, hard right rudder."

"Hard right, sir." Lupien spun the wheel, hand over hand. *Mistral*'s nose swung to the right with increasing speed.

At the rail, Bernat was taken by surprise, but grabbed a suspension rope in time to avoid falling overboard. *Mistral* really was nimble in a turn, which was a credit to her ugly sardine shape, but a quicker turn also increased the stress on her superstructure.

"Do clip on, my lord," Josette said. Her eyes were on the rudder wheel, her fingers wrapped loosely around the keel girder above her station.

"She's hard over, sir," Lupien said. "Rudder's a bit mushy."

Josette had already felt it in the pops and sprangs echoing down the keel. The ship was bending in the middle, shortening the direct length between bow and stern, which created slack in the rudder cable.

It was perfectly normal. Ideal, in fact, for the keel had to bend so it wouldn't break. "Hard left rudder," she said. "Elevators up full."

The bow angled up and the ship reversed its turn, rising in a tight spiral. Bernat looked like he was about to puke.

"If you're not feeling well, go up into the keel," Josette said. It was good advice, though she really just wanted him and his stupid notebook off her deck. "You only feel sick because you're looking out at the horizon, but if you—"

She felt a sharper pop in the girder under her fingertips. She relaxed slowly, and was nearly convinced it was only her imagination, when there followed a flurry of snaps echoing along the girder. It reminded her of the sound of a handful of dry pasta being cracked in half.

"Rudder amidships!" she called, spinning on her heels. "Level elevators!" She was already halfway up the companionway and running hard. "Landing stations!" She leapt into the keel and sprinted aft.

Jutes's voice cracked as he repeated, "Landing stations!" He shouted it once toward the stern and once down the companionway to the deck.

She was past him now and around the gearbox. All along the keel, the crew froze as terror splashed across their faces. Everyone, even the rookies, knew what an unscheduled call to landing stations meant.

It meant the ship was going down.

"Work party aft! Planks and cable!" As the crew scrambled, Josette saw Gears ahead of her, already rushing aft but at half her speed. The bisected catwalk amidships was too narrow for her to get past him. She was just short of running into him when she planted her hand on the steamjack housing and vaulted over it to the other side. The skin on her palm sizzled against the hot metal, and the passage left her trousers smoking where they had skidded across.

The pain didn't slow her down. With a clear path on this side, she ran even faster, past the boiler, streaking through the sleeping berths, pushing past Corne, who stood wide-eyed in the middle of the walkway, frightened and overwhelmed.

She could see the damage now. In frame two, just forward of the tail cone, the five longitudinal keel girders, the girders that made up the very spine of the ship, were twisting as if an invisible colossus had grabbed the ship around the middle. Splinters spit out of the strained girders as she ran. She was a few yards away when one of the two overhead keel girders failed entirely, shearing in half with a hard crack, like the report of a rifle. The shock went through the ship, buckling the catwalk under her feet and sending dust and splinters flying up all along the keel. The jagged ends of the broken girder tore a long gash in the number-two luftgas bag immediately above it.

She could see the plywood already splintering from the adjacent overhead girder as it took the strain from its broken neighbor. It was not a great deal of force, but it was in exactly the wrong place, and in another second this girder would snap too, transferring its strain to the three girders below, which would then snap in turn. The whole affair might take a minute, if that, and then the entire tail cone would tear open from top to bottom, shredding the four aftmost gas bags and sending *Mistral* spiraling to the ground.

In those fractions of fractions of seconds, in the space between two pounding heartbeats, Josette still ran toward the broken girder, not because she could do any good, but because it had simply not occurred to her to stop. She was barely in frame two when the other overhead longitudinal snapped, one broken end ratcheting upward to tear a second gash in the bag above, while the other just vibrated like a plucked guitar string.

Here it comes, she thought.

Another heartbeat thumped in her chest. In her head, she saw the forces that were tearing her ship apart with amazing clarity. She could have written an exacting scientific paper on them, if she'd only had the time. It would certainly save the engineers in Kuchin a lot of guesswork as they picked through the wreckage.

It was with this thought in mind, and not hope for herself or even for her crew, that she leapt and grabbed for the second severed girder, pulling herself up as if onto a tree's lowest branch. She wrapped her arms around the near end of the break and her legs around the far end, her body spanning the empty space between to hold her ship together with mere flesh and bone.

But it was not the strength of her body that she now utilized. It was her weight, small but precisely placed, that countered the forces acting on the failed girder. With that weight, she took enough of the strain off the remaining girders to put off their failure for a few precious seconds.

"Grab me around the belly and pull!" she cried as Gears finally reached frame two. Before he even had a chance to hesitate, she added, "Now!"

Standing on the catwalk, he reached up, wrapped his arms around her, and pulled.

"Pull yourself all the way up, goddamn it!"

She groaned as he put his full weight on her abdomen. The man weighed a ton, and thank God for it. She held on, half expecting him to rip her in two.

Grey, the mechanic's mate, had come with line under one arm and a plank under the other, but it would all be meaningless if they couldn't relieve the stress on the tail. "Pass the word," she shouted. "Elevators hard down." Three people relayed the order simultaneously. "Now bring that line here!"

Josette, her arms occupied, pointed with her nose to the first failed girder. "Lash the ends of the break to the keel girders in frame three, wherever they can stand the strain." She noticed that she was speaking in a ridiculous, high-pitched voice that might have been comical at another time. It meant they were losing luftgas from the number-two bag, but that was a distant worry.

She felt some of the strain come off the girder as the ship pitched down, but she didn't dare allow Gears to let go. Grey was making quick work of the lines. The carpenter arrived and, instantly assessing the situation, lashed another rope to the spot just beyond Josette's head.

Now Martel arrived. For a moment, Josette worried there was too much weight in frame two, but instantly damned herself for her own stupidity. More weight under the break might delay the next girder failure, and they needed every second. "Nic," she said, "send Kember aft to shift weight out of frame one."

Ensign Kember, the lightest person aboard and therefore the most qualified to venture aft without breaking the tail off, stepped quickly but lightly into frame one, and began throwing everything that wasn't tied down forward along the keel.

The repair party lashed line after line, and as each line was pulled taut, Josette could feel the strain coming off. In the time between, though, it seemed the strain was creeping back in, robbing them of all their progress. Or even outstripping it, she thought, when the girders gave an ominous creak.

She couldn't imagine what could be increasing the strain, until she suddenly realized that the culprit was the luftgas leak in bag two. She should have known that immediately, and would have if she'd spent a second thinking about it before dismissing the leak as inconsequential. The diminishing lift in the leaking bag was reducing the support on the tail, causing it to droop. "Martel!" she called down the keel, her voice squeaky and breathless. "We're hogging! Bring a work party and patch these leaks." As she spoke, her vision narrowed into a tunnel, the inert luftgas having robbed the outside air of its vitality as they mixed.

"Sir," Gears said. "Getting a bit dizzy, sir. I'm not sure I can hold on any longer."

"Goddamn it, man, not now! We're right on the edge here!" Stars swirled in front of her eyes as she spit out the words, and her vision narrowed until all she could see was a pinpoint of light. But even as her vision failed, she could hear the creak of the girders growing louder. There was a thump as Gears fell to the catwalk, and then even her hearing faded.

She was insensible for what seemed only an instant, but when she came to, she was staring into the face of Private Grey. "Captain," Grey said, as she slathered a cloth patch with steaming pitch and positioned it over a puncture in the bag.

"Private." Josette nodded back. She must have been out for at least a minute, but she was still hanging from the girder. "I didn't let go?"

Grey looked away. "Er, not as such, sir," she said.

Josette became aware of an odd, steady pressure against her back, like a lumpy hammock holding her up. She noticed a pair of hands on the longitudinals on either side of her head, and looked down to see another pair of legs wrapped around the girder on the other side of the break. Some quick-thinking crewman must have grabbed on underneath her, relieving Gears and becoming a human hammock to hold Josette's insensible body up. Their combined weight had kept the keel stable when otherwise it would have snapped.

"Whoever these hands belong to," she said, "I hope you know you've saved all our lives."

The work party became strangely quiet. From somewhere forward, she heard Gears clearing his throat.

"Is that so?" asked a squeaky but still ostentatious voice directly below her head. "Saved everyone? Well, I shall have to write Mother about this. She'll be thrilled."

Only then did Josette notice the frilly ruffles on her savior's sleeves. She closed her eyes and thumped her aching forehead into the girder.

HE COULDN'T SEE her face, and the luftgas made it difficult to read her voice, but Bernat had a very good read on Dupre's carriage, since he was pressed rather firmly against it. And, though everyone warned that the ship would crash if he let go, he could tell that Dupre was on the fence about shrugging him off.

She said in a quiet hiss, "I swear, if that isn't a roll of coins in your trousers, I will throw you overboard and tell everyone it was a tragic accident."

The object in his pants was, in fact, a roll of coins—part of his first week's payment from Uncle Fieren. "My dear captain," he said, loud enough for the entire work party to hear, "take it as a compliment."

She tensed even more. "Are all aristocrats such uncouth animals?"

"If I have given any offence," he said, "you need only call me out, and I will happily offer satisfaction."

This elicited some snickers from the crew, which Dupre

silenced with a glance. "I take that to mean a duel," she said, "and I am sorely tempted by the thought."

"Would you prefer pistols at dawn, or shall I visit you in the night with my longsword?"

"Chips!" she called. "When the hell will this goddamn girder be braced?"

"Very soon, sir," the carpenter answered from directly under them. He stood up with a plank under his arm and, climbing on a pile of sandbags, positioned it over the girder and tied it across the break. Chips added three more planks, one to each side of the girder, spanning the break. "There you are, sir. Better'n new."

"That means you can let go," Dupre said, after hardly a second.

"Sorry, I'm . . . just a little stiff," Bernat said, as he slowly uncoiled from the girder. He put his feet on the sandbags and stood.

Before he could even brush off his coat, Dupre was down and pushing past him. "Reinforce the rest of this frame," she said, and went forward at a brisk pace.

Bernat sat on the sandbags and massaged the feeling back into his legs. "So we all nearly died, did we?"

Most of the work party simply nodded their heads respectfully, but Grey smiled at him and said, "We would have, if not for you, my lord."

"I only saw everyone's distress and followed the captain's example," Bernat said. "It was she who saved us." He didn't want to bolster Dupre's image with the crew, but he detected a certain bashfulness in Grey's voice. It suggested a romantic sentiment, which he wished to head off as soon as possible.

"My lord is too modest," she said.

He gave her a purposefully strained, neutral smile and then went forward. It was a damn shame she'd chased him off, too, for he'd come up with a particularly biting line about Dupre "fainting in the midst of a crisis, and so endangering all souls aboard" and he wanted to duck into his berth and jot it down before he forgot.

Instead, he continued forward, receiving accolades from the crew through the entire length of the ship. These were men of a station who would otherwise have shied away from even speaking to an aristocrat unless spoken to first, but passing them on the narrow catwalk necessitated physical contact, which they now seemed to take as an invitation for handshakes and pats on the back. He made it to the companionway just in time to watch a pigeon being released, and to hear Dupre say, "Of course; it would have to be Durum."

She was examining a map with Martel, in the relatively calm air of the keel forward of the companionway. "Durum's shed is on the small side, but it should hold us," Martel said.

"It's not that. It's . . ." She trailed off, tracing a bandaged finger over the map. Her left hand was wrapped in linen. "It doesn't matter. We'll overfly the semaphore station at The Knuckle and then set course for Durum."

Martel nodded and went down to the hurricane deck to order a course change, reminding Corporal Lupien to "turn her easy."

Dupre stowed the maps and spread a diagram of the ship's tail out on the bench. She began marking it with a pencil.

Bernat hit his head on an overhead girder as he approached her, and felt one of the little sideways bits of wood cracking from the force of it. Dupre was close enough to hear it but didn't pay it any mind, so he supposed it wasn't a terribly important part of the ship. "I've always wanted to visit Durum," he said, looking down at her map.

"Just say the word," she said, without looking up, "and I will happily arrange a long vacation for you."

"Tempting," he said. "I would like to meet the former lover you left behind."

The timbre of her annoyed sigh told him that he'd guessed wrong. She didn't have a former lover in Durum. Well, of course she didn't. He should have known that. With this woman, there would likely be no future lover, either.

"Not a lover," he said, tapping his chin thoughtfully. "Then it must be . . . a disappointed father."

She snorted. "Wrong again. My father died in the army."

"Really? Which battle?"

Dupre put her head closer to the diagram. "Syphilis."

He thought. "I don't remember that one. Oh! You mean the pox." He chuckled. "I thought you meant a battlefield. Isn't that funny?"

"We all thought so," she said, hunching so close to the diagram that she couldn't possibly see it clearly.

Bernat's chuckle caught in his throat. "I, uh, I didn't mean . . . please accept my apologies."

"For this alone, or for the sum of your behavior during these trials?"

He might have given a pithy reply, but he was flustered from giving accidental offence. Intentional offence he would certainly have reveled in, but this misunderstanding left him somehow unbalanced. "I think I'll take a walk," he said, going down the companionway.

"Pray don't stop at the rail."

Bernat went down and took his habitual station on the right side of the hurricane deck, where he could look out at the horizon.

Lieutenant Martel was on deck, standing in the captain's spot. "Thank you for your quick thinking earlier, my lord."

Bernat was just about to deflect the credit onto Dupre, as he had when Private Grey complimented him, when he remembered that he wouldn't have to worry about romantic entanglements with Martel. Probably not, anyway. He nodded politely.

Miles of hill and countryside went past below. It was quite relaxing, now that he'd purchased a spare pair of goggles from Jutes and could keep the wind out of his eyes. He would also invest in one of those dashing leather caps at the first opportunity, but for purely aesthetic reasons. The fluttering of his tightly cropped hair hardly bothered him anymore, but he felt himself in some small way an airman now, and wanted to look the part.

The airship's shadow stretched far to the east by the time they crossed the semaphore system at a place the crew called "The Knuckle." As Martel dictated a report from the captain's notes, Kember relayed it by signal lamp, reporting the exact circumstances and details of *Mistral*'s mishap. Bernat hoped his name would be included favorably, but the report stuck to such phrasing as "the carpenter" and "the officer of the deck," which seemed to be represented by abbreviated signals requiring only a few flashes on the lamp. He supposed it too much to ask that there be a signal-lamp abbreviation for "the achingly handsome gentleman of high birth who saved the ship."

When the report was finished, Martel lifted his telescope to read the reply. A grin grew on his face as he read, silently mouthing the words. Bernat couldn't make out most of them, even watching Martel's lips, but he noticed "enemy" and "Durum" repeated several times.

Martel lowered the telescope. "Ensign, you have the deck." He went up the companionway stairs, taking them two at a time.

Bernat followed him, to where Dupre was still poring over structural diagrams.

"They've confirmed the report of an enemy scout over Durum," Martel reported.

Dupre looked up. "Then take us west, away from it. We'll hold station over The Nose. If the scout isn't gone by midnight, we'll divert to Arle." She went back to her diagrams, but Martel lingered. Without taking her eyes off her work, she asked, "Is there anything else, Lieutenant?"

"No, sir. It's only . . . well, I had thought we would have a go at them, sir."

"In this ship?" She scoffed. "Apart from the damage she's already suffered, we haven't finished our trials, so we don't know what other nasty surprises *Mistral* will have in store for us when subjected to the stresses of aerial combat. No, Lieutenant. Glory can wait for another day."

The carpenter came forward, moving like a man on a mission as he passed Jutes at the head of the companionway. "I hear somethin' about an enemy scout, sir?" Chips asked, touching knuckle to forehead. The rumor had spread through the ship faster than a person could walk. Bernat looked back along the keel, where the crew seemed to be divided into two factions: half of them were looking eagerly at Dupre, relishing the thought of battle, while the other half shot wary glances at each other.

"Do you have something to report, Mister Rosen?" Josette asked.

Chips gave his old-fashioned salute again, so great was his excitement. "We're in good shape for battle," he said. "Frame two's stronger now than it was before it failed. Used half the line and timber in the ship to brace it. Won't fail again, sir, I can promise you that. Been over every inch of the tail cap, too, and she's right as rain, sir."

"Thank you," Dupre said. "It's laudable work, but we won't put it to the test just yet."

The carpenter looked so blank for so long, Bernat began to worry a blood vessel had burst inside his brain.

"Oh, and Chips?" Dupre said, looking up from her diagrams. "Lord Mooncalf here has sprung one of the struts above you. Wrap it up when you have a chance, please."

Chips turned to Bernat. "Ain't nothin' to be ashamed of,

my lord. Happens to a lot of people, their first week aboard."
He saluted Dupre for the third time, turned, and shambled aft.

THE DAMN FOP continued to linger after Chips and Martel
left. Josette tried to concentrate on the diagrams, but found
the thought of his eyes on her too infuriating.

Then again, it wasn't just the fop infuriating her, was it? It
was the behavior of her crew. Their enthusiasm didn't bother
her, for everyone knew chasseur airships were filled with
bloodthirsty bastards who relished a good fight. This set them
apart from the regular army, where the average soldier was
quite sensibly terrified at the prospect of impending combat.
The all-volunteer chasseurs, on the other hand, were populated
by roughly equal measures of the suicidal, the heroic, and the
brutal. Although, she reflected as she looked back along the
keel, her own crew wasn't quite representative. Her crew
seemed to be split between those who resented her because
they thought she was going to get them all killed, and those
who resented her because they thought she wasn't going to let
them kill anyone else.

The two factions only agreed on the necessity of questioning their captain's every goddamn order. Captain Tobel, in
this situation, would have given the same order she had. He
would have protected his ship first. She was certain of it, and
just as certain that Captain Tobel's order would have been
obeyed without question, without grumbling, without second-
guessing, and without irate glances.

So why was she getting all of that in spades?

Perhaps, after all, there really was something missing in
women officers—some intangible air of command naturally
present in male officers, which she couldn't acquire even by
saving everyone aboard from certain death. Everyone was pat-
ting the fop on the back, congratulating the little bastard for

his quick thinking. How did he merit such respect for coming late to the scene and understanding nothing of the situation, but merely following Josette's example? She couldn't explain it, except to wonder if he, for all his uselessness, had something that she lacked.

Her mind was racing so fast now that it jumped that track and landed on another. The goddamn shooting contest! The late Captain Tobel couldn't hit a pagoda with a rifle if it was right under his keel, and had anyone thought the less of him for it? No! Of course not! But Josette had gone seventeen shots with the Deadeye Dandy and only lost by a nose, and they were calling her a bungler—if not with their mouths, then with their goddamn eyes.

"You seem to be turning red."

Her head whipped up and she saw the fop smiling at her. "What?" she asked.

"You're turning an alarming shade of red," the fop said, still smiling amiably. "I just thought you'd want to know, while there's still time to release the pressure." He winked at her, made some note in that blasted book of his, and went down the companionway.

"God damn him," she muttered. Soon they would take her ship away. She was convinced of that now. They would take her ship, and she'd be lucky if they gave her command of a goddamn blimp.

Jutes left his post and approached.

She looked up at him and sighed. "All things considered," she said, "this flight could have gone better, eh?"

"Cap'n," he said very quietly, "might be wise to reconsider that decision."

Not Jutes too, goddamn it. "It's the same decision Captain Tobel would have made. Surely you see that."

Jutes seemed to think about it. He nodded. "Aye, but it ain't the decision you have to make."

"And what if I do make the other one?" she asked. "What then? I'll only be trading one set of malcontents for the other."

"Mayhap that's so, sir, but a tidy little victory ought to sort that problem right out. The crew? They've heard of this fighting captain, this woman warrior who charged her ship into an entire company of skirmishers. Whatever they may think of her, what they're wondering right now is where that woman has got to. Truth be told, I'm wondering too."

Josette laughed. "When last I saw her, she was lying on top of a hill, somewhere south of Arle."

"Well, that ain't but a day's flying from here, Cap'n. We could swing by and try to find her again."

She looked down at her diagrams. "I don't think she made it, Jutes."

"Cap'n, I wish you'd—"

"That will be all, Sergeant."

Jutes touched his knuckle to his forehead and hobbled back to his post.

She took her work and retreated to her cabin in the stern. There, she sketched out a new tail configuration that would prevent a repeat of this afternoon's girder failure, at a small cost in weight. Perhaps she'd be relieved of her command by semaphore signal before she could even put the Durum shipyard to work on it, but she'd try, damn it.

She was almost finished when she heard Kember clearing her throat outside the curtains of her cabin. "Lieutenant Martel sends his compliments," the ensign said, "and we've arrived over The Nose."

"Thank you, Ensign," she said without opening the flap. She could hear Kember walking forward.

She finished marking up her diagrams, the work of a quarter hour, and then went forward herself. Alighting on the hurricane deck, she looked out to see the pointed outcrop of The Nose casting its shadow toward the east. The fop was staring at it with the awe and wonder of a true idiot. She looked west at the sun, still high in the afternoon sky, and then east, to where Durum lay over the horizon.

Why did it have to be Durum?

"Ah, to hell with it."

Martel tilted his head. "Sir?"

She didn't answer him, but only looked out over the deck crew. "Bring us east to ninety-five degrees on the compass. Pass the word to the mechanic: increase steamjack to full power."

Jutes grinned back at her before he relayed the order. Everyone on deck only looked at her with confusion and trepidation, as *Mistral's* nose swung around to point east.

She returned their looks, each one in turn, though they all looked away when her eyes met theirs. She took a long breath and said, her voice loud and hard, "Rig for battle."

7

THE CREW ADJUSTED the rigging, brought water and fire blankets forward, readied the bref guns, secured the small-arms racks to the rails, and loaded the rifles.

Bernat wondered if any of them questioned Dupre's feeble pantomime of a brave captain, and suspected they didn't. They hadn't seen the real Dupre, hiding in the bow, fretting until she turned red. The crew, no doubt, thought she'd been planning this all along, that her hesitation was part of some elaborate stratagem. He would have to mention that in his letter. Perhaps he'd add something about "permitting the deceit and vanity natural to her sex to rule over her other faculties, such as they are."

As he was contemplating this, the woman herself appeared before him and shoved a rifle into his hands. "Here. Make yourself useful and help the loader."

Bernat looked at the crewman who was busy loading rifles, then at Josette. He was thoroughly confused.

She sighed and spoke very slowly. "Load this rifle, please."

He took the rifle, but could only stare at it. "And how does one go about doing that?"

She narrowed her eyes. "You must be joking."

"At the palace, we have someone to handle these sorts of trivialities."

She snatched the rifle back. "If he can't find any other utility, my lord will perhaps lower himself to firing a shot or two at the enemy?"

"That sounds delightful," Bernat said. He didn't relish the thought of going into battle, but it seemed he had no choice, so he might as well kill a few Vins while he was at it. It would, at least, give him something to brag about.

The ship drove on, gaining altitude so quickly the change caused a pain in his ears.

"Passing through five thousand," Corporal Lupien said. Bernat was beginning to suspect the men and women of the signal corps simply enjoyed making pointless announcements.

Martel, posted along the forward rail of the hurricane deck, suddenly put his telescope to his eye and cried out, "Enemy sighted! Two points starboard at about four thousand."

Bernat looked in the direction he was pointing and, by squinting, could barely see a speck in the sky. "Tallyho!" he cried. But when he looked about, only blank stares met his enthusiastic grin.

"Tally-what?" Martel asked.

"It's what one says on a fox hunt, when the quarry is sighted." His grin diminished. "You know, 'tallyho!' I thought everyone knew that."

"Come to one hundred and twenty degrees on the compass," Dupre said. The bitch was ignoring him.

Lupien made a few turns on the wheel. The ship came about, but not far enough to point directly at the enemy. Bernat asked Martel, "We aren't going straight for them?"

"Cap'n wants to keep us between them and the sun," he said, handing the telescope to Bernat. After a bit of fumbling, Bernat found the enemy ship in the glass.

He'd been expecting something smaller, perhaps some weathered little blimp covered in patches. But the thing Bernat saw through the telescope was an airship, comparable in size to *Mistral* and bristling with guns.

"She has a fierce broadside," Bernat said.

"Three per side," Martel said. "But they're only swivel guns."

"What a comfort," Bernat said. When he looked into the telescope again, the ship was turning toward them. "They've seen us! They're attacking!"

Martel snatched the telescope back and looked out. "No, no," he said. "They're only turning to keep near cloud cover, but the weather isn't doing them any favors today." Indeed, the mottled cloud cover had been shriveling up all afternoon. The cloud bank near which the enemy lingered was one of the largest in the sky, but only a few miles wide at that.

"Range?" Dupre asked.

"I make it five miles."

It seemed to Bernat that an hour or more had passed before Martel called the range at two miles. Consulting his pocket watch, however, he found that the elapsed time had only been four minutes.

Dupre nodded and ordered, "Crew to stations. Mr. Martel, please send a bird to Arle with the following message: 'From *Mistral*: have engaged Vin scout over Durum.' "

Lieutenant Martel patted Bernat on the back, in a most uncomfortably familiar manner for a commoner. "Don't worry, my lord. Everyone's a little nervous, their first time." He trotted up the companionway ladder and disappeared into the keel.

The gun crews stood in their places next to the cannons, except for Corne, who had found Bernat standing in his spot and didn't know what to do about it. Bernat had sympathy, but not enough to move. If Corne wanted the spot so badly, he should have gotten there earlier. Martel came down carrying a pigeon. He released it over the rail, then went back up the companionway to take station aft.

They were on the outskirts of Durum now, passing over farmland and old, flooded quarries. The Vinzhalian ship hovered below and to the east, just beyond the old stone wall that surrounded the town. Just south of the town was Durum's aerial signal base. Its airship shed was a pitiful little thing compared to Arle's, but it was still the largest building in sight, and would have been the tallest if not for a rather excessive spire on the town's pagoda, most likely added to keep the shed from being taller.

Bernat saw something fall from the enemy ship. He thought they must be bombing the town, until Kember said, "Scout dropping ballast! Sandbags . . . and now water. They're turning away." She put the telescope to her eye. "And they've released a bird. It's heading east, toward Vinzhalia."

"Range?"

"To the bird, sir?"

"To the scout ship, Ensign."

"Over a mile, I'd say. A mile and a half. No, maybe less than that. A mile and a quarter. Maybe a little over a mile and a quarter." Kember's voice had a noticeable tremor in it.

"Thank you, Ensign," Dupre said.

The girl winced. Bernat deigned to pat her on the shoulder. "Don't worry. I have it on good authority that everyone's nervous their first time." They were close enough now that, even without a telescope, he could see a port opening in the tail of the enemy ship. It was suddenly lit by a brilliant light, from which emerged some small object, streaking toward them and trailing smoke. "Good God," he screamed. "They're shooting at us!" Only then did the shriek of the rocket reach his ears.

Behind him, Dupre sighed and said, "It would be more remarkable if they weren't, Lord Hinkal."

The rocket arced up until it was hidden from sight behind *Mistral*'s own envelope. He heard a bang in the distance and saw burning scraps of rocket falling about half a mile in front of the bow. The next rocket was even less accurate, turning hard right as soon as it was launched, spiraling around to explode nearer to the enemy ship than to *Mistral*.

"They're at about four and a half thousand feet," Ensign Kember reported. "Still dropping ballast, climbing fast. A bit under a mile away, I think."

"Let's try a ranging shot," Dupre said.

Ensign Kember cleared her throat at Bernat and said, "Excuse me, my lord. We'd like to shoot back, if you don't mind."

"Oh, uh . . . yes, of course. Please do." While the gun crew ran out the port cannon, Bernat scooted to the right, edging between the starboard cannon and the railing. He looked down to see the town below. They were nearly over it now, with the scout well past the city and running for the clouds to the east.

"Thank you for making room, my lord," Dupre said as she walked up behind him and held on to the corner deck cable. "Although, in general, it's considered unwise to stand in front of a loaded cannon." She patted the starboard gun, which was pointed directly at his posterior.

"Ah, yes," he said, and promptly scooted to the right. He wouldn't have made that mistake if he hadn't been so nervous. Why was he so bloody nervous? None of the enemy's rockets had yet scored a hit, and *Mistral* was about to reply with a cannon. Ensign Kember was already sighting along the barrel, holding her hand up to signal steering corrections to Corporal Lupien.

"Oh, and . . . my lord?" Dupre said. "You really ought to clip on."

Kember stepped aside and pulled the lanyard. The cannon's mouth exploded in smoke and flame as the deck came out from under Bernat's feet and the forward rail hurled itself into his belly. Only Dupre grabbing his safety harness at the last moment kept him from going overboard.

"Short!" Dupre called, and coughed as the smoke blew back into her face.

The gun crew was already reloading the cannon as Dupre returned to her station. Bernat looked forward. He hadn't even seen the cannonball in flight. "How can you tell it was short?"

"You look at their envelope and watch for the ball streaking in front of it," Dupre said.

He was about to ask how the hell she could keep her eyes on the enemy with a cannon going off next to her, when he heard the shrieking whistle of a rocket and looked forward to see it explode directly in front of *Mistral*. A moment later he heard the bang, and, for all that he had been expecting it, it still made his heart skip a beat. "I do wish they would stop doing that," he said, and heard his own voice crack.

Dupre said, "Make a request in writing. We'll send it over on the next cannonball."

"Maybe three-quarters of a mile now, sir," Kember said. "And the gun's warming up. Should increase the range."

Dupre nodded. "Port gun, commence firing. Fire as she bears." While Kember set to aiming, Dupre looked at Bernat and said, slow and loud, as if to a child or a foreigner, "My lord, may I once more remind you to clip on. If I have to save you from going overboard every time we fire a gun, I won't have time left to command the ship."

Good God, he couldn't believe he had forgotten again. He grabbed the clip at the end of the life line hanging off his harness and looked around for someplace to attach it. The first thing he saw was the thick suspension cable holding up the corner of the hurricane deck, but the little hook wouldn't fit around it, and then another one of those damn rockets was going off, its shriek so close now that he was certain it would hit, and he knew he was doing something wrong with his clip, but he couldn't think with all the damn noise around him. Unable to fasten the hook, he held it to the cable with his other hand, not because he thought it would do him any good, but from a fervent belief that he had to do *something* or he would surely perish.

The rocket exploded and he held on so hard the clip's metal hook bit into his hand, cutting his palm open. He looked up to see fragments of the rocket falling a hundred yards off the starboard bow, tendrils of smoke trailing behind them. Only then, when he was sure he wouldn't die in the next few seconds, did he noticed the jack line hanging above his head, so close it almost brushed his hair. The line was perfectly sized to fit the hook, but he had to make several attempts to clip on, so severely were his hands shaking.

Kember pulled the lanyard again. This time, Bernat was ready for it. He stared at the enemy ship, so close now that it looked like a long white cigar below and in front of them. Through the smoke of the shot, he could see a blurry streak pass just behind the scout's cruciform tail. "Short," he said. "But not by much, I think."

"Thank you, my lord," Dupre said, her voice strangely sincere, for once. "Starboard gun, commence firing. Fire as she bears. My lord, will you please join us back here, well away from the cannons?"

While the crew reloaded the port gun, Bernat went aft and leaned over the starboard rail to keep an eye on the enemy ship. Kember fired the starboard gun and Bernat saw another blurry streak against the enemy's tail. "Still short," he said.

The scout fired another rocket, this one coming on straight and level. Bernat wanted to run, for all the good it would do, but he was frozen against the rail, eyes locked on the oncoming missile. When it seemed the rocket would fly straight through him, it exploded so close that the bang followed instantly. He tucked against the rail, held fast, and closed his eyes.

And heard a shower of metal bits clink against the forward wicker railing, as if someone had thrown a handful of nails at it.

"Rockets are a sign of desperation," Dupre said without

concern. "Terribly inaccurate weapons. Mainly meant to rattle us."

Bernat stood and brushed himself off. He cleared his throat and willed his voice to be steady. "Does it ever work?"

She glanced at him. "In some cases. But the Dumplings are as likely to set themselves on fire with those rockets as they are to do us any harm."

"Dumplings?"

"The Vins."

"Oh, I see." Bernat pondered it, and in his nervousness he pondered aloud. "Because they eat dumplings?"

Dupre made no reply, unless rolling her eyes counted.

"I've been known to enjoy a good dumpling, myself. I hope that's not unpatriotic."

The port bref gun fired, its report followed by a sound from the enemy ship like a pane of glass breaking. Kember rushed to the rail and looked out. "Hit! Hit!" she cried. "Hit on the tail!"

"Very good, Ensign. Let's put the celebration off until we finish the job."

Bernat looked out to see the damage they'd inflicted on the enemy. There didn't seem to be any. No, now that he looked carefully, he could see a small hole in the scout's tail, edged with flapping fabric. It seemed a pitiful little injury. "Doesn't seem like much," he said.

"It adds up," Dupre said. "Besides which, we can only fire round shot at this range—solid iron cannonballs. When we get closer, we'll switch to explosive shell, and then you'll get some real fireworks."

The starboard gun fired. Bernat watched another hole appear in the scout's tail. "Hit on the tail fin," he said. "The one on the right that goes up and down. It doesn't look broken, though." Bernat didn't know if calling the fall of shot was needed or even welcome, but he desperately needed to do something.

The next cannonball hit the Dumplings in the aft section of their envelope. Bernat thought the scout, pierced through, would surely go down, but it didn't. In fact, it continued to rise. Before long it had risen to a mere a hundred yards or so below *Mistral*, and perhaps six hundred ahead.

"Reload with shell," Dupre said. This order brought the gun crews a positively salacious joy. The powder monkey ran down the gangway with a smaller gunpowder charge, along with a length of fuse. The powder went to the cannoneers, while Ensign Kember took the fuse, measured it against markings carved into the gun carriage, and shortened it with a knife.

The powder monkey made a second trip to deliver the shell itself. Kember inserted the custom-length fuse, and the shell was loaded into its gun. When they fired, the shell's burning fuse traced a thin line of smoke in an arc through the air. The shell exploded above the scout's tail, bursting into fragments that peppered the envelope, piercing it in half a dozen places and showering it with burning embers.

"Hit! Hit! Hit!" Bernat cried.

"She's turning to starboard," Kember said.

"Starboard as hard as you dare, Corporal Lupien," Dupre said crisply, as if she had been expecting this. She reached up and laid her fingertips on the girder above her.

The Vin ship swung right and *Mistral* followed, but *Mistral*, with her compromised tail, couldn't turn quite as lively as the smaller scout. Bernat saw the scout's broadside swivel guns come into view along the length of her keel. They were so close he could even see the cannoneers standing behind them, already aiming their swivels right at *Mistral*'s hurricane deck.

The bref guns fired two more shells, one exploding short and the other doing some small damage to the enemy's tail, and then the Vinzhalian ship was too far to the right for *Mistral's* bref guns to bear. *Mistral* could no longer use her fangs, but the prey was about to show hers.

"Lord Hinkal," Dupre said, "we should like you to take up station with the riflemen now. I suggest you aim for their cannoneers, for they will surely be aiming at you."

Bernat picked up a rifle, put it to his shoulder, and aimed for the nearest Vinzhalian cannoneer. The range was perhaps two hundred and fifty yards—not so difficult a shot, if only he could steady himself. He knelt and rested the rifle on the rail. It helped, but the shaking was not only in his hands. A continuous quiver had taken up residence in his chest, just below his heart. It coursed out in waves, through his shoulders and out to his hands. No matter how much he tried to calm himself, how precise and controlled he made his breathing, his heart raced and his entire body vibrated like a struck tuning fork.

He tried to swallow the fear, but it wasn't only fear that robbed his composure. It was the energy of the moment, the way it felt more real, more *now*, than anything he'd ever experienced before. It seemed that he resonated with the frequency of the battle itself.

He judged the wind as best he could from the rustle of the trees far below, and aimed just to the left of his target, at a point from which wind—if it was the same above as below—would nudge the bullet just enough to send it squarely through the man's chest. He'd nearly steadied himself when the rifleman next to him fired, and the crack of the rifle set him to shaking again.

The Vinzhalian ship was noticeably closer now, her unscathed cannoneers still aiming their swivels at him, waiting only to come within range. Bernat sighted again, shaking even more. And when his sights were wobbling in front of his target, he fired.

And missed. He knew he'd missed before the smoke had cleared, knew it even as he pulled the trigger, for he had repeated the very first mistake he'd ever made while firing a rifle, the first mistake his marksmanship tutors had trained out of him: firing off a hasty shot in the fleeting moment when unsteady aim happened to swing the sights across the target. He hadn't accounted for the wind either, and not because he'd forgotten.

So why the hell had he fired? Because he knew the swivel guns were coming closer and that soon they would be in range, and during that barest instant in which a decision had to be made, some part of him calculated that a wasted shot fired in time was better than an effective shot fired too late.

It was madness, and he knew it was madness, but somehow the madness had taken hold of him, and still had hold of him. He threw his rifle to the deck in his haste to take a fresh one and get another shot off before it was too late.

"Steady." Dupre's voice seemed to come from another time. It could not possibly be coming from this one, for she was far too calm for the current situation. "The battle is very much in our favor," she said. "It couldn't be going better."

But she was wrong, for that was the moment Private Corne decided to blow his hands off.

ANOTHER FEW MINUTES *ought to do it,* she thought. The Vin airship was already sprung aft and losing gas, her tail cone a wreck of splintered girders and smoldering shell fragments. A ship in that condition could not sustain such a tight turn for long. She'd have to straighten out soon, and then *Mistral* would have her.

There was the matter of the swivel guns, but their range was scarcely longer than pistol shot, so her riflemen would have time to work on the Vin cannoneers before they came into range. The swivels might have proved troublesome if *Mistral* were carrying mere muskets, but with rifles aboard, Josette hardly needed to think about it.

"Hurry up on that gun, please." The starboard gun crew, their pace slowed by the inexperienced Private Corne, was taking an eternity to reload. Private Kiffer, on the left side of the cannon, had just set the powder charge into the bref gun's bore. Corne, after trying to use the wrong end of the rammer, finally had it positioned correctly. He rammed the charge home, and was just pulling the rammer free when the cannon went off unexpectedly and the whole world turned to smoke and noise and heat.

The cannon, run all the way back and locked into its carriage for reloading, couldn't recoil smoothly along its slide. Instead, the force of its accidental firing was concentrated into a single, furious moment as a quarter ton of metal shot back under the impetus of a full pound of exploding gun powder, but had nowhere to go. The hanging deck swung back so fast it came out from under Josette's feet. The forward martingales, the lines meant to limit the deck's movement, snapped and whipped against the envelope.

The gun kicked up hard and came off its mount, its barrel pirouetting through the air to smash into Private Kiffer's leg. It bent his femur back on itself and kept falling, pulling Kiffer with it, its trajectory barely deviating from the impact. It hit the deck, plunged straight through the reinforced wicker, and fell into open sky, tumbling end over end as it returned to earth. On the way, it had pulled Kiffer's leg through the hole, but the edges of the wicker flicked back once the cannon was free, trapping the jellied limb just above the knee. Kiffer was the first to scream.

Then Corne, his face crisp and black with powder burns, opened his eyes and began to whimper. Of his left hand, there was nothing but a misshapen stump. The right one still had a few fingers, though it was hard to distinguish them in the amorphous, bloody mass of tissue and splintered bone above the wrist.

There followed several seconds of quiet, in which nothing moved but the wind. Even Josette was stunned into inaction, until she noticed that her ship was on fire. The bref gun had been run all the way back to its loading position when it had gone off, well behind the gun port, so the cone-shaped blast from its muzzle had blown apart the railing and deck in front of it. The edge of the damaged area had smoldered until the blast of air across the hurricane deck stoked it into flame.

Josette unclipped herself, snatched a fire blanket off the deck, and ran forward, dropping across the flaming rail with the blanket held in front of her. Despite her goggles, she reflexively closed her eyes in the face of the fire. When she looked again, it was smothered, and she was staring at the ground through a mile of sky. She could see the cannon still tumbling far below, and its ejected rammer arcing away in front.

She scrambled back from the abyss, leaving the fire blanket in place. She took one look at Kiffer and called up the companionway, "Get Chips down here! Tell him to bring fine sail thread, a sharp knife, and a good saw!"

"No!" Kiffer grabbed at her harness.

She found that she couldn't look the man in the eye, but she spoke as softly as she could. "There's no way you're keeping that leg, Private. Better to have done with it right now." She looked to Kember. "Take Private Corne back to his berth."

Ensign Kember was helping Corne up into the keel when Chips arrived. His eyes bulged when he realized what the saw was for.

"Goddamn it, man, hurry up," Josette said.

Josette felt a vague obligation to help with the amputation, but she was far too preoccupied. The elevatorman was struggling to keep *Mistral* from rising after the sudden loss of five hundred pounds of bref gun. The enemy scout was fifty yards below them and a little farther to starboard, looking up at the underside of *Mistral*'s deck and envelope. They'd be within swivel range in seconds.

And something was missing. She realized what it was with sudden anger: none of her riflemen were firing. They were, in fact, staring at Kiffer with mouths agape.

Chips was just making the first stroke with his saw, but Kiffer's scream couldn't match Josette's when she cried, "We're still in a battle, goddamn you! Shoot! Shoot, damn you, or I swear I'll throw you all over the side myself!"

Bernat and the other rifleman turned and fired simultaneously, so fast they couldn't possibly have aimed properly. They each took a fresh rifle and sighted more carefully before firing again. And yet, though the Vins were nearly within pistol shot, a quick glance over the side showed that her crew had so far failed to hit a single enemy cannoneer.

The punishment for their laxity —for Josette could think of no other way to describe it—came seconds later, when the scout's swivel guns popped off together, and dozens of musket balls hit *Mistral*'s hurricane deck from below.

A cluster of them hit the empty starboard gun carriage, not a yard from Kiffer. One pinged off Chips' saw and left a splatter of new blood, having passed through Kiffer's already-wounded leg. The growing blossom under Kiffer's armpit spoke to yet another wound, where a ball had gone into his shoulder. One of the Dumpling bastards must have aimed his swivel at the spot where Kiffer's leg stuck out.

Her eyes scanned the deck, looking first to the suspension cables. One had been hit and was frayed, but holding. The girders above it were splintered in several places, but they too held, at least for the moment. Above the catwalk, the bags and envelope must have gotten a good peppering, but that damage could wait.

Bernat was standing and still firing, to his credit, but one of her riflemen was down, a wound in his foot and a graze across his head. Corporal Lupien called forward, "My cable's cut, sir." He spun the rudder wheel. It turned without resistance.

"Transfer aft," she called back. "Continue this turn."

Lupien went up the companionway. The elevator steersman turned to follow.

"Is your cable also cut, Private?" Josette asked him.

He turned and shook his head.

"Then I will thank you to remain at your station on the hurricane deck."

She went to the rail, where Bernat was retrieving a fresh rifle for himself. Her second rifleman, as well as her loader, were kneeling over the wounded rifleman.

She tapped the loader with her boot, though some might have called it a kick, and said, "He'll live. Drag him out of the way and get back to work, both of you."

Bernat fired another shot. His sixth, she thought. She looked across to the enemy ship, where all three swivel guns were being frantically reloaded by unscathed cannoneers. How in hell had this battle turned so bad, so fast?

"You haven't hit anything?" she asked. "What the hell's wrong with you? When the target was road markers, you couldn't miss, but when it actually counts, you turn into an incompetent?"

Bernat looked at her, his face red. "It's different. That . . . that . . ." He pointed to the nearest swivel gun port on the Vin ship, and shouted, "That's a person!"

"It is different." She took a rifle and brought it up to her shoulder. "People are a good deal larger than markers."

She did not aim at the nearest of the enemy swivel ports, around which a cluster of holes showed the meager fruits of Bernat's rifle work. She aimed instead at the farthest port, the one nearest the scout's bow and *Mistral*'s stern, where the Vin cannoneer's next shot might spring a tail girder her ship couldn't afford to lose.

Josette was just about to shoot, when Kiffer redoubled his screaming. She paused just long enough to push the sounds out of her mind, aimed again, and fired. The rifle kicked into her shoulder and her vision filled with smoke. She didn't wait for it to clear. She held out her rifle and exchanged it for a fresh one.

She aimed at the farthest port again, but as the smoke cleared, all she could see there was a swivel gun rocking back and forth on its mount, without a cannoneer to service it. She swung the rifle forward to the middle port, where the Vin cannoneer was ramming a bag of musket shot into his muzzle.

She fired. The flash burned her cheek and singed her hair. The loader, in his haste, must have put too much powder in the rifle's pan. But the gun had fired, so she ignored the pain, held her spent rifle out, and exchanged it for another.

At the farthest port, the swivel was still unmanned. No one had relieved the dead cannoneer. The middle port was also empty. She swung her rifle aft along the enemy ship, to the swivel port nearest her. She found herself staring across the gap between ships and straight down the barrel of a loaded swivel gun. The cannoneer was staring back at her, sighting along the thick barrel as he scrambled to cock the flintlock. He was terrified, working frantically.

Josette did not hurry. She aimed directly at the cannoneer, as there was no need to account for wind or gravity at this range. She took a breath, let half of it out, and squeezed the trigger.

The instant the smoke leapt from her rifle's barrel, she dropped her calm demeanor along with her rifle. She grabbed Bernat and dove headlong for the deck, expecting the railing to explode into splinters under a hail of musket balls.

But nothing happened. She lifted her head to see Bernat sitting up, brushing off his coat. He looked at her and cleared his throat. "I was just about to say, that was a very clever shot. Got him right through the head before he could fire."

She sat up and looked around. "Thank you." She sprang to her feet. A crewman had already thrust a fresh rifle into her hands.

Bernat was only now rising. "I believe that puts you three shots ahead of me, for today."

She handed him the rifle. "You can make it up if you keep them from remanning those swivels." She looked over the side. The Vin scout was about to cut across *Mistral*'s wake, a position from which the Dumplings could rake her stern.

Josette looked up the companionway to Jutes. "Pass word to the rudderman: left rudder, as hard as he dares, and then another turn past that." When Jutes relayed the order, she added, "And tell Kember to get back to her goddamn post."

Jutes didn't have time to relay that order. Ensign Kember was already coming down the companionway, her uniform smeared with blood. She stopped at the bottom and stood at attention, but her eyes were locked on Chips's saw as it rocked forward, cutting through the last splinters of Kiffer's femur. She said, "I got tourniquets around Private Corne's wrists. I think he's going to live."

"It's an unjust world," Josette said. She regretted the comment before it was even out, but not quite enough to stop herself from saying it. "If you would kindly man your gun, Ensign."

Mistral was already swinging around to port. Aft, her tail swung past the scout from bow to stern. Josette heard one of the swivel guns firing, then another, accompanied by the patter of musket balls piercing the canvas and striking girders in the tail. She reached up to feel a girder, her eyes on Jutes.

Jutes was looking aft along the keel. When he looked back, he gave her a reassuring nod and said, "Tail's holding, sir."

Now she had them. She went to the port rail, Bernat following with a rifle. They both looked out. The scout had come full circle and farther still, and was not reversing its turn, but heading for the cloud bank to the east.

Too late for that, though. If the Vins had come out of their turn heading straight east, and resisted the opportunity to rake *Mistral*'s stern, they would have made it into the clouds before *Mistral* could come within canister range. As it stood, *Mistral* would certainly get one good canister shot in.

She returned to her spot just as Chips, the powder monkey, and a cannoneer from the port gun dragged Kiffer past. Even when dragging the wounded man, they detoured around the captain's spot, leaving a curved trail of blood behind them. Kiffer had stopped screaming at some point, she couldn't remember when, and was now staring blankly ahead, his face ashen.

The leg still lay embedded in the deck. "Get that, would you?" she asked one of the idle cannoneers. Unwilling to touch the thing, the man pushed at it with a rammer until it fell free.

To her left, Bernat fired his rifle, then stood waiting for the smoke to clear before he took another. "Blast," he muttered. He fired again, and twice more as *Mistral* came about. Her remaining bref gun had almost come to bear before Bernat, squinting through the smoke from his next shot, said, "My God, I hit him." He lowered the gun, still holding it tightly in his hands. His tone wasn't of jubilance or even surprise. It was horror.

"Well done, my lord," Josette said. She looked forward. "Ensign, we've lost the rudder cable, so you'll have to fire as we swing past." They still weren't close enough to deploy their most deadly munition—canister shot—so they'd have to make do with medium-range shell shot in the meantime.

Kember was already crouching behind her gun. *Mistral's* turn brought the gun to bear on the scout ship, and Kember pulled the lanyard.

Without martingales to hold it steady, the deck rocked wildly with the recoil. As the smoke cleared, Josette could see the narrow trail of smoke left by the shell as it curved directly into the top of the enemy's envelope. It had gone straight through without detonating, and the smoke trail sputtered out on the other side—the mark of a faulty fuse.

"Reload with canister," she ordered. The port gun crew was a man short, so she went forward and swabbed the gun herself, picked up the rammer, and pushed first the linen bag containing the gunpowder charge, then the cylindrical canister shot down the barrel. *Mistral* had by now swung past the target. She called to Jutes as she pulled the rammer free, "Pass the word: right rudder!"

This was the last shot she'd have before the scout reached the relative safety of the clouds, but with this single shot of canister, *Mistral* would return twice as many musket balls as the scout had fired so far during the entire engagement.

Josette remained forward, looking over the rail as the crew ran out the gun. Kember wrapped the lanyard an extra turn around her hand. This one final shot would determine whether *Mistral's* next dispatch would contain news of her first victory, or be filled with excuses for paying such a high price in blood and materiel for no gain.

The bref gun was almost aligned when a port opened on the scout's tail. Josette thought they were going to fire another rocket but, just as the ships were lined up, a Vin officer stuck his head and shoulders out and shot off a flare.

"Hold fire!" Josette said, but it was too late. The lanyard was pulled, the flint already sparking. Inside the gun, the priming ignited the charge, and the outer tin casing of the canister shot disintegrated under the force of half a pound of gunpowder. Eight-score musket balls were released and careened down the barrel to spread into a cone of destruction that billowed out in front of *Mistral* and tore into the scout's tail.

The flare from the Vin ship burst inside the cannon smoke, filling *Mistral*'s hurricane deck with the brilliant blue light that signaled an airship's surrender.

Kember gasped when she saw it. "I thought it was a rocket," she said. "I thought it was a rocket."

"It's not your fault," Josette said. The smoke cleared to reveal a tangled mass of wreckage where the scout's tail had been. The top fin now hung below the rest, suspended by its control line, swinging pendulously back and forth. The other three fins were bent and inoperable, leaving the scout lurching down and to starboard in an uncontrolled spiral. The man who'd fired the flare was gone. Just gone.

"I thought it was a rocket," Kember said.

Mistral was passing above the stricken ship, but Josette wanted to keep it in sight. "Pass the word: rudderman come to seventy-five degrees east." She ran to the side rail and leaned far over. The scout hadn't torn itself apart yet, so it still had a chance. It was buckling and losing gas at an alarming rate, but if the Vins could drop enough ballast, they just might come to a hard but survivable landing.

A cheer ran along *Mistral*'s keel, as word spread aft from the hurricane deck. Underneath that sound, and underneath the cry of the steamjack and the thrum of the airscrews, something caught Josette's ears. It was a strange hissing, wailing sound. Perhaps a leak in *Mistral*'s condenser? No, that wasn't quite right; as it grew louder, she knew that it wasn't coming from *Mistral*.

"I thought it was a rocket," Kember said, next to her.

"Shut up."

Josette retrieved the speaking trumpet, put the mouth end over her ear, and pointed it at the scout. The Vins were still spiraling downward, more slowly now that they were tossing everything but the keel girders over the side. Josette closed her eyes and pushed all other noises out of her mind, to focus on that one keening sound.

Her eyes opened. "We've shot away their governor."

From across the deck, Bernat asked, "Were they carrying politicians?"

"It keeps their steamjack from spinning too fast and tearing itself apart."

Bernat joined them at the rail, as Kember turned her attention to the scout. "Why don't they just open the boiler safety valve?" she asked. It was the obvious solution. With the valve open, the pressure in the boiler would fall, and the scout's steamjack would come to a stop on its own.

Josette watched, inching along the deck to keep the scout in view as *Mistral* turned toward it. She was expecting, at any moment, to see a jet of steam from the safety valve. It didn't come, and she suddenly realized why. "We killed their mechanics," she said. She looked back. "Four degrees down angle on the bow. Pass the word to Gears: reduce engine power to one-quarter." She was about to order Kember to rig the signal lamp, but when she turned, she saw the ensign already doing it.

Mistral dove after the Vinzhalian ship, her bow pointed down at the center of its spiral descent. The wailing keen was growing louder now, warbling in bizarre ululations that silenced the celebrations aboard *Mistral*.

Then there came a new sound: grinding, as some damn fool on the stricken ship disengaged the airscrews. He probably meant to save their gearbox from tearing itself apart, but he'd only made the peril worse by removing the only thing that held the steamjack's speed back—the last force that was keeping it from spinning out of control.

The grinding soon stopped, but the wail rose in pitch,

becoming a scream so loud it echoed off the ground half a mile below, returning as a hollow whistle. And then there was another new sound, a screeching, nails-on-slate noise below the others. Together they tore into Josette's ears and seemed to claw at the very bones of her skull. No banshee's wail could be so painful or so disquieting.

Kember had the signal lamp ready to transmit, but Josette took the lamp personally and asked Bernat, "Do you know how to say, 'open your boiler's safety valve' in Vinzhalian?"

Bernat thought for a moment. "I don't know their word for boiler, or valve. What about 'open your kettle's safety opening?'"

"It'll have to do. Spell it out for me, letter by letter."

He called the letters out and she relayed the message, shutters clacking open and closed in front of the quicklime lamp.

"Again," she said. The nails-on-slate sound was growing to eclipse the others. Halfway through the second transmission, there was a crash from the scout ship. A turbine blade had come free of the dying steamjack. It tore upward through the scout's envelope, rose past *Mistral,* and then fell in a long ballistic arc, trailing smoke. Josette completed the second transmission and said, "Again."

She made it through three letters before the Vin steamjack spun apart, shedding ragged strips of twisted, smoking metal that shot through the scout's keel and envelope as if they were insubstantial. A second later, the boiler blew apart with such force that the sound was felt more than heard.

Before the eye could perceive the split, the scout was in two pieces on either side of an expanding, obscuring white cloud. A second fat column of steam blew directly upward. It looked like the smoke from a cannon.

It reached high enough to cross directly in front of *Mistral's* path, and it was too late to turn out of the way. *Mistral* hit the column bow-on and was buffeted skyward in the sudden updraft. The steam swept along the envelope and over the hurricane deck, hot enough to sear the face and burn the lungs. Only her goggles allowed Josette to keep her eyes open.

In seconds they were through it, the cool air on the other side as soothing as ice. Josette ran to the back of the deck and looked down over the taffrail to see fires glowing, incongruously beautiful, in the heart of the cloud.

Above, droplets of boiler water pattered against the top of *Mistral*'s envelope. Below, tendrils of thick black smoke traced the paths of the burning wreckage through the larger cloud of steam. A large section of the scout's envelope fluttered gently downward, still buoyed by luftgas within and destined to come to a gentle landing, but there was nothing attached to it but ropes and fragments of girder.

Of the scout's crew, there was no sign. Josette could only hope that they had all died in the first moments of the blast.

She backed away from the rail, retreating until she stumbled against the companionway steps. There, she lingered a moment before saying, very softly, "Rig for landing."

BERNAT COULDN'T SAY why he followed Josette up the companionway. Perhaps he just wanted to be off the deck and away from the spectacle that filled the sky behind them.

"This ship is cursed," the captain said as she passed Jutes.

"If it's a curse," Jutes said, "I think the Vins bore the brunt of it, sir. That's not a bad curse to have."

But Jutes had only seen it in glimpses. Jutes hadn't *been* there. Not really. Not the way Captain Dupre had been there. Not the way Bernat had been there.

The mood in the keel was jovial. Crewmen slapped each other on the back, laughed, joked, and embraced. Even the stony face of their captain couldn't stop the festivities. As Bernat went past the condenser, someone slapped his ass. Probably Grey, but he wasn't sure, and he didn't look back to check.

Even in the sleeping berths, where the wounded had been taken, there was more cheer than Bernat could tolerate. Corne and Kiffer lay in their cots, alive and optimistic, even as the sight of their fresh stumps made Bernat want to vomit. The wounded rifleman glanced at the celebrations along the keel, clearly tempted to join in despite his perforated foot.

Was that really all of them? Only three wounded? Somehow it felt like more. At times it had seemed that *Mistral*'s entire crew would be hit, with the last man obliged to drag himself to the berths.

In Bernat's own berth, he saw the curtain had been shredded, and splinters and sawdust were scattered across his bunk. He slid the tattered curtain aside for a better look, and found that one of his bags had a dozen holes in it. Hastily unpacking it, he found that his best fall jacket—the lovely orange cashmere that went so well with his golden brown skin—was another casualty of the battle. The poor thing had taken the brunt of a swivel-gun shot, and was beyond all hope of mending. At least it had died a hero, standing in the way of bullets meant for *Mistral*'s vulnerable tail girders.

At the reservoirs, a young crewman was hunched, quietly scraping shit from the inside of his trousers. The captain took pains to not notice him, looking straight ahead at the auxiliary control area. Martel was there, standing at his station, with Lupien on the rudder wheel.

"Not a bad butcher's bill," Martel said, "assuming Private Kiffer lives."

"Could've been worse," the captain agreed. "Let's get the revelers into a work party, and patch up the bags. And I want a full damage report before we land."

"Yes, sir." Martel went forward, tipping his head and saying, "My lord," as he passed Bernat.

It was only then, as Captain Dupre was pulling back the curtain on her cabin, that she seemed to notice Bernat. She left the curtain open and sat down in one of her cabin's two hammock chairs. She occupied herself with prying a musket ball out of the small table between them, indicating the open chair with a flick of her head. "Have a seat, if you'd like."

It took Bernat a moment to get into the cumbersome little chair. The captain leaned over and opened a stern port, helping to clear the smell of shit from the aftmost frames and revealing the thick woods passing below them.

"I wonder why the king doesn't harvest these woods," Bernat said, not because he cared about the subject, but because he felt obligated to say something.

The captain finally pulled the musket ball out and idly examined it. "Your idea has merit," she said, "but I'm afraid it would make Durum good for something, and we can't have that." She turned the ball over and over, until Bernat got the distinct impression that, despite where her eyes were pointed, she wasn't looking at it at all. "Durum hasn't exported anything in over a century. The people can barely even feed themselves. It's a convenient place for a signal base, being so close to the border, but if not for that, you could wipe this place off the map and the rest of Garnia would shrug and move on, assuming they even noticed."

Bernat smiled. "No love like the love for a hometown." He desperately wanted a glass of wine, but his wine was in a bag in his berth, and he couldn't stomach the thought of seeing those bloody stumps again.

A crewman approached, stepping gingerly. "Mr. Martel sends his compliments, sir, and says we're on approach to the base."

The captain nodded and tossed the musket ball out the open port.

"Leaving so soon?" Bernat asked, sounding rather more desperate for companionship than he'd intended.

She stood. "Feel free to use the cabin. Nothing you find in here could make your uncle think any less of me than he already does."

"I promise I won't—"

"I just said that it doesn't matter."

"Nevertheless," he said to her back, as she walked away.

He didn't think she'd respond, but then she turned and spoke quietly. "Oh, if you are staying in the keel, will you keep an eye on the crew for me? Victory tends to get the blood up. There may be attempts at . . . mingling."

"Mingling?"

"*Mingling.*"

"Ah," he said, and exhaled. "Mingling. I shall stand ready with a bucket of cold water."

MARTEL SALUTED HER as she came down the companion-way, then stepped away from the captain's station. "The leaks are under control," he said, "the rudder cable is spliced, and the girders are sound, sir. The ship's still very light, which will make the landing tricky." By which he meant that *Mistral* was too light to settle gently to the ground, and had to be driven down with the engine. That, or vent luftgas, which everyone knew was a mortal sin. "I've brought us into the wind and signaled the base with our status."

"Very good," Josette said. They were coming in toward the setting sun. "Elevators down five degrees, steamjack to full power." To their right, cheering townsfolk were gathered on Durum's city walls, waving their handkerchiefs.

Ahead, on the edge of the airfield, a dozen yardsmen pushed ten times as many part-timers into their places. The part-timers would only be farmhands who'd been conscripted into yard duties for the evening, and hardly skilled enough to grab onto lines when commanded.

Mistral descended, passing them overhead at no more than a hundred feet. Josette ordered, "Cast lines." Crewmen in the corners of the hurricane deck and at ports along the keel dropped rope to the men below.

Lieutenant Martel looked a little nervous. "Have you stood the deck for an evening landing in a light ship before, sir?"

"Mister Martel, in my previous rank of auxiliary lieutenant, I was absolutely forbidden from performing such a dangerous operation." She looked straight ahead. "So I've only done it seven times."

While yardsmen below yelled directions at the rabble of part-timers, *Mistral* continued to descend toward the base's single mooring circle. As more men below put their weight on the ropes and held fast, the ship's buoyancy decreased, and it took less downward elevator to keep her from rising. If the elevatorman misjudged the angle, or failed to correct properly for a gust of wind, he might strike the mooring mast, or even fling the ground crew a hundred feet into the air.

"Stand by bow lines," Josette called up the companionway. She heard the monkey rigger run forward above her. "Disengage airscrews and rig for reverse." The airscrews slowed but the ship continued to glide forward on momentum, bow pointed straight at the mooring mast in the center of the landing circle, where a single brave yardsman waited to receive their line. When they were so close that a collision seemed impossible to avoid, Josette shouted, "Engage airscrews!"

The airscrews engaged in reverse gear, blasting the hurricane deck with their wash. The ship lurched, slowed, but did not yet halt. It slid on, kissing the mast before it finally began to reverse, playing out a line, which, at the moment of contact, had been passed between mastman and monkey rigger.

"Disengage airscrews!"

The airscrews stopped but the steamjack continued to spin, ready to bring the ship back under power at a moment's notice. The bow line was winched in, drawing the ship to the mast, until a sudden shudder spoke to the nose cap's connection. The monkey rigger's report was passed a few seconds later. "Secure to mast, sir."

As the sun went down, the yardsmen dragged her—mast, ship, and all—across the yard and into Durum's shed.

IT WAS NEARLY dark by the time Josette left the ship. The base commander, a junior lieutenant, was waiting at the foot of the ladder. As she hopped off the last rung, he only stood there, hardly glancing at her.

When Martel descended, however, he snapped a salute and spoke with bubbly energy. "Congratulations on your victory, sir! Sorry sir, I've neglected to introduce myself. Lieutenant Garand, sir. We don't get to see that kind of action every day, sir, let me tell you, sir! The way you took care of that Dumpling bastard, sir! Amazing! Anything you need from me, sir, you just name it!"

Lieutenant Martel said nothing. He only cleared his throat, tapped the single wing on his collar badge, and pointed to Josette.

Garand turned to her as if seeing her for the first time. His eager expression shattered when his eyes found the two wings on her collar badge. "You're a woman," he said.

Josette looked down at herself and saw some meager evidence of the accusation. "It would appear so." She pulled a folded sheaf of papers out of her jacket and handed them to him. "Here are the repairs and modifications I'll need."

She was not technically entitled to the yard's assistance in modifying her airship, but she outranked him, she'd just given Durum a show the likes of which it had never seen before, and she had nothing to lose.

"My carpenter is already familiar with the changes," she

said, "and my crew will be at your disposal, once they've so-
bered up from the bacchanalia they'll undoubtedly enjoy this
evening. Say, I don't suppose you have a spare twelve-pounder
bref gun in stores?"

Garand looked up from perusing Josette's sketches and
shook his head.

"Oh well," she said. "I think I remember where we dropped
ours."

Garand pointed to one of the sketches. "We only have four
airscrews of this type in stock."

"Lucky for both of us that we're reducing the number of
Mistral's screws from six to four, then."

Garand still wasn't happy. "The point is, you'll run my
stock dry if we make these modifications."

"That's what the stocks are there for," she said.

"Actually—" he began.

She cut him off. "We have wounded aboard. Don't take
them to the town surgeon, if by some misfortune he's still
alive. That man is an idiot. Take them to Heny the midwife.
You know her?"

Garand shook his head.

"She's in the cottage near the north gate. The one with the
plants growing out of the roof. I'm sure you've noticed it. Now
if you'll excuse me, Lieutenant, I must find billets for my
crew." She snatched up her bag, turned, and left the shed.

Martel caught up to her halfway across the base and said,
"I can handle the billets if you'd like, sir. Anyplace in particular you'd like for your personal quarters?"

"Regrettably," she said, looking uphill to the town, "I
already have a billet waiting."

"I see," Martel said, though it was clear he didn't.

As they approached the town's south wall, throngs of
townsfolk crowded around them. In the faint evening light,
she didn't recognize any of them, and she hoped they wouldn't

recognize her. They didn't; more merciful still, they pressed toward Martel, all wanting to shake his hand or profess their love and admiration for the "hero captain."

Josette separated herself from the crowd and, walking backwards, shouted over the din, "And you can handle"—she waved her hand vaguely at the throng—"this whole situation?"

"Yes, sir!" Martel said, seeming to enjoy the accolades.

"Very good. Carry on."

She entered the city through the south gate. Inside, the narrow stone streets and close-packed buildings made Durum look like a more substantial city than it really was. But she knew half the buildings were empty. Some had been vacant for generations, and were now filled to their moldering roof beams with decades of neighborhood trash. Farther into the city, entire blocks were nothing but empty, weed-ridden plots, or used only for vegetable gardens, whose manure-fertilized furrows made the whole town smell like shit.

As she walked the streets, Josette found it difficult to believe that, hundreds of years ago, before the long wars, Durum had been an important city. Straddling the border between Garnia and Vinzhalia—though back then it was on the Vinzhalian side—it was a center of trade and a boon to both nations. Trade goods crossing the border in this region had passed through Durum by edict of law, and in Durum they were taxed, tariffed, and skimmed.

Merchants' gold came in by the bag, and the king's gold left by the bag—often the very same bag, albeit with its burden substantially reduced during the short trip across town. The nomadic horse lords that once terrified the countryside became caravan masters, not because they were subdued by martial force but because the money was so much better. The local guilds flourished, the people thrived, and the town grew so fast they had to move the city walls out six times in as many generations.

Or so her father once told her. She had searched the town for the forgotten foundations of those older walls, and only ever found four. She'd spent half her childhood looking for the other two, rummaging in empty lots and digging archaeological pits across public streets in the middle of the night, searching for buried remnants.

She was tempted, even now, to spend the night looking for them. But it would be wasted time now, as it had been wasted time then, to search for something no one else even cared about in a town that everyone else had forgotten.

And then, quite suddenly, she found herself at her destination. It was a two-story brick-and-stone house sitting at the end of a lane—a much narrower lane than she remembered. She dropped her bag, took a deep breath, and knocked on the door.

Josette was looking slightly up when the door opened, and had to tilt her head back down when she found the woman who answered was of the same height. The woman had Josette's dry, wavy hair, but it was longer. Her eyes went from Josette's face to the bruise on her forehead, down to the bandage around her hand, and then to the bag at her feet.

The woman stood staring, thin lips pressed together, for several seconds. Then she swallowed and asked, "So, what'll you be wanting?"

Josette sighed and said, "Nice to see you too, Mother."

BERNAT WAITED UNTIL the wounded were offloaded, sitting quietly in the captain's cabin and pretending interest in the view from the stern ports. They looked out on nothing more than a bare shed wall, blackened by mildew. It wasn't much to look at, but Bernat couldn't see it anyway, as hard as he stared at it. What Bernat saw in its place was an expanding cloud of steam that had been an airship, alternating with the puzzled, strangely indignant expression of the man he'd shot through the neck.

After they finally took Kiffer out on a stretcher made from his own bunk, Bernat went forward to make use of the writing materials near the bow, then gathered a few essentials and disembarked.

It was strange, walking on solid earth again after nearly a week in the air. The ground seemed to lurch and sway underneath him. The crew had warned him of this. They called it "air legs," but to Bernat it seemed that the ground itself had disinherited him, and was refusing to recognize him as a child of the earth after his time in the air. It got better, though, just as the airmen said it would, and was gone by the time he passed through the south gate of Durum.

What a lovely little town it was.

The houses, workshops, and stores were tightly packed in this side of the city, no doubt due to its desirable southern exposure. It reminded him of his favorite streets in Kuchin, where quaint little buildings had been protected and preserved down through the centuries by wealthy families. Yet this was so much better. It had none of the bustle of Kuchin, none of that feeling of being shoved into a barrel with the other fish.

He took a winding route through the southern quarter, losing himself in the tangle of narrow streets. The town only became better the farther he wandered. Closer to the center of the town, the streets widened, and the press of buildings gave way to a checkerboard of beautiful open lots. Some of them were even furrowed into lovely gardens, whose rich, earthy aromas blanketed all of Durum, speaking to its deep connection with the land.

Perhaps, if he could find a good tavern and a gambling house, he might even stay for a while. Certainly, what he would earn from the letter tucked into his coat pocket would set him up in lodgings for as long as he wanted. Even if that hadn't been the case, he'd rather live in the poorhouse than go up in that accursed airship again.

Now he came to the town square, with frogs croaking in the decorative pond at its center. He walked the edge of the square, looking for the post office, but couldn't find it. He thought that it might lie inside the town hall, but that was locked up for the night. Fortunately, there were a couple of men seated on its steps, having a lively political debate. What a wonderful town this was.

As Bernat approached, the younger of them seemed flustered. "What do we want with Quah, anyway?"

The older man harrumphed. "Apart from it's our goddamn birthright as Garnians—something your generation just don't seem to understand—think of the iron and gold in those mountains."

"But we must have already spent half of that wealth in conquering and holding the damn place, if not all of it."

"All the more reason to keep fighting, by God! 'Cause if you don't—" He blew a short, rude note between his tongue and upper lip. "All that investment's just wasted."

Bernat was going to have to remember that smashing line of argument for his own use. "Excuse me, gentlemen," he said, stepping up to them. "I don't mean to interrupt, but could either of you direct me to the post office?"

They directed him down a scenic lane off the square, to a squat house halfway down the block. He arrived there to find no sign on the door, no indication at all that this was a government building. He strolled the length of the lane, thinking there had been some mistake, but found nothing that looked any more like a post office. With nothing left to do, he knocked on the door.

An old man answered. Fresh gravy clung to the corners of his mouth, and he had a crust of bread in his left hand. Inside, the table was set for dinner.

"My apologies," Bernat said. "I didn't mean to bother you. It's only . . . someone told me this was the post office. You don't happen to know where it is, do you?"

The man took a bite from his bread crust and spoke around it. "Right they are, sir. This is the post office, and I am the postmaster."

"How delightful," Bernat said, beaming a smile. "How charming!"

The postmaster took another bite and chewed with his mouth wide open. His dull eyes ran over Bernat's clothes. "New in town, sir?"

"Why, yes," Bernat said, "and I'd like to send a letter to my uncle." He fished into his pocket and brought it out. "It only needs to go to the garrison in Arle, and the army will forward it along to him." And shortly after that, he reflected, Captain Dupre's career would be over.

"I'm sure it will, sir," the postmaster said, reaching out to take the letter. "Very good at getting things where they need to go, the army is."

Bernat pulled it back, flushed, and said, "I, uh, I don't even know what it costs."

"One dinar to Arle, sir."

Good God, that was cheap. A few lines sent by semaphore had cost him over a hundred times as much. No wonder there was no proper post office—the pocket change the mail brought in could never justify the expense. He held the letter just out of the postmaster's reach. "I'm not convinced it's worth the price," he said.

"The price is the price, sir."

Bernat stared, his eyes unfocused. "Quite so."

"I tell you what, sir," the postmaster said, looking impatiently back at his dinner table. "You take the night to think about it, and if in the morning it seems worth the cost, I'll still be right where you left me."

He smiled. "A wonderful idea. Thank you." He was just turning to leave, when he suddenly snapped his fingers. "I don't suppose you know if there's a Dupre living in this town? A widow, perhaps?"

The postmaster narrowed his eyes. "And why would you be wanting to know, sir?"

"I'm a friend of the family."

The postmaster's directions brought him to a lovely little cottage at the end of a lovely little lane. He took a moment to listen at the door. The voices on the other side were elevated, but the words were not clear through the thick oak. He gave it a few hearty knocks.

The voices stopped and Captain Dupre threw open the door. No, not Captain Dupre; but in the faint candlelight coming from the cottage, he could see why he'd been mistaken. They shared the same angry, tawny, sharp-featured face that bore the same go-bugger-yourself scowl, but the woman in the doorway was perhaps two decades the captain's senior, with longer hair and plumper features, dressed in a humble peasant's shift. He was half in love already.

The actual Captain Dupre was behind her, on the other side of an old loom. Bernat smiled to both of them in turn and said, "I brought wine!"

The captain did not smile back, but asked, "Did you bring a sense of propriety?"

"Must have left it in the ship." He flashed another dazzling smile to the woman in the doorway. "And you must be the ravishing Mrs. Dupre."

"Oh, it's just Elise. 'Mrs. Dupre' makes me sound so . . ."

"Unavailable?" the captain suggested.

"Dowdy," Elise said, throwing a nasty glance over her shoulder.

"So very pleased to meet you. Allow me to present myself, seeing that the dear captain appears unwilling. I am Lord

Bernat Manatio Jebrit Aoue Hinkal, son of the Marquis of Copia Lugon." He bowed low enough to scrape the ground.

Elise was stunned into complete silence. She just stared at him, eyes wide.

Rising from his bow, Bernat gently took her hand and kissed it. "I would present myself as your servant, madam, but to a woman of your beauty, I am but a slave."

"Oh, good God," the captain muttered.

Elise, if not positively enchanted, clearly suspected that a tremendous amount of money was standing on her doorstep. She returned his smile, and he noted with delight that she still had all of her teeth. "Please come in, my lord," she said. "We were just sitting down to dinner."

Bernat entered and bent to sniff at a stewpot on the stove. By the crust around the edge of the pot, he judged that the stew had been bubbling away, unstirred, for at least half an hour while the two women shouted at each other. "I have just the red to go with this," he said. "And please, call me Bernat."

"What are you doing here?" the captain asked.

Bernat sat at the table and dug into his bag. "Joining you for dinner," he said. "And I have a lovely cheese to go with the stew. I think you'll like it. It's from the south of Kibril and perfectly aged."

"Don't interrogate him," Elise said, sitting across from Bernat. She looked at him across the table. "You're welcome here, Bernat."

"My God," the captain said, pacing a few steps and staring out through a small window set in a deep sill. "Of course he is. Of course some fop from the other side of the kingdom is more welcome in your house than I am."

"You mind your tongue!" Elise scowled, but it melted away as she looked into Bernat's eyes. "Bernat is no fop."

"Quite right," he said cheerfully. "At most, I'm a dandy."

He looked about the room, whose corners and edges were deep in shadow. "Could we perhaps get a bit more light?"

"She says she doesn't want to waste oil," the captain said.

But before the captain could even finish her sentence, Elise had leapt from her chair and was adjusting the lamp to produce a brighter flame. The light revealed the grime on her shift, which she seemed aware of. She bounded up the stairs two at a time, saying, "I'll be back down with candles and another lamp."

The captain took a deep breath. "For me, she doesn't want to waste oil."

"I'll have a fresh jar sent over in the morning," Bernat said. "And I do apologize for the intrusion, but I simply had to know what put you in such a state of dread at the thought of coming to Durum. Now I see that you were afraid I'd steal your dear mother away and take her home with me. Well, you may put your mind at ease, Captain. It's such a lovely town, I think the two of us will live here."

The captain rolled her eyes. "If it would get you off my goddamn ship, I would happily give you my mother, and throw a couple of aunts into the bargain."

"Your generosity is admirable, Captain. But really, it's not such a large house. One aunt will do, I think."

She leaned toward the stairs and shouted up, "Mother! Does Aunt Yvette still live in town?"

Elise's voice was strangely muffled when she called back, "Why do you want to know?"

The captain's eyes shifted to Bernat, and back to the stairs. "Just wanted to catch up."

Bernat was wondering just how long she could keep this going, when his thoughts were suddenly arrested by the sight of Elise coming down the stairs. She had changed out of her shift and into a green linen gown. It was a simple thing, really.

In Kuchin, it would have been laughed at, but in Durum it was surely the height of finery.

Bernat found himself unable to take his eyes off it. Perhaps Elise had purchased the gown from a slightly slimmer woman, or perhaps it had been fitted to her years ago, when she was her daughter's size. Whatever the reason, it was deliciously tight on her frame and snug around her features.

"Oh, good God," the captain said, accentuating every word. "You went upstairs for candles."

Elise stepped delicately to the bottom of the stairs. "I made it to the top of the stairs when I remembered that I keep them down here, in the cabinet." She fluttered her eyelashes at Bernat.

While she lit candles and set them about the room, the captain asked, "My lord?" in a suspiciously accommodating tone.

"Hmm?" he asked, pouring himself a glass of wine.

"You should really take the place at the head of the table."

He coughed. "Thank you, but, ah, I'm quite comfortable where I am."

Captain Dupre walked behind him and tugged with seeming helpfulness at his chair. "No, my lord. You're my mother's guest; you should be seated at the place of honor."

Bernat held the chair firmly in place. "I don't like this side of you," he said. He wondered if she would behave this way if she knew he held her destiny in his breast pocket. No, he concluded after a moment's thought, she would be worse.

"Leave him alone, Josie!" Elise said. Looking at Bernat, she added, "She's always been such a bully."

"I had an excellent tutor," the captain said.

Bernat took a long sip of wine, to forestall the expectation that he comment on any of this. Captain Dupre chose that moment to lean in and whisper in his ear, "Don't worry yourself, my lord. I'm sure she'll take it as a compliment."

Bernat choked and spat a fine mist of wine across the table.

"Is the wine not to your liking, my lord?" the captain asked, taking the seat at the head of the table.

"No, no. It just needs to breathe," Bernat said, panting. "It just needs to breathe."

"We are speaking of the wine, are we not?" the captain asked. This earned her a cuff from her mother, right across the back of the head. She was, for a moment, too shocked to move.

"She's always been a vile creature, ever since she was a girl," Elise said, standing next to the remaining chair but not sitting down. "Traipsing through the forest. Digging up the streets. Running off with men."

"Boys, mother. They're called 'boys' when they're the same age as you. You make it sound like, well, like something you would do. You were how old, again, when you married Dad?"

Elise returned a sneer.

"Oh, I'm sorry. Was that uncouth? Let me rephrase it: how old were you when you had to marry Dad to avoid a scandal?"

The captain directed her gaze at Bernat, who'd been hoping that if he pushed himself far enough down in his chair, they would forget he was there.

"Not that it worked," the captain continued. "Heny says I was born six months to the day after the wedding. Proof that there are some things you just shouldn't put off."

Bernat really didn't like this side of her. He stuffed a piece of cheese in his mouth so he wouldn't have to answer. A bubble plopped in the stew, still left unstirred in its cooking pot.

And that was when Elise began to cry.

It came as a surprise to the captain. She swallowed hard and began stuttering out an apology. But before she could form it, her mother stared balefully at her through brimming eyes and said, "Get out of my house."

For a moment, Bernat could see resistance in the captain. She clenched her fist and seemed on the cusp of a tirade. But then she sighed and said, in a very soft voice, "Gladly." She rose, gathered her things in silence, and left.

When she was gone, Bernat stood and walked around the table to sit next to Elise. She was not merely crying now, but sobbing.

He put an arm around her, cradled her head against his chest, and said, "She isn't very nice to me, either."

9

JOSETTE BILLETED IN the tavern that night. She woke in the morning on the grimy bar floor, her head throbbing, her uniform soaked in ale, and the footsteps of the barman pounding in her ears.

"Barman," she said, barely recognizing her own ragged, phlegmy voice, "I don't suppose I could beg the use of a basin to rinse my uniform? I can't quite remember the details, but somehow I've come to smell like a brewery."

The barman, a man she didn't recognize from her years in Durum, paused and leaned on his broom. "Just give 'em to the missus to wash. She'll do it good and proper, with soap and everything. And I'll fetch you water and a bottle of Heny's best hangover cure."

"That's too kind," Josette said, clutching her head as she rose.

"Not at all, Cap'n. Only good business. Your festivities last night will see my family through the winter. With the price of food and coal going up so fast, I wasn't rightly sure we'd have enough money to make it, until you came from the sky, like a flight of drunken angels."

Her memories of the night before were vague, but she remembered, at several points, wondering how the tavern keeper could possibly make a profit from the pittance he was charging for drinks. Now she suspected he'd gouged her, at least by local standards.

She wrote a report of the previous day's battle while sitting on a barstool in her underclothes, while the barman's wife washed her uniform. When she was finished, the barman offered to have the report sent to the base for her, but she had no time to linger, so she donned her damp clothes and took it over herself.

At the base, the repairs and modifications were coming along well. The dearth of trained yardsmen should have slowed the work, but Martel had drummed the crew awake at dawn and put them to work, despite their aching heads.

As she made a tour of the ship, Josette heard them grumbling. One crewman complained that "t'wasn't fair to do this to us, when t'was the captain who got us drunk in the first place."

She couldn't recall getting any of her crew drunk—could not remember them being at the tavern at all. But it was the only tavern in town, and they had clearly been drinking, so she didn't doubt their story. She could only hope that she hadn't done anything to permanently hobble their nascent respect for her.

She informed Martel of her intention to go into the woods and look for *Mistral*'s wayward cannon, and refused his suggestion of an armed escort, but agreed to go armed herself. In truth, she'd been planning to take a rifle anyway, and hoped to bring home the officers' dinner.

Martel must have suspected, for he asked, "I thought east of Durum was all King's Woods?" Meaning that all lumber and game there was the property of the Crown, unavailable for exploitation by the locals, and certainly not the personal sporting grounds of an army lieutenant.

She snorted. "If I see the king out there, I'll give him your regards."

She cut through the town to save time, but lost whatever she'd gained when she spotted Bernat strolling jauntily into the town square from Postman's Lane, and she had to duck behind the tall weeds in the pond to avoid speaking to him. He looked insufferably cheerful this morning, and whatever conversation he might offer would do her aching head no good.

When he was gone, she continued on and left town by the east gate, the only one of Durum's gates which had been properly maintained and improved over the years. Just outside the gate, there was a small triangular redoubt, a defensive fortification that sheltered the gate itself from direct artillery fire. The redoubt's sharp end pointed straight down the road, in the hope that any cannonballs coming in from an emplacement there would hit at an oblique angle and glance off. The redoubt had its own cannon, a modern twelve-pounder, with two older guns supporting it from the walls on either side of the gate.

The other gates had no such redoubts, but this was the gate facing Vinzhalia, where people looked when they thought of invasion. It wasn't entirely rational, for the Vins could cut a path through the woods and attack the town from any direction they chose, but Josette understood the sentiment all the same. Though this road and the thick woods around it were Garnian territory, she felt incredibly exposed. Even after years of neglect, the road was still wide, flat, and straight. A Vin cavalryman—and there might easily be cavalrymen in these woods even now, for airships weren't the only kind of scout the Dumplings had—could hide in the underbrush and see for miles up and down the road.

In fact, there was a small but very real possibility that she was being observed by the enemy at this very moment. The thought made her recheck her rifle's flint and the powder in the pan.

After a few more miles, she began to see signs of the previous day's aerial battle. There were charred fragments of envelope and splinters of plywood. The cannon couldn't be far from them, so she left the road and went into the woods. After another mile spent trudging through the underbrush, the squawks of ravens led her to Kiffer's black and bloated leg, which was being pecked at in the upper branches of a tree.

She was glad to see it, because it meant the cannon couldn't be far off. She traced a zigzag path through the woods, keeping her eyes on the canopy to look for splintering or other signs of a heavy object falling from the heavens. It took another two hours of searching, but she finally spotted a thick branch that was broken and dangling by a thread of bark.

Under it, there was no bref gun, but there was a bref-gun-shaped hole in the ground, impenetrably dark and deeper than her arm was long. At least, she consoled herself, the cannon had landed in soft earth. It was most likely intact down there, and could be returned to service as early as tomorrow, if she brought a work party back in the morning.

She was about to make her way back to the road when she realized that the hulk of the Vin scout ship had to be nearby. Once she thought of it, it didn't even occur to her not to look for it, and it was the work of a mere quarter of an hour to find the wreck.

The aft half of the ship lay twisted and bent in the midst of a burnt-out clearing. The charred underbrush crackled beneath her boots as she approached the remains of the girders. Farther on, she could see the bow had crashed amid ancient oaks. Being only a semirigid, the envelope had collapsed, but the forward keel segments were intact and their fabric skin unburnt.

As she approached, she heard something rooting around inside. Probably a fox. She readied her rifle and stepped quietly around the wreck. A fox would not do for the officers' supper—and certainly not this fox, considering what it was most likely eating in there—but the pelt might be worth a rial or two.

She maneuvered wide of the wreckage, between the trees,

trying to get a shot at it through an opening in the keel, but most of the forward section was still covered by canvas. She chose her steps carefully, rounding the bow to look along the other side of the downed airship's keel. It was only then that she noticed the horse.

It was staring back at her from atop the remains of the scout's hurricane deck, where it was tied to a limp suspension cable. When it saw her, it whinnied and pawed the ground.

A man—a Vin hussar, judging by his blue coat and fur busby cap—came out of the keel. Josette froze. The hussar glanced about the forest, but didn't see her in the dim light under the canopy. He walked to the horse and stroked the animal's neck, saying soothing words to it in Vinzhalian.

When he finally noticed Josette, she was already squeezing the trigger of her rifle.

As the smoke cleared, the horse pulled free of its bonds and galloped away, running headlong through the forest, stumbling over roots and uneven ground. The hussar lay on the ground, blood gushing from the hole in the center of his chest.

"Oh hell," she said. The hussar would have been a valuable prisoner. If she'd had half a second longer to think, she would have tried to wound him.

It was then, as she cursed herself for her inattention, that she finally noticed the second horse.

It was farther away than the first and hidden by a kink in the wrecked keel, but she could hear it plainly enough. She began to reload, but didn't even get the powder down the barrel before another hussar appeared, squeezing his shoulders through a hole in the wreckage.

She gave up all hope of reloading in time and simply ran at him, holding the rifle up like a club and shouting one of the few Vinzhalian words she knew, a demand for surrender.

He was evidently unimpressed by her vocabulary, for he

vaulted from the wreck and made a dash for his horse, where he had a carbine musket and the biggest goddamn cavalry saber Josette had ever seen.

She could see already that he was going to reach them before she reached him. If she kept running, he'd shoot her. If she stopped, he'd shoot her. So she kept running until he drew the carbine, and then she suddenly veered away into the trees. She heard him fire, and heard the bullet smack into a tree just behind her.

She looked through the trees to see the hussar toss aside his carbine and vault onto his horse. He drew his saber and charged. Though the horse had some trouble maneuvering in the forest, she knew it wouldn't matter. The Vins were renowned for their cavalry, and she'd just picked a fight with one of them. She was a mere signal officer, while the hussar was a finely honed instrument of death.

But he was a finely honed instrument of death mounted atop a horse—a weird, skittish creature that was only half sane on its best days.

She saw a thick tree trunk ahead of her, wide enough to hide behind, and she stopped short, her boot digging into the soft earth in its shadow, the hussar only seconds behind. The rifle was still clutched in her whitening hands. She held it over her head and, as the horseman charged past, she brought the butt around in a crushing swing that drove not into the hussar, who was expecting that blow and ready to parry it, but onto his horse's head.

The animal's dark brown eyes filled with blood. It turned away from the sudden pain just as Josette ducked the hussar's counterattack. His saber went high and buried itself into the bark of the tree. He tugged at it, but the horse pulled away before he could free the blade.

Josette did not pause or stop to assess. She ran after him, swinging her rifle with a savagery she'd never before experienced, striking a solid blow against his shoulder. Before he could get clear, she swung again in a scything motion that hit him in the belly just as his horse reared on its hind legs.

The hussar fell, landed on his head, and crumpled. Josette stood over him, poised for a death blow. She shouted another demand for surrender.

He didn't answer her. He only lay still. Perfectly still.

She slumped against a tree, gasping for breath. "Goddamn it," she muttered. Before she could think to restrain it, the wounded horse ran off as well, and wouldn't return no matter how loudly or angrily she shouted at it.

Feeling a powerful thirst born of her sudden exertion, not to mention a resurgent headache, she checked both hussars' canteens, but lamentably found only water. It was just her luck, at a time like this, to have killed the only sober cavalrymen in all the world.

She searched their jackets and rucksacks, taking every piece of paper she found. She even slit open the usual hiding places, the secret pockets and doubled-over cuffs into which money and messages might be sewn.

All told, she found several papers and a cache of Garnian coins, no doubt meant to pay for bribes and informants. She slipped them into her pocket. She searched the ship, too, but their orders had been destroyed—probably the moment they spotted *Mistral*—and the maps were uninformative.

She headed for home, examining the papers as she went. Most were meaningless to her, just line after line of scribblings in a language she didn't understand. One was a mundane promissory note, for gambling debts if she knew anything about hussars.

Another was, of all things, a lumber survey stolen from Durum's record house. It even had an official city stamp on it. The survey divided the King's Woods to the east of Durum into plots and listed the types and qualities of the trees in them.

She couldn't fathom why the Vins would be interested in such insignificant minutiae of Garnian affairs, until she read to the bottom, where the surveyor provided an estimate of the time and effort required to clear back roads to reach the choicest lumber.

"Oh God," she said, suddenly understanding.

"Oh God." She stuffed the papers into her jacket and ran. By the time she reached the road she was already panting, but she pushed on even faster.

"Oh God." She ran until she thought she might pass out from the pain in her feet, the pain in her legs, the burning of her lungs, and the lightness in her head. But finally she spotted Durum in the distance. She couldn't stop. She couldn't slow down. It was probably too late anyway, but if it wasn't, then minutes might make all the difference.

The gates were wide open. She tripped over a jutting stone where the compact dirt of the road turned into the cobblestones of the city, but caught herself before she fell. She staggered on through the streets, down alleys that she'd known since childhood, taking precious shortcuts that shaved time, second by second, off her sprint for the south gate.

She ran into Martel coming the other way, heading into the city from the signal base. Thank God it was someone competent, someone she could trust. She was dizzy now and misjudged the distance between them, so that instead of skidding to a stop in front of him, she barreled into the man and knocked him to the ground.

He laughed as he sat up, but one look at her face silenced him. He jumped to his feet and held out a hand to help her, but she waved it away, gasping for breath. "Message," she managed to spit out between gasps. "Run and send a bird to Arle . . . and a rider to the . . . to the nearest semaphore sta—"

The last word caught in her throat. She was wracked by a string of hacking coughs.

"What message?" Martel asked, poised to run.

She gulped air and said, "From Durum: Vin attack imminent."

WITH MARTEL ARRANGING for a horse messenger, Josette was forced to deal with Lieutenant Garand herself.

"Have you replaced our sprung girder?" she asked, her voice still showing signs of breathless exhaustion.

"Perhaps you should sit down and have a drink," Garand said, taking short steps despite his longer legs. It made him look like he was trotting to keep up with her.

"I'm fine. Did you hear my question?"

He assumed a more dignified gait. "It was the first thing we finished."

"Good man," she said, suspecting that Martel had insisted on that priority. "Get to work on the booms and airscrews. The rest can wait."

"But I've just sent the yardsmen home."

She eyed him. "Then get them back. I intend to have my ship in the air come morning. We need eyes on the Vins. They're coming, Mr. Garand. They're coming soon."

No spy, after all, would be so brazen as to steal documents from the records hall if the matter weren't pressing. Even if a lumber survey wouldn't be missed, there was the risk of being caught with a document that told precisely how long it would take an invading army's engineers to cut a road through the woods and bypass Durum.

She thought of the papers in her jacket. "I found a number of other documents, but they're all in Vin. Do you have anyone trustworthy who can translate them?"

Garand frowned. "Plenty here who speak Vin, but not many who can read it. Maybe if someone sounds it out for them?"

Just as she'd feared. "It's worth a shot if we can't find anyone else," she said. If no yardsman or trusted local could translate the documents, the alternative was unthinkable.

She went into the shed to look over her maps. The more she studied them, the more she thought the Vins' real target was still Arle, and Durum just happened to be in the way of their next line of attack.

If Arle fell, it would be a hard loss for Garnia, least of all because of its essential industries. It was no wonder the Vins were persisting in their efforts to take it, for it would deprive Garnia of her largest signal base and a critical rail hub.

Josette scanned the map, checking the roads and towns along likely routes of attack. The Vin city of Kamenka was across the border, only two days' march from Durum, and from Durum an army could march to Arle in three days more. But how would the Vins get an army to Kamenka in the first place? They didn't have extensive rail infrastructure along this stretch of the border. There was little economic reason, since Kamenka was hardly bigger than Durum, and produced nothing that was worth moving by rail.

The nearest rail line was a week's march from Kamenka, and the roads too rough and narrow to move a sizable force very quickly. An army assembling in Kamenka would take months to trickle in, something even Garnian intelligence—such as it was—would have surely detected by now.

She ran her finger between Kamenka and the nearest known Vin railway line. The road from that line to Kamenka was poorly developed, but it ran straight for most of its length, perfect for building a branch line. Could the Vins have managed that since the last time the area was scouted?

The yardsmen and crew were beginning to arrive and return to work. They were just hauling the outboard airscrews down when an older man came in through the shed door. Despite two extra decades of wrinkles and gray hair, Josette recognized him immediately as Kadi Halphin. Even if she hadn't recognized him by sight, she would have recognized the attire of office: the wide, gold-colored wool belt and that ridiculous red fez. On several occasions as a child, she'd tried to toss pennies onto its flat top, but they had always bounced off.

"Your Honor," she said, presenting herself with a snappy little bow and hoping to God he wouldn't recognize her. "You have a spy in your town."

Halphin laughed. "Just the one?"

"One who stole this," she said, handing him the purloined survey.

He examined it, not seeming to understand the implications. Then again, he didn't seem to recognize Josette, either, so she counted her blessings.

"It tells the Vins how long it'll take to cut a road through the woods. I expect they'll be on a very tight schedule, so they want to know whether it's faster to bypass us or just capture the town."

He grinned. "If they try that, they'll find that no one builds walls like ours anymore."

Josette attempted to keep her chagrin hidden. The kadi was right. No one built walls like Durum's anymore, because Durum's stone walls would shatter under a few hours of cannon fire. The Vins wouldn't even bother to emplace their siege guns. Mere field artillery would be sufficient.

"And if they do get in, my militia will send them packing."

Said militia was comprised of about half the male population of the town and was an absolute rabble. "You can't honestly expect to resist an entire Vin army," Josette said.

Halphin didn't answer, but only gave her a patronizing look. It was the kind of look she'd long since become accustomed to. It said that she should see to her gears and luftgas, and leave the hard work of strategy in better, or at least more masculine, hands.

"Perhaps as a precaution," she said, "in case they bombard and burn the town rather than risk an assault, you should evacuate the civilians, make preparations to fire the shed, and spoil any food that can't be carried away?"

He was on the verge of dismissing the idea, when doubt crept into his face. "They wouldn't really shell us, would they?"

She was certain they wouldn't. It would take longer than capturing the town, for one thing, and a Vin army on the march preferred pillage over destruction. The spoils of a good pillaging raised morale and helped keep the soldiers fed. Nevertheless, she put on a dour face and said, "They would happily shell your town, Your Honor. They're brutal, you know. And cowards. And no wall can stop a shell that's lobbed over it, or one that's dropped from an airship above. They'll burn Durum to ash, having never set foot within a mile of it, and they'll sleep soundly afterward. " She thought of telling him how much they liked to eat babies, but decided that it might be going too far.

"I'll consider an evacuation of the women and children," he said. "Good day, Lieutenant."

As Josette was returning to her maps, Lieutenant Garand ran in and stopped next to her. "We found someone who can translate the documents," he said. "University educated."

She stopped and closed her eyes, taking a deep breath. At this moment, there was certainly only one man in Durum who was university educated.

"I hope this is important," Bernat said, strolling up and speaking in that insufferably cheerful tone of his. "The Dupre household was just sitting down to dinner."

BERNAT WISHED HE had stayed at dinner, for the Vinzhalian documents turned out to be entirely mundane. Captain Dupre was exasperated, but what did she expect? That Vinzhalian scouts would wander through Garnian territory carrying their own battle plans?

"Perhaps," he suggested, "if I could have a word with the prisoners?"

The captain stared at him. "What prisoners?"

"The prisoners you took these documents from."

"I'm afraid they're dead."

So she'd tortured the poor devils to death. How ghastly. "Did you write down anything they said before they died?"

The captain looked at him in that petty, patronizing way of hers. "Why yes," she said, "I have their last words right here." She made a show of shuffling through some papers. "One said, 'Ow, you've shot me,' and the other said, 'Tell Madeline I love her.' Or it might have been 'Marianne.' It was rather hard to hear. Bad acoustics in the woods, you know. Which is a shame, really, because now the girls will never know who he was thinking of while being beaten about the head with a rifle butt."

To Bernat's shame, he sat staring stupidly into the air for a while, before he realized she was mocking him. To his further shame, it took him longer still to realize what she was getting at. "You killed them in the woods?" he asked.

She snorted and said, "Well, it would have been rude to kill them in the town, wouldn't it? It was so far out of their way."

He suddenly understood that she wasn't angry at him. She was angry at herself, and taking it out on him, which meant things were getting back to normal between them. "What were they doing out in the woods?"

Well, *now* she was angry at him. "The woods are where you go when you're scouting Durum for an invasion force." She spread a map with a tempestuous flick of her wrist and looked it over. She scribbled some calculations on the table and shook her head.

"What's the matter?" he asked.

She pointed to a spot on the map. "Here we are in Durum. Vinzhalia is directly to the east, with the border stretching north and south. Arle is a few day's march from here, to the southwest. So why haven't they come through here and attacked it before now?"

He thought for a second, and then said, "Lack of initiative."

She ignored his answer. "Because it's a wilderness east of Kamenka. Assembling an army of any decent size would be a nightmare. But . . ." She ran her finger along a road running east out of Kamenka. "If they have a rail branch here, they can assemble in a matter of days." She tapped it a few times as she thought. "If they do, there might be an army of fifty thousand marching toward us at this moment. They could arrive at Arle in five days, before we can assemble a comparable army to meet them."

Bernat frowned. "I would think five days would be more than enough time to bring troops south. It's only a few days by train from Quah."

"You're right. Five days is more than enough time for an efficient, professional army to gather for a defense of Arle. And if Garnia ever possesses such an army, God help the rest of the world." She pointed to Arle on the map. "In *this* army, my message will reach Arle in about a day, and will most likely be put at the bottom of a big damn stack of papers, because they aren't expecting critical information from *Mistral*. When someone does eventually read it, it'll be passed to Colonel Bellamy, the commander of the Arle garrison. Bellamy has always hated the signal corps, which hardly makes him unique in the top ranks. He thinks that all the money spent on the signal base and luftgas would be better spent on what he likes to call the 'real army'—a truly hilarious sentiment coming from a garrison commander. In any event, he'll mistrust the message from the start, pull out his maps, and conclude that a Vin surprise attack couldn't possibly originate from Kamenka. I have to admit, he won't be entirely stupid for thinking it, but he'll be stupid for ignoring us. Then tomorrow we'll go hunting for that new rail line, and if we find it, they'll know about it in Arle a day after that, but Bellamy will have already made up his mind by then, and won't make any special haste in passing the message up the chain of command." She paused, thinking about it. "In fact, I expect Durum to fall, and the news of that to make it to General Fieren before my report does. Even then, Lord Fieren won't think the Vins have enough troops on this part of the border to threaten Arle, for all the same reasons he didn't think they'd open a second front in the first place. By the time he works out the truth, it'll be too late to bring a force south. The defense of Arle will be left to the garrison and the militia—a force comprised of all the men who've managed to avoid being conscripted into the regular army—and the Vins will march over them like so many blades of grass. And once they have Arle, we haven't a chance, so I really might as well have taken my time getting back here with this." She waved something in his face that looked curiously like a lumber survey.

"So," Bernat said, staring at the map, "an entire war will be lost, due to ego and bureaucracy?"

"If you read between the lines of your history books, my lord, you may find it's more common than you think."

"But surely my uncle . . ."

Now she was shouting at him. "Will not arrive in time. Or he'll arrive without a goddamn army. At best, he'll manage to move a few regiments from Quah to Arle, not enough to make a difference, and those regiments will only be trapped inside the siege lines, ducking shells and starving to death." She jabbed at the map with her finger, growing even more agitated. "The Vins don't even have to take the city to cut the rail hub. And without that hub, we can't move regiments fast enough to answer their attacks along the second front. They can threaten Kuchin itself, or crush us piece by piece if they prefer. And do you know why?"

He crossed his arms over his chest. "Pray tell."

"Because your idiot uncle finds it inconceivable that the Vins would open a second front!"

Bernat frowned. "I've just been wondering about that. I mean to say, why would they open a second front?"

She leaned toward him in a manner he found threatening. "Because," she said slowly, "that's the sort of thing you do when you're winning."

"But Garnia hasn't lost a war in . . ." Something about the way she narrowed her eyes warned him that he was about to take his life into his hands. "I mean to say, even if that's true, why would the Vins risk siphoning troops from the Quah campaign?"

"I expect they're hoping to get the matter over with." She slumped against the table. "If they threaten Kuchin, they can name their own peace terms. They'll take Quah at the bargaining table and head home to rest up for the next war."

"Perhaps if I could find a way to send your message directly to my uncle . . ."

She rolled her eyes. "He'd ignore it outright, not coming through the proper chain of command. Even if he did read it, do you think he'd trust me? Didn't you know, he put a spy on my ship to keep an eye on me?"

Bernat fidgeted and said, "Really, a spy? I'd hate to be him right now." He gave her a moment to simmer, then stepped to the other side of the table, where he could look across at her even when she retreated to the cold comfort of staring at her maps. He was waiting for the question that he knew she must ask. He'd seen it coming from the moment he stepped inside the shed.

She suddenly looked up and asked it in a sharp whisper. "Did you sleep with my mother?"

He laughed very softly and spread his arms. "The moment you left," he said. "In every corner of the house, with particular care taken to defile the places where you have fond childhood memories. They were the most scandalous and, dare I say, the most imaginative sexual escapades ever envisioned. It was a carnal adventure the likes of which I've never before experienced."

Josette stared at him, obviously trying to find the truth in his face, but Bernat was too good at cards for that. Finally, she resorted to something near pleading. "Truthfully," she said, her voice quiet and low.

He looked back, impassive. "I don't suppose it's really any of your business."

"Good God," she muttered. "She's my mother."

He shrugged. "Then ask her yourself."

She put her hands on the table and stared down into the mess of papers and maps. After several long breaths, she asked, "Will you be remaining here?"

"Certainly not! If this mission of yours is so important, then I'm coming with you." He suddenly felt very nervous, because he knew in his heart that he was doing a very stupid thing. "You need another rifleman, and perhaps I have a bit of trouble aiming at people, but that fellow shooting next to me, the one who was hit in the foot? Well, he didn't hit anyone, as far as I could tell, so . . . I'm at least as useful as he was."

She looked skeptically at him. "You can't even load a rifle."

He smiled. "Actually, I can. Your mother taught me." He knew instantly that revealing this was a mistake, and his smile turned into a foreboding frown.

But she only sighed and asked, "Does this sudden fervor for duty mean that you'll perform your service as a rifleman, or will you continue to conspire against me whenever the opportunity arises?"

He smirked. "My dear captain, I couldn't possibly conspire against someone who sprang from the most magnificent set of loins I've ever laid eyes on."

"Don't push your luck, my lord."

"Oh, don't say 'my lord.' That sounds so formal. Perhaps you should just call me 'Dad.' "

"Perhaps I should allow you on my ship for just long enough to drop you from half a mile up?"

He held his hands up and said, "Just 'Bernie' for now, then?"

10

MISTRAL ROSE THROUGH the morning fog. As she slid back from Durum's mast, the wind clawed at Bernat's eyes and he fumbled with his goggles. The wash from *Mistral*'s new airscrews—four of them, each with four relatively stubby blades—had turned the hurricane deck into a roiling tempest worthy of its name. The fog streamed in turbulent rivers past the deck.

"Is it just me, or is it a bit windier than last time?" he asked, shouting over the noise.

"You have a true talent for detecting the obvious," Josette said. She looked up the companionway and called, "Pass the word to Gears: full power forward."

The whine of the steamjack grew higher and louder, and *Mistral* leapt forward in a lurch that made Bernat stumble. When he regained his footing, he shot Josette a sour look and said, "If that was retaliation for my insightful comments, then perhaps I'll just stop making them."

Her eyes were jumping back and forth between the foggy view forward and the kinemeter above her head, but she spoke without looking at him. "It was retaliation."

Amid the cluster of instruments above the captain's station, Bernat saw the kinemeter needle climb through fifteen knots. "Did you get a chance to see your mother last night?" he asked.

That comment took her attention away from the instruments, if only for a moment. "I was too busy seeing to the refit."

"Did you get any sleep?" he asked.

"Thank you for your concern," she said, "but I have a mother too many as it is." The airspeed rose above twenty knots. The corners of Josette's mouth twitched upward, threatening an actual smile. Her eyes were now locked on the instruments.

Bernat watched the airspeed reach twenty-five knots and keep going. In this soup of fog, though, the acceleration didn't seem real. The instruments and the blast of air whipping across the hurricane deck were the only indications of speed, for now the deck underneath felt perfectly stable under this steady acceleration.

As they passed through twenty-seven knots, *Mistral* burst from the cloud cover into a vast, empty dome of purple and blue. Ahead of them, the morning sun was still below the clouds, visible only as a ruddy brightness on the horizon that shot a dozen beams of sunlight into the heavens. Below them, a carpet of clouds stretched to the ends of the world.

"My God," Bernat said. "It's the most beautiful thing I've ever seen."

Josette grinned—actually grinned. "Isn't it, though?" she asked, but her eyes were not on the sky or the clouds. She hadn't taken them off the instruments.

Bernat tore his eyes from the heavenly sight outside to look at the kinemeter. It was twitching past thirty knots and somehow still increasing. It stopped at thirty-two.

"Level her off," Josette ordered.

As the steersman brought *Mistral* out of her climb and into flat, level flight, the airspeed needle slid even further, to settle down at thirty-three knots.

"Six knots faster than her old speed at full power," Josette said. She let out a little laugh and shook Bernat so hard it made him dizzy. "She's a charger! I knew those airscrews were holding her back. Sergeant Jutes, pass the word. She's a charger!"

* * *

SOMEONE WAS SHAKING Josette's shoulder. Someone thoughtless and unkind.

Josette told them how she felt, in a colorful manner.

But then one of the thoughtless, unkind person's words stuck in her mind. "Kamenka." Kamenka was important somehow.

Her eyes snapped open and she was instantly awake, alert, and ready. "Thank you, Ensign," she said.

Kember saluted unsteadily, her face drained of blood.

"Oh, and Ensign?" Josette said, before the girl left. "That request for you to throw yourself over the side and fall straight to hell was not a formal order. You may feel free to disregard it."

Kember nodded and swallowed. "Yes, sir. Thank you, sir."

Josette put on her jacket and harness, stowed her suspended cot in the girders overhead, and went down to the hurricane deck to find a bright, clear day. With the morning haze burned off and not a cloud in the sky, *Mistral* had a clear view for scouting, but everything else in the sky or on the ground had an equally clear view of her.

"Ah, Captain," Martel said, vacating the commander's spot on deck. "We're still well to the north of Kamenka, but I thought you'd want to see that." He pointed.

Josette looked out. Ahead of *Mistral*, winding through the Vinzhalian countryside, was a single-track railway, where the map said there should only be a road. It was a spindly little rail, but the Vins could move three or four regiments a day on that track, given sufficient trains and half-decent coordination. It was a direct connection between the Quahnic front to the north and the new second front on Garnia's eastern border. "Send a bird," she said.

Martel nodded and went up the companionway.

"Watch for Vin airships," she said. "With the cloud cover this sparse, we may as well trail a banner that says, 'We're spying on you. Please come and kill us.'"

Bernat looked up from his customary spot on the starboard rail and said, "They'll have to catch us first."

That comment seemed to please the deck crew, who chuckled and nodded to each other. But he was wrong. As fast as *Mistral* now was, Josette had no intention of deviating from the mission until she found the army she knew was out there—an army watched and shepherded by Vin chasseurs.

They wouldn't have to catch *Mistral*. *Mistral* was coming to them.

M ISTRAL WAS JUST north of Kamenka now, so close that they had come within range of the city's high-angle guns. Josette assured Bernat that they were perfectly safe at this altitude, and that the guns weren't accurate enough to kill a ship a mile up; so far, the Vinzhalian cannoneers were proving her right.

"There's a camp down there!" Martel said. "That's one hell of an army."

Josette and Ensign Kember crowded to the forward rail, looking down with their telescopes. Bernat followed and leaned over. He thought he must be looking in the wrong place, for all he saw was a flat field. Martel handed him a telescope, but Bernat still saw only a rail yard, and beyond that, only green fields with rows of yellow squares in them.

"The yellow patches are tents, my lord," Martel said, noticing his confusion. "Or, rather, where the tents were. The army's already marched."

"Good God," Bernat said. "There are thousands of them."

"Turn us west, Corporal Lupien," Josette said. Her telescope was already turned that way, toward the old arterial road that led from Kamenka to Durum.

Bernat trained his glass onto it. Even he could see that an army had marched here, trampling the road to muck under the boots of the infantry and cutting deep ruts under the wheels of the wagons.

"Mr. Martel," Josette said, "send another bird to Arle. Message reads, 'Army bivouac in Kamenka. Estimate fifty thousand men, now decamped. Composition unknown. Disposition unknown. Marching on Durum.' Can you fit all that on one roll?"

"I'll write small, sir," Martel said, and went up the companionway.

Bernat asked Josette, "Shouldn't we send a bird to Durum as well?"

She lowered her telescope. "Carrier pigeons only fly back to their roosts, and our pigeons all come from Arle. They'll relay the message to Durum."

"How long will that take?"

She didn't quite look at him as she answered, "We'll get there before it does. Which may be for the best, in any event."

"Oh, indeed." Bernat nodded his head. "When telling someone their home is about to be overrun by fifty thousand bloodthirsty Vins, one ought to convey that personal touch you just don't get in a letter."

SHE KNEW THE Vin column was close. She could smell it. Quite literally, she could smell it, as fifty thousand men don't march hard for days, eating questionable food and drinking even more questionable water, without leaving an odor in their wake.

Jutes shouted down the companionway, "Crow's nest reports

airship ahead! Bearing one point starboard at ten thousand feet. Range, thirty miles. She's turning. Lookout can't tell if it's toward us or away."

"That'll be their high altitude scout," Martel said. "If we've seen them . . ."

Josette nodded. "Then they've certainly seen us. Up angle three degrees. Bring us to three thousand feet." She noticed the disappointed looks from the steersmen. The crew, over the past couple hours of hunting for the column, had somehow gotten the impression that their captain planned to overfly the Vins at low altitude, strafing and bombing as she went. She had to admit that such a course would be very cathartic, right up to the moment the Vin escort ships closed in around them. After that, it would become notably less cathartic.

"Is there anything I can do to help?" Bernat asked.

"We can always use another set of eyes in the crow's nest," Josette said. "If you think you can make it up there, that is."

"Of course I can," he said with a smile, and pranced up the companionway.

As they gained altitude, the horizon widened. A little under a thousand feet up, she spotted the cloud of dust kicked up by the column. Word came from the lookout of a second airship ahead, just coming over the horizon. That would be the Vin's rearguard escort.

At two and a half thousand feet, she could see the column itself, seven miles long and marching for Durum. She lowered her telescope and said, "There's still a chance they'll turn back when they get to Mother's house."

"Sir?" It was Martel. She'd forgotten he was there.

"Nothing," she said. "We should have spotted the vanguard airship by now." Ahead of the column, a bank of afternoon clouds was forming. It was already thick enough to conceal an airship or two, which it surely did.

Martel seemed to read her thoughts. "If we run fifty miles

north or south, then make a run for the cloud bank, we can get around whatever's lying in wait in those clouds."

But it would mean getting no closer to the column. That meant no composition or disposition reports—no regiments identified, no count of cannons, horses, and wagons. She looked at Martel, who was already grinning, having read her mind again.

"Send another bird," she said. "Message reads: 'Column sighted, marching west. *Mistral* will close and develop target.' And give our position." She looked at him. "The fastest way home is straight ahead."

"KIND OF COZY up here, isn't it?"

Bernat nodded sheepishly. *Mistral*'s crow's nest was indeed cozy. Before he'd experienced it for himself, Bernat had imagined a platform large enough for three or four people, but this was merely a wind-blasted hole in the top of the ship and a rope ladder barely wide enough for one person. Two people simply couldn't fit on it without their hips rubbing together.

Grey had taken great advantage of the narrow space, pressing her body to his and "accidentally" brushing her cheek against his on no fewer than four occasions in the past fifteen minutes.

As he turned his head to scan the cloud line, she did it again. "Sorry, my lord," she said, but with mirth in her voice.

He sighed. This was surely God's punishment for some particularly vile sin. He only wished he knew which one.

Grey put her telescope to her eye. "My lord," she said, "will you look at this and tell me what you see?"

He saw nothing but clouds. Then she shifted, and he felt one of her breasts pressing against his chest. "Private," he said, "I don't think the officers would appreciate your . . ." And then he saw it. It was the same white color as the clouds, but once he saw it, he couldn't believe he'd missed it before; it was so obvious. "That's an airship," he said.

"I thought so," she said. She yelled down the keel. "Airship in the cloud bank! Four points to starboard at four thousand feet. Range, twenty miles."

She waited and listened for a few seconds before Jutes's voice came back. "Cap'n says to look for another one, four points to port on the other side of the column."

"Acknowledged," Grey said. She pointed. "That'll be right about there, my lord."

DESPITE THE HUNTERS closing in on them, Josette's eyes were on the ground. She had her telescope steadied on the starboard rail and was studying the column. Martel was next to her, doing the same. They were only three miles away from it now, close enough to distinguish individual men through the ship's best spyglass.

"Not as many wagons as I expected," Josette said. "They're putting a lot of faith in their supply lines."

She counted the artillery pieces. There were over two hundred guns of various calibers, but no large siege guns. The Vins might be planning to move them up later, once they had Arle encircled. Or perhaps they didn't intend to capture Arle at all. Perhaps, angry at Vinzhalia's recent defeat, they were content to shell it into oblivion. Armies had done worse, and with less cause for bitterness.

She turned her attention to the infantry. Most of them were conscripts or ordinary fusilier regiments, judging by their blue trousers with white jackets and vests. But there were half a dozen fully manned battalions, at least six thousand men in total, wearing blue jackets with yellow vests and trousers trimmed with red—the uniform of the elite Vinzhalian Royal Guard. As the name implied, their primary occupation was protecting the royal family, but they could be detached as need or opportunity dictated, and what an opportunity this was. These men, so hardened and experienced that the king of Vinzhalia trusted his life to them, would smash the garrison at Arle on their own. Bolstered as they were by ten times their number of regular infantry, they wouldn't even have to stop to reinforce afterward, but could march right on to Kuchin.

Josette looked back to the cloud cover, now fifteen miles away. It was midafternoon and, though the sun was not in her eyes, it was reflecting off the tops of the clouds with dazzling intensity.

She walked to the aft end of the hurricane deck and looked out. Now that *Mistral* was past the column's trailing supply wagons, the Vins' rearguard airship had left its protective position and was sweeping around to come in behind *Mistral*. It wasn't angling to attack, though. It was cutting off their retreat, closing the circle.

She stepped into the captain's spot and said, "Mr. Martel, would you say that we've done just about enough of this horseshit reconnoitering?"

Martel was stunned for a second, but then he grinned and said, "Captain, I was just about to suggest that we've done about enough of this horseshit reconnoitering, though not half as eloquently as that."

She looked out into the clouds, where the hunters were surely waiting for them. "Then be a dear and rig for battle."

At the sergeant's whistle, Grey closed the crow's-nest opening and said, "My station's at the engine. Captain'll probably want you on rifles."

As she was climbing down, Bernat asked, "Who's going to keep a lookout here?"

"If the captain wants one, she'll send one up," Grey said,

already off the ladder and scrambling down the girders toward the engine.

"Doesn't seem very prudent," Bernat said as he climbed mindfully down, always thinking of the gigantic luftgas bag immediately below the crow's nest. Jutes had explained that, if he fell into the fragile bag, he would fall through the edge of the envelope and out the bottom—if he was lucky. If he was less lucky, he would go straight down the middle and land on the keel. If even less lucky, he would fall through the top of the bag, land inside it, and drown in the unbreathable luftgas.

"Anyway, don't fall," Jutes had told him, before he went up. "It'll be a pain to patch the leak."

He was at the end of the rope ladder now, and within leg's reach of a longitudinal girder. He put his foot on it and swung out to grab another with his hand. Once he'd transferred himself, he climbed slowly down, girder by girder, always taking care not to step on the delicate struts holding them together. All the way down, the bulbous gas bag pressed into his back and pushed his front against the ship's fabric skin.

It was damn irritating, but he finally made it to the keel. On his way to the companionway, Martel waved him over.

"If you're heading to the deck, would you mind releasing her, my lord?" Martel asked, handing Bernat a perfectly docile little pigeon. "Here, just hold her like that, so she doesn't get loose in the keel, and let her go at the rail. She'll do the rest."

The bird cooed at Bernat as he went clumsily down the companionway. It was somehow comforting, holding this delicate, warm little creature in his hands. He stepped to the rail and gave her a toss to help her on her way.

He frowned when he saw which way she was going. The airship to starboard had broken free of the clouds. The pigeon was heading right toward it.

"I've heard they do that sometimes," Kember said, stepping to the rail next to him. "Curiosity, maybe."

"She isn't going to land on that ship, is she?"

"I . . . don't think so, my lord." Kember's voice was strangely sympathetic. Bernat watched as four puffs of gun smoke appeared off the enemy's hurricane deck.

Bernat could just make out the pigeon as she fell, a tiny dot spiraling downward. He pointed an accusing finger at the enemy ship. "They shot my bird!" His head whipped around to stare at Kember. "Can they do that?"

Ensign Kember cleared her throat. "I believe they just did, my lord."

He watched the bird dwindle and then disappear against the background of the forest below. He slumped against the rail and said, "But she was unarmed."

Kember turned crisply to the captain and said, "We lost the bird, sir."

"Run up and send another," Josette said.

Bernat was perfectly aware of how silly his grief was. He'd shot hundreds of birds in the woods around Kuchin, but the death of that brave little pigeon seemed deeply unfair somehow.

He walked slowly back to stand next to the rifle rack. Josette noticed his expression and said, "War is hell."

He looked about the deck for anyone who might commiserate, but his search was interrupted by a sudden stab of smoke from the nearest enemy airship, the same ship that had shot his bird. Something screamed past below as the booming sound of the cannon finally reached them. "Aren't we going to do something about that ship?" he asked.

"I'm more worried about the ship they're herding us toward," she said, staring not at the ship that was firing but into the wall of clouds ahead. "There's probably a two-gun chasseur cruising around in there with only its crow's nest poking above the clouds, waiting for us to pass so it can come in from behind and rake our tail."

"But we can outrun it, yes?"

"Not without a tail."

He remembered what a single shot of canister had done to that poor scout over Durum. The memory gained an even sharper clarity when he heard a crash behind him and turned to see splinters of girder erupting in a spout from the port side of the keel, amidships. The ship to starboard had them zeroed in.

He looked to Josette, who had her eyes closed and her hands on the girders above her head. She opened her eyes and gave him a reassuring look, seconds before Jutes shouted down, "Sprung two longitudinals in frame four, sir. Chips is reinforcing them just in case, but *Mistral*'s taking it like a champ."

She looked to Bernat. "Rather different from being shot at with pop-guns, isn't it?"

He nodded and said, "Speaking of which, aren't we getting rather close to that ambush you mentioned?"

The cloud bank ahead, which had seemed blanket-thin from a distance, now towered above them, a cliff face of solid white. "Now that you mention it," she said, "I think we are." But she ordered no change of course.

"What does one wear to an ambush?" he asked. "Is it a formal affair? I ask only because I can't seem to decline the invitation."

Josette glanced at him and said, "You're fine in what you have on."

"Wonderful," he said. He picked up a rifle, checked the flint and the powder in the pan, and held it at the ready.

He scanned the sky behind them. The Vin rearguard ship was directly aft now, but couldn't seem to close the distance and come into firing range. The high altitude scout was somewhere above them—he couldn't see it through the envelope—but no one seemed worried about that. And then there was the ship to starboard, firing away while they sauntered past its single cannon.

Another plume of smoke hid the starboard ship's hurricane deck, and a moment later a cannonball tore through the envelope above Bernat's head, its screaming wail turning high-pitched as it passed through the number-seven luftgas bag. Bernat ducked reflexively, though the ball came nowhere near him. It would have been too late anyway. The cannonball was already falling away to port before he even got his head down.

Ensign Kember was just coming down with a fresh bird. This one did better than the last, ignoring the enemy ship and flying southwest, right into the cloud bank. He was contemplating how the bird could even see where it was going in there, when the ship to starboard fired again. It was a shell this time, not a cannonball, but it exploded short, sending smoky trails arcing under *Mistral*'s keel.

Still *Mistral* did not reply, her single cannon pointing uselessly at the clouds ahead. Those clouds filled the sky now, fluffy white cliffs so tall and so close that Bernat could no longer see where they ended, above or below. A flash to the right caught his eye, and he saw the reedy trail of smoke from a shell coming toward them. He crouched behind the rail in time to miss seeing its explosion, but the sound of it hit him in the chest hard enough to make him gasp.

When he put his head up, the ship was already passing the smoke from the shell, but he thought he saw more smoke coming from the envelope itself. He clipped on, slung his rifle, and leaned over the edge. He could just make out an orange glow.

"I, ah, I do believe we're on fire," he said, in as mild a voice as he could manage.

Josette joined him at the rail, leaning out even farther than he did, despite her shorter height. "It's only a little one. Jutes!

Have the riggers put out the fire in frame four, starboard, please."

Bernat could see the silhouettes of riggers against the bottom and side of the envelope, their shadows cast onto the canvas by the glow of the fire. They put it out just in time to receive the next shell, which exploded twenty feet off the starboard side.

The keel bent inward in front of the blast, then snapped back like a released bowstring. The hurricane deck rocked below Bernat's feet, sending the rail into his stomach and flinging him back.

Then the screaming started. It came from one of the riggers fighting the fire and sounded like a baby's cry: a long, high-pitched wail, a quick gulp of air, then the poor bastard was wailing again.

Jutes called down, "Damage to the condenser. Grey is patching it up. Gears got a blast of steam to the arm, and Private Bashir's been hit in the gut."

Bernat saw red embers clinging to the perforated canvas where it had been pierced by the shell fragments. They grew brighter in the wind, and suddenly burst into life. "And we're on fire again," he said.

He heard Jutes calling aft, "Fire in frame five, starboard!"

"When will I have full power?" Josette asked.

Bernat hadn't even noticed it until now, but the kinemeter had dropped below thirty knots and was still falling.

"Grey says three minutes."

"God damn it," Josette said.

Bernat looked at those clouds ahead, which had seemed so close until just now.

"My lord," Josette said, "if you would be so kind as to kill the men loading their cannon. This next shot will be another shell, but the one after that will be canister, which we do not wish to receive, as it would ruin your clothes for the ambush."

The other rifleman joined Bernat at the rail, the loaders standing ready. He watched the Vin chasseur bearing down on them, its single gun like a cyclops eye. The range made it a very long rifle shot, even for Bernat, but he thought that he might at least send a ball past their ears to rattle them.

He chose the cannon itself as his target, fired, and was rewarded with the crisp plink sound of a bullet hitting metal. As the smoke cleared, he saw a man on the deck of the enemy ship holding on to his leg. The bullet must have hit him on the ricochet. "Ha!" Bernat said.

A loader took Bernat's rifle and slapped a fresh one into his hand. As he aimed his second shot, the enemy's hurricane deck disappeared in cannon smoke. For a fraction of a second, Bernat hesitated, but he still had a clear picture of the cannoneers' positions in his mind, and he found it somehow easier to shoot at men through smoke than to stare at them while he fired.

He squeezed the trigger and knew immediately he'd hit his man. And when the smoke cleared, there he was, slumped over the forward rail of the enemy ship, his rammer still halfway into the cannon.

Mistral's other rifleman fired and missed. Bernat stole a glance at the kinemeter. It had dropped to twenty knots and was still falling.

"Focus," Josette said from his other side. She had come up on his left while he was shooting and had taken a rifle of her own.

Something cracked overhead, and a shower of splinters rained down on the hurricane deck from the keel girders. When Bernat looked, he saw a hole in the catwalk above and another in the deck below. "What the hell was that?" he asked.

"Cannonball from the rearguard ship," Josette said. "Now that we've slowed, she's catching up to us."

He'd forgotten all about the ship behind them. He tried to forget it again as he aimed for the flanking ship, straining to keep his focus.

A trio of shots rippled down the line of rifles. No shot hit anyone aboard the enemy ship, but the cannoneer who'd ventured out to grab the rammer ducked and slunk back, afraid to expose himself.

"Keep it up," Josette said. "They're no danger if they're too afraid to load their gun."

On the enemy hurricane deck, Bernat could see one of their officers—their ensign, he thought—run forward to grab the rammer himself. Bernat was drawing a bead on him when he suddenly realized the brave little lad was no older than thirteen. He paused, trying to work out what he should do.

While Bernat hesitated, Josette shot the boy through the head.

"Condenser's back up, sir!" Jutes called. "We're at emergency power!"

Bernat hardly registered the news. He only stared at Josette, mouth agape. Before he could say anything, the world went white, then gradually darkened as they slid deeper into the cloud bank. Soon Jutes called down, "Stern is inside the cloud, sir."

Josette handed her rifle to the loader, patted Bernat's arm even as he continued to gape at her, and said, "You did well, my lord. If they'd managed to put a shot of canister into our steamjack, we'd never have made it. Thank you." She looked out into the cloud. "Now all we have to do is avoid being ambushed."

"Is that all?" Bernat asked.

"Decrease power to three-quarters," Josette said. "Ensign, worm out that cannonball and reload with canister."

As Ensign Kember set her gun crew to work, Josette could only wait and hope the ambushing ship would mistake *Mistral*'s speed. If the trick worked, they would never realize she had decreased her power, and they'd fire too far ahead. But if

Mistral decreased power too much, the ambushers would hear the difference in the pitch of her steamjack and make the proper adjustment.

Behind *Mistral*, two cannons fired in quick succession. The first shot missed cleanly, but the second sent scores of musket balls tearing through *Mistral*'s forward frames. Josette looked forward in time to see the envelope ahead of the hurricane deck burst open in a gout of splinters and sawdust, sprung girders sticking out at odd angles. Josette didn't need a damage report to know that the number-eight bag was a total loss, already hemorrhaging luftgas.

But it was not a fatal wound. Already, the riggers were shifting ballast to compensate. Josette reached above her, found the pull-ropes for the forward emergency ballast, and put all her weight on them. In response, water cascaded from ports in the bow. She could barely see it through the cloud, but she could hear it, and she counted off four seconds before releasing the ropes to stymie the flow.

In those seconds spent hanging from the pull-rope, she had not been idle. She'd been plotting the likely angle and distance to the ambushing ship, working from the assumption that they meant to fire one shot at her steamjack and put another through her hurricane deck.

Judging from the distance they'd missed by, they were close enough to recognize the error, or at least know they'd made one, since they could plainly hear that *Mistral* was still flying. They only had to correct their mistake, and their next volley would bring *Mistral* crashing down.

"Ensign, you have the deck." She leapt up the companionway ladder and ran, the wicker catwalk flexing under her feet. "Be ready to rig for hard braking," she told the mechanics on her way past the steamjack. She continued on to Martel's station, all the way back in frame three. "We never did complete our trials," she said.

"No, sir," he said.

"That's unacceptable."

He looked at her strangely.

"I will tolerate no excuses, Mr. Martel. I want you to prepare for the braking trial immediately. Best we do it before they reload their guns, as I don't anticipate having the time after."

He grinned, suddenly understanding. "Right away, sir."

She ran forward, past the wounded Bashir, who was mercifully quiet now; past Gears, wincing as he saluted with his bandaged right arm; past the riggers, stretching new cloth over the fire-damaged sections; past Grey, still working on the condenser.

None smiled. All saluted her, though this wasn't required or expected when rigged for battle. All of them wore blank, cold expressions as she passed.

What the hell did it take to please these people? An hour ago, they'd been disappointed when *Mistral* had passed up the chance to make a suicide run on a Vin column. Now they were sulky because they'd been roughed up a bit? She wished for whatever quality Captain Tobel had possessed that gave him the ability to get the crew on his side. Whatever it was, she seemed to have the opposite talent. She could earn their ire no matter the circumstances.

She stopped at the top of the companionway, where she could keep an eye on the deck and on the preparations with the steamjack. Jutes didn't salute her, thank God. If he had, she wasn't sure she could resist the urge to push him down the companionway ladder, gimpy leg and all.

"Morale's a little low," she said.

His expression didn't argue the point. "They'll perk right up when you put your plan into action."

She arched an eyebrow. "How did you know I have a plan?"

He smiled and stood even straighter. "Can't imagine a world where you don't, Cap'n."

She grinned as she looked back. Gears and Grey had abandoned their previous tasks and were prying the cover off the gearbox. Martel was visible near the boiler. He gave her a thumbs-up signal.

"Rig reverse gear! Steamjack to full power!" she shouted. She shot Jutes another grin and went down the companionway. On the hurricane deck, everyone stood at their posts, looking into the impenetrable fog of cloud all around.

The gearbox made a rattling, grinding sound as the entire ship shimmied. The steamjack's whine increased to a truly painful volume, and the hurricane deck became a swirling vortex of airscrew wash. Josette counted the seconds, watching the kinemeter needle swing left, until it dropped to zero and sat hard against the pin.

By her best estimate, she was now moving backward at a little under twenty knots, closing distance with her erstwhile ambusher at a combined speed of almost a mile per minute. Visibility was zero, but she only had to close her eyes to see the ship, plain as day behind them. Accounting for the time it took to brake and the probable reaction time of the enemy, she would pass under their keel in just about . . .

"Elevator fins up full!" she ordered. "Steamjack to emergency power! Everyone hold on!"

The elevator steersman spun the wheel, hand over hand, as fast as he could. The stern began to rise, at first so gently that the ship's inclination went unnoticed for want of a horizon. Then the back martingales creaked in their anchors on the taffrail. An unsecured wrench slid forward along the catwalk. The slope of the ship was impossible to ignore now, for it threatened to pitch the entire deck crew over the forward rail and out into the white nothing below.

"Make sure those rifles are secure," Josette said. She held on to the girder above her with both hands as the tilt of the ship took the deck right out from under her feet. She held on, her legs rocking farther and farther forward along the deck, until her toes were pointing down at the cannons and railing.

The rest of the deck crew were clipped on, which was all that saved Kember and one of the less experienced cannoneers from falling out. The unsecured wrench made its rackety way through the keel behind them, until it reached the companionway and fell through. It didn't even hit the steps of the ladder on its way down, so extreme was the ship's tilt. Josette swung out of its way as it fell past her. It clanked off the cannon and got stuck against the forward rail. A rifle that Bernat had not been able to secure in time followed it and nearly went overboard.

"Elevators level," she ordered, when she heard water sloshing out of the tops of the ballast bags.

"Stern is clear of the clouds!" Jutes called down, his voice strained with the effort of keeping himself upright.

The hurricane deck followed in seconds, bursting from whiteout conditions into perfectly clear air. The dazzling brightness of the receding clouds filled the sky forward, but to either side there was clear blue sky above a skewed horizon.

When Bernat looked out and saw how steep their stern-first climb into the heavens really was, he unleashed a stream of vomit that arced ballistically over the forward rail. When the last of it was clear of the ship, he spat, rubbed his mouth, and said, "Please don't interpret that as a lack of enthusiasm."

But Josette's attention was already fixed to starboard. There—less than fifty yards away, cruising through the clouds like a shark—was the enemy ship. Only its upper surface was visible, the rest a pale shadow beneath. *Mistral* rose to pass her, soaring tail-first into the heavens.

"Elevators down full! Rudder, put us right on her ass!"

"Right on her ass! Yes, sir!" Corporal Lupien answered.

The Vin ship was now in reverse, turning in a desperate attempt to bring its cannons into action, but they'd been following too closely to react, and now *Mistral* had the legs of her. The slope of the deck eased under Josette. Her boots touched down. *Mistral* leveled off just above the enemy, right on her ass, with both ships running in reverse and *Mistral* pulling slowly away.

"Reduce steamjack to full power! Corporal, line us up to fire."

The enemy ship turned wildly, trying to shake herself free of *Mistral*, but Lupien had his eyes on their rudder and matched them move for move.

"I have you now, you son of a bitch." Josette was staring at the enemy's stern. It lay half in the murk of the clouds and half out, right under *Mistral*'s bow. "Ensign, you may fire when she bears."

Josette hadn't even finished the sentence before Kember stepped out of the way of her gun's recoil and yanked the lanyard. The muzzle spat flame, sending eight-score musket balls screaming at the enemy in an expanding wedge of pure destruction that tore through fins, girders, cloth, and men.

The smoke cleared to reveal a ragged hole in the enemy's stern so wide Josette thought she could shoot through it and pick off the crew. But a look down the crippled ship's keel showed that there was no one aft of the boiler to shoot at. No one left alive, at any rate.

The enemy's stern drooped, and its speed fell off. The shot must have pierced two or three of their luftgas bags, but there weren't enough crewmen left to shift ballast to compensate. The Vin chasseur's tail sank, tilting the ship so that she seemed to hang in the air by her bow, her tilt growing more extreme than *Mistral*'s had been when she left the clouds. A good third of the enemy ship's length was above the clouds now, but sliding slowly back into them. It pirouetted in an uncontrolled turn as it sank, coming around to show its belly.

Jutes called down, "Mr. Martel sends his compliments and

he says . . ." Jutes ducked his head past the hatch and gave her a baffled look. "He says, 'Think we can check that one off the list,' sir."

"Tell Mr. Martel to go ahead and check it off."

While Kember's crew hurried to reload the bref gun, Josette kept her eyes on the enemy's hurricane deck, which was above the clouds and just turning into sight. She could see the crew over there, hanging by their harnesses or crawling along the sloping deck to stick their heads over the railing. She waited for the blue flare of surrender.

Instead, she saw three stabs of smoke and, before she could even make sense of their significance, a mist of blood splashed her face and Ensign Kember fell to the deck, choking and holding her neck with both hands as crimson oozed between her fingers. Farther forward, one of her cannoneers dropped a canister shot and slumped against the gun as a dark patch grew on his chest.

Josette ran forward, stepping not *to* but *over* Ensign Kember and the fallen cannoneer. She went straight to the bref gun, grabbed the dropped canister, and pushed it into the bore. The cannoneer with the rammer hesitated to come forward and expose himself to more musket fire, but when Josette reached out to take his rammer and do his job herself, it seemed to shame him into action. He took his place by the gun and rammed the canister home.

Before he'd even finished, Josette took Kember's place and sighted down the length of the cannon. It was aimed at the enemy's envelope, well above their hurricane deck. "Bow angle down three degrees." While she waited for *Mistral* to pitch down, Josette pointed at the enemy. "Bernie! Put some goddamn fire on that ship!"

Bernat was kneeling over Kember. When he heard Josette, he hesitated for a second and then ran to pick up a rifle. He went forward, knelt in front of the rail, and fired.

Josette took Bernat's place, kneeling over Kember, who was still choking and writhing on the deck. To get at the wound, Josette had to pull the girl's hands away from her neck by brute force. Underneath, the bullet had torn a divot from the skin on the right side of her neck, which now hung open like a bloody door, laying bare the grisly strings of muscle, tendon, and blood vessel below. The open cavity filled with blood as Josette watched, but the largest vessels were not severed—none spouted blood in those rhythmic spurts that meant death within seconds.

Josette slid the divot of skin back over the wound, lining up the torn flesh as best she could and pushing down on it. She did this not from any surgical instinct, but from a vague notion that it had come off, and therefore had to be put back. She tore off her flight harness, removed her jacket, and tied it into a loop around Kember's neck and under her armpit.

The ensign looked at her with wide, terrified eyes. She struggled to speak, but could only manage a croak.

Josette put a bloody hand on her cheek and said, "You'll be fine." She looked up and motioned to the remaining cannoneers. "Take her back." Josette really had no idea whether the girl would be fine. She might still burst a blood vessel and bleed out, or the wound might putrefy and go septic.

A bullet plinked off the cannon as Josette moved forward. She ducked, keeping her head below the railing as she heaved the dead cannoneer clear of the gun. He fell facedown onto the deck and a moaning gush of air escaped his lips. For a moment she thought he lived, but it was only that the fall had pushed the breath from his lungs.

"We're three degrees down, sir!" the elevator steersman called. He and Lupien were keeping their heads down, manipulating their wheels from a crouch, steering by the inclinometer and the hematic compass.

Josette sighted down the cannon. It pointed directly at the

enemy's hurricane deck, which was just about to swing out of sight and be eclipsed by the spinning envelope.

She stepped out of the way of the recoil and pulled the lanyard.

The bref gun fired, its bellowing report followed instantly by snapping, scraping, and screaming sounds. The smoke cleared to show the Vin hurricane deck hanging by its rear suspension lines, with the forward lines cut; the bottom side of the deck was slapping against the envelope, wafting back and forth like a sheet on a clothesline. Below it, the last man to fall was just passing into the clouds.

No, not the last. There was one man still clinging to a control cable, dangling above the abyss and pulling himself up, hand over hand. "Bring me a rifle," Josette said, stepping to the rail. Bernat slapped the gun into her hand without hesitation or judgment. She lifted it to her shoulder, leaving a smear of Ensign Kember's blood where she held the stock.

She cleared her mind and waited patiently, until her aim was at its steadiest. She took a breath and let half of it out.

And did not squeeze the trigger.

She lowered her rifle, watching as man and deck and ship sank into the clouds, out of sight. With any luck, the survivors could free-balloon their wrecked ship to a survivable landing.

On her way to stow the rifle, Bernat took it and said, "I'll see to that."

She nodded, avoiding his eyes as she went up the companionway, following the men who were carrying the cannoneer's body aft. "Take the deck," she said to Jutes as she went past. "Bring us to five thousand, and continue on course for Durum at cruising power."

"Yes, sir" was all he said.

11

BERNAT INSISTED ON helping tend to the wounded, but refused to feed them the hard-tack porridge and pickled beef the rest of the crew were eating for dinner. Instead, he dipped into his own stores to prepare some lovely little sesame-stuffed mushrooms for Bashir and a savory broth for Kember, heating it atop the boiler.

He was kneeling next to the ensign, about to spoon steaming broth into her mouth, when she gave him an odd look, took the spoon, and sat up to feed herself. He wasn't sure why he'd assumed she couldn't.

She tasted the broth and gave an approving nod, letting out a croak that sounded vaguely like, "Good."

"Old family recipe," he said. "At least, that's what it said on the can."

He looked across the catwalk, to where Bashir had perked up considerably and was chomping away at his mushrooms. When he saw Bernat looking at him, Bashir lifted one in a sort of salute. He grimaced when the movement hurt his wound, but returned to eating in short order.

It cheered Bernat. The only sour note was the dead cannoneer, whose body lay not ten feet from him, wrapped in canvas and concealed in a sleeping alcove with the curtain drawn.

The presence of the dead man had barely dented the ebullient mood on the ship, which Bernat found odd. Yes, they'd done a hard job—escaped an ambush, sent an enemy chasseur plummeting to earth—but the victory against the scout over

Durum had been more complete by any measure. It had
cost less and accomplished as much, and hadn't left the after-
taste of an enormous army bearing down on Garnia. Yet he'd
felt miserable after that victory, while he was positively buoyant now.

Élan was a fickle bitch. It reminded him of Josette, in
fact.

He wondered if he could get his letter back from Durum's
postmaster, or if it had already gone out. How frequent could
the post be out here? He pushed the matter to the back of his
mind. There was nothing he could do about it until they
landed in Durum, and by then he might not want it back in any
event.

With the wounded doing so well, Bernat made two cups of
tea and went forward. Grey was on the starboard side of the
engine, so he went around to port, but she followed after him,
aiming to ambush him at the gearbox. He walked faster and
made it there ahead of her, then pressed on to the companionway without looking back.

On deck, he found the sky dark and the captain leaning
over the front rail. He went to stand next to her.

"I missed the sunset," he said, handing her a teacup. With
a hand free, he covered his own cup to stop the wind from
spraying hot tea into his face.

"By several hours," she said, nodding her thanks. "Another
hour and we'll be in Durum."

"Time flies when you're tending to the sick," he said. "But
Private Bashir is looking better."

She was in the middle of a sip when she stopped and stared
at him. "Bashir's going to die."

He shook his head. "No, I've just come from him. He looks
much better."

She finished her sip and lowered the cup below the rail, out
of the wind. "Men with gut wounds can rally, sometimes.

They get better and have a good day. But it takes them in the end. He'll be dead by next week."

Bernat swallowed and looked away, off into the moonlit mountains of cloud below. "I didn't know," he said. "Does Bashir know?"

She took another sip of tea. "If he doesn't, don't tell him."

He wasn't sure he liked that, but he nodded.

She must have read the doubt in his expression, for she said, "Everyone says they want to know how bad it is, to know whether or not they're going to make it, but it only makes them miserable when they find out. Give him his one good day. Not just for his sake, but for the morale of the crew."

"You really care about them, don't you?"

She whipped her head around and screwed up her face. "Of course I care about my crew. Why would you ask that?"

He was about to answer frankly, when he remembered her advice about not telling the wounded how bad it is. He said instead, "You come off as a bit cold." If he'd been giving his full and honest opinion, it would have involved comparisons to icebergs.

"I . . . admit that I'm not good with people."

"You're quite good at killing them," he said. "Perhaps if you'd put that kind of energy and attention into, say, smiling . . ."

"I smile!" she said, belying the assertion at that very moment.

"You smirk from time to time," he said, "but I've seen you smile only twice. Once in response to the improved speed of your airship, and once when you saw a cloud that resembled a certain part of a man's body." He waggled his eyebrows at her. "You thought I didn't notice that, but I did. The point is, you never smile at *people*."

She snorted. "Perhaps not at you."

"I don't expect a miracle," he said with a smirk.

"I just . . ." She trailed off, then started up again. "I just

don't know how to please these people. Everything I do seems
to make them dislike me more. *Osprey's* crew loved Captain
Tobel. They would have done anything for him."

Bernat laughed. "You think these people wouldn't do anything for you? In the last twenty-four hours, your crew has
done four days' worth of repairs in one night, overflown an
enemy column, and gone cheerfully into battle for you."

"Are you suggesting they secretly adore me?"

"The exact opposite, in fact. They'd do anything for you
because they wouldn't dare disappoint you. I don't know if
you've realized this, but you're scary when you're angry."

She didn't seem to like the thought of that. She looked at him
sourly and said, "It was never my plan to make them fear me."

Bernat smiled. "But you have a knack for it, and that can
be even better than a plan." A moment's thought brought a
grave expression to his face. "What would it do for your hap-
piness, do you suppose, if you actually got your wish?"

The question caught her completely off guard. She couldn't
even formulate a response.

Bernat ran his finger across an imaginary newspaper article as he recited, "*Captain Josette Dupre, the most popular officer in all the army, adored by her crew, loved by her fellow
officers, today hanged herself out of misery.*"

This extracted a chuckle from Josette. "I suppose I hadn't
thought the matter through. But, you know, I would appreciate the occasional—" She went suddenly quiet and looked
toward the horizon.

Bernat heard a sound in the distance. It reminded him of a
morning during his childhood when he'd found an empty
wine cask by the front door and had upset the entire manor
by rolling it across the marble floors of the entry hall. It had
rumbled along until, once per turn, the barrel went up on its
cork bung and came down hard, sending a hollow boom echo-

ing down all the halls. That was the sound he heard now: a long, rolling rumble punctuated by sudden clashes. "Thunder?" he asked.

Josette narrowed her eyes, looking forward. "Not thunder," she said, handing him her teacup.

He watched her as she returned to the commander's spot on deck. "That column couldn't have gotten ahead of us, could it?" he asked.

"Not that column." She looked up at the instruments. "The other column. The one we never spotted. A vanguard force sent ahead to secure Durum. Goddamn it, I should have known."

He looked forward again, gaping. He could just barely see flashes of light through the clouds.

Josette called up the companionway, "Increase steamjack to full power. Rig for battle."

JOSETTE LOOKED THROUGH her night glass as soon as *Mistral* broke through the bottom of the clouds. A mile up the road, four field guns were firing on Durum from the absolute worst emplacement she could think of. They were placed right in the road, where they were in the way of reinforcements coming from Vinzhalia, exposed to counter-battery fire, and could only fire on Durum's stronger eastern wall—the only wall with a semblance of modern fortification. It was a foolish location from which to attack the city, but the Vins had a schedule to keep, and had apparently decided that, lumber survey or no, they hadn't the time to cut a road through the woods.

The Vin battery fired a rippling volley. In those brief moments of light, Josette could see that the battery's only protection was a single wall of rubble-filled wicker gabions, but she could also see that the inexperience of Durum's defenders had preserved the attacking artillerymen from annihilation. By the light of another volley, she saw gouges torn in the road ahead of the battery from shots that had fallen short. A couple of gabions had been hit and were split open, spilling the dirt and rubble within. A shattered carriage wheel spoke to at least one good shot from Durum that had dismounted a Vin gun earlier in the exchange, but the Dumpling bastards already had the gun repaired and firing again.

The Durum battery returned fire for the first time since *Mistral* had broken below cloud cover. None of their three shots hit anything, and the Vin battery replied with two more volleys before the defending cannons were loaded and fired again. Despite their seemingly suicidal placement, the Vin guns were throwing eight shots for every three returned. Josette couldn't see where the Vin shots fell, but the obvious target was the redoubt and, as soon as it crumbled, the gate beyond.

Muskets fired below her. She could hear perhaps a dozen men on the road, excited and shouting. A bullet whizzed past her ear. She returned to her station and said, "Bring shells forward for bombing. Long fuses and slow match."

The powder monkey and one of the cannoneers went up the companionway, coming back with two shells each in the crooks of their arms. They set them into ready racks along the side rails and then went up to fetch more. When they returned again, Ensign Kember followed behind them. She stopped at the foot of the companionway.

"Sir?" she croaked. "I'd like to take my station." The ensign coughed and instantly winced at some pain it must have caused inside her neck.

Josette was not pleased, but she could hardly refuse. She nodded and said, "Just don't shout your orders. I don't want that wound reopening."

"Yes, sir," Kember said, her voice a tatter. "Oh, and I believe I owe you a uniform jacket, sir."

Josette didn't meet her eyes. "Don't worry about it."

WHILE THE CREW cut wide beechwood fuses and hammered them into shells, Bernat quietly asked Josette, "Is this entirely safe?"

"May I remind you that you're aboard an airship," she said. "Nothing we do is entirely safe."

He frowned. "I mean to say, where would we be if a stray spark set off one of these shells?"

She stared at him. "Technically speaking? We'd be in a lot of places. The surrounding woods and countryside, to begin with. If these winds hold up, parts of us might even make it to Halachia."

As Bernat watched another load of shells being carried down from the magazine, he said, "Well, I've always liked to travel."

Kember croaked out the order: "Light match." The cannoneers lit their slow matches and placed them into buckets within arm's length of the gunpowder-filled shells.

"Bow down seven degrees," Josette said. "When ordered, bombers will throw for the guns, not the cannoneers. Aim your throws but don't wait to see where they fall. Just go right on to the next shell. Everyone understand?"

The bombers nodded and took their stations, three to a rail. Perhaps a quarter of a mile ahead, the Vin cannons fired, briefly illuminating forest, road, and cloud cover.

"Light fuses," Ensign Kember said. At the order, the bombers put slow match to their shells. The fuses hissed and spit sparks, and it seemed to Bernat that they were burning down toward the gunpowder-filled shells at an alarming rate.

"Fire carcass," Josette said, and quickly covered her eyes.

Bernat followed her example, and only looked after the gun fired. He wasn't sure what to expect when he heard "carcass," but it turned out to be an incendiary round, a bright yellow comet streaking toward the cannons, now only a hundred yards ahead. It skipped off the road just behind the Vin artillerymen and sailed over their heads to land on the far side of the protective gabions. From there, it skittered off into the woods, where it continued to burn and illuminate the battery.

"Good enough," Josette said, just before a trio of musket balls pierced the deck from below. The carcass round had illuminated her airship as effectively as it had the Vin cannons.

Looking down, Bernat found the soldiers on the road even less visible than before. They were too far from the carcass round, which had ruined his night vision. Only when one of them fired could he pick the man out and shoot back. So he took a rifle, waited for a flash, and then fired at it.

Only after the smoke cleared did it occur to him that it was pointless to shoot at a man who, having already discharged his musket, couldn't hope to get another shot off before *Mistral* was out of range. As he traded his rifle for a fresh one, Bernat quietly hoped that he hadn't hit his target. It was one thing, after all, to shoot at a man who might otherwise kill him or his crewmates. What he was doing now, however, struck him as something akin to murder.

"Ready bombs," Kember said.

The bombers at the rails hefted their first shells, holding the heavy spheres against their collarbones, with fuses fizzing inches from their faces.

The captain's eyes were fixed on the gun battery closing fast ahead, where the Vin artillerymen were already abandoning their pieces and running for the cover of the woods. She held her hand up. *Mistral*'s bow was nearly over the guns before she shouted, "Now!" She brought her hand down, though only Bernat saw it in the darkness.

"Drop!" Kember shouted, her enthusiasm winning out against the captain's advice and common sense.

The bombers hurled their shells forward. They picked up the next shells and had them over the side before the first ones even hit the ground. Then they dropped the next, and the next. By the time the bomber nearest Bernat loosed his fifth shell, he didn't so much throw it as hastily dump the smoking bomb overboard, double-handed.

The shells bounced like leaping fleas, the mass of them nearly keeping pace with *Mistral* as they skipped over the road below. Many of them, perhaps more than half, deflected uselessly into the woods on their first or second bounce. A few plopped into muddy spots and stopped well short of the guns. The remainder skipped or rolled or skidded into the battery, either stopping against the gabions or coming to rest between the gun carriages.

Bernat ducked as a volley of muskets peppered the rails. When he looked again, *Mistral* was past the battery and moving away fast.

Josette stood at the taffrail, looking back. She pointed and said, "Shoot that fool!"

The other rifleman fired immediately, but it took Bernat a moment to realize just what he was supposed to shoot at. It was a man—an artilleryman, he thought—running between shells, pulling their fuses out.

"Shoot him, Bernie!" Josette shouted, taking a rifle.

The range grew noticeably longer as he aimed. Josette fired but missed. Bernat fired. When the smoke cleared, the artilleryman was down, and desperately dragging himself away from the battery.

A shell burst in the woods. Another went off behind the

battery, and then all the rest seemed to go off together. The guns were hidden behind the flash and the smoke. The gambions disintegrated, throwing rubble a hundred feet in every direction. One shell was kicked upward by the detonation of its neighbors and exploded a hundred feet in the air.

As the last few straggler shells exploded in the woods, Josette turned to Bernat and said, "Just like bowling ninepins."

Bernat looked back on the destruction. "I've bowled ninepins," he said. "I can't recall a game that ended like that, no matter how much wine was invol—"

He was cut short by a sudden punch to the gut, striking harder than he'd ever been hit, bringing more pain than any he'd ever felt. As he stumbled against the back of the companionway ladder, reeling, he tried to sort out who had struck him and what sort of hammer they'd used.

And then he noticed the distant firelight shining through a hole in the wicker taffrail, where a musket ball had passed through on its way to his stomach. He slumped down to the deck, muttering, "I'm shot, I'm shot." Some corner of his mind was earnestly worried that no one would know if he didn't tell them. "Oh God, I'm shot."

And not merely shot, but gutshot. Gutshot and facing that slow, lingering death sentence that came with it. He stared back at the stern, eyes blank while Josette knelt in front of him, frantically tearing his shirt away.

She cleared the area around the wound and, staring at it, grew strangely quiet and serene. Then she looked away, felt around on the deck around him, and held something in front of his nose.

His eyes focused on it. It was a bullet.

"Spent," Josette said. She let out a breath, fell back to sit splay-legged on the deck, and smiled. "It's spent."

Bernat looked down and felt his stomach. Just touching it was agony, but there was no blood, no ragged hole torn in him.

Fired by one of the Vin fusiliers they'd left behind on the road, at extreme range for a musket, the bullet with his name on it had lost its lethal fury during its long flight.

A thought occurred to him, and he grinned despite the pain. "You were worried about me!"

Her relieved expression fell away to leave a poor imitation of her usual stone-faced countenance. "I'm responsible for you, is all."

"You smiled! You actually smiled! And not a prick-shaped cloud in the sky!" He tried to laugh, but the pain of doing so was too great, so he merely chuckled.

"I suppose I might have been a little relieved," she said, grimacing at this small admission. "We can't afford to lose a rifleman. And the crew seem to be fond of you, for what reason I surely can't fathom."

"Ah yes, of course. The crew. Such a sensitive bunch, they are."

"Are you done now?" Josette asked. "Would you like to go to the sick berths?"

He shook his head. "I think I'll just rest a while here, if it's all the same to you. Though if someone could fetch a bottle of wine from my bags . . ."

JOSETTE LEFT BERNAT to his wine and went to the forward rail. *Mistral* was just passing over Durum's east gate, where the Garnian defenders atop the wall raised a wild cheer. She didn't see how she merited such a reception. Yes, it would take the Vins hours to make their battery operational again, but they would make it operational. She had only given Durum a respite in what still promised to be a very short siege.

She recognized Kadi Halphin, dressed in his full colonel-of-militia regalia, standing atop the gatehouse with his hands on his hips. Someone rushed a speaking trumpet to him, and he called up to Josette, "I see, after all these years, you're still tearing up my roads!"

So the old bastard did recognize her. She ordered the steamjack power to station keeping, which would balance their air speed with the oncoming wind and so allow them to hover in place. She called for the ship's speaking trumpet. When she had it, she called back, "Bet you can't find a man who'll testify against me."

This produced a wave of laughter that spread along the thin line of defenders manning the wall.

"Are the civilians evacuated?" Josette asked.

The kadi shrugged his shoulders. "Everyone who'd go," he said.

Josette knew what that meant. It meant the truly stubborn jackasses were refusing to leave their homes. Knowing Durum, that was most of the town.

"Have you seen any Vin airships?" she asked.

He shook his head.

"Then we'll stay here as long as we can," she said.

The kadi took off his hat and waved it at her, which set off another cheer among the defenders. *Mistral* crept onward, out over the town.

"Steer for that house over there," Josette told Corporal Lupien.

As they passed over a granary, Josette noted with approval that it had pitch-splattered cordwood stacked around its foundation, and militiamen standing guard, ready to burn the grain rather than allow it to feed the Vin army.

She looked back at Lupien and said, "Turn right down this street. At the end, turn us into the wind and lie to."

Lupien was baffled, but he obeyed, tracking the street precisely until it came to a dead end, then turning into the wind. The ship hung nearly motionless.

Josette pointed her speaking trumpet at the brick-and-stone

house at the end of the lane and shouted, "Mother, come out. I know you're in there."

A window on the second floor opened and Josette's mother stuck her head out. She yelled something and waved the ship away.

"You have to leave town," Josette called. "You have to leave town before the Vins cut the road."

Her mother yelled again. Josette couldn't make out the exact words, but they seemed nasty.

Bernat approached the rail, taking tiny steps and clutching his stomach as he walked. He looked over and saluted with his wine bottle. "Good evening, Elise," he shouted.

Josette's mother looked somewhat less angry when she saw Bernat, but she only shook her head and muttered something. When she disappeared inside and closed the window, it was obvious that she wasn't preparing to leave.

"That woman is impossible," Josette said.

Bernat offered Josette the wine bottle without saying another word. She took a long swig and handed it back.

Returning to her place on the deck, she ordered, "Increase to one-quarter power. Run a circuit around the edge of the town at fifty feet. Lookouts on deck."

Mistral began its circumnavigation of the town, running from corner to corner to corner, like an attentive night watchman. On their fourth circuit, a lookout saw movement in the fields to the south. Josette, even looking through her night glass, thought at first that the jumpy lookout had seen only stalks of grain swaying in the darkness.

But it would do to be cautious. "Put a carcass shot into it," she said.

"Why in hell do they call it 'carcass'?" Bernat asked, waving his wine bottle to accentuate the question.

But no one was paying any attention to him, for the burning carcass round had sailed over the heads of a full company of Vinzhalian fusiliers and landed amid a second. The shot bounced, trailing smoke and fire, to finally burst in front of a third company that was following in the rear.

Josette stared, wide-eyed and slack-jawed. "There's half a battalion out there." That was several hundred men against half as many Durum militiamen.

Trumpets and whistles sounded amid the Vin companies, and they sped to a quick march. Quick-thinking Vinzhalian soldiers quenched the fire set by the shattered carcass round with dirt, but not before Josette spotted ladders and the glint of axes. So the attackers had never intended to wait for the cannons to do their work. The cannons were only there to hold the attention of the defenders, to fix their eyes eastward, while the real attack snuck through the woods and across the fields to the south.

"Reload with canister," Josette ordered. "Pass the word to increase steamjack to full power. Bring us over the gatehouse."

The colonel was already redeploying his men to cover the south wall when Josette overflew him, calling down her report. He nodded his acknowledgement and called out more orders before joining the militia in their rush to the south wall.

A bright light drew Josette's eyes to the signal base, where a plume of flame was rising from the shed. Half of the giant shed collapsed around the explosion as she watched, and the other half was already catching fire. In addition to the destruction she could see, Josette knew that thousands of liras' worth of luftgas had just been released and was rushing invisibly upward, to be lost forever in the rarified air above.

"They've blown it up," Bernat said.

"We've blown it up," she said. She looked at the base through her telescope and saw, in the light of the burning debris, half a dozen men running for the south gate. "That'll be Lieutenant Garand following his standing orders."

Mistral passed over the southeast corner of the wall on her way toward the Vin companies. By the light of the burning shed, Josette could see the attackers, at first only as a reflection of firelight off a hundred bayonets. But soon they came marching out of the darkness, casting long shadows behind their loose files. In the gloom, their tall shakos seemed a part of their heads, and their bayonet-tipped muskets melded with their shoulders. They looked like monsters from a fable.

But the defenders had the wall, a cannon emplaced next to the south gate, and an airship over their heads. Josette was beginning to feel the itching, nervous sense of responsibility that comes with a slim hope.

Before they overflew the Vin companies, she ordered steamjack power to be reduced, and took the ship up higher. There were just too damn many fusiliers down there to risk their fire, at several hundred musket balls to a volley and three volleys per minute.

Just before the hurricane deck rose into cloud cover, the south-gate cannon fired, and Josette saw the cannonball pluck an attacker out of his rank. His body went tumbling, arms and legs flailing like a rag doll, and slid to rest ten yards away.

"That's one down," Bernat said. He seemed genuinely disappointed when no one made a response, and finally he attempted it himself. "That only leaves . . . err, how many of them are there?"

"Steamjack to full power," Josette said. She didn't wish to ignore him, but she wished even less to indulge him in that stale old quip.

"Well," Bernat said, "that leaves only that many, less one." He still received no reaction. "Quite a few remain, at any rate."

"Bow angle down ten degrees," she said. She heard scattered shots below.

"By which comment I mean to draw ironic attention," he said, pressing on, "to the fact that, despite having drawn first blood, the odds are still very much—"

"Let it go, Bernie."

He looked a bit petulant, but took up a rifle, saying, "Consider it gone."

"If you're not too drunk to see them, please aim for the ladder parties," Josette said. "Ignore the ranks and the axemen. Whatever you do, just don't shoot your foot off."

As they began their descent, more musketry crackled from the ground. She heard bullets hitting the bow. A second later, *Mistral*'s hurricane deck burst out of the clouds. Below them, three escalade parties were carrying their long ladders, illuminated by the shed fire and by torches atop the wall. Here and there, a shot from the Durum militia found its mark and a ladderman fell. This slackened the ladder's speed only a little, however, for men trailing behind jumped over the dead man and ran forward, racing each other for the honor of taking his place. Such valor was not surprising, for ladder parties were usually mustered from volunteers. Thus, they were filled with men either trying to make a name for themselves, or seeking to commit suicide by way of the army.

Kember directed the steersmen, lined up her gun, and fired. The smoke swept back along the deck to reveal three dead at the front of the nearest ladder. The next man back tripped over their bullet-ridden bodies, and with four men down, the front of the ladder dropped and stuck in the ground. The laddermen behind piled up against it.

"Up ten degrees!" Josette ordered. The hurricane deck was already receiving a peppering from the reserve companies, assembled a hundred yards from the wall.

In the few seconds it took for the members of the stricken ladder party to sort themselves out and get moving, *Mistral*'s riflemen and the militia on the wall took advantage of the stationary targets they presented and shot four more of them.

The ground disappeared as the hurricane deck rose into

cloud cover, though the musket balls continued to hit farther aft for several seconds, until the whole ship was hidden.

"Level off elevators, left rudder," Josette ordered, beginning the wide turn that would bring them around to come in from the rear of the attackers. She estimated that the ship had taken something like fifty musket balls. She could hear the riggers above, already climbing through the superstructure and groping in the dark for the holes. *Mistral* could handle this sort of damage for a while—with the reinforcements made to her stern, she was proving to be a tough ship—but too many passes like that and they'd have to stop and put all their efforts into repairs.

Mistral completed her turn and, at Josette's order, slashed downward. The clouds swept aft to reveal all three Vin ladders now propped against Durum's south wall, men packed onto them. Except . . . the ladders weren't quite high enough. They came just short of the top of the wall, forcing the man at the top of each ladder to stand on the shoulders of the man below and look for handholds in the uneven stone. And while they searched for someplace to hold on to, the militiamen atop the wall stabbed down with bayonets and smashed at their fingers with musket butts.

Josette was uplifted by the sight—not only because it greatly improved the odds, but because it meant the Vin army was as capable as her own at making a complete cock-up of a job that ought to be trivial.

Mistral approached the Vin reserve ranks, which were now giving fire to support the men going up the ladders. Many of them adjusted their aim when *Mistral* passed overhead, and the peppering began again in earnest. It increased as the ship dove lower and lower, until most of the deck crew were crouched with their heads below the rail.

But behind the bref gun, Kember was unfazed, her hand indicating the minutest course corrections to the steersmen.

She dragged it out for so long that Josette was near to ordering her to just fire the damn thing already, when finally she pulled the lanyard.

"Up ten degrees!" Josette ordered, then stepped through the smoke to see the canister shot's effect.

It was worth the wait. *Mistral* rose over a score of dead and wounded Vins, all piled around a broken ladder at the base of the wall. Four attackers who'd already made it onto the wall were left orphaned there. They fought bravely on, but were hopelessly outnumbered.

Only two ladders remained. Josette could see Kadi Halphin, sword in hand and truly dashing in his colonel's uniform, right in the thick of the fight at the next ladder over. As *Mistral* slipped into the clouds and began her next turn, it seemed the odds had shifted and were now stacked impossibly against the Vins. Durum's militia needed only to press in around the Vins as they came up the other two ladders, and wait for *Mistral* to dispatch them. As long as that press held, the militiamen who were not so engaged could pour leaden death into the attackers as they filed up the ladders, and into the axemen who chipped away at the south gate.

But when *Mistral* next descended out of the clouds, Josette saw a changed battle. Atop the wall, the attackers were being cut down in ones and twos. It should have been encouraging, for most of the Vins who came up the ladders fell to the defenders' bayonets. But the men waiting on the ladders couldn't see that, couldn't tell what the odds were—not until they were up and over, and by then they had no choice but to fight or die.

And so the Vins kept coming, man after man, in that pathetically slow trickle. But they came over the top faster than they fell to the defenders, and now the small nucleus of Vin attackers on the wall had swelled until there were half a dozen around the top of each ladder.

As she watched, Josette saw the attack reach that critical inflection point, that moment when the next soldier cresting the wall met not the bayonets of the defenders, but the backs of his friends. And while his friends were still outnumbered and might be bayoneted at any moment, even by their deaths they kept the defenders occupied long enough for another man to scramble onto the wall without resistance, thus making room for the man behind him, who in his turn had enough time to lend his hand and help the next man up. And so the attackers came up faster and faster, and soon it would be the defenders who were outnumbered.

"Aim carefully," Josette said to Ensign Kember. There was still hope. If the defenders only kept their heads, held the wall long enough for *Mistral* to take out the remaining ladders, then Durum would remain Garnian—at least until the main column arrived.

The peppering of musketry was lighter now as the reserve companies went forward to go up the ladder themselves. Kember sighted and fired.

If anything, her shot was more perfectly aimed than the one before it. As the smoke passed astern, Josette could see a cluster of pockmarks on the wall behind the ladder. The destructive wedge of the canister shot hit it dead center, turning the men there to butcher's meat. But the ladder itself held.

When the defenders on the wall realized that it still stood fast, and that the Vins were still coming at them from two intact ladders, fear began to take hold of the militia. It started with a few men at the back, farthest from the fighting. For, unlike the defenders in the thick of it, hemmed in by their comrades behind them and a fifty-foot drop to either side, the men in the back had space to run.

It began, as it almost always did, with only a few of them. But their flight spread fear and panic, unhinging a few more, who ran after them. And now that it had started, it couldn't be stopped. Men who would not otherwise have run suddenly imagined themselves abandoned by their comrades and fighting alone, and they, too, fled. Soon, even the most stalwart militiamen had no choice but to run or be pushed off the wall by the press of their comrades.

And so the Durum militia dissolved into a stream of terrified men, pouring down the steps and into the streets. *Mistral* passed over the wall, where Kadi Halphin alone fought on, surrounded by a score of attackers, still alive only because they hesitated to finish him.

Josette was too stunned to order *Mistral* up into the safety of the clouds. Not that it mattered. The attackers were ignoring her airship in their enthusiasm for the hands-on slaughter in front of them.

Beyond the wall, the nearest granary was flamed, and then the guards joined the rest of the militia in their rout. The city's other granaries went up almost at once.

"At least Durum's grain won't feed the Vins," Bernat said. She looked at him, but he didn't take his eyes off the city.

Mistral outran the spreading wave of Vins, and then outran the militiamen they were driving in front of them. The ship slid over Durum, the sound of her steamjack and airscrews echoing back from the empty cobblestone streets below. The ship passed the north wall and only then turned west, into darkness.

Josette was not at her post, not standing upon that mystical spot on the deck that made her a captain. She was standing at the taffrail, staring back at a tiny brick-and-stone house at the end of a narrow lane until it receded into a single point and disappeared behind a mist of cloud.

12

BERNAT SLEPT WITH a bottle cradled in his arms, but all the wine in Garnia couldn't have kept him asleep for more than a couple of hours. He woke before dawn and lay quietly in his bunk, staring into darkness and listening to the sounds of the airship. The steamjack and the airscrews made a continuous din, but one that he hardly even noticed by now.

Instead, his ears were occupied with the snoring of three of the sleeping crewmen, and the occasional emanations from Ensign Kember. Air scoops were drawing a breeze forward, and open ports releasing it aft, so Kember's contribution to the olfactory bouquet aboard ship was always transient, but somehow that made it even more offensive. If the smell were constant, he thought, he might eventually become accustomed to it.

Kember wasn't alone, either. She was merely the worst of them. They all did their part, and after a week aboard, Bernat could already tell the crew members apart by the unique character of their gas. He couldn't even remember all their names, but he'd know any one of them in the dark if they'd only oblige him by breaking wind.

He tried to remember why he'd embarked aboard this ship. In his hazy, half-awake state, he couldn't think of anything to justify the decision.

Presently, the watch changed and the crew stirred from their bunks. Despite the increased bustle aboard, Bernat managed to catch half an hour's sleep before something altered in the nature of the activity and drew him back to consciousness. After a few minutes listening to men drag equipment over the narrow catwalk and back to the tail, he rose to investigate the matter himself.

He ran into Josette coming the other way, and asked, "Something the matter?"

"Nothing at all," she said, not stopping.

He followed her forward, past anxious-looking crewmen. "It's only . . . I sense a bit of tension."

Without looking back or slowing at all, she said, "We're in the middle of a night landing in a village with no mooring mast or ground crew. It's an operation that falls somewhere between 'extremely dangerous' and 'impossible,' depending on which reference you consult. The village is in the way of the Vin advance, so it will certainly be occupied by enemy dragoons within the next few hours. If we're still tethered when they get here, we'll all be captured or killed. Besides which, the sun rises in an hour and the vanguard of the Vin airship escort will be hunting us. If they find us on the ground, that's the end of us. Even if we survive all that, we plan to transfer gunpowder from ship to ground with the airscrews turning, which means static, which means sparks, which could blow us all to hell. Then, of course, there are still tens of thousands of angry Vins less than fifty miles away, coming to destroy all we hold dear, and rape our cows, and suchlike. I'd say a certain amount of tension is justified."

By this time they were nearly to the companionway. "But there's nothing the matter?" Bernat asked.

At the head of the companionway, she paused and turned to him. "Of course not. Why would there be?"

He shrugged. "Only asking." He followed her down the companionway to the hurricane deck. "Though we did leave your mother stranded in occupied territory not eight hours ago. That's liable to make a person, even a person as ascetic and bitter as yourself . . ." At the bottom of the companion-way, she whirled to stare at him, eyes hard and lips pulling back into a sneer. ". . . worried," he finished. "Understandably worried."

She held him there, staring with such intensity that he wanted to shy away and drop the subject. But as much as he wished to retreat, he held his ground and returned her stare, glower for glower.

"That particular matter is not on my mind right now," she said, and walked aft along the hurricane deck. He followed her to the taffrail and, as his eyes adjusted to the dark, he saw that *Mistral* was dragging a canvas bucket through the river below, tethered by a long line. It seemed, as far as he could deduce, to work on the same principle as a drogue anchor on a naval vessel, slowing the ship to a crawl while maintaining its maneuverability.

"How in hell can it not be on your mind?" he said, after the distraction of this odd sight wore off. "She's your mother."

"She's only one person," Josette said, watching the drogue line carefully. "By now, the Vins are scouring Durum, flushing out surviving militiamen from their bolt-holes and bayoneting them. By lunchtime, tempers just might cool enough to merely take them prisoner, steal their boots, and send them on a forced march over fifty miles of trampled road to Kamenka. By evening, the same story will be playing out in this village, and will soon happen in every other settlement along the Vin line of march. Thousands of people will be killed, forced from their homes, or left to starve in a countryside stripped bare by Vin foraging parties. By the end of the week, the column will reach Arle, and tens of thousands will be trapped inside the siege lines, without food or hope of rescue, and under artillery fire." She turned from her examination of the drogue to look at him. "Amid such chaos, I haven't the right to worry about one woman."

Bernat looked back, his hard expression softening as he said, "Yes, you do."

"That is your opinion, Lord Hinkal." She pushed back from the taffrail with both arms and spun about to stride forward.

Again, he followed. He could see a settlement ahead, hazy amid the light fog. Four cottages were clustered near a water mill and granary. In what passed for the village square, men were gathered with torches. Bernat would hardly even call it a village, though it did possess a sturdy stone bridge. Too sturdy, he thought, with its single arch spanning the entire river in one graceful curve. Though he didn't wish to be sidetracked, he was too curious not to ask, "Is that a Tellurian bridge?"

"I suppose it is," Josette said, her eyes on the village. "I don't imagine the locals built it. Not many first-rate architects around here, you know."

He gasped. "Amazing. I've always wanted to see such a bridge. My God, it must be at least two thousand years old. Imagine what skill the Tellurian architects and stoneworkers must have possessed, that their work still stands after all this time."

"Indeed," Josette said. "It's a damn shame we're here to blow it up."

His eyes nearly shot out of his skull. "What?"

She looked at him as if he were an idiot. "What the hell did you think we were doing here? Dropping in to purchase some rustic handmade quilts?"

"But . . . but . . . you can't do this! You're just going to blow it up—all that history—without a second thought?"

"Yes," she said. "Welcome to the army."

"That little bridge? What good could it possibly be to the Vins?"

"It's a bridge," she said, as if that were explanation enough. "It's wide and sturdy enough to send cannons across."

He slumped down, more dejected than ever. "What will the villagers say about that?"

She snorted. "I should think they'd be rather displeased. One of the local quirks in these parts: the people don't like having their bridges destroyed and their homes showered with rocks. You'd know that if you read more. It's in all the guidebooks."

"Are you lashing out at me or are you—"

"Yes," she said, quickly. "Yes, I am. Because you're a truly phenomenal annoyance, in answer to your next question."

In spite of it all, he smiled at her. "Now you sound like *my* mother."

Josette's eyes were still on the village. "She seems an insightful woman. I hope I'll have a chance to visit her in exile, after the Vins take over."

"Don't talk like that," Bernat said. "I'm sure destroying this treasure of the ancient world will stop the Dumpling hordes in their tracks."

Her hard façade cracked, just a bit. "No," she said. "There's a fording point west of here."

His jaw dropped. "So this will slow them down by . . ."

"Perhaps two hours."

He looked out at the bridge, where villagers and farmers from the surrounding country were gathering to watch the airship, then back at Josette. "Don't blow it up, then."

She didn't meet his gaze. "Two hours is two hours," she said. "And it's not just that. The attitude of a defender, as much as their force of arms, may check an invasion, if the invader is cowed by their ruthlessness."

"So you think this will cow them?"

He could already see the answer in her posture. "No," she said, confirming it.

"Then don't blow up the goddamn bridge!" He spoke loudly enough for everyone on deck to hear.

"Pray control your voice," she said, her own voice calm and mild.

He leaned in and spoke in a harsh whisper. "You don't have to blow up this goddamn bridge to avenge your mother, who is in all likelihood sitting safe and sound in her house at this very moment. Probably the worst thing that's happened to her is that the soldiers have stolen all her lingerie, and that only if Corporal Lupien is correct about the habits of the men in the Vin army."

"A point starboard, and pass the word to ease back on steamjack power," Josette ordered. And then she spoke to Bernat. "I thought I made it clear that this has nothing to do with my mother."

"And I thought I made it clear that you're a terrible liar."

She ignored him, watching the bridge come up. When it was under the bow, she ordered, "Power to station keeping! Break out pistols and sabers for the landing party!"

"Pistols and sabers, yes, sir," Jutes called back from the keel.

"Are you expecting the bridge to put up a fight?" Bernat asked.

Keeping a keen eye on the river and the ground, she said, "The villagers will. These people don't care who rules over them. It doesn't matter to them whether Leon or Yuslan is their king. They'll still live in filth, moan about the grain levy, and die having never once seen a two-story building. If any man in this village actually gave a damn about king and country, he'd have run off to volunteer a long time ago."

"The other side of that coin," Bernat said, "is that they're innocents in this affair, but you plan to punish them, regardless."

"Not punish," she said, with a sharpness that made him jump. She quieted herself when Jutes came by, handing out weapons to the landing party. He handed Josette two pistols,

a sword, and a waist sash to tuck them into. When he was clear, she went on. "I have nothing against these people. They happen to depend upon a strategically important bridge, which is unfortunate for them. The Vins would blow it up too, if they were in my position, not because they're monsters but because they're soldiers. They loot because they're greedy, they shoot because they're trained to, they bayonet fleeing miliamen because they've just watched their friends die, and they storm the walls because those are their goddamn orders. It isn't personal." She spoke softly now. "Whatever they may have done to Durum, or to my mother, it wasn't personal."

He smiled back at her. "Make sure you explain that to these people, when you blow up their bridge."

She snorted and called to the steersmen, "Two points right and bring us down in the square. When she rises again, put her back over the river. I don't want to snag the drogue on the bank."

The ship swung right, out over the village, and the bow pitched down. With her keel tethered to the drogue, *Mistral's* airscrews drove the ship into a smooth descent.

While still fifty feet in the air, Josette swung herself over the rail, one hand on a suspension cable. She glanced once at the ground, then back at Bernat. "These bumpkins may not care which side of the border they're on, but I do. If destroying some old bridge can better our odds by the minutest fraction, you may consider that bridge destroyed. I'll destroy their bridge, and their mill and their granary for good measure, and I'll do the same in every goddamn village and hamlet from here to Arle. And if I run out of bridges and mills and granaries, I'll burn the crops in the fields, poison the wells, kill the animals, and foul the meat. And when the Vins send out foragers, I will hunt them down by twos and threes, and hang them at the side of the highway as a warning to the others. I

tell you, I will do whatever is necessary to tip the scales, and I won't stop until every one of those goddamn Vin bastards either retreats to his lands or lies dead on mine."

Bernat just looked at her for a while as the ship drove down. "I thought it wasn't personal?" he finally asked.

She looked back, her façade cracking wider and deeper. She drew a deep breath. "To them," she said, and looked down. "I said it wasn't personal to them."

And then she jumped overboard.

JOSETTE LANDED ON her feet in the village square. Private Grey, Chips, and six cannoneers and riggers followed, jumping as the ship brushed the ground. Only one of them hesitated and, by the time he worked up the courage to let go, the ship was lighter by half a ton of crew and rising fast. He fell hard and let out a sharp gasp when he landed.

He was back on his feet in only a few seconds, unhurt save for scrapes and bruises, but he'd landed on the flat of his saber and snapped it in two. As Josette approached the congregated villagers, she could hear him behind her, bickering with Private Grey.

"Give me your sword."

"No. You already broke one."

"What the hell are you going do with a sword, anyway?"

"Well I'm not going to break it in half, for a start."

"Good morning," Josette said to the villagers. "Who's in charge here?"

None stepped forward, but many stepped back from the oldest of them, a man of perhaps fifty, give or take ten years. She was not confident of even this approximation, for the man had a wrinkled, leathery face, weather-beaten beyond its years.

She looked up at him and said, "The Vins are coming. Take your people and get across the river."

"Vins don't have any quarrel with us," the man said.

"They will shortly," she said, indicating the bridge. "Take whatever you want, but don't waste time. You have as long as it takes us to blow that bridge, and not a second longer."

She turned away without another word, half expecting to find a pitchfork in her back at any moment. But she walked away safely, perhaps because the village elder thought her unworthy of wasting a pitchfork on. As she called her party to the bridge, she could hear the elder shouting up at the airship. "Hey! I want to talk to whoever's in charge up there! Your goddamn harridan wants to blow up my bridge!"

The goddamn harridan took her landing party to the water's edge, where Grey and Chips were busy surveying the underside of the bridge. By the time they finished, only one family had crossed to the safe side of the river, but more had crossed from the other side, going the wrong way. They seemed to be farmers from outlying cottages, drawn by the commotion and unwilling to listen to Josette's admonitions about an oncoming army.

Chips made his report to Josette. It consisted in total of the statement, "Never blown up a goddamn bridge before, and don't know how neither. Sir."

Grey's report was somewhat more specific. She said, "I suppose two casks of gunpowder might do it, sir."

It struck Josette as conservative. "Are you sure?"

Private Grey considered it for a moment, then said, "No, sir. I've never blown up a goddamn bridge before, either. But it's an arch, built to take force from above, not below. If we can put the charge on the underside, it should blow the keystones out, and the rest of the bridge will fall over on its own."

"Let's make it three casks. What else do you need?" Josette asked.

"A boathook and about fifty yards of rope," she said without another second's thought.

Josette looked up at *Mistral,* where Ensign Kember was keeping an eye on the landing party. Josette communicated the ground party's needs with a wigwag signal, dipping her outstretched arms left, right, or forward to spell out her message. Kember acknowledged in the same way, and a minute later *Mistral* was descending toward the bridge.

The deck crew pitched Grey's shopping list to the ground. As the bottom of the hurricane deck kissed the side of the bridge, Kember lowered a line to her captain.

Josette got a shock when she touched it, the static spark visible as a blue flash in the predawn darkness. She lowered the end of the rope into the river, giving the static fire a clear path to the ground that she hoped would spare the gunpowder from any subsequent spark. She signaled and the crew above tied casks to the line. They lowered them through the fog and onto the bridge, string-of-pearls fashion. In lieu of untying them, she cut the rope, all the more swiftly to sever its perilous connection with *Mistral.*

With the line cut and most of the danger passed, she bent to inspect the casks for damage and was promptly hit on the head by a length of slow fuse and a flannel bag. She could just hear Kember shouting above her as the airship rose: "Sorry, sir!"

Josette cut a minute's worth of fuse and delicately filled the bag halfway to the top with gunpowder from one of the casks, making a charge of about half a pound. She took this and a party of two crewmen with axes to the mill, while Chips and Grey set to work on the bridge.

She entered the mill alone, the villagers ignoring her in favor of her male escorts, whom they variously harassed, harangued, or kicked at. They conveniently soaked up all the villagers' abuses, leaving Josette entirely unmolested as she set her gunpowder charge inside the eye of the millstone and lit the slow fuse. As it burned down, she slung a bag of flour over her shoulder and left, closing the door on her way out. "Keep them well back," she said to her escorts.

She put her fingers in her ears a few moments before the charge went off. The blast sent the mill door flying off its hinges and geysers of flour dust spewing from every window. The water wheel continued to turn, but its axle thumped and grated against the shattered mechanisms inside. On the second full turn, the axle came off entirely and the wheel fell into the river.

While the villagers variously gaped and shouted, Josette strolled to the granary. It was a small, stout building, held a foot off the ground by stones at the corners. Apart from these smooth cornerstones, made to keep rats from reaching the grain, the entire thing was made of wood.

"Should we call for some kerosene, sir?" asked one of her escorts.

"We have plenty of fuel," she said, tossing handfuls of flour onto the roof. "But hack open the walls and spread the grain as thin as you can."

The escorts looked at each other through the fog, seeming to think their captain had gone mad.

"What, you never made flour bombs when you were kids?"

They apparently hadn't, but they went to their jobs regardless. As they swung their axes, cutting through planks and watching the grain spill out, the crowd of irate villagers grew larger and more irate. Josette even spotted a couple of pitchforks. There were something like twenty men gathered now. Where they had all come from she wasn't sure, but they were angry, ugly, and closing in around the granary.

"I would step away from there if I were you," she said, spreading spilled grain with her foot and dusting it with flour.

The only men who moved were the ones muscling between her men and the granary, pushing the axemen away and forming a barrier around their spilled harvest.

Josette snorted. "Don't say I didn't warn you." She drew one of her pistols, which finally checked the crowd. They didn't back away, however, and without another thought she tossed her last handful of flour into the air and fired.

The bullet went high over the villagers' heads, a danger to no one, but the powder lit the flour hanging in the air. It took flame with a dull, loud whooshing sound and a flash that lit the entire village as bright as the noonday sun. The brief fireball kindled the dusting of flour spread on the grain and atop the granary roof, and within seconds it was all ablaze.

"Come on!" Josette shouted to her escorts, while the villagers were still flash-blind and trying to find their eyebrows.

One of her escorts seemed to be having some trouble finding one of his own. "Respectfully, sir," the man said as he ran, "you ever try not enraging people so much?"

"Once," she said, looking over her shoulder. "It didn't work."

The village mob had recovered itself and was right on their heels now, but the bridge party had already formed a line with their weapons drawn. Josette and her escorts darted between them. When the villagers caught up, they faced swords, pistols, and half a saber.

With her escorts taking up station in the protective line, Josette went to check on Chips and Grey.

"We're ready, sir," Grey said, her eyes flitting to the horde of angry villagers. "But the casks are only tied around the bridge. All they have to do is cut the line and they'll all drop into the river."

"Then we'll just have to keep them from it." Josette looked up at *Mistral,* hanging motionless in a sky turned gray by the first morning light. She signaled for them to back away, then ordered Grey to light the fuse.

With her ship retreating to a safe distance, Josette stepped into the no-man's-land between her crew and the villagers. It wasn't only anger she saw in them now. It was fear, anxiety, and pleading. They were begging her not to destroy the last vestige of their livelihood.

She didn't give a damn.

"I will personally shoot the first son of a bitch who takes a step onto this bridge," she said, drawing her second pistol. "Do not try me. I have had a very bad week, and I am a very good shot."

The village elder took a step forward. This, Josette knew, was the deciding moment. If he attacked, the rest of the villagers would follow, and she couldn't shoot all of them. Nor were her crewmen likely to fire on fellow Garnians.

But the villagers didn't know that, so she raised her pistol and held it an inch from his nose, her eyes daring him to move.

He stood for a time, staring balefully. Then he stepped back, and in that moment the fight went out of his men. She could see it when she glanced at their faces.

Josette counted in her head, and when thirty seconds had passed in terse silence, she said, "I heartily suggest you all run for cover."

She nodded to her own people, who found shelter behind the bridge's own stonework or leapt into the nearest convenient hollow. The villagers ran. When she saw that everyone was reasonably safe, Josette crouched down and covered her head.

The charges went off with a resounding crack, like a knife stabbing at her ear. The center of the bridge disappeared in smoke and dust. Fragments of stone scattered through the air. The largest pieces went straight into the river, but fist-sized chunks rained down around Josette. One hit a crewman on the back and inspired a flurry of curses.

The ancient bridge crumbled from the center out, stone

after stone tumbling into the water until there was nothing left but a pair of abutments facing each other across the river. A three-foot-high wave ran upriver and down, swamping the banks for a hundred yards in either direction.

And then, as the sun rose through dust and haze, *Mistral* returned to pick up her landing party. In the village, a bucket line had formed between river and granary, and the villagers were desperately trying to put out the fire.

It was hopeless, of course. As *Mistral* pulled up her anchor and turned west, the granary roof caved in, sending sparks and embers swirling into the fog.

13

"LOOKOUT REPORTS ENEMY ships closing in," Jutes called from the companionway. "Firing range in five minutes."

Josette couldn't see the ships from her station on the hurricane deck. They were above and behind *Mistral*, attacking from the best position they could have asked for. She caught some of the deck crew sneaking worried glances at her.

"We will hold course and speed," she said, committing her ship to come under enemy fire. There was cloud cover two thousand feet above, and she could still make it in time to avoid a pummeling. But it would mean giving up what was perhaps her last chance to slow the Vin column cresting the horizon behind them.

She'd kept ahead of that column all day long, destroying a second bridge late in the morning and two more granaries in the early afternoon. Now she had entered hilly countryside dotted with farms and windmills. A stone granary directly ahead trailed a thin line of smoke from its charred, collapsed wooden roof.

Bernat came down the companionway. He was wearing a silk robe and had a towel draped around his shoulders. His chin was shaved to exquisite smoothness, his face scrubbed, his hair damp. He wrung the towel around his right ear and asked, "Is there to be a battle?"

Josette had to look twice before she believed her eyes. "Hoping to leave a good-looking corpse?"

He grinned. "I couldn't avoid it if I wanted to." He looked

ahead, to the smoking granary. "I see the campaign against the Vins by way of the common folk continues."

Josette fixed her eyes on the smoldering granary. "Actually, it was like that when we arrived. The villagers have fled. They tried to set fire to their granary before they left, God bless them, but they proved woefully untutored in arson."

"Well, what do you expect? The schools out here are terrible." He stood next to her, invading the space that was hers by right of command. "Would it have affected your actions, if they were still here and defending the grain with their lives?"

She didn't answer him. "Try a shot," she said to Ensign Kember. "You might hit it on the bounce."

Kember lined up the cannon and fired. The shot skipped on the rocky ground and smashed squarely into the granary.

Josette looked through her telescope. The stone wall, apart from a cracked stone where the cannonball had hit, stood firm and true. "Who the hell builds a granary like that?"

"Someone thinking ahead, to the day when rats finally discover artillery," Bernat suggested.

She'd hoped to split the wall with cannon fire, spill the grain within, and drop lit carcass rounds to ignite it. Now she had no idea what to do. She could attempt to ignite the grain without cracking the granary, but the villagers had already attempted that without success, the fire having burnt itself out in the confines of the silo.

The granary was coming up fast. She couldn't hope to land a party, or even to circle around for a second pass, with those Vin chasseurs so close on her heels. She was so desperate, she resorted to asking the advice of Bernat. "Can you think of any way to spoil that grain?" she asked in a whisper.

He pondered for a moment, then said, "I hear Vinzhalians won't eat anything with pesto on it, if that's useful."

She shot him a harsh look. "Did you come down here to help, or just to badger me?"

"Primarily the latter." He smiled, and before she had a chance to hurt him, added, "Though, if we lack for pesto, we might consider the contents of the aft reservoirs."

Kember fired another shot. It struck the granary, but did no more damage than the first.

"Cease fire," Josette ordered. "Steersmen, take us directly above the granary. Steamjack to idle." She held the pull-ropes to the aft reservoirs and waited for *Mistral's* momentum to carry them over the granary. The roofless structure slid by below. Josette looked back along the ship, waited until just the right moment, and yanked on the pull-ropes.

The entire volume of *Mistral's* wastewater—a fetid mix of feces, urine, and shaving powder—cascaded from the ballast ports and into the open granary. Some dropped on the far side of the structure, and some on the near side, but enough went right down the middle to make anyone think twice about consuming the grain within.

Josette released the ropes and ordered, "Emergency power. Up elevators. Maximum climb." Then she looked to Bernat and said, "Thank you."

"Not necessary," he said, and bowed. "The unending adulation of yourself and your crew is thanks enough for me."

The ship, lightened as it was, rose quickly toward the clouds. But forward speed had to be sacrificed to maintain maximum climb, and now the enemy ships were catching up. By Josette's estimation, *Mistral* would have to endure several minutes of concentrated fire, and it was going to begin any second now.

She heard a cannon fire in the distance. A second passed with no impact, and no screech of round shot flying past. Only then did she realize that something was wrong about the sound of that cannon. It was too close, and it had almost seemed to come from . . .

She looked up, just as Jutes called down, "Crow's nest reports another ship coming out of the clouds above us." Several tense seconds followed. "It's one of ours! He thinks it's the *Ibis*!"

"Rudderman, come about," Josette ordered. "Continue climbing. Cannoneers load round shot."

The odds were still in the enemy's favor, with *Mistral* over a thousand feet below them and more Vin ships on the way, but the sudden appearance of *Ibis*, combined with *Mistral*'s aggressive turn to engage them, proved sufficient to unnerve the attackers. They declined battle, coming about and returning to their column after exchanging only a few shots.

Mistral rose to meet *Ibis*, and they slipped into the clouds side by side.

"Where the hell have you been?" Captain Emery shouted across the gap, when the ships converged close enough for speaking trumpets.

"Out fighting the goddamn war," Josette shouted back. "Where have you been? Cloud-watching?"

This elicited chuckling between Captain Emery and his first officer. Emery raised the speaking trumpet and said, "Is that the young Lord Hinkal behind you?"

Josette glanced over her right shoulder, where Bernat and Martel were speaking to each other. "The very same," she called back.

"My thanks and compliments, Lord Hinkal," Emery shouted. "If not for your warning about the Vin army, they'd have caught us with our pants around our ankles. But thanks to you, we have a chance."

Josette spent a moment rolling that statement around her head. She slowly lowered her speaking trumpet and turned around. Bernat's eyes were wide, like a deer surprised in the forest. Lieutenant Martel took a step away from Bernat, as one might step gingerly away from a smoking bomb, and discovered a sudden, absorbing interest in the aneroid altimeter above his head. He reached up to tap it, then stroked his chin thoughtfully.

"My memory may be faulty," Josette said, "but I seem to recall that it was my warning."

Bernat looked to the side and cleared his throat. "I, ah, I do also seem to recall that, now that you bring it up." He cleared his throat again. "I also recall your worries regarding the time it would take a warning to move through proper channels, so, ah . . . it's possible that, before I boarded the ship, I hired the fastest horse and best rider in Durum, and it's possible that he carried a substantial bribe to the staff of the nearest semaphore station, and it's possible that, in appreciation of that gratuity, they sent a message of highest priority to friends of mine in several cities to the north, where I thought my uncle might be quartering. I may have offered a rather generous reward if they found my uncle and delivered a certain warning, that may or may not have said something about a Vin horde practically at the gates of Durum. It's possible that this expedited our army's response to the crisis."

She didn't answer. She only stared at him as his gaze wandered about the deck from place to place—everywhere but her—and waited for more details to fall from his mouth.

He finally met her eyes. "This report may have been grossly exaggerated, as to the number, proximity, and certainty of the enemy forces, but I do recall very firmly that I decided not to make an account of the hundreds of Vin war elephants I imagined were among their number. In the interest of credibility." Unable to sustain the force of her glare for long, his eyes wandered back to the deck. "A shame, really. I had a masterful line about 'a plenitude of adamantine beasts, stampeding together in gargantuan fury, to the abominable trumpeting chorus of their unmanning battle cry.' It was really quite moving."

She waited a little while longer, but no further details fell out.

"Is everything all right over there?" Captain Emery called from the *Ibis*.

She turned, nodded, and made a thumbs-up gesture.

"I . . . I'm sorry," Bernat said.

"For what?" She gave him an approving nod. "You did well, Bernie. As Captain Emery said, you gave us a chance."

A wave of relief seemed to pass through him. "So, you're not going to throw me overboard?"

"Oh, I'm certainly going to throw you overboard," she said, "but on your way down, I want you to know that you have my admiration."

He smiled, put his hand over his heart, and said, "I will hit the ground a contented man."

Josette turned and lifted her speaking trumpet. She shouted to the *Ibis*, "He says you're too kind, Captain."

Emery looked at his first officer, who handed him a stack of papers. "Oh yes, I have orders to relay to you, Captain Dupre. Order dated three days ago: '*Mistral* return to Arle.' Order dated two days ago: '*Mistral* return to Arle.' Order dated yesterday . . . well, they go on like that. The most recent ones are from General Fieren himself."

Now it was Josette's turn to look like a frightened deer. She lowered her speaking trumpet and said, "He's going to take my ship away."

14

WHEN THEY MOORED at Arle, the general's aide was waiting for them in the shed. "That'll be the constable, here to keep me from making a dash for it," Josette said to Martel. "You may have to see to the repairs yourself."

"Don't worry, sir," Martel said. "I'll keep the hands at it until the work is done."

She considered it. "No. Let the yardsmen do the work. The crew are going to have a hot day tomorrow. Let them get some rest."

Martel, once he'd recovered from his surprise, said, "Yes, sir, but I'm not sure how much rest they'll get."

Her only answer was a mild smirk.

"Lieutenant Dupre," Captain Katsura said, hailing her from the shed floor. "General Fieren requests the honor of your presence."

She leaned over the hurricane deck railing and called back, "We're just about to offload our wounded, sir. I'll be down directly after that, unless the general is in such a hurry that he'd have them linger on the ship, rather than suffer a delay to his schedule."

"He's a compassionate man, Lieutenant, to be sure. By all means, see to your casualties."

Private Bashir was offloaded and sent to the hospital on a stretcher, for there wasn't a cart to be had on the entire base. They watched him go, babbling in a hazy delirium, and then Katsura led Josette and Bernat to a luxurious open carriage, which carried them out to the streets of Arle. The city was not yet in a complete panic over the second Vin army to threaten it this month, but a sense of anxiety and dread pervaded the air, and the usually bustling streets were quiet. Indeed, Josette appeared to be riding in the only carriage left in the city, which struck her as particularly immoderate when they rode past the stretcher-bearers still laboring toward the hospital.

Captain Katsura smiled at Josette and said, "That reminds me. I must congratulate you on your aerial victories."

It took Josette a moment to remember what he was talking about. As recent as they were, those victories seemed to belong to a different person. "Thank you," she said distantly.

"Somehow," Katsura said, infusing the word with accusation, "the papers obtained an account of them, and your ever-growing exploits have been the talk of the Garnian rabble. You hit just the right note for a heroic victory. Not enough casualties to make it another bloodbath, but not so few that it looked easy. Masterful work."

She put her elbow on the carriage rail and her chin on her fist as she watched the streets go by. "It wasn't easy to get it right, sir. In the end, I had to shoot Private Kiffer myself, to make the numbers come out."

That shut Katsura up, and he was remarkably quiet for the rest of the journey. A few times, she caught him studying her face, as if he harbored some doubt that she'd been joking.

The carriage came to a halt in front of the Arle Museum of Art and Antiquities. Josette groaned when she saw it.

Katsura led them inside, straight through the galleries and into a back hall. He stopped in front of a door. "If you'll wait here," he said, "the general will be with you in a moment." He stepped through and into a small private viewing gallery, locking the door behind him.

They waited a great deal longer than a moment. An entire hour passed, during which staff officers came and went, and

Katsura stuck his head out once to beg their patience. The only conversation that passed between Josette and Bernat was her occasional mutter of, "He's going to take my damn ship away," to which Bernat could only respond with comforting platitudes.

Another hour passed with no conversation at all, albeit with the frequent exchange of troubled glances. Staff officers continued to come and go, in ones and twos and threes.

In the third hour, Bernat first sat and then lay upon the tile floor. Josette, accustomed to long watches spent on her feet, remained standing, taking only short walks as needed, to keep the blood flowing in her legs.

Halfway through the fourth hour, Katsura stuck his head through the door. "It'll only be another minute," he said. "The general is terribly sorry, but he has so much to do, what with the Vins coming."

Bernat only stared at the ceiling. "The Vins," he said, his tone detached and distant. "I think I remember them, from my life before the museum."

"Thank you, Captain," was all Josette said.

After five full hours had passed, Josette was finally invited in. She entered to find General Fieren sitting at an old desk and Katsura standing next to it. On the wall hung a large painting of a man being stripped naked and stabbed by an angry mob. According to the plaque, the painting was titled *The Death of Gesshin Grassus, Champion of the Plebeians.*

Subtle, she thought.

"Ah, Lieutenant," General Fieren said, without looking up from his papers. "Thank you for waiting."

She saluted and stood at attention, saying nothing.

"You've had an eventful little cruise." General Fieren looked up from a slim, leather-bound book that she recognized as *Mistral*'s log. One of the officers coming and going must have had it in a satchel. "You engaged two enemy airships," the general said, "came under fire from several more, dashed into Vinzhalian territory to scout Kamenka, and reconnoitered a column." His voice pitched up at the end of every item in a lilt of admiration. "You bombed an artillery battery, strafed troops escalading the wall at Durum. You destroyed two bridges, four granaries, and a mill." He gave his mustache a flick and nodded his head in appreciation.

Josette stood perfectly still, looking straight ahead and waiting for the hammer to drop.

"Only one thing troubles me," General Fieren said, his chair creaking as he leaned forward. "And it's this: I can't, for the life of me, remember seeing orders for any of that." He looked at his aide-de-camp. "Do you recall seeing orders for any of that, Gaston?"

"No, sir."

The chair creaked again as he leaned back. "That's an odd thing, indeed. Lieutenant Dupre, you did receive orders instructing you to take those actions, didn't you?"

Josette didn't flinch. "No, sir."

She counted two beats before General Fieren exploded, right on schedule, rising from his chair so quickly that it tipped over and hit the floor behind him. He slammed his hands on the table and bent across it, shouting, "Then what in the holy hell do you think you were doing out there, woman?"

"Commanding an airship, sir," she said without pause.

"And you think that gives you the right to go off and do whatever the hell you please?"

"Absent instructions to the contrary, sir, and within the scope of my orders, I understand that it does."

General Fieren was not impressed. "You destroyed two Garnian bridges, Lieutenant. Do you know what it costs to rebuild two bridges?"

"I'd have to ask the Vins, sir. I expect they're the ones rebuilding them."

"Oh, very droll, Lieutenant. And you were ordered to return to Arle several times before you complied. Gaston, how many times was Lieutenant Dupre ordered to return to Arle?"

"Six, sir."

"Six," he said. "Six times. Lieutenant Dupre, I'm sorry if the needs of the army were an inconvenience to your whirlwind tour of western Vinzhalia, but I cannot countenance blatant disregard for orders."

"Sir, as my logs indicate, I responded promptly upon receipt of those orders, proceeding with all practical speed to Arle."

"Received them from . . ." General Fieren began, and then snapped his fingers. "Gaston, which semaphore station relayed our orders to *Mistral*?"

"You're mistaken, sir," Captain Katsura said. "The orders were relayed by the airship *Ibis*."

The general frowned. "How odd. I was under the impression that such orders were usually relayed by semaphore. Gaston, did we neglect to send *Mistral* her orders by semaphore?"

"No, sir."

"How very, very odd. It's almost as if *Mistral*'s captain was deliberately avoiding contact with our semaphore stations, in order to extend her little jaunt across the countryside, and only through a chance encounter with another airship was she brought to heel."

Josette had remained quiet through most of this, knowing that it was all a play, and her character didn't have any lines. But here she spoke up. "It was not a chance encounter, sir."

The general arched an eyebrow.

"*Mistral* and *Ibis* were on intersecting courses, sir."

"You know that for a fact?" the general asked.

Josette did not know it for a fact, but she had very little to lose by guessing. "Yes, sir. *Ibis* was ordered to destroy the same string of bridges, granaries, and mills that *Mistral* was engaged in destroying on our way south. Thus, the two ships were bound to sight each other, visibility permitting."

"*Ibis*'s mission is not your concern, Lieutenant, and I will not tolerate another whit of your smarm or insolence."

"Yes, sir."

"In addition to those transgressions," he said, closing the logbook and picking up a stack of papers that looked curiously like the thin parchment used aboard airships, "you neglected to set your auxiliary officer and female crewmen safely down before commencing battle, failed to complete your ship's aerial trials, wantonly endangered your ship and crew, and ordered unauthorized modifications to reduce first the length and then the number of airscrews."

The entire list was an absurd collection of puffery and technicalities, but the last item she simply could not abide. "Those modifications increased *Mistral*'s top speed by six knots, sir."

General Fieren laughed. This was not the mimed laugh of his earlier theater, but a genuine, hearty belly laugh that set his mustache to quivering. "Are you really going to stand here and tell me, to my face, that you increased your ship's speed by taking airscrews away?"

"It's all in my logs, sir."

"That's the most absurd thing I've ever heard," he said. He laughed again and turned to Katsura. "Taking away its airscrews makes an airship go faster. Did you know that, Gaston?"

Even the stalwart Katsura laughed. "If only she'd removed the remaining four, sir, perhaps her ship would have broken an airspeed record."

The general laughed and shot a patronizing look at Josette. "Thank you for your time, Lieutenant. If you'll wait in the hallway, I'll have new orders for you shortly. Oh, and do send Bernie in."

She saluted and turned for the door.

On her way to it, she heard the general ask Katsura, "Think there's anywhere for her?"

The aide replied, "Outposts in the fever swamps always need quartermasters and whores. We'll be killing two birds with one stone."

She stepped into the hall, closed the door behind her, and promptly collapsed, her legs turning to jelly.

BERNAT CAUGHT HER as she fell.

He almost asked what happened, before he realized what a stupid question it was. Instead, he simply helped her back to her feet. By the time she could stand upright again, every trace of despair had been wiped from her, and she bore the same stolid, stone-faced expression she wore under fire. "He had a letter from someone," she said, looking him hard in the eye.

"Ah," was all he said.

"You sent it?"

He swallowed. "I was going to get it back when we landed again in Durum, but . . ." He looked at the floor. "I was really hoping it hadn't gone out, or was still in transit. Why does the mail only move quickly when you don't want it to?"

Her cold face hadn't warmed. "In the normal course of events, I imagine it would have been stuck in Arle for a week, waiting to be forwarded along to General Fieren. As it happened, Fieren came to it."

"Ah," he said again.

"Do enjoy whatever reward you've earned for this. He wants to see you, and I'll likely kill you when he's done." Even to Bernat's honed eye, she showed no sign of jesting.

"Sounds fair," he said.

His uncle stood waiting for him inside, and gripped his hand in a hearty shake as soon as he entered. "Do close the door, Bernie."

Bernat did so, saying, "Hello, Uncle. What a lovely painting."

His uncle turned to admire it. "You like it?" he asked. "Gaston, inform the museum that I'm buying this painting, and have it sent to wherever Bernie is staying. Would you like some tea, Bernie? Gaston, fetch Bernie some tea."

Gaston was sitting at the desk in front of the painting, writing something out. He began to rise, but Bernat stopped him, saying, "That's quite all right. I already drank my own urine while waiting in the hall."

His uncle laughed and slapped him on the shoulder. "Terribly sorry about the wait, Bernie, but it couldn't be helped. I would have seen you earlier, if it was at all possible."

"Naturally," Bernat said. "I'm sure the invasion has set everything on its end around here."

"Quite, quite," his uncle said, changing to a more serious tone. "We have no shortage of problems."

"Is that so? I recently learned an interesting way of dealing with problems, Uncle."

"Oh?"

He grinned, sly and assured. "You shoot them."

His uncle laughed. "Quite right, Bernie. Quite right. Though there are a few problems that can't be shot." He took the top paper from a stack on the desk and looked it over. "Such as this band of leaderless militia. They're unattached men from the surrounding counties, mostly. We formed them into a scratch regiment, but we need a colonel to lead them. Someone with noble blood, you know. The men don't respect anyone else." He held the paper out to Bernat. "So what do you say, Bernie? Are you up to it?"

Bernat hadn't understood what his uncle was getting at, right up to the moment when he offered him command of a thousand fighting men or more. He looked at the floor and gathered his thoughts as the shock slowly wore off.

"Or, if that doesn't suit you, perhaps we could see about

adding some gratuity to your payment, instead. In light of the . . . additional services you've provided. Perhaps another hundred—"

Bernat shot him an angry look and very nearly growled at him.

And his uncle recoiled. "Let's make it another two hundred. No, two hundred and fifty. That'll set you up nicely for a while, won't it, Bernie? And there'll be no need to mention the finer details of any—"

"I don't want the money," Bernat said, cutting him off. "I want to stay aboard *Mistral,* and I want Captain Dupre commanding her."

His uncle looked at him strangely. Gaston, who'd been diligently scratching away with his pen behind the desk, stopped and looked up.

"Bernie," his uncle said, "why in hell would you want to go up in one of those things, with a real battle coming?"

Bernat was asking himself the same question, and had been from the moment he stepped off the ship. "I'm not entirely sure," he admitted, "but I think it has something to do with the contrast between Vin and Garnian choices in footwear." He tried in vain to remember how that thread of logic went, but everything he came up with seemed much less convincing than he remembered.

His uncle had by now recovered some of his composure. "Now see here, my boy, don't think your little notes entitle you to this sort of insolence. The ground you're standing on isn't half as firm as you think."

Bernat grinned. "Isn't it?" he asked.

"It is not," General Lord Hinkal said, loud enough to make Bernat flinch. "Whatever you may think, no one's going to blame me for failing to foresee a second Vin attack on Arle, should some little weasel let that rumor out. No one could have known they'd attack again so soon."

"Yet many did," Bernat said, beginning to walk slowly back and forth in front of his uncle. "And those who didn't will soon pretend differently. Indeed, people who until yesterday said that a second front was an impossibility, will tomorrow say it was inevitable and obvious to anyone with half a brain. And they'll draw attention away from their own hypocrisy by mocking the failure of others. So I wonder, just how would that sordid little stew taste, if we seasoned it with the news that the vaunted General Lord Fieren Hinkal would have left Arle entirely defenseless, had he not been called back by a note from his foppish little nephew?" He stopped, turned on his heel, and looked straight at his uncle.

"If you think you can sink me, boy . . ."

Bernat laughed. "I handed you enough to sink Captain Dupre, Uncle, and I had less to work with, believe me." He held up his hand just as Fieren was about to yell at him, and said, "On the other hand, if General Hinkal *had* displayed the foresight, the strategic vision, the military brilliance to anticipate the second attack on Arle? Well, I suppose he'd get some sort of medal or something. Whatever it is they usually give to legendary heroes."

That checked his uncle, but he clearly still harbored reluctance. "Why this sudden affection for Dupre? What, are you giving it to her?"

Bernat reddened. "A gentleman would never say, were it true."

This comment seemed to restore a large fraction of his uncle's esteem for him. Fieren slapped Bernat on the shoulder so hard, he had to step to the side to keep his balance.

"So," Bernat said, "will you order her back aboard her ship? And forget all this nonsense about the fever swamps?"

"Of course, Bernie," Fieren said. "In fact, those are exactly the orders we were about to give her. Weren't they, Gaston?"

At the desk, Gaston crumpled the paper he was writing on and dropped it into a waste bin. He took a clean sheet and began writing again. "They certainly were, sir."

"I COULD HAVE sworn that man was going to take my ship away," Josette said, as she read her orders on the museum steps. She looked to Bernat, who'd just delivered them. "I would have bet any amount."

Bernat only shrugged and said, "People can surprise you. Perhaps under that brash exterior, there beats in General Lord Fieren Hinkal a tender heart."

"No doubt he cries at the theater, and is kind to stray kittens as well." She went down the steps and turned to him. "Thank you."

Bernat, for once, seemed to be at a loss. After a long silence, he said, "Thanks may be premature, if they're even deserved. I had the strangest impression, toward the end of my interview, that he means to kill us."

She shook her head. "No, no. He'd never try to kill us." She turned and began to walk down the street. "He'll just order us to our deaths in tomorrow's battle."

"Oh," Bernat said, following after her. "How uplifting."

"You don't have to come along, you know. There's nothing obliging you to stay aboard *Mistral*."

"I should think there is. Now more than ever."

She turned her head away, so he wouldn't see her smile. "You're a good man, Bernat."

He sighed. "No, but I get there in the end."

They walked on. The city felt different, and not only because of the lengthening shadows as evening approached. The place had regained its vibrancy—if not in fact, then in her impression of it. It had sloughed off the character of an elaborate gallows that it had possessed when she was being escorted to her appointment with General Fieren. For, whatever tomorrow might bring, today she was captain of a king's airship.

"Oh, blast!" she said, as the full implications sank in.

"What?" Bernat asked.

"I'll have to deal with that bloody-minded quartermaster now. That would have fallen to Martel if I'd lost the ship."

"My condolences."

They made their way to the signal base, where they found the quartermaster's office bustling. Staff officers were filling out paperwork on every flat surface, while yardsmen and crew were dashing in and out of the adjacent warehouse. Lieutenant Bowden was yelling at all of them from behind her desk.

By the door, Josette found Captain Emery of the *Ibis*. "Just got in," he said. "It's madness in here. Has it been as bad all day?"

"I couldn't say. I've only just arrived from receiving my orders from General Fieren."

Captain Emery was perplexed. "Why doesn't he pass them down the chain of command, like he does for everyone else?"

Josette shrugged. "He's a peculiar man. Likes to take meetings in front of paintings, you know."

"Oh, one of those." Emery scanned the ruckus. "Quite a scene, though, isn't it?"

Josette sighed. "I have a hard enough time getting my stores when it isn't like this. I'm down a bref gun, you know."

"I noticed. How did you lose it, by the way?"

"Dismounted over Durum when some damn fool didn't swab it out properly. Damn fine gun, too." She finally noticed Bernat, who'd been trying to catch her eye. "Oh, Captain Emery, I suppose you haven't been formally introduced to Lord Bernat."

"A pleasure," Emery said, bowing to Bernat. "Of course, you know, I've heard something of your warning of the Vin invasion, but I wonder if I may ask—what is your position aboard *Mistral*?"

Josette spoke before Bernat could. "Ship's spy."

Emery was brought up short. "Oh, uh, a pleasure," he repeated.

Bernat bowed and said with a smile, "Your servant."

"I don't suppose you know how many airships the Vins will have tomorrow?" Emery asked, not seeming to understand just who Bernat was spying for. When Bernat only returned a mysterious expression and a shrug, Emery looked back at Josette. "How does one merit one's own spy aboard ship?"

"You have to be on the general's good side," she said.

"The first step, of course, is finding it," Bernat added.

A lull in the bustle provided an opportunity to confront the quartermaster. "I see an opening," Josette said. "I'm going in."

"Godspeed," Captain Emery said.

Josette went straight for the quartermaster's desk, steeling herself as if for a charge into cannon fire. She would get her new bref gun no matter the resistance. No excuse or bureaucratic tangle would deter her. She was going to plant herself in this office and not leave until her ship had what it required. She stepped to the desk, fixed Lieutenant Bowden with a stare that could melt iron, and said, "*Mistral* needs a replacement bref gun, and I'll not take any of your usual piffle about it."

The quartermaster looked up from her paperwork with strangely wide eyes. "Oh, thank God," she said, relief showing on her face. "I don't suppose I could convince you to take two of them?"

Josette was loaded and ready to return a volley of resolve and defiance, so this instant acquiescence caught her unawares. At first, she thought it must be a new gambit, meant to throw her off balance. When the quartermaster's steady, pleading eyes finally convinced her that it wasn't, she said, "Where the hell would I put a third bref gun?"

"I don't know," Bowden said. "Perhaps you could point it out the back?"

"Point it out the back?" Josette peered at her, incredulous. "What the hell is going on here?"

The quartermaster let out a tired sigh. "We've been ordered to move all our stocks and stores, to keep them from falling into enemy hands. But by the very same order, we had to hand all our carts and carriages over to the goddamn infantry, may the villains rot in hell. They took them when they marched out this morning, with every able-bodied whore in the city following. Can you believe it?"

"Quite," Josette said. "Be that as it may, *Mistral* can accommodate only two bref guns in total, but we have suffered considerable damage and expended many of our stores. I'll be quite happy to relieve you of the best of your cordage, planks, fabric, and powder."

"How much?"

"We are, as always, severely limited by weight, but we can top off our standard allotment."

The quartermaster looked down at her ledgers, forlorn and desperate.

Josette sighed. "If it'll help, I'll replace some of my sand ballast with any compact, easily handled stores you might have, with the understanding that we'll drop them over the side like any other disposable ballast should the situation call for it. In fact, I've been saying for years that we ought to do that, but who the hell ever listens?"

Lieutenant Bowden's eyes began to swim. "Oh, bless you. Bless you, Captain!"

"You don't seem very happy about this," Bernat said, as they accompanied the yardsmen dragging a fine new bref gun on a fine new gun carriage.

"Of course not," Josette said. "That was the most surreal and disturbing experience of my entire life. Makes me wonder if I haven't, in fact, been shipped to Utarma, and I'm lying in a hallucinatory fever even now."

"If that is so," Bernat said, "then you should enjoy it as long as it lasts, as it's likely to be your final opportunity." They passed into the shed, where Captain Emery's ship—*Ibis,* he thought—was tied up next to *Mistral.*

Martel met them halfway to the shed door. "All repairs are complete," he said. "We only need to top off the ship's stores. Ah, but I see you've already taken care of that."

More yardsmen were filing in with spools of rope, lumber, or small barrels on their shoulders.

When Martel saw the quality and quantity of the stores coming aboard, he whistled. "How did you manage this, Captain?"

Josette's expression didn't change. "I took a firm line, and wouldn't budge an inch until she finally gave in."

Bernat had no intention of contradicting her, though he was so amused that he couldn't contain a grin, even when she shot a nasty look at him. "Why don't we all go out to dinner at Oceane's, to celebrate your unlikely victory?" he asked. "My treat, of course."

"Thank you, but no," Josette said. "I'll have my dinner out of the ship's stores."

Martel, on the other hand, was quite interested. "Are you sure, Captain? This may be our last chance to enjoy their cuisine before they're forced to go to an all-dumpling menu."

"Yes, do come along," Bernat said. "Your ship is practically ready, your orders are in hand, and you've defeated the quartermaster with your firm resolve—as any witness would surely testify to under oath. What's the harm in taking an hour off to eat something that hasn't been pickling in a barrel for who knows how long?"

Bernat wasn't sure whether it was the force of his logic or the veiled threat that did it, but Josette relented. "Very well," she said. "But if I return to find the yardsmen haven't seated our new bref gun properly, I'm holding you responsible."

"On my own head be it," Bernat said.

So they fetched up Kember and headed off, but arrived at Oceane's to find the owner locking the place up.

"You can't possibly be closed," Bernat said. "It's not even dark yet."

The old man looked up from his padlock and tipped his head to Bernat. "Our chefs are all in the militia," he said. "So naturally, most of them have run for the countryside, and the ones that got caught marched with the army."

Martel put his hand on his chest. "My heart glows with pride at the thought of our brave fighting militiamen," he said. "Doesn't your heart glow with pride, Ensign?"

Kember considered the matter carefully and said in her still-hoarse voice, "If you say so, sir."

"Oh well, back to the ship then," Josette said. "If we hurry, we'll be just in time to supervise them balancing out the guns."

"No, no, that won't do," Bernat said. "I promised dinner and I intend to deliver. In fact, I know just the place. Nobody in the militia there at all." In fact, he knew of no such place, but he certainly couldn't return to the ship—the rations were terrible and his wine had run out. And there had to be a tavern open somewhere in the city. He led the party through the streets, seeking out his usual haunts, finding them all closed, but walking past as if they were only on the way.

"I do believe he has no idea where he's going," Josette said, after they'd made their fourth consecutive right turn.

"I know exactly where I am, dear captain. The hospital is just ahead, and beyond it lies . . . well, I think I'll just leave it as a surprise."

"Because he has no idea where he's going."

"Vicious slander."

As they passed in front of the hospital, a wiry-haired little dog came out of the alley ahead and crossed the street in front of them. They all stopped to watch, not because the dog was in any way exceptional, but because it was dragging a decomposing human arm over the cobblestones. The arm was severed just below the elbow, where the rotten flesh had already been gnawed on.

After the dog and its baggage had disappeared into the alley opposite, nearly a full minute of silence passed while the party looked variously ahead or into the darkness of the alley. Finally, Josette said, "I do believe the Tellurians would call that an omen."

"Good or bad?" Bernat asked, drawing the scornful eyes of the rest of the party.

"Dogs must have dug up the pit where the amputated limbs from the last battle were buried," Martel said. "The whole city will be strewn with finger and foot bones by morning."

"Pray tell me this was not your destination for dinner," Josette said.

Bernat smiled. "No, it lies farther ahead."

"Do lead on, then."

Bernat had by now run out of establishments that were known to him, and only hoped to happen across someplace before the officers lost faith. They were on the brink of mutiny when he spotted a taproom with a lamp burning in the window. "Here we are. One of my favorite places to enjoy dinner." He could only hope they served food.

Josette looked it over. The placard was blackened by soot from the manufactories, the name unreadable. "By what name is it called?" she asked.

"Hmm?"

"What is this establishment called?"

Bernat smiled as he held the door open. "Let us never trouble ourselves with such trivial details."

"Come on, Captain," Martel said. "Should prove interesting, in any event."

She shook her head, but entered anyway.

The inside was so gloomy that Bernat could hardly see, even after his eyes adjusted to the dark. The oil lamp in the window was the only light in the place. "Hello?" he asked the shadows. "Are you open for dinner?"

"Eh?" a ragged voice came back. "You lot from the army?"

Before the others could warn him against it, Bernat said cheerfully, "Why yes, we are."

"Then get the hell out!" the voice said. A man limped out of the gloom and stared balefully at them. "Goddamn army. Your friends have already been through, ate and drank half my stock on credit, and ran out on me. When I sent someone to find them, they'd already marched. And food costing me what it does now."

Bernat continued to smile. "You're mistaken about us, my good fellow. We can pay."

The man snorted and spat on his own floor, near Bernat's feet.

"Oh come now," Bernat said. "We mean to spill blood for your protection on the morn. The least you could do is offer us a pot of ale and a warm meal."

"Ha!" the man said. "Don't you try and play on my sympathies. I was in the army, lad, back in the day when we won our damn battles. I was even wounded a time or two, but you don't see me begging and stealing my meals."

"But we aren't begging," Bernat began, but was stopped by a hand on his shoulder.

"Come on," Josette said. "We'll just have to take our dinner aboard ship."

The man stepped closer and squinted at them. "Airmen, eh?" he asked. "That mean you go up in them balloons?"

"Airships," the officers said, all at once and rather loudly.

"Well," the man said, looking at the floor and seeming to think. "Always felt better with one of them over my head." He lifted his head and looked back into the gloom. "Marguerite!"

Footsteps sounded from the floor above.

The man led them to a table, lit the lamp there, and sat them down. He even pulled out the chairs for the ladies. "Marguerite!" he shouted again at the stairs.

"I am coming as fast as I can!" said a voice from upstairs. "And if it ain't the tax man or the supreme high priest down there, you're gonna be damn sorry about it, ya old bastard."

Bernat waited, more uncomfortable than when he was merely unwelcome.

A woman took a few steps down the stairs, then bent over to look into the taproom from ceiling level. "What is it?"

"Marguerite," the man said, "get these folk some stew, and whatever else they want." He was already behind the bar and pouring drinks, while Marguerite came down the stairs and went out the back, grumbling all the way.

"So," Josette said, "you're a frequent guest at this establishment?"

"One of my favorite places in Arle," Bernat said. "So quaint. So homey."

They enjoyed their ale, and earthen pots of stew whose ingredients might as well have been dug up from behind the hospital, though they were still superior to that horrible beef in the ship's stores.

Marguerite was clearing the plates and the party was on its second round of ale—except for Kember, whom Josette had cut off after the first—when a riot seemed to break out in the streets. The mob came closer until it was just outside the taproom, and then it burst inside, its members pouring through the door.

They were the crew of the *Mistral*, their numbers shored up by supernumeraries in the form of painted ladies hanging from the arms of male crew members. The one on Corporal Lupien's arm had to be helped over the doorstep, as she was missing a foot.

The vanguard of the group spotted Josette looking back at them, and stopped cold a few feet inside the door. The rest of the group ploughed into them from behind, nearly knocking them forward, before they too noticed their captain's icy gaze. They all froze, the crew growing more terrified by the second and the supernumeraries growing more confused.

"Who is this, Lupie?" the one-footed woman asked. "Another of your mistresses?"

Corporal Lupien snapped into a salute, nearly sending the poor woman to the ground. The rest of the crew instantly followed his example.

Josette continued to watch them for a while, then touched a finger to her brow. "Carry on," she said.

The crew let out their breaths as one. A quick inhalation followed, and then a hearty, spontaneous cheer. The crew spread out into the room, some going to the bar, others finding tables, and some going straight to the ninepins table.

Sergeant Jutes approached and put a knuckle to his forelock. "Don't worry, Cap'n," he said. "I'm keepin' an eye on them, and I won't let any of them drink more than he can handle."

"I know they're in good hands, Sergeant," Josette said. And without looking away from Jutes, she reached out to stop Kember from drinking the dregs out of Bernat's first mug of ale. Jutes touched his forelock and hobbled over to the dartboard where Gears was already waiting for him, defending the board from the rest of the crew.

Private Grey and the monkey rigger sat down near the back, at a secluded table next to the rear door. This concerned Bernat greatly, for he'd been just about to get up and visit the privy, and now he had to either go past Grey or explain to his tablemates why he'd gone around the front instead. He decided to put the matter off as long as possible and hope for a change of circumstance.

"I've been curious since Durum," he said, raising his voice to be heard over the din. "Why is a hole in the luftgas bags of such small concern?"

Josette answered, "You've seen for yourself why it's no concern. We only need to find the hole and patch it."

"Yes, yes," he said. "I know that. What I wish to know is, why does the gas not escape all at once? It seems to me that a single musket should be enough to sink us." He was genuinely curious, but his primary interest in asking was to distract himself from the needs of his bladder.

"It's because it keeps the same pressure as the air," Ensign Kember said, as if she were reciting it from a textbook. "In a rigid, anyway, and it's not much higher in a semirigid or a blimp."

"It only escapes at all by mixing with the air, and because it wants to spill upward," Josette said, "just as water in a damaged rain barrel spills down."

The example just had to be spilled water. He crossed his legs and said, "Interesting."

"But if you imagine the effect of a small hole in a rain barrel the size of one of *Mistral*'s bags, well, it would take a year for it to dribble dry. Drip by drip." She approximated the sound of running water.

Did she intend to torment him as a punishment, or did she simply have a natural talent for it? In either event, he stood up and said with annoyance, "Thank you very much for that most edifying lesson."

As he moved quickly for the rear door, he heard Kember ask, "What's the matter with him?"

"Just a soggy sort of fellow, I suppose," Josette said.

Kember began to laugh, but Martel only asked, "What have I missed?"

Bernat didn't hear the answer, as distance and the noise of the room finally drowned out their voices. Just in time, as it happened, to bring him within hailing distance of Private Grey. "My lord!" she called as he approached. "Sit and have a drink with us."

"Another time," he said as he went past. He reached the door and pulled on it several times, before realizing he had to push. He did so and stepped out into the blessed quiet of the night.

No, not quite quiet. He could still hear the room through the thin walls of the tavern, and in particular he heard the monkey rigger saying, "He didn't seem very interested."

To which Private Grey replied, "He'll come around."

He fled as quickly as he could to the privy, not certain at that moment whether he ever meant to return. It took him some time to find it in the dark, but he was reasonably sure he relieved himself in the privy and not the kitchen.

He paused at the door on his way back in, steeling himself for the return trip past Private Grey. While he was waiting, he couldn't help but hear more of her conversation with the monkey rigger. He could perhaps have helped putting his ear to the wall to catch everything, but it was all of a piece.

"Persistence," Private Grey said. "That's what my father always told my brothers. Keep at them until you've worn them down."

"Does he tell you the same, though?"

"I'm sure he would. He doesn't speak to me much. But all my brothers are married, so it must work."

"Didn't you tell me your sisters-in-law were all miserable? That they all regretted ever marrying?"

"Well . . ." The rest of Grey's answer was drowned out in a clatter of skittle pins falling, and the congratulatory cheers that followed.

Bernat went around the building in the dark, and stopped only when he saw Private Davies pissing in the street. He walked up to him, but had to dodge aside when the man snapped a salute without interrupting his previous activity. "Oh, it's only you, my lord," Davies said, returning the balance of his attention to the task at hand.

"If anyone asks after me," Bernat said, "I'll be back at the base."

And there he went, to wait aboard *Mistral* until the crew returned. They arrived in the middle of the night, snatched a few hours' sleep at the insistence of their sergeant, and rose in the predawn darkness to rig for launch.

15

MISTRAL HELD STATION at nine hundred feet in calm winds, just below the cloud ceiling. Her captain stood leaning on the rail between the new bref gun and the old. She looked down on General Hinkal, mounted on his white mare and parading in front of the thin Garnian line. The general's speech was inaudible to the crew of the *Mistral,* drowned by distance and the unceasing whine of the ship's steamjack turbine. It was, Josette reflected, probably lost on the men in the line as well.

"Why parade in front of the line, giving a long speech that any man can only hear a few seconds of?" she asked.

Bernat looked down and said, "You're missing the point. The men may only hear him for a few seconds, but he hears himself the entire time."

She looked through her spyglass at the Vins, assembling by battalion on the other side of the boggy field.

The first elements of the Garnian army had arrived a day ahead of them, and had immediately set themselves to improving their position. Fieren meant to create a killing ground by burning out the vegetation for two hundred paces on the other side of a little stream that cut across the fens, but the brush there was too damp to take a flame. The men—already tired by their forced march from Arle—had to spend the entire day cutting and uprooting shrubs. By sunset, with the skin on their hands rubbed raw, they'd cleared only fifty paces in front of the stream.

And their ordeal had not been over. With the Vin horde due

in the morning, they and every subsequent regiment had gone to work building earthworks. They dug entrenchments on the near side of the stream, shoveling and packing the dirt into a wall in front. No regiment, no matter how late it arrived, was allowed to retire for the night until they'd built their earthen wall to shoulder height.

Still, it would have been well worth the effort, if not for the rain that began around four in the morning. The downpour, sweeping in from Lake Magdalene, washed hours of hard work right into the stream. By daybreak, when the airships arrived, the only defensive works still standing were the lumber- and gabion-reinforced walls constructed by army engineers to protect the artillery batteries.

But while the Garnian infantrymen now stood completely exposed, envying their comrades in the artillery, they could at least take consolation in the condition of the field. The rain had turned the already-muddy terrain into a slurry of boot-sucking muck, which the Vins would have to cross under fire.

"What do you suppose he's saying?" Josette asked. Below, General Fieren's horse had become mired in the mud for the third time since the speech began.

Bernat thought for a moment, then spoke in a passable impression of his uncle. "Harrumph. Harrumph. Men, I know you're worried, but you have nothing to fear. For, let me reassure you, the moment the fighting starts, I will take my mustache safely behind the line, there to be guarded by ten stout sergeants, each with a halberd in one hand and a tin of wax in the other. Harrumph. Harrumph."

Josette put her hand over her heart and said, "I feel better already."

"So, what are our chances?"

Josette assessed the battlefield for the tenth time in as many minutes. Then she looked southwest to the village of Canard, its wide dirt streets packed with supply and artillery wagons coming from Arle. Garnian infantry regiments were still trickling in along the road.

"I'll say one thing for General Fieren," she said, "he has a talent for finding a beautiful piece of ground and compelling the Vins to fight him on it." She pointed to the fields around Canard, behind the Garnian line. "If the Vins try to flank us, Fieren can pull back and redeploy across solid ground, while they're still slogging through the bogs out there. So wherever they go, he'll be waiting for them and already dug in. And with more of our soldiers arriving from Arle every hour, the Vins must either attack now on Fieren's terms, or turn around and go home."

Bernat said, "Yes, yes—but do we have a chance?"

Josette ran her eyes across the thin defensive line below, then the seventy-thousand-strong Vin army massing across the field. "I never liked Arle that much anyway," she said.

"Ah," Bernat said, and sighed.

General Fieren finished his speech and returned to his staff tent. Josette clapped her hands together. "All right, everyone. The inspiring speech is over. Back to work."

Crewmen who'd been sitting on the bref guns or nibbling hard tack suddenly leapt to their posts.

"Captain," said Luc Lupien at the rudder, "what if I don't feel inspired yet?"

Josette eyed him and said, "I anticipated that eventuality, Corporal, and I've made a particular effort to be inspired enough for the both of us."

Lupien smirked, but kept his eyes forward. "Awfully thoughtful of you, Captain."

"Message coming in," Kember called, her voice throaty, the words rattling in her mouth. She was stationed on the starboard rail to observe messages flashed by quicklime lamp from the staff tent. "To St. Camille militia, left flank: withdraw your three leftmost companies to one hundred paces and form a reserve column. To 83rd Fusiliers, arriving: fill line and form reserve to left of St. Camille militia."

"Relay it," Josette said to the crewman posted on the port railing. He pointed his quicklime signal lamp and flashed the messages to their recipients.

"Pray tell," Bernat said, "why are the militia regiments not given numbers, like the regulars?"

Josette considered this, then said, "I suppose they'd give them numbers, if militia officers knew how to count."

With the arrival of the 83rd, about half the Garnian line was now regular army regiments, and the other half militiamen. Some militia regiments—those whose aristocratic sponsors could afford the expense—wore the standard Garnian uniform: a blue vest and jacket with brown trousers. It made them look almost like real soldiers. Other militiamen wore rough, undyed uniforms, and the worst of them wore no uniform at all, but only their own tattered farmers' clothes.

Regardless of dress, all any of them could do was wait until the Vins attacked. In the meantime, the Garnian artillery positions tried an occasional shot at extreme range, and *Mistral* reported on its lack of effect.

And every quarter of an hour, Josette fired off a white flare, to keep the other airships of the squadron on station. There were four of them, hidden above the cloud ceiling in a line astern of *Mistral*. Closest in line were the one-gun chasseur *Lapwing* and the two-gun *Ibis*, whose captain commanded the squadron. Next was a lightly armed, semirigid scout ship, the *Grouse*. In the rearguard were a pair of inauspicious blimps, too insignificant to merit formal names, but unofficially dubbed the *Swamp Hen* and the *Nowhere Express*. The poor blimps didn't even merit the expense of luftgas. They were buoyed by inflammable air, which the merest spark might set off.

Mistral, in the vanguard position, was the only ship yet revealed to the enemy. She hung stationary and exposed above the infantry, there to relay messages, report enemy movements, and inspire the troops by her presence. The custom was to rotate the ships of the squadron into and out of this vulnerable position, so as to share the risk of enemy artillery equally. In this case, however, orders had come directly from the general, ordering *Mistral* to hold the station until given further instructions, which would arrive shortly. That had been an hour ago, and no further instructions had yet arrived.

AT NINE IN the morning, the sun broke out over Lake Magdalene, thirty miles away, but the cloud ceiling above the battlefield stubbornly refused to disperse. As the sun climbed somewhere behind them, the clouds glowed with a diffuse red-orange light that seemed more gloomy, somehow, than the murky dawn preceding it.

The air had calmed to perfect stillness. The battlefield, cast in that strange orange light, had the surreal quality of a dream. More than once, Bernat tried to wake himself up while he watched the Vins unlimbering their artillery.

And then it began to rain fire, and he knew he was awake, for he'd never had a nightmare that could produce the stomach-tightening dread of shells exploding on every side. The Garnian cannons replied, but their fire passed over the grand battery to fall scattershot into the Vin infantry's assembly area. Indeed, the cannons on each side seemed entirely uninterested in shooting at each other, but directed most of their fire at the enemy infantry.

While he contemplated what seemed a strange kind of professional courtesy, a shell exploded directly to starboard, sending smoking, red-hot fragments so close he heard them hiss as they sailed past.

"Enemy in sight!" Kember called. As Bernat was wondering how she'd managed to miss them until now, the ensign reported, "Looks like a chasseur. Dead ahead, just breaking cloud cover."

"That'll be our counterpart," Josette said. A shell exploded above, and she had to raise her voice over the noise. "How do you say 'good luck' in Vin?"

Bernat spelled it out and Kember sent the message by signal lamp.

He turned to Josette and said, "I thought you were of a mind to sweep these Vin bastards from our lands, kill them to a man, make them pay for what they've done, obliterate them, eviscerate them, and et cetera."

She shrugged. "I am, but there's no reason to be impolite about it."

"So, is it personal?"

She didn't answer.

"Message from the Vin chasseur," Kember said. She spelled it out for Bernat.

He frowned. "They say, 'Good luck. Looking forward to killing you. Love, Dimitri.' Huh. Not a very sentimental people, the Vins."

A fresh flight of cannonballs hit the Garnian line, leaving man-wide gaps in it. A blast above made Bernat jump, and soon several crewmen in the keel were shouting, "Fire!"

"Form a party and put it out," Josette said, firmly and calmly.

Bernat felt his guts twist even tighter. He looked up, hearing crewmen climb through the girders.

Whereas Josette stood watching the enemy lines, stone-faced, not bothering to inquire about the damage, as if a little thing like a fire was nothing to worry about.

Soon Jutes called down, "Fire's out, Cap'n. Some damage to the envelope. A few small holes in bags six and seven."

"Very good," Josette said. "Continue repairs."

"Shouldn't we at least make ourselves a moving target?" Bernat asked.

"Our orders are to keep station."

"Lovely."

Kember lowered her telescope. "The Vins are forming columns of division. Six battalions up front and more following behind. Big sons of bitches."

"Send it," Josette said.

The signalman on the starboard side flashed the message to the command tent.

Bernat went forward to look, but soon wished he hadn't. When he heard "columns of division," he imagined a formation akin to a column of march, but these columns were something else entirely. The front of each was made up of something like two hundred musketmen, arrayed in a battle line that was three men deep and about sixty across. Following fifty paces behind them was another line of the same form and complement, and fifty paces behind that another line, and then another, and another, until each column resembled the rungs of a ladder—if the rungs of a ladder bristled with muskets. He counted the number of rungs in each column. The smallest had fifteen. He couldn't say how many the largest had, for he lost count at thirty. The damn thing was half a mile long, and at the back the individual lines blurred together in the morning haze.

And all at once, they were on the move, marching smoothly out onto the battlefield. When the front ranks were past the grand battery, a screen of loosely spaced men spread out in front of them, while a similar screen of riflemen left the Garnian lines and ventured into the field to meet them.

These skirmishers, Garnian and Vin, moved with none of the coordinated precision of the columns. Once they closed in and came within range of each other in the middle of the field, every skirmisher sought cover independently. They traded shots, but the action was too far away for Bernat to make much sense of.

"Who's winning?" he finally asked, when Josette joined him to observe from the rail.

"Given the numbers involved, I imagine they are," she said quietly.

It wasn't long before she was proved right. The Garnian skirmishers were pushed back, and farther back, until they reached the clear ground in front of the stream. From there, they ran back to their own line, each one stopping once along the way to kneel and fire off a hasty shot, as if to inform the enemy that this was a withdrawal, but certainly not a retreat.

Whatever it might have been, many fewer men crossed the stream coming back than had crossed it going out, and the Vin skirmishers were close on their heels. "Rifles to the forward rail," Josette said, as they came within range.

As a loader handed a rifle to Bernat, he heard a twang near his feet and looked down to see the frayed edges of a bullet hole. Josette was already kneeling behind the rail, so he joined her.

"Forget they can shoot back?" she asked.

He had, actually. He scooted along the rail and glanced over to take a shot. The Vin skirmishers had advanced to near two hundred paces from the Garnian line, and were pelting it from outside effective musket range.

Yet muskets suddenly crackled in uncoordinated fire from several places on the line.

"God damn it!" Josette shouted. "Signal those idiots to cease fire!"

Bernat looked out at the Vin skirmishers to see the effect of the musketry. Despite thousands of balls loosed on the enemy, hardly a man among the Vin skirmishers was hit. On the other side of the field, the Vin airship was already flashing signals, no doubt reporting which sections of the Garnian line had fired, and thereby identifying the points where the defenders were the least experienced and most poorly disciplined.

"Can we reposition the weak units to spread them out along the line?" Bernat asked, trying to look on the bright side.

Josette only stared over the rail and said in a hushed tone, "Not before *that* gets here." A rolling thunderclap punctuated her words.

Bernat looked out past the Vin columns to their grand battery, which was now invisible behind a spreading, impenetrable cloud of smoke.

Dozens of cannonballs split the air below. They struck the line, streaking over or tearing through the diminished earthen wall to cut men down by ones and twos and send them flying back, often in pieces.

Bernat heard a crash above him, and looked up to see a ball tear a furrow down *Mistral*'s keel, snapping struts and sending splinters in every direction as it plowed through to exit just behind the hurricane deck. Another ball hit on the starboard side, the whistle of its passage becoming an unnerving, high-pitched squeal as it tore through three luftgas bags.

And the volley wasn't even over, for now the howitzers' shell shot arrived. As the shells exploded, Bernat was not ashamed to cower between the two bref guns, as most of the deck crew was doing the same. Even the steersmen had ducked down, squeezing as much of their bodies as possible behind the scanty protection of the wheels.

"Under the circumstances, can we not move?" Bernat shouted over the booming of the shells.

Josette returned a grave look and called up the companionway, "Get Chips to work on these girders. I'd rather my ship didn't snap in half." Blood was running from a wound on her forehead. She noticed Bernat's eyes on it and, as she reached up to pull a splinter out, said to him, "It's shaping up to be a hot day, Bernie."

* * *

CHIPS SAWED A plank on the catwalk above and ahead of Josette, sending a fine sprinkling of sawdust into her face. It was not the most irritating thing about standing in the open during an artillery bombardment, but after the deadly metal fragments flying in every direction, the sawdust was a close second.

Third was the goddamn music.

The Garnian national anthem floated up from a regimental band somewhere below, mingling discordantly with "Patriot's March," which was being played by another regiment's band farther along the line. Josette didn't know how well these regiments would do in a fight, but she hoped to God they fought better than they played the fife.

A cannonball shrieked past below, cutting the national anthem short with the sound of a shattered snare drum. The melody was replaced by sounds of agony, and she reflected that the music had not been so bad after all.

A peppering of rifle bullets hit the hurricane deck. A bullet hole opened in the wicker, not a yard from Josette's place on the deck. The gun crews sheltered in the shadows of their cannons, and were rewarded for their prudence when a ball that might have struck one of them skipped off the port bref gun instead, leaving the barrel ringing like a bell. Most shots missed the deck entirely and spent themselves in trivial damage to the bags and envelope. Cruising behind the line at an altitude of nine hundred feet, the crew members on *Mistral*'s hurricane deck were a long shot for even a skilled rifleman. Thank God Fieren hadn't thought to specify the altitude they were to hold station at, and had merely ordered them to remain below the clouds.

Which consoled Josette only a little as she stepped to the rail, into plain view of the Vin skirmishers, and looked out on the battlefield. She knew the situation was bad, and thought herself prepared, but the sight still staggered her. The Vin artillery, concentrating its fire on the weakest sector of the Garnian right flank, had torn bloody swaths through the line. In places, there were only enough men left to make a single rank where there should have been three. In a few spots, there was no line at all—only craters and corpses.

The reserve companies, who should have been plugging holes in the line, were instead huddled at the rear. In the chaos, perhaps, no one had ordered them forward, or perhaps they simply refused to advance into that smoking hell.

A thousand paces away, the six Vinzhalian columns marched on as if powered by clockwork. She saw a well-aimed Garnian cannonball tear through a file of men, but the files on either side stepped in to fill the gap, taking the place of the dead without orders or hesitation.

Her eyes flitted across the color guards dotted down the middle of each column, their regimental flags hanging limp in the light airs. By drawing a mental line from one flag to the next, and extending it until it intersected the Garnian line, she could see where each column would deploy. As she suspected, one or two aimed to keep the left flank occupied, while the rest would attack the right flank, where the Vin artillery was already eviscerating the weakest parts of the Garnian line.

A bullet hit the rail near Josette, snapping her away from her thoughts. She pulled paper and a short stub of pencil from her jacket pocket and began sketching the enemy disposition.

"Good God," Bernat said. He'd come up from behind and was now staring at the carnage below.

"It isn't as bad as it looks," she said, even though it was exactly as bad as it looked. "Our gun batteries are still firing."

And that, at least, was true. The Garnian cannons were in decent shape, dug in amid their little bastions all along the line. But they could not answer the concentrated fury of the Vins' grand battery, for each Garnian battery was an island unto itself, two to four guns projecting slightly ahead of the line, and they could not easily coordinate their fire with the other batteries.

She finished sketching the enemy's disposition and discreetly wrote a note in the corner that read, "Right flank will break at first contact with the enemy." She underlined the note and placed the sketch into a tin cylinder with a red streamer attached, which she then dropped over the side. Within a few minutes, an ensign on horseback came along, fetched it, and galloped back to the command tent. Ten minutes after that, the command tent's signal lamp began to flash.

"Orders coming in," the starboard signalman said, then winced as a shell exploded off the bow. "*Blimps will take up picket positions. Scout will take up relay position. Chasseurs will support the right flank.* Mistral *in vanguard.*" The signalman looked despondent. "Why us again?"

Josette ignored the lament. "Acknowledge the message. Send up a green flare and when *Ibis* breaks cloud cover, relay our orders."

Ibis appeared below the clouds and received the orders. After her acknowledging flash, there came an additional message which read, *How you holding up, Jo?*

"Signal *Ibis*: *You'll know too well shortly.*" The signal was sent and, true to prediction, *Ibis* came under fire soon after.

Ibis signaled each ship its orders as they broke cloud cover. The three chasseurs proceeded to the weak right flank, *Mistral* foremost, to add the pitiful fire of their bref guns to it. *Grouse*, the scout ship, was ordered to the relative safety of the rear, where it would take over for *Mistral* as signal ship.

The unweatherly blimps broke cloud cover last of all and farthest from their proper stations, and upon receiving their orders went forward to screen the chasseurs. They hadn't been given this job because they were the most capable, Josette knew, but because they were the most expendable. Their only mission was to warn of approaching Vin airships, by signal flare if practical, and by exploding under enemy fire if otherwise. The little *Swamp Hen* struggled along on *Mistral's* port side, and Josette was tempted to move her ship farther away from it, in case a lucky shell set off its inflammable air.

The blimp had no keel, only a gondola slung twenty feet below the bag, to keep a wide space between bag and boiler fire. On the prow of the blimp's gondola stood her captain, a fresh-faced junior lieutenant. His feet were on the rail and he leaned forward over the abyss, holding a martingale with one hand. When he saw Josette watching him, he saluted with the other.

Josette put her heels together and returned the salute. *Swamp Hen's* captain gave her a toothy grin that invited no sympathy or pathos, but only reflected an unrelenting commitment to this grim job that some poor bastard had to do.

"Steersmen, fall in ahead of *Swamp Hen*," Josette ordered.

"Uh, Captain?" Lupien asked, eyeing the explosive little blimp. "How far ahead?"

"Directly ahead, if you please." She noticed the trepidation in the deck crew. She lifted her voice to address them collectively. "Make no mistake, men, it's guts and glory from here on out. Anyone who doesn't like it is free to get off now." This elicited only a few polite chuckles, but the words did their work, steadying her crew.

When the squadron came within range of the columns, *Swamp Hen* split off and rose into the clouds, while *Mistral* and the other chasseurs took their new stations. Josette ordered, "Riflemen to the starboard rail. Bref guns commence firing."

Kember pulled the lanyard and the cannon spat its round shot into one of the center columns, slicing down a file of men, hitting the first in the head, the second in the shoulders, and the next in the guts. Kember fired the other gun to lesser but still brutal effect.

The column's foremost divisions chose to return the favor, firing a volley that must have numbered in the thousands of muskets. *Mistral*'s envelope fluttered with the impact of the bullets, most of which failed to penetrate even as far as the luftgas bags—their sting much reduced by nine hundred vertical feet. Josette leapt as one hit the deck under her foot. "God damn it," she shouted, hopping to the companionway and sitting down. Bernat and a signalman ran to help, but she waved them away.

A keening shriek came from the stern, drawing all eyes. Jutes shouted down the companionway, "Private Davies is hit, sir."

"How bad?" Josette asked, rubbing her foot.

"Not mortal, sir," Jutes said. He hesitated. "Didn't even get through his clothes. He'll be back on his feet in a few minutes, but in the meantime, if you need someone to sing soprano . . ." On the deck, every man winced in sympathetic pain.

THE VIN OFFICERS marched apart from their men, making them easy prey for Bernat. After firing six shots, he thought he'd killed a major and wounded a captain, and he could have kept it up if he hadn't run out of loaded weapons. As he helped reload, the drums drew his attention out to the columns.

Those damned columns were endless. He could shoot officers all day long and there would still be plenty left. As he watched, round shot from a Garnian cannon tore a swath through the column nearest *Mistral*, killing three men outright and knocking more off their feet from the concussion.

And now the columns had drawn near enough for the Garnian howitzers to blast at them with canister. Bernat saw a canister shot that must have killed twenty men at once, cutting through three ranks as easily as a scythe cut wheat.

But the column didn't stop, didn't even slow down. The files stepped in to close the gap and the ranks behind stepped briskly over the bodies of their comrades. In seconds, the column was as firm as ever and marching on to the beat of the drums.

Mistral's bref guns now coughed their own canister shot, adding to the butchery. To starboard, *Ibis* fired her two guns, and further on *Lapwing* did the same with her one. But the holes in the columns filled in with men as soon as they were made. There were always more men. Vins were dying by the score, but the bastards kept marching into fire, so cool they might have been on parade.

Bernat finished loading and raised the rifle to his shoulder, searching for a target. The spacing of the columns tightened up now, until the rungs were only a few paces apart. It was harder to spot the officers in that tangle of soldiers, but he saw a sergeant marching apart from the column.

As he took aim, a shell went off above and fragments tore through the envelope. He heard a scream from the keel. Gripped by a now-familiar desperation that goaded him into firing a shot, any shot, before it was too late, he fired hastily at the sergeant. He knew he'd missed.

"Goddamn it," he muttered, and set to reloading.

"Calmly," Josette said, stepping up behind him. She looked over the rail and nearly lost her own composure. "Oh, hell!"

Kember and Bernat both looked at her.

"Oh, hell!" she cried again. "Signal relay ship: *Columns on our right flank are not deploying into firing lines. Anticipate immediate bayonet charge.* Keep repeating that until they acknowledge."

Bernat swallowed, wet his lips nervously, and said, "I had thought that open-field bayonet charges were not quite the thing these days. I don't suppose you might be mistaken?"

She shook her head. "No. They're in a hurry—the cocky bastards—so they'll just tighten up their formations and charge straight in. They think our line is too ragged and undisciplined to stand up to a massed charge, and they have the proof in front of them."

There was another scream from above, and Bernat heard a saw grating on bone. "Who's hit?"

Josette just looked at the columns and said, "Concentrate on reloading." The bref guns fired and she turned around. "Reverse airscrews. Left rudder. Keep us in front of the column."

Bernat tried to concentrate on loading his rifle, but the sight below had a magnetic pull on his eyes. The front line of the Vin advance had reached the edge of the clearing, where the killing field was prepared for them, but the columns themselves were still so deep that it seemed impossible for the narrow, fractured Garnian line to hold against them.

As the Vins entered the clearing, the Garnians unleashed a ragged musket volley, the columns' front ranks hesitated, and their advance was checked—but for seconds only. The Vin formation had closed up even tighter in anticipation of the coming charge, and the next line of three ranks was only a few paces behind. That second line closed the gap and pushed against the first line, and then the third line pushed against the second, and in the end the hesitant men in the front had no choice but to advance or be trampled.

Some of them returned fire, but they had to shoot on the move, for the column advanced like a single beast. It was a monster made of men, possessing the sum of their rage but hardly any of their fear. And now it broke into a run, screaming with thousands of voices as it charged toward that thin line of Garnian defenders.

Josette raised her voice. "This is the moment of truth, everyone. Give our boys on the line a cheer!"

On the deck and all along the keel, the crew of the *Mistral* shouted together in a whooping battle cry.

"Better than that!"

Jutes added, "Shout or I will make you shout, I swear to God."

Airmen strained their lungs to be heard from so high above, to outshout the steamjack and the cacophony of battle. For all their effort, Bernat could hardly imagine the cheer arriving at the ears below as more than a faint yowl, and yet it seemed to buoy the spirits of the defenders, for they returned it with gusto. Bernat had his rifle loaded now, and was seeking targets in the columns when their front ranks hesitated again. He looked down to see a Garnian reserve regiment, its courage bolstered perhaps by the airship above it, dash into the line and fill the gaps. A band began to play the Garnian national anthem, which Bernat had never before cared for, but which now roused pride and steel in his heart.

The reinforced Garnian line fired a volley, and under that withering fire, the crisp cohesion of the Vin columns showed the first sign of wavering. As men fell, those behind had to slow to step over them, but the effect was not equal across the fronts of the columns. Where the casualties were few, the men ran on, as fast as the boot-sucking mud would allow. Where the casualties were high, the men behind were brought to a standstill as they picked their way across the tangled mass of the dead. Men who found themselves ahead of their comrades instinctively veered in the direction of their regimental standards, and so turned their neatly dressed ranks into a disordered blob. But even in disorder, the columns advanced. Quick or slow, they marched together across that killing ground, with their sergeants and corporals prodding them back into formation on the move.

The most advanced column reached the stream, and only had to charge through the water and smoke to break the Garnian line. But the front ranks stopped at the water's edge, as if confused by it, and in that moment the Garnians unleashed another devastating volley. Even through obscuring smoke, the range was under ten yards, and they could hardly miss.

The column's front ranks were flayed alive. The men who stepped up to replace them did not march on, but stopped to aim their muskets and return fire. Bernat saw the sergeant he'd missed earlier, screaming and pushing at his men from behind, urging them to charge. He took careful aim at the screaming man, steadied himself, and fired. This time there was nothing to distract him, for the Vin guns had shifted their fire to avoid hitting their own columns.

The smoke cleared to reveal the sergeant alive, but crawling through the mud and leaving blood behind him. His men, who'd advanced only a few paces under his coaxing, now stopped mid-stream to reload. They were jostled by the men behind, but fear had rippled back through the ranks, and the attack stalled in open ground.

The Garnian batteries made them pay for it, pouring hot iron and lead into their flanks. The small artillery batteries, spread out along the line in a manner that until now had struck Bernat as inefficient, were now perfectly positioned to fire slantwise into the columns. Canister and round shot, fired at point-blank range, tore furrows across the Vinzhalian ranks.

Yet the sight did not give him hope, for the column could stand amid this punishment for a quarter of an hour and still have enough men left to overpower the Garnian line, if they only charged across the few remaining yards.

So why didn't they charge? If they only charged, the cannons couldn't fire on them, and the volleys would stop, and the clash of cold steel would send the Garnians running. In a charge, they would find not just victory but safety. But they only stood there, paralyzed by fear.

"Break," Josette said. "Break, you bastards, break."

And they broke. It started in the column's rearmost ranks, which had taken the most punishment from the brisk Garnian cannon fire. For a time, the surviving sergeants had pushed all the harder, urging their men forward. But now even they seemed to despair of ever advancing out of this hellscape, and if the column was not to advance, where was there to go but back? So they stopped pushing, and when the men felt the pressure on their backs ease, and looked back to see their once-stalwart sergeants contemplating retreat, they gave up hope and decided the matter for themselves. The rout moved forward through the column in a wave.

Only one column had broken, and it was the smallest one at that, but to see even the least of those unstoppable beasts running away was enough to raise a victory cry aboard the airships. The enthusiasm spread to the defenders on the ground, who surely couldn't see a damn thing through the smoke, but who knew from the cheering above them that something had changed.

Ibis flashed a report to the command tent, and another message came back. Bernat didn't know what it was, but the men below fired one more volley before fixing bayonets. The defenders, not just inspired but ebullient, splashed forward through the stream. As they emerged from the smoke of their last volley, every Vin column but one broke.

Bernat stared in disbelief. It didn't seem possible that this pathetic, thin line of Garnians could charge at the unstoppable columns, much less send them running.

The single remaining Vin column delivered a devastating volley of its own and stood firm to receive the charge, but as the Garnians wrapped around the column and hit it from the flanks, and the airships concentrated all their fire on it, even this last, most courageous formation turned to flee the field.

They'd done it. God damn it, they'd done it. The rifleman next to Bernat grabbed him by the sides of the head, bellowed a triumphant whoop, and kissed him squarely on the mouth.

Some of the gun crew were dancing a little jig between their still-steaming cannons. Another was twirling a rammer over his head, hitting every man within arm's reach.

Josette's voice cut through the celebration. "Steamjack to emergency power! Elevators up full!"

Bernat looked forward. With the columns retreating, the Vin grand battery had renewed its fire. The first of the round shot shrieked past below.

THEY WERE COMING back.

Despite their losses, the Vins still outnumbered the Garnians by a wide margin. Their infantry was shaken, yes, but their fears would calm and they would be sent back out, reinforced and more determined than ever.

And when they came back again, they'd take the time to deploy properly, and they'd advance with Vin airships over their heads. The Vins hadn't risked their fragile, expensive ships in the first assault, when they were confident of an easy victory, but this time would be different. She scanned the cloud ceiling with her spyglass, looking for signs of them.

"Sir, can't we ascend into cloud cover?" Kember asked, her voice a whisper. The ensign was just coming down the companionway ladder.

Their orders said otherwise. "I believe I asked for a damage report, Ensign, not advice."

"Yes, sir," Kember said, swallowing. "That last shell cut a piece out of the steamjack housing, but it's still spinning. There are slow leaks in several of the bags, probably from musket balls, but the riggers haven't found all the holes. And . . . sir? It looks like Private Chase will live. Chips is getting pretty good with legs. But, ummm, Private Allard was bleeding out so fast when I saw him . . . I think he's, uh, probably gone by now, sir. And there are plenty of minor wounds to go around."

"Thank you, Ensign."

"*Ibis* signaling," a crewman at the rail said. "We're to come alongside her and receive relayed orders."

They maneuvered alongside and Captain Emery looked across the gap, his expression dark. He called through a speaking trumpet, "Doing all right?"

"We're holding together, sir," Josette called back. "But I'm worried they'll throw their chasseurs into the next attack."

Emery nodded. "To bomb our cannon batteries, I expect. The cannons are all that stopped the bastards last time. If they can knock a few batteries out from the air, or even just tie them up . . ." He trailed off, with the speaking trumpet still at his mouth.

"I'd like to take *Mistral* forward to join the pickets, sir." It was what Emery had been about to tell her, anyway. She'd just saved him the trouble of working up to it.

"Granted," he said, "and I'll send *Lapwing* to keep you company."

"Thank you, sir." She saluted.

Emery returned the salute. "Good hunting."

16

BERNAT PEERED INTO the soup of cloud, seeking signs of the enemy. He pointed to a darker area in front of the bow and asked Kember, "Is that one?"

"That's a cloud, my lord," the ensign said.

He looked into the solid cloud cover, blinked several times, and said, "Aren't they all?"

Ensign Kember was listening intently to another dark area in the clouds. "Not all. I think we'll make contact with *Nowhere Express* in a minute or two."

They soon made contact, but with *Swamp Hen* rather than *Nowhere Express.*

Kember looked disappointed in herself. "My ears must be a bit dull from standing so near the cannons."

Bernat attempted consolation by saying, "Not your fault. The two blimps sound identical, do they not?"

This elicited a roll of the eyes from not just Kember, but also Josette and half the deck crew.

Mistral came alongside *Swamp Hen* and, when the hurricane deck was even with their gondola, Josette called across, "Any sign of enemy chasseurs?"

"No, sir," the junior lieutenant in charge of *Swamp Hen* said, cupping his hands around his mouth. He had no speaking trumpet. The little blimp apparently didn't merit one.

"Well, they're coming," Josette said. "Go silent and keep a good lookout. If you see anything, run first and drop a flare when you can."

"We all have muskets, sir," the commander of *Swamp Hen* said.

"Good," Josette answered. "You can drop them along with the rest of your ballast. It'll help you gain altitude."

"Sir," he began.

"You understand your orders, Lieutenant?"

After a few seconds of gritting his teeth, the man nodded.

Mistral came around in a sweeping turn that only ended when she was pointed back toward the Garnian lines, and took station so far from *Swamp Hen* that Bernat could see no sign of the blimp through the clouds. Josette then ordered the steamjack to be shut down.

"Now we just wait for a ship to go past," she said to Bernat, "spin up the steamjack, come in behind them, and put two in their stern."

The steamjack shut down with a shuddering rattle. The airscrews creaked to a halt. The boiler issued a last whistle. The artillery still thundered somewhere below, but that battle seemed to belong to a different world now. The only sounds that felt real in *Mistral*'s world of impenetrable cloud were the creaks in the suspension cables and the sharp, staccato plinking of the bref guns as they cooled.

Bernat jumped in fright as Josette broke the spell, saying, "Now's a good time to get a drink of water, if you're thirsty."

He *was* thirsty. Parched, in fact, though he hadn't noticed until that moment. He began to wonder what else might be wrong with him that he wasn't aware of, but decided it was better not to think about it. He nodded to her and went up the companionway, where Jutes motioned for him to stop.

"If you'll just hold up here, my lord, it'll only be a minute. We have to mind the trim when we're free-ballooning."

Bernat nodded. "Of course, of course." He searched desperately for some topic on which to make small talk. "So, how're we holding up?"

Jutes gave a skewed grin and punched an overhead girder, disturbing sawdust all along its length. "Beautifully, my lord. She's a bitch, but she's a tough bitch."

Bernat glanced surreptitiously down at the hurricane deck. "Are we talking about the ship?" he asked.

The sergeant's grin grew. "Yes and no, my lord. Yes and no. Ah, there we are." He raised his voice. "Ballast coming aft!"

"Ballast coming forward!" Martel called from the stern.

"There you go, my lord," Jutes said.

Bernat started along the catwalk, past a gaggle of riggers working to patch a gaping, burnt-out hole in the envelope. He took the left fork around the gearbox, because he saw Grey working on the other side. He kept his eyes forward as he passed her, but when he spotted a ragged, two-foot gash in the steamjack housing, he couldn't help but stop and stare.

"Don't worry, my lord," Private Grey said, her head popping up behind the steamjack as if she were spring-loaded. "These things are built to take a beating." She gave the top of the steamjack a reassuring thump, which must have caused something to pop out inside the housing. Grey's face froze as some bit of metal tinkled down through the turbine blades, bouncing from one to the next, hitting a dozen on its way down, until after several long seconds it finally reached the bottom of the housing and began rolling back and forth inside. "Shit," she said.

Bernat walked on without saying a word, passing crewmen coming forward. In the sleeping quarters, he passed a recent amputee whose name he couldn't remember, and a bunk with a blood-soaked blanket spread over its unmoving burden.

Farther aft, crewmen were already lined up and slurping from the drinking reservoirs. As Bernat waited his turn, he gave a polite nod to Lieutenant Martel in the first officer's station near the auxiliary controls. "How goes the action?" he asked.

"Took a beating from that artillery," Martel said, "but we're in fine shape. With the stern reinforced, she's sturdy as an ox." Martel cocked his fist, aiming it at a girder.

Bernat held up his hands to stop him. "Pray do not punch the ship. I cannot imagine why the habit is suddenly so popular, but you'd be shocked at how little reassurance it has inspired up to now. I don't suppose, though, that you know how long we'll be waiting here?"

"Depends on how long it takes the Vins to organize their next attack. Might be as much as an hour."

"That long?" He frowned. "You should really think of having some food prepared, then. It's getting on lunchtime."

"You'd have to talk to the captain about that, my lord."

It was Bernat's turn at the reservoir. He drank his fill and then waited to go forward. He didn't have to wait long, for the deck crew had formed a line at the companionway, waiting to come aft and drink.

He stopped at his bunk to retrieve something to eat, but the man coming aft to counterbalance him didn't know that. He continued on, until the imbalance of weight brought the ship low by the tail, and the catwalk tilted at a noticeable angle.

A chorus of annoyed shouts drove Bernat to haste, and he grabbed the first foods he found in his baggage: a tin of date cookies and a jar of olives. He rushed forward with his pickings.

As he passed the steamjack, Grey held a bolt triumphantly toward him. "Found it!" she said in a cheerful tone. Her smile crumpled when she looked at the steamjack. "Now if I can just figure out where it came from." He left her with her eyes twitching back and forth across the engine.

On deck, Josette was at the taffrail, staring into the clouds. Her goggles were pulled up to her forehead, leaving clean circles around her eyes that, against the sweat-streaked soot covering the rest of her face, gave her a fixed appearance of surprise.

"Would you bring me the speaking trumpet?" she asked before Bernat could get a word in. He delivered it and stood by while Josette put it to her ear and listened.

He munched on his cookies and olives, waiting patiently for her to finish. But she only went from rail to rail, pointing it into the depths of those strange orange clouds and listening in every direction. When she came back around to his spot on the starboard rail, he leaned out and spoke into the end of the trumpet. "Would you like a cookie and an olive?"

She lowered the trumpet and looked at him, then at the food. "You nobles have the strangest culinary habits," she said, and went back to pointing her trumpet at clouds.

"I'll have an olive, my lord," Kember said, coming over from her station at the forward rail.

He gave her one and, after she'd eaten it, she spit the pit into her hand and slid it into a pocket of her uniform jacket. "Pray tell," he asked, "why don't you toss that pit over the side?"

The girl looked at him as if he were suggesting a homicide. "You can't do that, my lord. Oh, tell me you haven't been doing that."

Bernat did his best to look innocent.

"That's ballast, my lord. You should never drop ballast over the side, unless the captain orders it. That's . . . that's . . . that's as bad as venting luftgas, for that's what we might have to do to make up the difference in weight. Do you know what an olive pit's weight of luftgas costs, my lord?"

Bernat spread his hands. "Is it a lot?"

"Might as well throw dinars over the side."

"Oh my," he said. "Well, I've never been any good with money."

Kember went back to her station, shaking her head all the way.

Bernat finished his olives, taking care to spit the remaining pits into his handkerchief. He wondered about all the times

Josette had threatened to throw him overboard, and considered whether his value as ballast might have saved him.

With his olives gone, he ate his cookies. Then, with nothing left to occupy his time, he sat down at the rail and leaned his head against it. Looking out at the orange-red sky, he found it strangely peaceful. The cannons were still firing below, but they seemed to belong to an entirely different world, and had been firing for so long in any event that he hardly noticed them anymore. The only real reminder of danger was Josette, going from rail to rail with that absurd trumpet to her ear.

"I think I'll just rest my eyes," he said. "Let me know if we're all going to die."

Presently, he woke to a boot prodding his posterior. He gave a final snort and his eyes shot open to find the situation much the same as when he'd closed them. He blinked several times.

"Damn," he said, "and I was having the most wonderfully erotic dream."

The boot prodded him harder, this time in the ribs. It was attached to Josette, who shot him an irritated look.

"No one you know was in it," he lied.

"Everyone, back to your stations," she said. "Quietly."

Word was passed from man to man down the keel, and the ship became silent. Even the creaking of the deck suspension stopped as crewmen gripped the cables and put steady weight on them. The gun crews wrapped fire blankets around the cannon barrels, muffling the plinks as they cooled.

Bernat heard the thrum of airscrews coming from the direction of the Vin lines, behind *Mistral*'s tail. The sound grew louder, and was joined by a steamjack. The deck crew turned their heads as one, tracking the steamjack as it came nearer and passed to starboard.

A sudden anxiety showed on Josette's face. As the sound of the enemy airship receded in front of them, her head scanned slowly back toward the stern. There, only now becoming audible, was the thrum of another set of airscrews. She held up two fingers to Bernat, silently mouthing the words, "Two chasseurs."

The sound of the ship in front abruptly stopped. A few words of Vinzhalian drifted through the clouds, but Bernat couldn't make them out.

The trailing ship continued on for a little while, coming right abeam of *Mistral,* so close its amorphous shadow could be seen inching through the clouds above and to starboard. There, it shut down its steamjack and went silent. Now, with airships listening off the bow and abeam, silence on deck became a matter of survival.

After an eternity of waiting, there came a hiss from the clouds ahead, and the lead ship's steamjack spun up. Everyone listened off the stern, waiting for the other ship to restart its engine.

But it didn't. It just hung there, so still and so silent that Bernat lost track of where its shadow lay, and could no longer find it amid all the other vague and varied patches of shadow within the clouds.

The sound of the lead ship's steamjack had been growing fainter ahead, but now seemed steady. Josette moved to the forward rail and listened there. She suddenly whipped her head around to Kember, described a wide sweep with her hand, and mouthed, "They're circling back." She followed that with a series of intricate hand motions.

The ensign must have understood immediately, for she became pale and returned a questioning look. Josette only narrowed her eyes, and Kember moved quietly up the companionway. She came back a minute later, carrying a rocket nearly as tall as she was. Several crewmen went silently to her aid, moving the thing down the companionway and across the deck.

By the time Kember got it to the starboard side, the starboard gun crew already had a fire blanket draped over the rail and an impromptu launch rack made from the cannons' worming rod. They fit the rocket into the rack. As Josette lined it up, Bernat could only recall her words above Durum: "Rockets are a sign of desperation."

Ensign Kember brought the slow match from its tub, blew on it until the frayed end was cherry red, and touched it to the rocket's fuse. She backed away quickly, pushing Bernat to a safe distance as she retreated.

The flame sizzled along the short fuse, inching up until it disappeared inside the rocket motor. For a moment, Bernat thought it had failed, and then it shot away in a brilliant streak of light. He only avoided flash-blindness because Josette clapped her hand over his eyes at the last second.

While crewmen stamped out embers on the deck and checked the nearest suspension cables for damage, Bernat followed Josette to the rail and leaned out to follow the rocket's flight. He could see the light from its motor through the clouds, corkscrewing wildly as it gained altitude.

It dimmed with an audible sputter, then exploded into a brilliant, lingering white light that he recognized from university as phosphorus mirabilis. It was actually too bright at first to see the other ship by, for the light scattered through the clouds and seemed to come from every direction. As it faded, the silhouette of the ship became visible.

No, two silhouettes became visible, one on either side of the illumination, casting long, slanting shadows through the clouds below them. Bernat looked forward, to where the lead Vin ship was barely visible as a single cigar-shaped patch of darkness in the illuminated mist.

"Three ships?" he silently mouthed as he turned to Josette. But she wasn't there. He twisted farther and saw her moving to her post.

"Emergency start on the steamjack!" she shouted. "Then give me emergency power!"

"One of them must be ours, right?" Bernat asked.

But Josette spoke as if she hadn't heard. "Drop all forward ballast! Riggers to the stern! Elevators up full! Right hard rudder! Man your guns!"

"How can there be three?" Bernat twisted farther, all the way around, to come back to the view off the rail. The light of the rocket had faded now, leaving only the impenetrable orange blankness of the clouds.

"I want those guns ready to fire, Ensign!"

"Yes, sir!"

"But . . . our ships will be coming to help, right? Now that we've illuminated the enemy?"

The steamjack came to life in a way he'd never heard before, with a painful screech rather than its habitual whine. It shook the whole keel as it spun up, roiling and rumbling as if it might explode at any moment.

"Faster than that if you want to live," Josette shouted up the companionway, then climbed up to shout her orders directly to the mechanics. "Cut the secondary condensers and tie down the boiler safety valves! And then climb out and disengage the starboard airscrews."

"Perhaps one of them's *Lapwing*? Or *Ibis* come forward to help?" Bernat was still staring into the mist and still seeing nothing. Whatever the mechanics were doing to the engine, it was causing gouts of steam to erupt from the keel and merge into the clouds in swirling, turbulent whorls and eddies.

He was about to mutter something about signaling for support from the Garnian artillery when Josette whipped her head around to face him and said, "Bernie, grab a rifle and shut up, please."

"RUDDER'S MUSHY, SIR," Lupien said.

"Then pull it over harder!" Josette had a hand on the girder above her, and could feel the sprangs and pops as the keel bent. If it snapped, there would be no need for the enemy to fire a shot. *Mistral* would go down in a broken tangle of girders and fabric.

But their survival depended on the speed of the turn. The nearest Vin chasseur, the one ahead and to starboard, was already inside canister range. The first ship to bring its guns to bear would live; the other would die in a hail of musket balls. It all came down to who turned the fastest.

The clouds darkened ahead. Josette ran to the forward rail, between the guns, and peered into the mist. The enemy chasseur's bow loomed off the starboard quarter. It was a full compass point closer to bringing its guns into action.

"Pass the word," Josette called back. "Every crewman get to the center of the ship, immediately. Run, damn you!" Ensign Kember turned to follow the order when Josette stopped her. "Riflemen and ensigns excepted. I need you here to shoot the bastards."

As Kember watched the others run up the companionway, she asked, "You don't actually expect this to help, do you?"

"The flight engineers will tell you that a ship turns faster with her weight in the middle, rather than at the ends."

"The same flight engineers who said our original tail could hold up to any maneuver?"

Josette returned a stoic look. "Afraid you'll feel silly on the way down?" She looked along the bottom of the envelope, out past *Mistral*'s bow. The enemy's bow was distinct now, its surface bone-white against the orange mist. With ballast redistributed, *Mistral* did seem to be turning faster, but she couldn't tell if it was enough. She could hear shouts in Vin from the other ship's hurricane deck.

Bernat had his eyes closed in concentration. "The Vin captain is yelling at his rudderman," he said. "I thought I knew all their curse words, but there are a few in there I've never heard."

A grin grew on Josette's lips. "We have them," she said. And now she could see it plainly, as the Vin bow slid to the left in front of hers, coming so close that for a moment she thought they would scrape together. "Ready starboard gun! Put one through her hurricane deck."

Whether in confusion or frustration, the Vins fired both their bref guns. The canister shot whipped harmlessly through the air ahead of *Mistral,* while the muzzle flash illuminated two instants of the scene on the enemy deck, showing a captain pulling desperately on a rudder wheel.

"Everyone back to their stations!" Josette ordered.

She saw Kember's hand tighten around the starboard gun's lanyard, and said in a calm voice, "Steady, Ensign." Too many chasseurs had wasted too many critical shots on an enemy's envelope, tearing open a gas bag or two, when if they'd only waited a few seconds longer, a critical spot would have come to bear. When it was life or death, there was always the urge to take action, any action, even if the moment wasn't ripe for it. The impulse had to be swallowed down. "Patience."

And Kember showed patience. She waited until the Vin deck was just visible ahead, the cannon lined up perfectly with it, and only then did she yank the lanyard.

The gun shot back on its slide, spitting metal and flame at so close a range that the Vin hurricane deck, already obscured by cloud, disappeared completely in the smoke. From within it came a sound like the patter of a hard rain, and the twangs that followed spoke to the damage wrought to control lines and suspension cables. "Hold fire," Josette said, when she saw Kember go to the port gun. "Save the next shot for their steamjack. Avoid the boiler. A boiler explosion at this range would sink us too."

When *Mistral*'s bow was pointed at the enemy's first set of airscrews, Kember fired. The canister shredded them, sending shards of mahogany flying into both ships' envelopes, while the spreading fan of musket balls flew on to pierce the enemy's condenser and steamjack. Their turbine coughed and rattled to a grating stop, as steam poured from the gaping hole the canister had torn in the chasseur's canvas.

Mistral shuddered as her bow struck the other ship, but it was a glancing collision, and the ships scraped past each other in the mist. As their hurricane decks passed, Josette looked over to see cables dangling limply from the deck, the steersmen stations in ruins, and the companionway riddled with holes. No living thing was visible on the other deck, but a soft, whimpering moan rose from somewhere between their bref guns.

Someone—Josette thought it was the first officer—ran boldly down the perforated companionway, and made it halfway to the deck before two red blots erupted on his chest. Bernat and another rifleman had fired simultaneously. The Vin officer fell the rest of the way, crashing down the companionway steps to lie tangled and still on the deck.

Both shooters stood stunned for a moment, their faces frozen in guilt, as if they were children caught at some mischief. The spell was only broken when the loader returned and handed them fresh rifles.

"Elevators up six degrees," Josette said. "I don't want to get an airscrew tangled in their wreckage." She put a hand on Bernat's shoulder and, after he leapt in fright, said to him, "Ask for their surrender."

Bernat shouted the message across. Within moments, a blue

flare rose from the chasseur's tail and fell through the clouds ahead of *Mistral*. From this distance, Josette could hear crewmen on the surrendered ship hauling on lines to open their luftgas vents. The Vin ship began to sink moments later.

Bernat turned to Josette and asked, "How do we deal with the other two?"

Josette lowered her voice. "I have a plan. Is your Vin accent convincing enough to pull off a ruse?"

"My tutor said it was the worst he'd ever heard."

"Damn. Well at least they won't shoot until they've sorted out who just surrendered."

As if timing themselves especially to make a fool of her, the Vin chasseur to starboard fired. Josette dropped to the deck and called, "Down!" as soon as she saw the stab of fire lighting the clouds, but it was a futile gesture, for the fury of the shot reached her ship before the word left her mouth.

The sharp, high sounds of metal smashing on metal stabbed her ears as a hail of musket balls tore through *Mistral*'s guts. The steamjack made a keening wail as turbine blades snapped off and were dragged by the still-spinning mechanism, scraping against the housing as they went. As the turbine came to a grinding halt, the airscrews stopped along with it, not coming to their usual gentle stop, but locking up abruptly, arrested by the shattered steamjack. Within seconds, the only sound from the engine was a long whistle broken by rumbling burps.

Josette ordered, "Keep the rudder hard over," before she was consciously aware of the logic behind the order. The rationale fell into place in the moments that followed: the ship to starboard had *Mistral* in its sights and wouldn't let go. Even if she had a working steamjack, no matter which way *Mistral* turned, no matter how she maneuvered, the Vin ship had to turn only a fraction as hard to track them. But *Mistral* might have just enough momentum left to finish her turn and point her guns back at them.

Above her, Jutes was picking himself up. He looked back along the keel and his mouth fell open. He called down the companionway in a broken voice, "Vincent is . . . Gears is hit bad. Someone else is dead."

"Who?" Josette asked. She hurried halfway up the companionway ladder, stuck her head into the keel, and looked back, her eyes level with the catwalk.

"Can't tell, sir," Jutes said, his face white.

It wasn't the other mechanic. That was what Josette needed to know. The mechanic's mate, whole save for scrapes and cuts, was kneeling over Gears, who was streaming blood from holes in his belly, chest, and arm. Gears was alive for now, but just one of the musket balls in his chest and gut would have been a death sentence, let alone the three or four she could see.

The other casualty had no head or neck, and only one shoulder. Its blood was pouring through the wicker of the catwalk to rain down on the inner side of the envelope, pooling there and soaking in.

Josette's mind continued to give orders, but she found herself paralyzed by the sight, and the words stuck in her throat. The commands piled up inside her, until she screamed within, cursing her weakness and demanding that she take charge of her own voice. But her eyes swung manically between the dead crewman and the soon-to-be dead chief mechanic. Her voice remained bottled up, while precious seconds ticked by.

Finally the pressure was too great, and it erupted from her in a rage. "Private Grey! Back to your fucking post and get my goddamn engine working!"

Grey looked confused, as if she hadn't heard right. She stared at the strips of twisted metal that, moments earlier, had been a steamjack turbine casing. "That thing? Captain, it's not going to run again."

Josette had now regained control, and she spoke with a cold precision. "It is going to run, Private Grey, and you are the one who must make it run. And if the suffering of Warrant Officer Sourdeval is what stands in the way of your duty, then I will shoot him in the head myself, to get you moving."

The chief mechanic's wide eyes turned on her. She'd made the threat in such icy tones that no one knew whether she might actually do it—she wasn't sure herself. Gears pushed Grey away, and nodded to her when she looked at him. "You can," he mouthed silently, blood bubbling at the corners of his mouth.

"Everyone else will assist the mechanic's mate in any way possible. All other repairs are pointless until the steamjack is spinning." She pointed at the decapitated body. "And for God's sake, someone put that over the side."

The nearest crewman leapt to the duty without hesitation, though the victim was a comrade and likely a friend, because no one wanted a corpse aboard in the midst of battle. Apart from the distracting smell of hot blood and shit, it was too much of a reminder of what might lie in store, and so it was shoved unceremoniously through a port in the keel, along with any fleeting decency still held for the dead.

She spent another moment assessing the damage. The steamjack was perforated in two dozen places, and really might never spin again. The boiler was dented but unperforated, and so would not explode—at least not in the next few seconds. The keel around the steamjack was a shredded mess, but it was holding together.

She returned to the deck. *Mistral* was slowing but still coming about. Her guns would come to bear on the enemy, but not before they got another shot off. "Anyone who is able will fire the guns when they bear," she said, giving authority to fire at will over to whoever was the least bullet-ridden when the time came. "Gun crews may shelter behind their cannons. Riflemen take the forward rail, stay low, and fire through the gun ports."

Bernat stepped closer, rifle in hand. "Fire at what?" he asked, motioning to the obscuring mist ahead, in which the enemy ship was only visible as a dark shadow.

"At wherever you think their gondola may be," she said. "It may rattle them."

"Perhaps I should fire rockets instead?"

She shot him an ironic look, but he went forward with the others. It would put more of her crew in a position of relative safety next to the gun carriages, at least, and keep their attention on the enemy ahead of them, when they might otherwise obsess over the other ship that must by now be coming in from behind. By her best estimate, the other ship would be in canister range within the next minute, and then *Mistral* would be raked fore and aft.

Bernat fired, and she heard his bullet plink off of the other ship's bref gun. In response, a stab of fire shot from the center of their deck. Josette, already primed for it, dove to the deck as musket balls tore through wood and fabric above her.

She lifted her head, expecting to find the gun crews, the riflemen, and herself flayed into a bloody mess. She scanned her eyes across them from left to right, then back again.

Not a man was hurt. Ensign Kember looked back at her, bewildered.

They'd fired too early. Josette laughed and said, "We're still in it!" She kept her eyes forward even as she yanked the pullropes above her, releasing emergency ballast to keep her ship in the air and the bow pointed at the enemy.

Above, she could hear the rush of luftgas escaping from burst bags. The damage was serious, but the stupid bastards had wasted their shot firing obliquely through *Mistral*'s envelope, when a few seconds more would have given them a shot at the hurricane deck.

"To your guns!" she called. "Don't make their mistake, Ensign."

She hardly needed to say it. Kember was the picture of sangfroid, staring coolly along the barrel of the port bref gun as it traversed with aching slowness across the mist-blurred enemy's belly. Only when it was perfectly lined up did she pull the lanyard and unleash a shot that cut into them amidships and came out through the tail. The enemy ship pitched up as buoyancy was lost from her stern, but she still floated and she still had teeth.

"Shift ballast aft! We'll put another one into her deck!" Josette cried up the companionway. Jutes repeated the order and *Mistral*'s weight shifted tailward as riggers ran aft along the catwalk, bringing the ship up by the bow.

Ensign Kember stood behind the starboard gun as *Mistral* tilted up. A musket fired on the enemy deck, and the ball hit to Kember's right. She flinched but held her ground. Bernat raised his rifle and fired; where the musket shot had come from, there now came a scream.

An eternity passed as *Mistral* pitched up and the bref gun slowly elevated, until finally the enemy's hurricane deck crept out of eclipse behind the bow and Kember fired her bref gun. The effect was worth the wait. Where the canister hit, the Vins' keel buckled, kinking the line of the enemy ship so that she caved in at the middle. Girders splintered all along their keel, bursting bags from one end of the ship to the other. She plunged downward with such speed that the suction of her passing pulled *Mistral* forward from a dead stop.

Bernat and half the cannoneers were leaning over the side, watching the other ship go down. Josette screamed at them to stay low, then called up to Jutes, "Make sure everyone's lying flat, Sergeant!"

Though confused at first, all her crew seemed to remember the third ship at the same moment. Josette looked aft, trying to find the ship that was coming to kill them amid the orange clouds. She couldn't make it out. It ought to be directly astern of them by now, but she could see only vague shadows.

She saw the stab of flame.

No, she saw four tiny stabs of flame, followed by faraway musket cracks. "Goddamn it, I ordered that blimp to run," she said. The third Vin chasseur wasn't engaging *Mistral* because *Swamp Hen* had engaged it. Now she saw the chasseur as it fired a flaming carcass shot that streaked across the sky from left to right.

She ran up the companionway. "Everyone back up! Back to work! I need my steamjack running right now!"

ONCE THE RIFLES were reloaded, Bernat went up the companionway to see if he could help, but Jutes stood in the way and shook his head.

"Might be best if you didn't venture aft, my lord."

While Bernat was trying to work out the reason for this, something sharp and heavy fell from the turbine assembly, landing with a crash in a detached section of the housing. Steam gushed from the space it left, until Grey ran to the boiler and closed a valve. Josette unleashed a roiling torrent of curses as she strained to lift the fallen piece with the help of two crewmen.

"There's that, for one," Jutes said.

Ensign Kember came up the companionway, moving past Jutes before he could speak a word of caution. "Sir," she reported to Josette, who was elbow-deep in the turbine assembly. "We're still sinking."

"Then toss the sand ballast and whatever's left of the stores," Josette said, without looking away from her work.

"We don't have any left, and we're about to drop below a thousand feet and lose cloud cover."

"Then toss the round shot!" Under the keel, the sound

of drums could be heard. "We won't need it in this soup, anyway, and you might even hit some Vin fusiliers going past below."

"Are we out of the fight?" Bernat asked Jutes, at what he thought was a low volume.

Josette's eyes whipped toward him. "What's that?"

He took a step back, nearly falling down the companionway.

"What did you say?" she asked again. Before he could answer, she went on. "This ship is not out of the fight. This fight will not last much longer by the sound of it, but by God, *Mistral* will be in it." She looked at Grey and the nearby crewmen. "Everyone understand that?"

"I, ah, I think I'll be on deck," Bernat said.

Jutes nodded. "That may be best, my lord."

At the rail, Bernat watched the battle between blimp and chasseur take place in the haze ahead. The action was moving steadily away, he thought. It seemed to be moving higher in the sky, too, but that might only be *Mistral* sinking.

As another carcass shot streaked toward the *Swamp Hen*, one of the cannoneers asked, "How the hell is that blimp still alive?"

"The chasseur's more interested in getting to our cannon batteries than fighting a blimp," Lupien said from the rudder station. "See how she's farther away every time she fires? And the blimp can turn faster than any chasseur. If she stays close, she can keep out of their gun sights. I pulled that trick myself a few times, when I was rudderman on a blimp in Quah."

Half a dozen skeptical eyes turned to Lupien.

"Well, once or twice," Lupien admitted. Under further stares, he caved. "Okay, once, for a few minutes, before a friendly chasseur rescued us."

The cannoneers were now tossing cannonballs over the side, and it was beginning to have an effect. When Bernat next saw the distant flash of the blimp's four muskets firing together, it was nearer to level. "We're rising," he said. "I think we're light."

"Give it a minute," Kember said. "With all the holes in us, we'll be heavy again soon enough." She was about to say something else when a cannon fired somewhere off the port bow. Unlike the incendiary carcass shot fired by the Vin chasseur at the inflammable blimp, this one exploded in the eye-searing starburst of shell shot.

Kember shouted back, "*Lapwing*'s joined."

When Jutes relayed the message, it did not elicit the enthusiasm that Bernat expected. Far from taking the pressure off, it caused Josette to erupt into another fit of cursing about getting *Mistral* into the fight before it was too late.

"I'd thought the news of another ship taking over for us would make her happy," he said to Kember.

Kember made an incredulous face. "You thought the captain would be happy to have another airship arrive late to the scene and steal our glory? Apologies for being blunt, my lord, but you're a very naive fellow."

He shrugged and said, "You may be right."

As Bernat watched the battle ahead, a slurping gurgle sounded from the keel, followed by a string of staccato clinks that only faded when eclipsed by a hellish scream rising from the steamjack. But when the screaming of metal on metal subsided, the steamjack was spinning. It was grinding as it turned, and making the most disconcerting honking sound at regular intervals, but it was spinning. And now that the gears were engaged, the airscrews were beginning to turn, and *Mistral* dragged herself forward.

"I don't know how long it's gonna last, Captain," he could hear Grey saying from the keel.

"You will make it last, Private," Josette said at the companionway. She came down the steps, still rubbing grease from her hands with a stained rag. "Corporal Lupien, steer straight at them."

MISTRAL LIMPED TOWARD the aerial battle, hemorrhaging steam and luftgas as the drums of the Vin advance played somewhere below. On the cusp of shell range, Josette heard a sound behind her like a musket ball hitting metal.

She immediately knew what had happened. They'd had to jury-rig several of the steam nozzles, and one of the damn things had come off. She could already hear it flying around inside the steamjack, striking blades and ricocheting in the tight space. If it caught in one of the gaps left by a broken blade, it might tear the entire assembly to pieces.

"Shut her down!" she called, turning to go up the companionway.

Grey was already turning valves to cut off the flow of steam. Now it was the private's turn to utter an unending stream of curses. She took up a wrench and began the tedious process of removing the housing to get at the steamjack.

Josette was about to go back to help, but saw several crewmen already assisting, and knew that she'd only be in the way of this operation. Only one person was required to get at the steam nozzle, and anyone else could only help by passing tools or holding a pan of loose bolts.

Josette returned to the deck. Ahead, *Lapwing* and the Vin chasseur were exchanging shell shot. If it were her out there, she'd want to close in and finish the matter with canister, but these two seemed content to dillydally at medium range. Flickering light suggested fires aboard both chasseurs.

"The ship to port is *Lapwing*?" she asked Ensign Kember, who had been watching without interruption.

"Yes, sir. She's having a hard time of it, but with *Swamp*

Hen pricking the enemy ship from the other side, I think she can hold on."

Josette stood and watched the exchange. It was all she could do, apart from yelling at the mechanic's mate to hurry up. She was about to do exactly that when a flickering light in the clouds ahead betrayed another fire. It was a little to starboard, which might put it on the tail of the Vin ship.

No. It was burning upward in a straight line, which meant it was spreading along a gondola's suspension cable. "Good God," she said.

"You don't think it's the blimp, do you?" Ensign Kember asked.

She'd hardly gotten the words out when she received her answer. The fire creeping up *Swamp Hen*'s suspension cable had reached the envelope, and now it flashed into a brilliant red spot, which bloomed into the outline of the blimp's envelope. For a moment, it illuminated *Swamp Hen* from within, making her look like some gigantic, festive paper lantern. In the next moment, the fire burnt itself out and left nothing but empty cloud. The noise of it reached them as a hollow thump, which struck Josette as a strangely subdued sound with which to send four men plummeting to their deaths.

She pushed the thought away and set her mind to how *Swamp Hen*'s loss affected the tactical situation. It doomed *Lapwing*, most likely, and *Mistral* as well, if it permitted the enemy ship to deal with them one at a time. So she had to bring *Mistral* quickly into the fight, in any capacity possible. "Fire the guns," she ordered.

"We can't aim them without power, sir."

"Thank you for that insight, Ensign. Now fire the damn guns."

It would at least give the enemy chasseur something else to think about. If they believed they were under fire, they might even return fire on *Mistral,* providing *Lapwing* a small window in which to take decisive action.

Bernat, standing at the rail and seeming to understand the implication of the order, asked, "Tell me, is 'sacrificial distraction' a higher or lower rank than 'ballast,' in the air corps?"

"Lower," Josette said, "but it comes with a free cannonball, if you can catch it."

"I'd like to decline that honor," he said, "but I'll be pleased to wave as it goes past."

Kember stood behind her cannon. She pulled the lanyard and the bref gun spit impotent smoke and fire into the clouds. She repeated the procedure on the other gun.

After a few quiet seconds, Bernat asked, "Did it work?"

A blot of flame colored the clouds ahead. "Down!" Josette shouted, before dropping to the deck. The enemy's shot tore through the space where her body had been, knocking the air out of her lungs with the concussion of its passage. It ripped through the companionway stairs behind her, showering the aft end of the hurricane deck with shards of oak.

As she gasped for breath, she heard Bernat say, "I forgot to wave."

She looked up to see him leaning against the rail. "I think you forgot to duck," she said.

He swallowed. "And that as well."

He helped her to her feet, and she stood staring at the demolition of the companionway ladder. The shot would have gone straight through her chest if she'd been standing.

"Shall I fire again, sir?" Kember asked.

Josette shook her head. "No. If we fire from the same place, they'll know we've lost power."

"And that would be a shame," Bernat added, "because they might lose interest in killing us."

"Precisely," Josette said, without irony. She turned and went up the companionway, stepping mindfully on only the intact steps. In the keel, Grey was bolting the housing back onto the steamjack.

Another cannon blast sent the deck crew, Bernat included this time, dropping to the deck. Josette half scrambled, half fell from the companionway. Yet no cannonball came. Instead, a shell burst about a hundred yards in front of *Mistral*, in the spot she would have been in if she were still under power.

"Where the hell is *Lapwing*?" Josette asked, returning to her station.

"She's that glowing patch over there, sir," Kember said. "I think she's taken advantage of the distraction to stop and fight her fires."

"Goddamn it!" Josette shouted. "Grey, where is my goddamn power?"

"Just bringing it up now, Captain!"

The steamjack came back online, spinning up with the same screeching complaints as before. Josette turned forward and watched for the next discharge. When it came, and the rest of the deck crew dropped to the deck, she remained standing, fixing her eyes on the spot and burning it into her mind.

The shell's explosion brightened the clouds around *Mistral*'s bow, making a wedge of shadow under it. Josette felt the superstructure shake with the concussion of the blast, saw smoking fragments of the shell casing rip through the bottom of the envelope, and heard shouts of "Fire!" from the forward frames. She could see the flame casting a flickering glow on the clouds ahead, even as the light of the explosion faded.

"Damage control forward," she ordered.

"Sir?" Jutes asked through the companionway. "It's in a bad spot. I think we should stop and put this one out."

"Like hell we're stopping. We just got moving again. Engine ahead, best possible speed. Ensign, load shell. Put your shot right there." She pointed her open hand at the bearing and inclination where she calculated the Vin chasseur would now lie.

As *Mistral* shuddered forward, the flames on her nose licked back along the envelope. The forward motion was helping to feed and spread the fire, but at least the ship was steerable and could point her guns.

Kember fired the port cannon. The shell whistled through the clouds and burst, casting the shadow of a chasseur back toward *Mistral*. "Long!" Kember cried.

The fuse was set shorter this time, the starboard cannon loaded. They fired almost simultaneously with the enemy ship, the shells whistling past each other in the air. The Vin shell burst above *Mistral* to send hot metal tearing through her amidships, while the Garnian shell burst at nearly the same time, but Josette couldn't tell where it had hit until the fires broke out and she saw the smoldering outline of a chasseur's bow. She'd hit them on the port side of their nose cone.

The enemy ship was now plain in the clouds, given away by the expanding ring of flame burning through its envelope. She imagined that her ship must look much the same, except that her ship was driving on, barreling down upon them, while the enemy chasseur had cut its engine and was coming to a halt.

"Reload with canister," she ordered.

"Sir, I really think we ought to stop," Jutes called.

"Tell the riggers to cut away the fabric of the envelope one frame ahead of the fire," she said, by way of reply.

"Which fire?" Jutes asked, a tinge of resigned irony in his voice.

"The big one."

"Which big one, sir?"

She looked up at him, and could see him haloed in red, illuminated from both sides by flickering light. She'd imagined the midships hit as something minor, but apparently it wasn't. "The front one," she said.

"Sir," he said, and relayed the order.

Another cannon sounded through the mist, not from the enemy chasseur but from close behind it. The Vin ship's flaming bow, now outlined as bright as day, heaved upward as if yanked by strings. It could only be due to a canister shot hitting her in the stern.

"I think we've shamed *Lapwing* back into action," Josette said to Bernat.

"That, or she envies the size of our fires."

Before Ensign Kember could add another canister shot to the mix, the enemy chasseur sent up a blue flare. She threw down her lanyard in frustration. "Damn it," she said as she watched the enemy ship drift slowly downward, "we came all this way for nothing."

"Cut steamjack," Josette ordered. "All hands, damage control!"

She turned and made her way up what was left of the companionway ladder. As she crested the top and looked along the keel, she could see her ship was already filled with choking black smoke.

Bernat was right behind her, but stopped short when he saw it. "My God," he said, the flickering flames reflected in his eyes.

"I'm sorry, Bernie," she said. "I fear I've killed us all."

17

GENERAL LORD FIEREN Hinkal sat atop his horse, his second mount of the day, and stared into his teacup. His first horse lay amid her own entrails, back at his command tent. The unlucky beast, worth more than five hundred liras, had been hit by round shot with him astride her, throwing him off and absolutely ruining his best jacket to boot.

He took a sip of tea, careful not to wet his mustache, and found it cold. He poured it out and called, "Tea!"

While one of his aides galloped off to retrieve a teapot, he looked out onto the field. From this little hillock behind the Garnian line, he could see the Vin columns advancing, their screen of skirmishers in front. And then there were his dragoons, closing in on the skirmish line from the right, firing their carbines at a trot instead of charging home like they should have done.

"Gaston!"

Gaston appeared at his side and saluted. "Sir."

"Gaston, what in hell is wrong with those horsemen? Why don't they charge?"

Gaston looked at the field. A shell exploding overhead made both their horses jump. "I believe they're having trouble in the mud, sir," he said when he had his horse under control. "The good news is the Vin horsemen have even farther to go, over ground just as muddy."

It was true. Hell, it was part of the reason he'd chosen this place to make his stand—it neutralized the Vins' advantage in cavalry—but he hadn't counted on conditions this bad. As he watched, the flank of the Vin skirmish line fired a rippling volley that put down dozens of dragoons. "Goddamn it!" he bellowed.

They were only skirmishers, which God in His wisdom had placed on Earth so they could be slaughtered by horsemen, and yet here they were, taking a piss on his dragoons.

Gaston had a telescope to his eye. He lowered it and said, "I fear we cannot blunt this assault, sir. We might think of an ordered withdrawal."

"To where, Gaston?" He paused to take a cup of tea from the aide he'd sent out. He sipped it. Nice and hot. Wonderful. "To Arle? To be trapped there by encircling forces? No, it's here or nowhere."

He could tell Gaston didn't agree, but Gaston was a good officer and said nothing of it.

General Lord Fieren sipped his tea, accidentally wetting his mustache when a round shot shrieked overhead and his horse shied. "Goddamn it," he muttered. "Can nothing go right today?"

"There's another one, sir," said the aide to his left.

He looked up to see an airship fall, burning, from the clouds. "Not a good day for airmen," he said. "Is it ours or theirs?"

Gaston was watching it through a telescope. "Hard to tell through all the smoke, sir. And I think its bow markings have burned away."

"Any chance it's that harlot's ship? The one my idiot nephew is aboard?" He'd asked much the same question of the other falling ships, but until now the big ones had all been Vin. He dearly hoped the answer would be different this time—that the Vins had rid him of that troublesome little bastard. If only that ship would do him the courtesy of going down with all hands, then he could make up any story he liked about the harlot's cowardice in the face of danger, end this foolishness about an integrated service, and go back to having a proper army.

"I think it may indeed be the *Mistral,* sir," Gaston said. "And I wouldn't put money on anyone escaping that wreckage alive."

General Lord Fieren sipped his tea. "What a terrible shame," he said. "Isn't that a terrible shame, Gaston?"

"I was just about to say what a terrible shame it is, sir. Just terrible."

The fires aboard the ship licked higher and it fell faster. The inert hulk landed on the field somewhere behind the Vin advance, its superstructure collapsing in on itself and sending up a swarm of burning embers. Looking through his telescope, General Lord Fieren saw no one escape.

"It crashed right in the line of their grand battery, sir," Gaston said. "The smoke may throw off their aim."

"It's nice to see an airship making itself useful for once," General Lord Fieren said, lowering his telescope. The comment brought a few polite chuckles from his staff. He turned his attention to dispatches and reports.

"Our dragoons are about to make contact with the Vin skirmish line, sir," Gaston said, a few minutes later.

He looked. "Too damn late to do any good." The skirmishers were finally dying under dragoons' sabers, and the line infantry in the rightmost column was forming square, a prickly formation which made them all but immune to cavalry attack, but from which they couldn't attack the Garnian line. But it was only that one column. The others continued on without missing a step, and would soon deploy, if he didn't miss his guess.

They came on through artillery fire, closing ranks as men fell, seemingly undiminished no matter how many died. Through his telescope, he could now make out the blue, red, and gold of a Vin royal guards regiment coming right for one of his artillery batteries. These battle-hardened veterans didn't blob up and veer away from the danger of the guns, as the conscripts had during the first attack, but marched straight into the dragon's maw.

"Goddamn," he said, collapsing his telescope with a slap of his palm.

"If we lose those guns," Gaston said, "we'll lose the whole flank."

"Goddamn!"

Just before entering musket range, the Vin columns deployed into mixed order, the rear ranks fanning out to form firing lines that would engage his infantry, while the front ranks massed together to assault and silence his artillery bastions. He had to admire the bastards. They deployed as if practicing on a parade ground, rather than marching through ankle-deep mud while under cannon fire.

And now they advanced calmly against volleyed muskets. Along the defensive line in front of him, he heard the crisp, satisfying bang of the regular army regiments firing by platoon, and the uneven crackle of the militia regiments doing their feeble best to fire together. The Vin front ranks had to be getting a damned good thrashing, but from this vantage point he couldn't see it for himself, for by the time the smoke of a volley cleared, the gaps were closed. All he could see were unbroken ranks of men in the Vin firing line, and forests of gleaming bayonets in the massed columns.

"Send any airship you can to attack their center," he said. "I doubt it'll do any good, but it can hardly hurt at this point."

Gaston took a small notebook out of his jacket pocket and consulted it. "Sir, those would be the *Ibis* and the *Grouse*. The *Grouse* is only a scout ship."

"Yes, yes, those," Lord Fieren said, waving his hand in the direction of the Vins.

Gaston scribbled the orders on a page, tore it out, and handed it to another aide. The aide galloped off to the command tent. When Gaston pushed the notebook into his pocket and looked up, his eyes caught on something ahead. "Sir," he said, and his voice trailed off.

"What is it, man?"

"Another airship, sir."

Lord Fieren followed his gaze. Above and behind the Vin formations, an airship emerged from the glowing brimstone of the low cloud. It streamed smoke and belched steam behind it, like some infernal demon escaping from hell. He looked through his telescope and could not believe the ship was still in the air. The damn thing looked like a burnt-out barn. Its nose was nothing but a charred skeleton of girders, and there were similar wounds on its flanks. Where the skin wasn't burnt out entirely, it was peppered with tears, large and small, that flapped in the wind as it drove forward.

"What ship is that?" he asked.

"Can't tell," Gaston said. "Its markings are burned away." A lamp began to flash from the ship's gondola. "It's signaling, sir."

"Well, I can see that, man! What's it say?"

Gaston lowered his telescope, frowning in confusion. "It says . . . 'Tallyho.' "

"HAVE WE SPOTTED the fox?" Bernat asked.

"Right there," Josette said, pointing to a battalion of elite Vinzhalian infantry directly ahead.

"That's, uh . . . that's not a fox," Bernat said. "Has an air of wolf about it, as a matter of fact."

"Whatever it is," Josette said, "it's heading right for a critical gun battery, and we're going to stop it."

Bernat looked back along the length of the ship. "In this?"

Josette had to admit that her ship was a wreck. *Mistral* was still streaming smoke from the extinguished fires. In several frames, the envelope was more ash than canvas. The steam-jack was barely working, and threatened to give out entirely at any moment. Two of the nine gas bags had burst outright, and the rest were leaking so fast she'd soon have to drop the cannons over the side just to stay in the air.

"She's still flying," Josette said.

"In spite of our best efforts."

"Elevators up another degree," she ordered. "Let's try to stay above effective musket range. Cannoneers, ready bombs. Shortest fuses, please."

Closer to the Garnian line, the Vins were in mixed order. That alone showed they were taking this assault more seriously than the last, and were not counting on the Garnian line to fall into shambles at their very approach. As a further caution, they had a second set of columns waiting in reserve, standing ready to make another assault if this one should fail.

Mistral sputtered and coughed along, coming at one of the reserve columns from behind. They cheered *Mistral* when she approached, and Josette had to laugh. "They think we're a Vin ship," she said. "Someone told them an airship was coming forward to support the attack, and here we are."

Ahead, one of the Garnian artillery batteries was already under assault. Amid the smoke from its four cannons and the hundreds of muskets firing from the flanking regiments, she couldn't tell who was winning. She only knew that the cannons suddenly stopped firing, their booming thunder replaced by the clash of swords and bayonets.

Mistral passed over the reserves and reached the rearmost ranks of the nearest Vin assault, where men who could smell victory were pushing their way forward, striving to be a part of it. "Cannoneers, light your bombs and drop immediately," Josette said. "Drop as soon as the fuse is lit. Don't wait." With the fuses so short, a cannoneer's hesitation might blow the entire hurricane deck apart.

The cannoneers blew on their slow matches, set the glowing ends to their fuses, and dropped the shells. One fell amid the ranks and would have killed a score of fusiliers if one of them hadn't leapt at the smoking shell and pulled the fuse out before it could detonate. Two shells exploded early. Hot metal fell into the ranks, hurting no one, but checking the advance of the rear ranks. A few of the men fired their muskets upward. Others, still under the impression that the ship was an ally, waved their arms and shouted at it.

The next shell did better, exploding ten feet above the Vins' heads to send deadly shards tearing through the ranks. Several more exploded harmlessly or were put out, before another burst at shoulder height. Its effect made even Josette wince. It made a crater in the middle of a mass of men, hurling them outward against their fellows, who in their turn fell in blue-and-yellow rows that lay as flat and motionless as trampled grass.

More shells followed, but they were over the gun smoke now. Whatever carnage they might cause below, from above they only appeared as flashes in a white cloud. "Cease bombing," Josette ordered. "Stow the remaining shells."

The Vin grand battery, now that *Mistral* had revealed herself as a Garnian airship, hurled shells at her by the dozen, until the air was again filled with flying metal. An explosion to port tore ragged holes in the envelope over frame six and sent a smoking shell fragment arcing through the air to land near Bernat's feet. As he prodded it with the toe of his boot, he said, "Oh, good. I was worried we were getting a bit too chummy with the Vin artillery."

Directly ahead, *Ibis* was flashing a message. "We're ordered to attempt a landing, sir," Kember said.

"Damn it!" Josette said. "This ship has plenty of fight left in her." Then a grin came to her lips, spreading into a wide and eager smile.

Bernat's expression fell. "Oh God," he said. "You're smiling. You're going to try to get us killed, aren't you?"

"You're the one who told me to smile more," she said. "Steersman, right rudder. Elevators down full. Pass the word to rig a drag anchor. Break out pistols and sabers. Oh, and acknowledge the order."

Bernat's eyes went wide. He looked over the side, down to a column packed shoulder to shoulder with hundreds of veteran soldiers—hardened killers who'd spent years or even decades perfecting the art of war. "No, no, no," he muttered. "There are too many of them."

"Nonsense," Josette said. "There's plenty of room in hell." A pair of cannoneers distributed weapons. Josette tied a sash around her waist, into which she tucked a saber and two pistols.

Mistral was well into her turn now, sweeping around to come at the artillery battery from along the stream. At the tail, they were lowering the canvas bucket that would serve as a drag anchor.

When she looked back, she saw Bernat taking a sword. "Joining us?" she asked.

He shrugged. "Mother always said a woman would lead me to ruin."

"Do you even know how to use one of those?"

"Of course," he said, raising the blade in salute. "I'm an aristocrat. We like swords."

She knew that, of course, but she had to talk to occupy her mind, or else she'd start to think about what she was doing and be overcome by anxiety. "Just remember to jump exactly when we do," she said. "If you hesitate, the ship will be a hundred feet in the air before you know it." She was about to add some words of encouragement, but she saw him staring with determination into the smoke ahead, and knew it was unnecessary.

Against all odds, Bernat was unafraid.

BERNAT WAS TERRIFIED, absolutely terrified, but he dared not show it. He hoped that if he just stared forward and looked determined, they wouldn't notice. He only wished he had Josette's natural courage. There she was, calmly speaking to the crew, chattering on as if this were any given day.

Ensign Kember walked into his line of sight and leaned far over the rail. "*Ibis* is signaling," she said.

"But you can't make it out," Josette said, before Kember could relay the message. "At this altitude, our envelope blocks the line of sight to their lamp."

Kember leaned back and nodded. "Yes, sir. I see now that it does."

"Ensign, can you handle both control wheels on your own?"

Kember looked nervous, but nodded. "I think so, sir, if I only have to fly a straight line."

"Good," Josette said. "Once we're off, just get her to the rear and set her down on the first flat piece of ground you come to. Vent as much luftgas as it takes to keep her there. Don't worry about the cost. We'll say it was lost in action, and God help anyone who calls us liars."

There was a jolt as the drag anchor hit the stream. Bernat looked back to see it filling with mud and blood-tinted water. The ship lurched and began to swing downward on the end of its anchor line, straight toward the thickest fighting on the entire Garnian line.

Lieutenant Martel, Sergeant Jutes, and most of the riggers rushed down the companionway and gathered weapons. Martel flashed a toothy smile at Josette. "Monkey rigger will cut the line as soon as we touch down, sir. And Private Grey would, uh, like to have a word with Lord Hinkal before we disembark."

"Make it fast," Josette said, looking at Bernat and pointing her thumb at the companionway hatch.

Bernat had to push through the crew, so many were now gathered on deck. There were more than a dozen here, leaving only the wounded and a few extra crewmen to fly the ship. Bernat pressed between two riggers and looked up through the companionway, where Grey knelt at the edge.

"Good luck," she said.

"Thank you," Bernat said, hoping there wouldn't be more.

There was. She swallowed and said, "My lord, do you think . . . I mean, do you suppose . . . that there's any possible way that someone like me, and someone like you . . ."

The deck suddenly quieted as everyone on it held their breath.

"No," Bernat said, before things got out of hand. "No, there absolutely isn't."

The moment seemed to hang in the air for several seconds, until Grey snorted and said, "Well, to hell with you then." She rose, turned, and went back to her engine without another word.

The silence on the deck persisted for some time after that, until Josette finally said, "This is why they shouldn't allow men aboard airships."

Sergeant Jutes snorted. "I'm startin' to see the wisdom in that line of thinking, sir."

"Are you sure you're up for this, Sergeant?"

He grinned at her. "Doctor back on base said I should stay out of the air with this leg," he said. "I'll only be following his instructions."

"Pass out rifles to the men on the rails," she said, then raised her voice to address the men packed in front of her. "Stand clear of the guns!"

Bernat took a rifle from Jutes and pushed his way to the rail. Musket balls were now hitting the envelope, fired by men in the rear ranks of the column.

"Left rudder," Josette called. "Down half a turn on the elevators."

Mistral twisted on her kite string until her guns were pointing just ahead of the battery, where Bernat could see the faint glimmer of tightly packed bayonets. There, where the attacking column had to climb the mud-slick fortifications in front of the guns, the Vin column was bunched up, the attackers packed in like fish in a barrel.

"Rudder amidships. Elevators down another half turn. Wait for it, Ensign."

The Vins on the shelf seemed to suddenly realize their peril. Muskets flashed in the smoke. Most were ill-aimed, fired not at the hurricane deck itself but at the massive shape looming out of the smoke above them, but not all the shots were wasted. The man next to Bernat fell, clutching his chest, and there was a cry of pain on the other side of the deck.

"Now!" Josette said.

Ensign Kember pulled the lanyard on the port gun. It threw the entire deck back and added its own smoke to the morass already ahead. Bernat could not see the shot's effect, but he heard a great, terrible groan rise up from the packed ranks as dozens of men cried out in pain together.

Kember ran to the other gun and fired it without delay. As soon as it recoiled, men rushed forward to fill the space on the forward rail.

Bernat knew the ship was still plunging downward, but in the smoke he couldn't tell how fast or how far away the ground was. He only knew that his stomach was rising into his throat, and the sounds of pain and battle were growing closer with every passing second.

"Rifles!" Josette called.

Along the rail, every rifle went up and fired, Bernat's last of all, for he sought a target in the smoke before realizing the futility of it. Following the example of the others, he fired blindly into the morass and hastily discarded his weapon on the deck.

Mistral's war cry began with Sergeant Jutes, but it spread across the deck, until Bernat found himself joining involuntarily, raising his voice and screeching out his own feeble shout. The sound of it, and the hollow roar of the steamjack behind, bellowed from *Mistral* as if she really were some baleful dragon descending from a fairy tale.

The bottom of the deck splashed into the stream, heaving Bernat up even as the keel came crashing down. The weakened companionway ladder, sandwiched between deck and keel, snapped in the middle, sending splinters flying.

And then the keel was bouncing back up and crewmen were leaping over the side into the veil of smoke. He felt a hand grip his arm and pull him forward, and he sprang over the rail to splash into the stream next to Josette. He looked up to see the ship already rising, becoming nothing but a dim silhouette above.

"This way, Bernie!" Josette called, drawing her saber and pushing through the knee-deep water.

He followed as fast as he could, wondering how the hell she knew which way to go. No matter which direction he looked, it was water for three feet ahead and only smoke beyond. He tore his goggles off and discarded them, but it didn't help. The smoke stung his eyes, parched his throat, and burned his nose with the intensity of its horrible rotten-egg smell.

Coming out of the stream and onto a muddy shelf, he tripped on the bank and fell into a patch of moss, nearly coming down atop his own sword. As he lifted himself up, he became aware of several pertinent facts. One was that he had tripped not on the bank, but on a severed leg. The second was that he had fallen not into moss, but amid a pile of bodies.

As he ran to catch his fellows, the glint of bayonets caught his eye to the left. There were hundreds of them, all held at the ready, their gleaming points aimed right at the spot where Josette and the *Mistral* crew had disappeared into the smoke. He knew he should run after them and help, but all his vigor fled from him in an instant.

The shouts and screaming began ahead. He wanted to follow, wanted to die with them, but he couldn't move from that spot. It was only by sheer force of will that he kept himself from falling to his knees and bursting into tears.

He heard feet splashing through the water behind him. He looked over his shoulder to see the metal badges of a hundred shakos looming out of the smoke, with more bayonet tips ahead of them. He ran, but they were faster. He spun around and whirled his blade in a wild slash at the nearest one, shouting, "No!"

A big hand came down on his shoulder and someone said, "This way, sir!" It took him a moment to realize that the voice was Garnian.

THE LITTLE GUN battery was more impressive from the ground. Two twelve-pounder cannons and two twenty-four pounder howitzers had been emplaced on dry, level ground, five feet above the stream. Anyone attacking the battery had to climb that slippery, shoulder-high earthwork, then negotiate the wood-and-gabion wall atop it. There were even planks spread across the top of the battery to protect the artillerymen from shell fragments. Vins who wanted to storm this battery would either have to break through the roof, fight their way past the entrenchments at the flanks, or climb in through the cannon embrasures.

All three of which they'd done, it seemed to Josette. The battery had become a charnel house, with dead infantrymen from both sides strewn across the ground, along with dozens of wounded Garnians whom the stretcher-bearers were still collecting. There was a notable lack of Vinzhalian wounded, which could only mean they'd all been bayoneted after their comrades had retreated.

"You'd better call back the gun crews," Josette said to the first officer she saw, a young lieutenant from the 24th Fusiliers. "We have to get these cannons firing."

"You're looking at the gun crews," the lieutenant said, pointing to several shirtless bodies lying here and there inside the battery. "General Fieren ordered them to stay with their guns and keep firing."

She sighed, suddenly feeling very, very tired.

"Are you from the airship?" the lieutenant asked.

"*Mistral,* yes."

He seemed to roll the name around his mind for a second, before suddenly snapping his fingers. "Hey, you're that lady captain!"

"Lieutenant," she said sharply, "there's a reserve column out there, forming for an attack right now."

He froze and swallowed. "Shit," he said. "We have to get these guns firing!"

"An excellent idea." Shouting so loud the young lieutenant covered one ear, she called, "Mistrals, to me!" She turned to shout in the other direction, and saw Bernat coming out of the smoke. "Bernie, where the hell have you been?"

Bernat stumbled as if drunk, and said in a distant voice, "Oh, here and there."

"It was a hell of a sight, wasn't it?" She slapped him hard

on the back, making him wobble. "A thousand Vins, running in terror from little old us. Of course, all those Garnian infantrymen charging in behind us probably helped, but I dare say it was our example that inspired them."

Bernat bobbed his head, his eyes pointing vacantly in whatever direction his face was turned. "My thoughts exactly," he said.

She slapped him again. "Ha! Well, if you want to be useful, refill those buckets from the stream. We have to get these guns firing, Bernie." She took a deep breath. "Mistrals! Get your lazy asses back here! There's work to do!"

The silhouettes in the smoke approached and resolved themselves into her crew. They'd never gone farther than twenty paces from her, but that may as well have been a mile in this smoke. The smoke was thinning gradually, but with no wind, it would take a while to disperse.

"Cannoneers, reload with canister over round shot," she ordered. "Riggers, assist the cannoneers. Act as powder monkeys or help clear out this mess. Lieutenant Martel, go back to the caissons and check on our powder supplies. If you see an officer from the reserve company, send him to me. And keep your sabers handy, men. This day isn't over." A cannonball screamed toward them and hit with a hollow thump against the front of the battery. She stepped under the shelter of the battery's roof as a shell exploded overhead.

Sergeant Jutes leaned against the inner wall for a few seconds to catch his breath, then went straight to a cannon, putting his thumb over the vent hole while another man swabbed.

Her cannoneers, used to the short, easily serviced bref guns, were having difficulty loading these big cannons, but they were soon assisted by a few artillerymen who'd retreated when their battery was overrun, as well as one who'd risen alive and well from the bloody mess of bodies after having played possum at the first sight of blood. He tried, shame-faced, to explain himself, but Josette only slapped him on the back and thanked him for his prudence.

A horse trotted up to the back end of the battery, right to Josette, and the man atop it saluted her. "General Fieren's compliments, sir, and would you 'kindly get your goddamn guns firing again.'" In the smoke, the horseman must have mistaken her for an officer of artillery.

"Most of the cannoneers are dead or wounded," she said. "My men are filling in as best they can."

When he heard her voice, the horseman leaned down to get a better look. With his face so close, she could see that he was hardly more than a boy. "What the hell are you doing here?" he asked. "There's a battle going on!"

"Thank you, Ensign, I had worked that out for myself." She took hold of the horse's bridle, to keep him from leaving. "There's another column coming right at us. I need the nearest reserve company up here to support these guns."

"Who's in charge of this battery?" the ensign asked, indignant.

She stared up and said, "I am, you pimply little twit!"

He only huffed at her and urged his horse on. Josette could have held fast to the bridle, but it wasn't worth it. Behind her, the battery finally renewed its fire.

As the ensign rode off, Martel emerged from the smoke, accompanied by a hulking, scar-faced captain of infantry in a mitre cap. "Captain Whetstan, Captain Dupre," Martel said, by way of introduction. On the ground, she was only a lieutenant, but she wasn't about to correct the record if misinformation could serve her.

In the few quiet moments since she'd sent Martel out, Josette had been trying to work out the best way to finagle the help she needed from the reserve company's commander. She would have to flatter him, of course; explain the circumstances carefully; and deftly imply—without lying outright—that the general had ordered the man's reserve company forward to support her.

Before she could speak, however, the scarred captain scanned the battery from left to right and said, "We have to keep these guns firing. I'll bring my grenadier company up to support you." He turned without another word and disappeared into the smoke.

Josette was left with her mouth hanging open. She looked at Martel and said, "Thank you, Nic, for finding the one infantry officer in this entire army who possesses a single morsel of brains."

Martel smiled and said, "My pleasure, sir. And the caissons have ample powder. Shall I attend to the guns?"

She nodded. "Canister over round shot until they're within pistol shot, then double canister." Unlike *Mistral's* bref guns, these sturdy cannons could be double-shotted, at the cost of a reduced powder charge and shorter range.

The guns were firing briskly now, but she had no notion of their effect on the attacking force, which was invisible out there in the smoke. If her cannoneers had miscalculated, they might be firing short—digging harmless divots in the mud, while the Vins took pinches of snuff and laughed at Garnian incompetence.

There was an impact on the roof and something rolled over it. It had to be a shell. "Down!" she cried, and leapt behind the nearest cannon as the shell burst, caving in the roof and sending the corner gabion tumbling into the stream. She came up to find two men down, one of hers and one of the artillerymen.

"Keep these guns firing!" she said, clearing a broken plank from atop the nearest howitzer.

The rightmost cannon fired, and the percussive force sent the weakened right side of the battery wall tumbling into the mud. Infantrymen in the trench below scrambled out of the way as logs rolled through their line. There was no repairing the damage. It would take a score of men to lift that lumber back into place.

Her eyes were drawn to a line of muskets flashing in the smoke. The bullets thumped against the forward wall, and she heard men in the trench groan or scream as they fell. And then came the sound of drums, and Vinzhalian voices cheering the advance.

"Don't let up!" Josette said, pulling a swab from the hands of a dead artilleryman and taking his place in the gun crew.

BERNAT SAW JOSETTE and Martel taking the place of fallen men, and the sight made him feel desperately useless. He'd filled buckets with bloody water from the stream until he ran out of buckets, and then had gone back to the caissons to fetch powder charges, but he couldn't tell one charge from another, and didn't know which to bring. Now he was casting about, looking for some way to be helpful.

He saw his chance in the motionless form of a man lying facedown in a trench. Someone from the reserve ranks had already taken his place on the line, so Bernat snuck in and took up the dead man's musket. Unable to tug the cartridge box free, he sawed the strap off with his sword.

He found a spot at the edge of the battery, out of the way of the cannoneers but with a clear line of sight over the remains of the defensive wall. He loaded and fired into the smoke, where he imagined the Vins were coming from, though he couldn't see them except when they paused to fire a volley. He resolved to never again complain about the smoke in Arle.

He had no idea if his aim was true, but it hardly mattered with a musket. Even a well-aimed bullet from this inaccurate gun might miss, or it might hit though misaimed. So he loaded and fired, loaded and fired, again and again.

The Vins were firing two volleys for every shot he sent at them. With every volley, men fell on the Garnian line, but every time more came from behind to fill their places. Above, he heard the drone of an airship, probably *Ibis,* and found its presence calming.

Which is not to say he was calm. Particularly not when there came, louder than the airship above, the roaring battle cry of a thousand frothing Vins. "Here they come!" a scarred Garnian officer called from the line. "Fix bayonets!"

Josette and Martel simultaneously held their hands up to stop the gun crews from firing. "Wait!" Martel said, while Josette shouted, "Save your last shot!"

Bernat was halfway through reloading. He redoubled his efforts until, seeing the brass shako badges and bayonets gleaming through the smoke, he realized the futility and tossed his musket aside. He drew his sword instead, and moved among the remnants of the wall, willing himself to be strong, to be brave, to face death with the dignity befitting a nobleman.

On the sides of the battery, the grenadier company was moving forward, unwilling to simply wait for the enemy, but massing to charge them head-on.

"Hold! Patience, men!" Josette shouted at the gun crews. They stood by their guns, now reloaded and double-shotted with canister. The Vin column emerged from the smoke just yards away, charging through the mud and the bloody froth, screaming their war cry.

Bernat found that he was screaming back at them, baring his teeth, spitting with rage and waving his sword over his head. He had no idea when he'd started to do it, but he couldn't have stopped if he'd tried.

"Now!" Martel and Josette called simultaneously.

The world turned to smoke and noise and fire as cannons, howitzers, and hundreds of muskets went off at the same moment.

And the front ranks of the Vin column ceased to exist; the men who had been there left no fragment of their corporeal forms that couldn't fit into a hat box. Their shattered remains tore into the ranks behind, where men were lacerated not only by musket balls but by splintered shards of bone that an instant before had been their friends.

It was the most horrible, the most gruesome, the most unnerving carnage that Bernat had ever witnessed, and some small part of him reveled in it. That part swelled to become his only focus, the sum of his existence on the battlefield. He gulped a breath and screamed a guttural, savage battle cry. Hardly aware of what he was doing, as if he looked out through another man's eyes but had no control of his actions, Bernat leapt from the battery and down into the bloody hole torn through the enemy column, his sword flashing.

He slipped on spilled guts and fell flat on his face, but was back on his feet before he even felt the pain. To his right the grenadiers were charging. Behind him he could hear the gun crews following his example. He wouldn't let them get in front of him, wouldn't let them beat him to the fight. He pushed on through the mud and shattered flesh, boots slipping with every step, nostrils burning with the smell of smoke and blood and shit.

But somehow he stayed upright, scrambled forward until, after what seemed an eternity of running, he saw the bayonets in front of him, pointed at him in two gleaming rows. There were more bayonets behind them, endless rows pointed at the sky, but they didn't concern him. He swung his sword at the glint of steel ahead, the one pointed at his heart, and grabbed the bayonet next to it with his bare hand, pushing it aside to make a space between.

The Vin in front of him pulled his musket back, but Bernat thrust his sword into the man's thigh and sent him stumbling to the side. Now, with a clear space in which to work, Bernat lifted his sword in both hands and brought it down into a hammer blow that cut through the shako of the man in front of him, knocking the gilded metal badge aside on its way into the soldier's skull. The dying man stared in disbelief as blood trickled over his forehead and down one side of his nose.

A bayonet came at Bernat from the second row, but these soldiers were reacting to him with such pitiful dullness and lethargy, as if they were moving in water and saw the world through frosted glass, while Bernat's world was crisp and sharp, his muscles primed, nimble. He twisted out of the way as the bayonet stuck harmlessly in his jacket.

He turned his eyes on the soldier who'd thrust it, and a vicious, sadistic smile came to his lips. The smile was reflected as terror in the soldier's face. The man struggled to free his weapon, but Bernat pulled his sword free and brought it down on him. The soldier screamed, let go of his musket, and tried to duck out of the way, but Bernat struck him on the shoulder, crushing through muscle and bone and sending the man crumpling to the ground.

The dead man twisted around and landed on his back, atop the first man Bernat had killed. There was an opening now, and Bernat pushed into it, tugging at his sword to free it from the second man's shoulder as he stepped forward.

He was amid them now, wedged so tightly into their ranks that they couldn't lower their muskets to attack him, nor could he raise his sword hand above his waist. This inconvenienced him only briefly, for he was soon slashing back and forth across their legs. There was no power in these wild swings— even the fabric of the soldiers' trousers was enough to turn the blade—but they recoiled from his fury all the same, pushing back against the ranks behind.

Their retreat opened a space just wide enough to bring his sword hand up to waist level. Though he still couldn't lift it high enough for a powerful swing, he settled for punching the weighted pommel into the nearest man's groin, doubling him over.

The soldier in the next rank back lowered his musket across the stricken man's back. Bernat readied himself to dodge the bayonet, but the soldier did not thrust. Instead, he reached for the trigger.

Bernat wrenched his sword hand up, but knew already that he couldn't do it in time. He gritted his teeth and stared balefully ahead as, in a flash of exploding gunpowder, his killer's face disappeared amid smoke and blood.

Bernat stood staring for a moment, then looked down at his unperforated body. Another shot went off by his ear, and another Vin fell in the rank behind. Bernat looked left to see Josette, a smoking pistol in each hand, pushing her way through the throng to stand even with him. She flipped her right-hand pistol into the air, caught it neatly by the barrel, and brought the handle crashing down onto the skull of the still-doubled-up man in front of Bernat.

"Thank you," he said, nearly breathless.

She only nodded, dropped both her pistols, and drew her saber. She pushed forward into the Vin ranks, her crew behind her, pressing into the gap Bernat had created. Farther left, the thin Garnian line crashed into its opposite number. To the right, the grenadiers had already charged home and were making their own gaps, pitting their miniscule force against the might of the Vin column. Bernat pushed onward, wedged shoulder to shoulder between Mistrals and grenadiers.

The fighting had begun to simmer, and was not so brutal now. That first burst of red-hot rage was ebbing away, and both sides were lulled into a strange, hypnotic dance in which bayonets were thrust and repulsed across a narrow no-man's land between Vin and Garnian soldiers. Bernat felt fear creeping back into him, in direct proportion to his sudden hope of surviving the day. And it was not just him. Trepidation was spreading up and down the Garnian line. They had poured all their fury into this countercharge, and still the Vins stood limitless before them.

He glanced at Josette, who looked back at him. By her eyes, he knew she felt it too. The entire Garnian force was sliding toward a rout. Their energy was spent, their terror swelling, and they might break now at any moment.

And suddenly, Josette grinned at him. She raised her sword above her head, all but inviting a bayonet in the belly, and screamed in a voice honed by years of shouting over engines and airscrews, "Just one more push and they're ours, boys!" She followed with a triumphant, whooping cry that promised victory.

Bernat raised his sword and joined in. He pushed forward, expecting at any moment to be skewered by a score of bayonets, but there were men to his left and right who were pressing forward with him, and in the face of that sudden onrush of steel, the Vins recoiled.

He slashed at them, his sword cutting notches in musket stocks, swiping across faces, hacking at the shoulders of men who scrambled back before him. Those men stepped back into the men behind them, and for a time the sheer weight of men in the column prevented any retreat.

Cannons went off overhead, spraying canister shot across the lines, killing as many Garnians as Vins. Following Josette's example, Bernat gave a cheer that belied the effect of the misaimed canister. And though the men nearest the carnage could not be fooled, those farther away, left and right along the Garnian line and toward the back of the Vin column, could only imagine what devastation must have been wrought upon the Vins, to elicit so much Garnian joy.

And through the smoke, Bernat saw the gleaming forest of

Vinzhalian bayonets begin to thin, as men in the column's rear ranks heard and believed those cheers, felt the momentum of the battle shifting away from them, and turned to run.

The thinning ranks encouraged the grenadiers to Bernat's right, spurring them into renewed cheers and charges, and as they charged, the left flank of the unstoppable Vin column melted like ice in a fire. The grenadiers ran in pursuit, and the men in the column who'd been standing firm suddenly heard Garnian voices to their left.

And they ran. The Garnian fusiliers to the left followed them, along with Josette's band of airmen. Bernat ran with them for a while, but the Vins were running with the speed of desperation, and what little stomach he had for stabbing men in the back wasn't enough to keep him going.

As he stood catching his breath, a scar-faced grenadier officer came out of the smoke in front of him, slapped him on the back so hard he nearly fell over, and said, "Ha! You airmen are the craziest sons of bitches in this army."

Bernat was about to inquire into this strange custom of slapping your comrades around after victory, but the officer had disappeared into the smoke, shouting, "Grenadiers, to me!"

Other infantrymen were coming back now, laughing and hitting each other with giddy excitement. Some were already looking through the pockets of fallen soldiers, ally and enemy alike. The stretcher-bearers trickled forward, seeking out screams in the smoke and carrying the wounded away. To his left, a large and rowdy group went past, clustered around two men with a captured Vin regimental standard stretched between them.

Bernat was turning to go back to the battery, when a massive shape loomed in the smoke ahead of him. It was a horseman, his blade drawn and held at the ready. He looked up and realized it was his Uncle Fieren, and he felt suddenly alone—as alone as he'd been when lost in the smoke after *Mistral* had set him down. The infantrymen had all gone back to the line or were chasing the Vins, leaving no witnesses here but the dead.

Fieren brought his blade up, and Bernat held his own sword tight, for all the good it would do him. He didn't suppose he could bring it up in time to parry. Fieren wore a savage grin, teeth and blade shining through the smoke. His mustache twitched one way, then the other. The blade came down.

Bernat tensed.

And Fieren's blade plunged smoothly into its scabbard, safe and out of the way. The general looked into the smoke, then back down. "Hot day, ain't it, Bernie?"

Bernat swallowed, letting his sword hand hang limp at his side. "I should think so, Uncle."

The mustache twitched. "Brought my staff forward to see to the battery," he said coolly. "It doesn't do for a general to always stay safe at the rear, you know." He grinned. "I hardly believed it when I heard your voice out here, screaming like a real devil."

Bernat stood still, unable to speak.

Another horse clomped up. The man atop it saluted the general. "There you are, sir," Gaston said. "I was worried we lost you."

"Was just having a word with my nephew," Fieren said.

Gaston leaned forward against his horse's neck. "Good God," he said. "What the hell is he doing here?" He then added a hasty "Sir."

Fieren bellowed out a laugh. "Fighting Vin guardsmen." He looked down. "Did you get any, lad?"

It took Bernat a full second to remember whether he had. "Uh, yes," he said, stammering. "Yes, I did."

"Good lad!" He laughed again. "That's the Hinkal blood, Gaston."

"Indeed, sir." Gaston waved his sword behind him. "We have them in full retreat, sir. Shall we pursue?"

"Yes, yes, send the cavalry in, before the Vins can organize theirs to cover the retreat. Let our men know they'll answer to me if they don't cut down at least five thousand of the bastards."

"As you say, sir." Gaston saluted, gave his horse a kick, and disappeared into the smoke.

When he was gone, Fieren leaned over and whispered, as if the smoke might have ears, "I saw the condition of your airship. Is that damn woman dead?"

Bernat held back a smirk. He looked very somberly up at his uncle and said, "Alas, no."

"I suppose you can't have everything you want." Fieren waved Bernat along as he turned his horse. "Come on, lad. Let's see if we can rouse up a cup of tea."

18

Dawn found Lieutenant Josette Dupre pacing the bulwark she'd defended the day before. The cannons were gone, and would be halfway back to Arle by now, bolstered by two-score guns the army had captured from the Vins. The battlefield was silent now, save for the trickle of the stream and the squabbling of carrion birds.

In the predawn gloom, shadowy figures moved amid the bodies in the field and picked through the still smoldering carcasses of three Vin airships. They were villagers from Canard, making up for yesterday's disruption with a bit of early morning looting. Some had stripped so many uniforms from the dead, they could hardly carry them all. Their bulbous, dark outlines lurched and staggered across the field, and she wondered how they remained upright under the weight. As a Garnian officer, it was Josette's duty to put a stop to it, but she knew what their lives were like, and knew the dead wouldn't begrudge them their meager finds.

A flight of crows scattered in front of the bastion, and she looked up to see someone moving amid the bodies, only a few yards away. He, for she saw now that it was a man, stopped at the edge of the stream and sat down. She watched in morbid fascination as he untied his pants and pulled them down, then began the same operation on a dead grenadier.

As much as she sympathized with the villagers, she could not abide the evil debauchery this one was planning. She shouted, "You there! Stop that! Stop that this instant!"

The shadow froze and looked up. "Captain?"

She recognized the voice. "Corporal Lupien?"

Lupien attempted to don the grenadier's pants and salute at the same time. He failed at both, caught his foot under the dead man's bare ass, and fell into the stream. He scrambled to his feet, holding the waistband up with one hand and saluting with the other.

Josette, at a loss for what else to do, returned the salute. "Corporal," she said, "what the hell are you doing?"

Lupien yanked the trousers up with both hands and tied them off. He looked up and, even in the gloom, Josette could see his teeth shining through an abashed grin. "Hard to find good trousers on a corporal's pay, sir."

She sighed and said, "Carry on, then."

She went on pacing until she grew tired of it, then sat on the shattered bulwark and watched the shadows retreat across the field as the sun rose. When it was above the horizon, Bernat approached, put his legs awkwardly over the bulwark, and planted himself next to her. "Mind if I sit?" he asked, after he already had.

She nodded. "I'm afraid I won't make very good company. I've always experienced the strangest melancholy after a big victory. I don't know why."

Bernat arched an eyebrow. "Mayhap it's the thousands upon thousands of dead, rotting in the fields?"

That was the obvious answer, but she didn't think it was the right one. Still, she shrugged her shoulders and said, "Perhaps."

"Or mayhap it's because you stay up all night and don't eat," he said. Something crinkled in his hands, and he handed her a sausage wrapped in paper. "I apologize that it isn't warm. Lieutenant Martel won't let anyone start a fire."

She dearly hoped not. *Mistral* and *Lapwing* had lost so much luftgas from their uncountable leaks that they could not be made buoyant. They would have to be refloated with inflammable air, which, unlike luftgas, could be manufactured in the field using generators hauled from Arle. It was a hell of a way to fly, but they only had to make it back to the signal base.

Bernat, who had been holding the sausage up while she reflected on this, finally said, "If you find the shape of your breakfast too intimidating, I will happily carve a smiling face on it with my pen knife."

She took it from him and bit off the end.

He smiled. "Ah, I see that you find the shape not intimidating, but on the contrary, quite stimulating."

She swallowed and shook her head. "You're a cad. No, not just a cad, but a cad among cads."

He gave a shallow but humble bow. He had his own sausage, and they ate together in silence until Josette finally said, "They're likely to give Nic his own ship."

Bernat swallowed a bite of sausage. "And you?"

She only shrugged. "They're letting me keep *Mistral*. That's all that matters."

Bernat seemed unimpressed. "No medals, promotions, honors? I thought they might even throw tradition to the wind and give you a knighthood."

"What do I need a knighthood for? Besides, there isn't room in the ship for a horse and all that armor."

"I'm . . . not sure those particular accouterments are strictly necessary, these days."

She said nothing.

Bernat fidgeted with his last stub of sausage, adjusting it in its wrapping. After a few false starts, he said, "I, uh . . . I had some time to speak to my uncle . . . yesterday." He fidgeted some more, then finally tossed paper and sausage alike into the mud. "He's had several reports from Durum, from refugees who escaped after the city fell. One of them was a militiaman who's now joined the army. I was able to find him before his regiment marched."

Josette braced herself, as if for an incoming canister shot.

Bernat hesitated, but pushed on, avoiding her eyes and looking out at the distant fens. "Your mother—she's been entirely impoverished," he said. "The soldiers looted everything she had, and the new Vin kadi gave the house to one of his underlings."

Having expected the worst, it took Josette a moment to grasp hold of the news. She ran the words over and over in her mind, checking to make sure she heard them right. "So . . . she's alive?"

Bernat jumped. "Oh," he said, suddenly apologetic. "Yes—yes, of course. I'm sorry. I didn't mean to imply . . ." He hit himself on the forehead with a closed fist. "God, what a fool I am. Yes, she's alive and unsullied."

"Thank God," Josette said. She let out a long sigh. "Finally, I can go back to hating her."

Bernat tilted his head.

"You have no idea how much of a strain it's been, to think well of her these past few days." Josette gradually released the wound-up tension from her body. "Although I must correct you on one point."

Bernat looked up, finally making eye contact.

"My mother," Josette said, "has never, to my knowledge, been unsullied."

His shoulders rose and fell with a chuckle. "Well," he said, "let us say that she's no more sullied than she was under Garnian rule."

"Did Fieren give you any notion of how far he was willing to pursue the Vins?"

"You mean, will we chase them until every one of those goddamn Vin bastards either retreats to his lands or lies dead upon ours?"

She shook her head. "I mean, will we retake Durum?"

"Ah," he said. He cast about for words, and bit his lower lip.

And she knew the answer. "Ah," she replied, taking a deep breath. "I suppose the general doesn't think Durum worth the effort of recapture."

Bernat's dour expression confirmed her conclusion.

"Oh well," she said. "I've always thought of her as more Vin than Garnian, anyway. And she does love dumplings."

Bernat shot her a smile that left her confused. He said, quite firmly, "She'll be fine. Women in your family have an uncanny knack for survival."

She looked again at the wreckage of the three Vin airships, rising like hillocks on the field. "That does seem to be true," she said.

Beside her, Bernat looked from ship to ship. In the light of the morning, thin wisps of smoke could be seen rising from two of them. "So?" he asked.

She looked at him. "So what?"

He shook his head, as if his meaning were obvious. "So," he said, indicating the field with a sweep of his hand, "is it personal?"

She looked out at it—at the blood, at the bloated bodies of Vin soldiers, at the crows feasting on eyes and entrails, at the once-majestic Vinzhalian airships whose few unburnt girders would soon join Canard's store of winter firewood. She lowered her eyes, taking no pleasure in any of it. "I don't suppose it is," she said very softly.

"So why do you do it?" he asked, his voice warbling, as if he regretted the question before he'd even asked it.

She spoke without hesitation, for she'd asked the same question of herself a hundred times through the night. "If I didn't, someone else would have to." She took a bite of sausage. "And they'd probably just muck it up."

He laughed softly. "I've just realized why I enjoy your company," he said.

She looked at him, eyes questioning.

He looked back and smiled. "It's because I find kinship in our shared humility."

They began to laugh, longer and louder than could be justified by the meager humor of the comment. The laughter went on until the sound of it attracted Ensign Kember. "Captain, there you are," she said, coming to a halt inside the empty battery. "I've been trying to find you everywhere."

Josette let her laughter trail off into a contented sigh, turned her head, and said, "Yes, Ensign?"

"Mr. Martel sends his compliments, sir, and we're ready to launch."

"Already?" Josette glanced at the sun, thinking that more time had passed than she thought. But no, it was barely above the horizon. "Mr. Martel's efficiency is laudable," she said, as she rose from the bulwark. She stuffed the last bit of sausage into her mouth and tossed the paper into a trench on her way out.

Mistral, riding a jury-rigged mast just beyond the village, looked like an old quilt. Her outer skin was patched with fabric from a dozen sources, including the army's old tents, blankets, and cloaks. Even so, there were still gaping holes amidships and on the bow, through which the gasbags could be seen.

Despite the ship's half-wrecked condition, a dozen children from Canard had gathered to gape at it. Well, that wasn't quite true. Some were staring up at the superstructure, while closer to the ship—close enough that they'd have to be dispersed before *Mistral* could take off—a trio of the smallest were watching something on the hurricane deck. Josette followed their eyes, to where Sergeant Jutes was inspecting an extra line rigged to shore up the martingales. She couldn't work out what they were so fascinated by, until Bernat smirked and said, "I believe this is the first time they've seen someone of Sergeant Jutes's rather, ah, northern complexion. Not very cosmopolitan out here, are they?"

As they drew nearer the ship, the smallest child, a little girl of perhaps five years, tugged on Bernat's sleeve to get his attention. She pointed at Sergeant Jutes and asked, "Is he a frost monster?"

"Yes," Josette answered, before Bernat could say anything. "And if you don't leave now, he'll turn your blood to ice."

Fortuitously, at that moment Jutes happened to look down from his work to see what the fuss was about. As soon as his gray eyes were on them, the three children bolted for the village, screaming all the way.

"See?" Bernat said. "I told you that you have a knack for it."

As she boarded over the side, she saw Jutes working on deck, and thought that his limp was worse after the exertions of yesterday.

Bernat followed her up the steps but lingered on the top one, with only his head showing over the rail. When he caught Josette's eye, he said, "I realize that, as an avowed spy, you hardly have cause to—"

She cut him off with a wave of her hand. "Are you asking for permission to come aboard?"

"Would that, perhaps, be something you might allow?"

"In the signal corps, you don't have to ask permission," she said, and reached down to take his hand. "A hundred and fifty pounds coming aboard." While the crew scrambled at some last-minute task behind her, Bernat came aboard in his usual uncoordinated style, requiring Josette's other hand to keep him from slipping on the deck.

"A hundred and fifty?" he asked, as if his feelings had been hurt.

"If it makes you feel better, I can add another ten for ego." Josette turned to the deck. She stopped cold when her eyes swept across it.

The whole crew was mustered there, standing at attention. Bernat, who seemed as confused as she, soon smiled and strolled to take position to their left.

Sergeant Jutes took a smart step forward. "Crew ready for inspection, sir." He touched his knuckle to his forelock and stepped back in line.

She nodded and, unsure what else to do, walked down the line, in what little space was left on the crowded deck. The signal corps didn't have such inspections, which she knew were common in the navy. So she walked down the line as she imagined a naval captain might, taking a look at each crewman in turn.

She noted the empty files, where the crew had left a spot open for a fallen comrade. She paused in front of the spot where Gears might have stood. Yesterday, she had helped move him onto a cart, and pushed a rolled-up blanket under his head for a pillow. He was bound for the hospital in Arle now, where he would die in the coming days, if he hadn't already. Four other crewmen had been killed in yesterday's battle, and another two would never fly again. Even the survivors bore an assortment of broken bones and flesh wounds. Fully half of them had one wound or another, and it showed in their bruised faces and bloodied uniforms.

When she reached Bernat, at the end of the line, he straightened his jacket and stood in his best approximation of attention, though his eyes repeatedly darted to the man next to him, to observe his example.

Josette walked to the opposite rail and turned to them. She looked over them again, studying each one with a critical eye. She looked at Kember, with her neck scarred and swollen; at Jutes, with his limp; at Grey, covered in layers of grime; and at Lupien, wearing a dead man's trousers. Few of them could be called fit for duty. Not one was in proper uniform.

"You people are a ragged mess," she said in a hard, harsh voice. She took a deep breath and let half of it out. A smile came to her lips. "I could ask for no finer crew."

Jutes stepped forward. She desperately hoped that they